Dear Reader,

This year has be[...]

particular brand of romance fiction [...]

in North America and the UK, and we are also reaching audiences as far afield as Russia and New Zealand.

So, what delights are there in store for you this month? Characters from Angela Drake's book *The Mistress* are featured in *The Love Child*. Naughty-but-nice Ace Delaney from *Game, Set and Match*, returns in Kathryn Bellamy's new novel, *Mixed Doubles*. (But don't worry if you didn't read the authors' earlier titles – both of these books stand alone.) We are also absolutely delighted to announce the return to writing of much-loved romance author Margaret Pargeter, with a brand new book, *Misconception*, written especially for *Scarlet* readers. And finally, we are proud to bring you another author new to *Scarlet*: Tammy McCallum has produced an intriguingly different novel in *Dared to Dream*.

I believe this time there is something to appeal to all reading tastes. But if there is a type of romance (say, time travel, ranch stories, women-in-jeopardy novels) we are not featuring regularly enough to please *you*, do let me know, won't you?

Till next month,

Sally Cooper

SALLY COOPER, Editor-in-Chief – *Scarlet*

About the Author

For six years **Tammy McCallum** and her husband Steve owned a multi-million dollar computer franchise in Houston, Texas. In 1989, they sold their business and, in search of new challenges, Tammy answered the creative voice that had nagged her for years and began a new career in writing.

Always interested in the unusual, and having a deep-seated love for historical and mystical tales, a story involving time travel seemed natural. The result was *Dared to Dream*, Tammy's first *Scarlet* romance and her first published novel.

The author's home is in McKinney, Texas, but she loves to spend her free time travelling, skiing and scuba diving with her husband of nine years and their three children. She's grateful to be able to work from home so she can keep an eye on her one-year-old dog, Katie (a creative blend of mutt), who has developed a taste for dining room chairs!

Other *Scarlet* titles available this month:

MISCONCEPTION – Margaret Pargeter
MIXED DOUBLES – Kathryn Bellamy
THE LOVE CHILD – Angela Drake

TAMMY McCALLUM

DARED
TO DREAM

Enquiries to:
Robinson Publishing Ltd
7 Kensington Church Court
London W8 4SP

First published in the UK by Scarlet, 1997

A copy of the British Library Cataloguing in
Publication data is available from the British Library

ISBN 1-85487-985-5

Printed and bound in the EC

10 9 8 7 6 5 4 3 2 1

I believe every woman should have
a hero in her life. I thank God
for mine everyday.
To my husband, Steve. I love you.

CHAPTER 1

Westbourne Castle, England
April, 1997

Damn, if the man didn't fascinate her.

It's too bad he's been dead for nearly five hundred years. Lauren Ferguson studied the painting hanging in the gallery of Westbourne Castle. A dangerous emotion shadowed the knight's dark blue eyes, as if he dared her to step closer. The sneer lifting his full mouth emphasized the legendary two-inch scar along his right cheek. In contrast to the other portraits of men in his time, who'd curled and waxed their hair, this man's black mane was pulled away from his face and tied with a strip of worn leather.

The only hint of wealth came from the jeweled belt strapped about his waist, accenting the black, long-sleeved tunic molded to his chest and arms. Large, rough hands clasped the hilt of a sword, angling it as if he meant to use it. On the gold pommel the words *Kenward, A Lion Rampant* were engraved. Lauren felt the overwhelming need to not

1

only take the dare and touch the painting, but the man as well.

Each time she visited her grandparents at Westbourne, she was unable to pass the portrait without sensing the knight's gaze fixed on her, following her every move, giving her the eerie feeling he wanted to speak to her. The hair at her nape prickled. What would he say if he could? Would his voice be refined, with the education of a lord, or harsh and commanding, like a knight inured to hardship and endless battles? She guessed the latter. But she knew what she'd ask him. The one question that had puzzled her for years. Why did he seem so angry? She blew out a breath, knowing she'd never know for sure.

And why do I care? She shook her head. It was certainly time she ended her fixation for the long-dead lord, but, she reasoned, fantasizing about him seemed safer than taking a risk with the men of her own time. *He* couldn't disappoint her, break her heart, or demand more than she could give.

As Lauren pushed away from the stone wall, a shrill voice broke the silence. Edith Milborrow, their tour guide, rounded the corner with a group of tourists close on her heels. She was leading the crowd past a sixteenth-century bronze statue of King Henry VIII. Lauren thought to herself that Edith was as much a part of Westbourne Castle as the weapons and tapestries that filled the monstrous dwelling. Sharing her knowledge of the castle's history was Edith's 'last remaining passion.' There wasn't a person alive who knew more.

'Everyone, come close now.' Edith fluttered her hands like the wings of a hummingbird to draw the straggling group together. Her corkscrew gray hair had rebelled against the chignon she'd forced it into, escaping to form mad curls about her face and frame the bifocals perched on the tip of her nose. 'I'll be tellin' you a sad tale about our most famous knight.'

'What about the armor, here?' one man asked as he clicked pictures with his disposable camera.

Sunlight pouring through the narrow windows glinted off the collection of suits of steel. The empty armor had fueled Lauren's childhood imagination. Especially one enormous suit of polished black metal, engraved with the Kenward crest.

While she was growing up there had been definite advantages to having grandparents who managed Westbourne Castle for England's National Trust. America had nothing so magnificent. The sight of the ruined curtain wall, the smell of musty hallways, the creak of worn floors had become a touchstone for her. During summer visits, she'd filled her days with imaginary knights, fair damsels and marauding blackguards. She'd searched every inch of the castle, convinced she'd find hidden passageways which would lead her to a secret tower filled with treasure, or perhaps the bones of a forgotten prisoner. Even now, at the age of twenty-four, she could still feel the twinge of disappointment at never having found so much as a peep-hole.

Turning her attention back to the group, she reminded herself she hadn't come to England to find a

3

knight, and she wasn't a damsel in need of protection. With her degree in hand, she'd crossed the Atlantic for what she hoped would be the last time to start a new life doing what she loved most. Practicing veterinary medicine. A remote English village near Westbourne seemed the natural place to open her surgery.

'Oh, the armor is grand, is it not?' Edith said. 'There's more on the tour I'll be tellin' you about. Now listen, please.'

Lauren moved closer to the group. She'd heard the story behind this painting so many times she knew it by heart. Still, she couldn't resist closing her eyes and envisioning herself as the heroine, ready to relive the love, the fear and the ultimate tragic ending.

'This handsome knight was none other than Lord Nicholas Kenward. He ruled these lands from the tender age of twelve until his violent death in 1530, at the age of twenty-eight.'

Lauren's skin warmed. She opened her eyes to see the knight's rugged face, tense with anger and another emotion she'd never been able to identify. His dark blue eyes stared down at her, holding her captive.

'Lord Kenward's father and older brother were ambushed and murdered by a Scottish reiver, a heartless thief named Bruce Armstrong,' Edith explained. 'The young lord vowed to wear black until he'd claimed his revenge. Thus, he became known as the Black Knight. For many years he ruled his lands, and his people prospered. The one time their faith in him wavered was when he took an outlander as his wife.'

Edith turned and ran her fingers over the gilt frame. 'The villagers were frightened of the woman at first. It's said she had a strange way about her. Not only was she Scottish, which was bad enough at the time, but some whispered she was a witch, possessing the power of second sight. But Lord Kenward loved her so much his people soon realized there was nothing to fear.'

'What was the woman's name?' a lady with the white fuzzy hair of a clipped poodle whispered.

'That I can't say.' Edith sighed and adjusted her glasses on her nose. 'The stories simply refer to her as "Lady Kenward." We don't know her first name or where she came from.'

Shrugging off the mystery, she continued, 'Since we are just nine miles from the Scottish border, there were constant battles between the Scottish and English. In 1530 Laird Armstrong laid siege to Westbourne Castle.' Edith's hand fluttered to her chest, as it did each time she reached this part of the tale. 'After hours of battle, an arrow pierced Lord Kenward's armor, fatally wounding him.'

A man whose attention Edith had managed to snare asked, 'That sort of thing happened all the time back then. Why is this man so special?'

Edith clicked her tongue. 'There is more to this story. Yes, Lord Kenward died that night, but his wife, heavy with their first child, lifted her husband's sword in anguished fury and rallied his men.' Edith's voice rose to a theatrical pitch. 'The soldiers fought back the Scots and won the battle.'

A chill swept across Lauren's skin. *Nicholas died.*

5

She looked into his painted face and imagined a desperate energy reached out toward her. Strength chiseled his features, but beneath the brawny physique and hard stare she sensed something else. A deep sadness, and perhaps loneliness. From where did it stem?

He'd had a wife he adored, a thriving community at his command. What had been missing from his life that would cause such an intense emotion? The puzzle surrounding Lord Kenward spun through Lauren's mind, pestering her like a buzzing gnat.

Edith continued, 'Once the wounded were cared for, it was discovered Lady Kenward had disappeared. She was never found or heard from again, thus ending the Kenward family line the day of Lord Kenward's death. What happened next no one can truly say, but there is a myth.'

Lauren smiled as the tourists, entranced, leaned forward to hear the rest.

'It's said Lady Kenward's tears woke the mystical Light Elves from their eternal slumber. Upon seeing the mistress's fiery red hair, they knew she was a *dergflaith*.' Edith paused with dramatic flair, then explained, 'A woman chosen by the Celtic goddess Arianrhod to possess the power of sight. Feeling pity for Lady Kenward, the Light Elves pleaded with Thorr, a champion among the gods, to ease her pain.

'Thorr swept her away to the celestial palace in a chariot of fire drawn by twelve white horses with golden manes. There, Lady Kenward bore a daughter and named her Aurora. It's said Aurora lights the

6

sky on the anniversary of her father's death, hoping his spirit will find them.'

A collection of sighs from the women echoed through the hall when Edith had finished. Dragging her gaze from the painting, Lauren saw several men roll their eyes at the fantastic ending.

Edith shook herself from her storytelling trance and ushered everyone down the hall, but stopped next to Lauren. 'How was I, dear?' the older woman asked in a conspiratorial whisper.

'Perfect, as always.' Lauren smiled despite the strange melancholy clinging to her. She didn't believe Thorr had carried the grieving Lady Kenward away, but – call it childish fantasy – Lauren wanted to believe Nicholas had found his wife again.

Clasping her hands together, Edith looked at the painting. She heaved a great sigh that threatened to pop the buttons on her knit jacket. 'I don't know what it is about this story that moves me so. You'd think after twenty years of retelling the tragic tale I'd be immune to it by now.'

Lauren followed Edith's gaze. The woman's words struck a vulnerable nerve along her spine. 'I know what you mean. It's like he's alive and can hear us. Sometimes I think his expression changes when you tell the story.'

Edith turned to study Lauren over the top of her wire-rimmed glasses. 'What a queer thing to say, my dear.' Clicking her tongue, she added, 'It's only a painting. Now, I must catch up with my group.' Over the tapping of her Oxford shoes against the

7

stone floor, she called, 'I don't want them to miss the new collection of pewter cups!'

It's only a painting. Lauren repeated the phrase over and over until the chill left her body and she became convinced Lord Kenward's eyes were nothing more than blue paint. Still, she wondered what it would have been like to be married to a man like him. A man brave enough to risk his life to save the woman he loved. *And leave her behind to carry on without him,* came her rational voice.

Forcing herself to turn, she walked away from the portrait. She had to forget about the man and his needless death. After all, it had happened nearly five hundred years ago. Nothing could be done about it now. She rolled her shoulders to ease the tension that had settled there. She needed to relax, and only one thing could dissolve the pensive mood thinking of Nicholas Kenward always created. A ride on her thoroughbred mare, Jessy.

Needing her jacket and hat, she headed for the office off the main hall.

As she drew near, the familiar sound of Grandma Morna's laughter rang out. Except this time she sounded like an excited teenager instead of a 67-year-old woman. Stepping into the cluttered room, Lauren spotted her grandparents huddled around a battered oak table, digging through a small, dirt-crusted leather-bound trunk.

'What are you two about?'

In unison, they looked up. Smiles broke across their wrinkled faces. Their eyes glittered with mischief.

'Come, see what we've found,' her grandmother said in a thicker than usual Scottish burr. ''Tis a thing of beauty.'

Lauren maneuvered through an assortment of broken spears, mismatched armor and piles of scarred furniture. She marveled at the way her grandparents clung to their Scottish accents despite having moved to England over thirty years ago. Although one hundred percent Scottish herself, Lauren had grown up in America and had never developed the Scottish lilt.

'What's in the box, Grandpa?' She peeked inside and caught her breath.

'We dinna know for sure,' Angus said. 'But we think it dates back to the early sixteenth century.'

'Lord Kenward's?' Lauren asked, hearing the whisper of hope in her voice.

Her grandmother shrugged. 'Who can say?'

Lauren reached inside the trunk and lifted the enameled box. She set it on the table and the three of them bent down for a closer look. 'It's beautiful.'

'Aye, 'tis the finest cloisonné I've seen on a jewelry case.'

Lauren grazed her finger over the gold scroll framing the lid. The enamel painting depicted a woman with waist-length red hair sitting in a field of purple heather. A young girl stood next to her and held out a bouquet of the colorful flowers.

Holding her breath, Lauren lifted the lid. The elaborate box was an incredible discovery. She didn't dare hope to find anything inside. Angus whistled low. Lauren and her grandmother gaped, speechless.

9

Nestled in purple velvet lay a gold ring bearing a lion raised on his hind legs. Surrounding it, the words *Kenward, A Lion Rampant* were engraved.

'It *is* Lord Kenward's.' Her hands shaking, Lauren picked up the ring. Light from an overhead bulb glinted off the smooth gold. She cradled it in her palm, wanting to believe the elegant piece had belonged to the Black Knight of her girlhood dreams. 'I wonder why he isn't wearing it in the portrait?'

'Are you sure he is not?' Angus asked as he leaned over Morna's shoulder for a closer look.

'I'm sure.' Lauren knew the portrait so well, she could close her eyes and see every detail. She slid the ring onto her finger, surprised by the perfect fit. The cool metal warmed against her skin, its weight oddly comforting. 'Where did you find it?'

'We were in the dungeon, cleaning it out.' Angus held up the painted box to the bare lightbulb.

Lauren wrinkled her nose and suppressed the urge to shiver. She hated the dungeon. Each time she ventured into the dark pits the damp walls, slick from mildew and decay, seemed to press against her, choking her. As a child, she had imagined the rush of wind against stone to be the moaning voices of dead prisoners, the constant dripping of water through the walls their tears.

'We thought it would be a good place for storage – after a bit of remodeling, that is,' he added. 'Your grandmother discovered a loose stone. When we pulled it out, we found this leather trunk inside.'

'I suppose you'll lock these in a display case.'

10

Lauren knew she couldn't keep such valuable heirlooms, but she resisted giving up the ring, liking the feel of it on her hand.

Grandmother Morna held out her palm. 'I must tag these and add them to our records.'

With a reluctant sigh, Lauren pulled the band off. On impulse, she checked for an inscription. She gasped as she read, ' "*My love, my life I give you. N.*" ' Dazed, she whispered, 'This must have been his wife's ring.'

'Oh, my!' Morna snatched it from Lauren's fingers. 'This is the only thing we have of the woman, except the legend.'

Turning to her desk, Morna sat and opened her leatherbound log book, the cover worn thin from years of use, and entered the latest castle treasure. Lauren stared at the ring in Morna's hand. How had the treasures become hidden in the dungeon? Who had put them there, and why?

Feeling bereft, Lauren picked up her hat and coat from a chair and headed for the door. 'I'll see you at dinner. I'm taking Jessy out for a ride.'

'Lauren?'

'Yes, Grandma?' She paused at the threshold, her gaze locking on the glint of gold in the older woman's thin fingers.

'Be careful. The weather's sure to change, and I know how skittish that horse of yours can be.'

Feeling strangely out of sorts, Lauren met her grandmother's worried frown. 'We'll be fine. I know how to handle Jessy.'

* * *

11

'Blast you, Jessy, I don't want to go that way!' Lauren tugged the reins to turn the mare toward the woods and away from the open glen. The horse halted and craned her head around. Lauren could swear impatience darkened the mare's large brown eyes. 'If you don't follow my lead, I'm going to turn you into a plow-horse.'

Jessy snorted and shook her mane, as if she understood the threat and didn't buy it.

'I don't want to go to Hadrian's Wall today.'

The chestnut mare stamped her hoof against the grass, tugged at her bit, and tried to head for the field.

Matching the mare's stubbornness, Lauren reined Jessy toward the stand of old oaks barely visible in the distance and nudged her flanks. Finally, Jessy broke into a canter. Cool wind brushed against Lauren's face and pulled at her braided hair. She breathed in fresh, crisp air and let the troubling thoughts about Lord Kenward and the mysterious ring fade into the background of her mind.

As the thoroughbred crossed the rolling moors, the springy grass became dotted with flowers. Stars of Bethlehem, with their milky-white petals, struggled for space among the rich green ferns and spreading ivy. Small clumps of purplish heather added soft splashes of color.

Lauren drew in the mixture of sweet smells. She loved this country, from its wooded valleys and swelling moorland to its temperamental weather. Each time she returned to Northumbria it was like coming home. She let her mind wander, refusing to think about anything more taxing than the sun beating down on her.

As they reached the edge of the forest Jessy faltered in her step, then shied away, refusing to enter the dense brush.

'Come on, girl.'

The sun's hot, drowsy rays vanished behind steel-gray clouds, casting shadows over the earth. A gust of wind brought the scent of rain. A chill swept over Lauren's skin as she drew the collar of her riding jacket up around her neck. 'Let's get out of the wind.'

Jessy took a hesitant step forward, as if afraid the ground would fall out from under her with the next step. The mare danced sideways, then pranced in a circle.

'What's the matter with you?' Lauren demanded.

A crack of thunder shook the ground. Holding onto her riding hat, Lauren tilted her head back just as moisture-laden clouds opened up. Icy rain stung her face and stole her breath. Digging her heels into Jessy's sides, she leaned over the mare's neck and forced her through a curtain of branches.

Jessy pushed deeper into the woods, dodging trees and leaping over fallen trunks. Limbs snatched at both of them. Lauren cried out when a sharp branch ripped her dun leggings and scratched her thigh. The horse jolted to a stop, but pranced in the tight space.

'Shh, girl.' Lauren stroked Jessy's slick neck until she calmed.

The canopy of entwined branches filtered the heavy rain to a fine mist. Rising wind tore at the treetops, but hardly disturbed the leaves around her. Lauren peered through the dense brush that seemed to shift in the changing light, growing darker, pressing tighter against her.

She'd never been so deep inside the woods before. As apprehension sharpened her senses, she wished she wasn't there now. Twisting in the saddle, she expected to see the path they had forged. Nothing but tangled vines and eerie shadows closed around her. The thick mulch of fallen leaves disguised the mare's hoofprints.

Lauren's heart thumped against her chest. She swallowed and tasted the musky scent of wet earth. With a start, she realized she had to be careful or they'd become lost. The forest encompassed miles.

Dismounting, she rubbed Jessy's muzzle. 'See, it's not so bad in here,' she said in a shaky whisper. 'At least we're out of the rain.'

She looked at the swaying treetops. A dusting of cold water settled on her face, making her shiver. Feeling as if she was intruding where she didn't belong, she gripped the mare's reins and listened. Despite the rustle of leaves and faint wind, a strange quiet surrounded her, as if the forest animals were watching her, waiting for a vulnerable moment.

She bit down on her lip and considered leaving the shelter of trees and braving the storm on the open fields. A powerful gust shook the giant oaks and sent a spattering of icy raindrops over them. Discarding the idea to leave, but wanting better protection, she led the mare deeper into the woods. Within minutes she discovered a granite overhang tall enough for her and Jessy to fit under. She dropped the reins, wrapped her arms around her waist and leaned against an ivy-covered wall. A miserable, damp cold crept through her clothes. She clenched her teeth to keep them from chattering.

Damp fir needles and bog-myrtle mingled with the clean scent of rain. Now that she was out of the drizzle, the bracing, earthy smells were reassuring, almost comforting. Almost. Beside her, Jessy nibbled on a long stem of ivy. The mare clenched the greenery between her teeth, then pulled an entire section away. The wall of vines relaxed, then with a quiet rip collapsed, sending Lauren screaming backwards into darkness. She landed on her bottom with a thud. Her hat flew off, disappeared.

'Oh, God!' Scrambling to her feet, she hurtled through the opening, startling Jessy. The mare danced sideways but Lauren caught the reins before the horse bolted. She turned and stared into the dark cave. Her hat was somewhere in the void. A wary inner voice told her to leave it, she could buy another one, but a stronger voice dared her to see what lay inside.

Jessy whickered low, then nudged Lauren's back.

'All right, I'm going,' she laughed, though her voice sounded as uneasy as her stomach felt. 'But if something's in there, I'll have your hide if you leave me.'

With both hands, Lauren pulled the vines until she'd revealed a large opening. Dim light bathed the shallow cave's smooth walls and stone floor. To her relief, there were no monsters or ancient wizards lurking inside.

15

Spotting her hat on the ground, she stepped inside to retrieve it. Straightening, she gasped and clutched the hat to her chest. Petroglyphs in dark shades of red and brown covered the walls. Men with spears hunted fat deer. Soldiers, armed with swords, battled one another. A religious ceremony depicting a small boy being sacrificed made her grimace in disgust.

Jessy's restless snort brought Lauren around. She grabbed the reins and led the horse inside the cave. The last thing she needed was to be stranded alone in the woods, inside a cave that probably dated back to the Druids. Moving to the rear wall, she spotted a picture of two staffs with snake heads that formed a large X. A six-spoked wheel had been painted in the top portion. Beneath it was the profile of a woman with long red hair.

Below the pictures, words were carved into the smooth rock. Lauren recognized them as Gaelic, but couldn't decipher them. Sounding out the strange dialect, she read, "*Co Sam-bith beir Arianrhod uachta gearr a bolg de uair scoilt curfola steach an de.*" Arianrhod,' she whispered, remembering the goddess's name from the myth about Lord Kenward's wife. Excitement rushed through her at having found it written here. *Did the woman or goddess really exist?* Could the drawings have something to do with the legend?

Wishing the walls could talk, she touched the cool surface and whispered the strange words again. She grazed her fingers over the pictures, then across the letters. A fine vibration pulsed up her arm. 'Who were you, Arianrhod?'

16

Jessy whinnied and tugged against the reins. The mare laid back her ears. Her eyes widened, showing their whites.

'What is it, girl?'

Then Lauren heard it, a high-pitched hum. It rose, then faded, rising again in an hypnotic rhythm. She glanced about the cave, but couldn't detect the source of the odd noise. The sound grew stronger, until it vibrated through her body, filling her, tightening her skin. Her blood ran hot and pulsed with each wave. An ache numbed her limbs, forcing her to stand still when she wanted to run. Her heart thudded hard and slow against her ribs. The air turned thick, smothering, coating her lungs. She drew in a breath, but it wasn't enough.

Jessy ceased her struggles and stood still, her eyes closed and head bowed. The urge to lie down and sleep overwhelmed Lauren. She fought to keep her own eyes open. Again, she tried to move, but her legs felt like lead instead of flesh and blood.

The droning hum continued. *I have to get out of this cave.* She willed herself to turn and face the entrance. The wind had picked up, sending leaves and branches flying through the air. Thick oak trees bent with the ease of willows. She heard a deafening crack, as if a tree had been ripped apart.

Lauren swayed, and her eyes slipped closed. She wanted to sleep. But something in her mind told her to resist. She opened her eyes a slit. The wind settled, leaving a heavy silence. Deep purple shadows gathered outside. The fading light pulsed in tune with the buzzing noise. The steady vibrations forced her mind to slow, her eyes to close.

I'll rest for a minute. The thought floated through her like a dream. *I have time.*

Something soft and warm nuzzled Lauren's cheek. She smiled and stretched her arms over her head. Rolling onto her side, she gasped when a sharp rock poked her ribs. Opening her eyes, she choked on a scream. Jessy's large velvety nose hovered above her. Before she could move the mare snorted, blowing a hot breath over Lauren's face.

Swatting Jessy away, she pushed herself to her feet, and only then realized she had been asleep. How strange. Frowning, she glanced around. Her thoughts careened when the cave floor tilted. The walls spun out of control. She gripped her head and stumbled. Bumping into the rock wall, she leaned against it and closed her eyes.

As the dizziness eased she dared a peek, and released a trembling breath when everything remained in place. She stared at her shaking hands. 'What's wrong with me?'

She recalled the strange buzzing noise and the eerie way it had thrummed inside her, lulling her to sleep. She glanced at Jessy, who was standing still, as docile as a lamb. That in itself was unusual. The mare always had to be tethered or she'd wander off, leaving Lauren stranded.

Curls of damp, tangled hair fell over Lauren's shoulder. She pulled the clip from her braid and shook her long hair loose. She pushed away from the wall, but her knees shook and threatened to collapse. Spotting her hat on the dusty floor, she carefully bent over and retrieved it, and felt the jarring wave of a headache.

An ominous chill crept down her spine. Something wasn't right. She stared at the Gaelic words. For some reason she thought she should know what they meant, that they were vitally important. The pounding in her head increased. White pain flared behind her eyes.

She pressed a hand to her temple and pulled herself into the saddle. Nudging the mare's sides, she decided she didn't give a damn who or what Arianrhod was. She just wanted to go home.

Letting Jessy find her own way out of the forest, Lauren rubbed her aching scalp, but could find no bumps. What was causing her headache? Had she fallen asleep? Or had she fainted? Turning to look behind her, she saw thick trees and heavy brush concealed the cave's entrance. Swallowing it as if it'd never existed.

But she knew it was there. Had something happened to her while she'd been unconscious? Jessy halted and her head snapped up. She sounded a low whicker. Lauren turned back around. They'd stopped at the edge of the woods. The mare's ears pointed forward. Her big body trembled as if she sensed something wrong.

Lauren looked past the few branches blocking her view and stared in disbelief. A hundred yards away on the rise of a hill stood a horse, his huge body covered with armor and his head tilted into the wind. But that wasn't what stunned her. An enormous man dressed in matching black armor was mounted on the stallion's back.

Armor she could swear belonged in Westbourne Castle.

CHAPTER 2

Nicholas Kenward reined Hades to a halt and listened to the high-pitched hum. It pulsed with a steady rhythm unlike anything he'd ever heard before. No lute or viol could make such a sound. This was hollow, yet deep. It pulled him, urging him to follow the noise and discover its source. He scanned the copse of oak trees but saw nothing through the dense brush.

The stallion danced sideways, rattling the armor covering his thick neck and sturdy body. His black ears were laid back in warning. Nicholas tightened his knees to still the horse, but the stallion reared and pawed the air. Dropping his forefeet to the ground, the animal gathered his powerful haunches and sprang into a run, heading for the forest.

'Hades!' Nicholas commanded.

The stallion balked, stepping sideways, but finally obeyed. 'This isn't the time to chase a stag.' Not now, when the perfect opportunity for revenge against Armstrong had been handed to him. Nicholas allowed a grin as he recalled the informant who had brought news of Laird Armstrong's daughter, Christel. The woman would be passing here on her way to Kelso Abbey in Scotland where her father had ordered her cloistered.

As if that would keep her safe from me, Nicholas thought with loathing. Once he had the wench he'd lead the siege against Laird Armstrong, recapture Gowan Castle and return it to its rightful English owner, Lord Wright.

Nicholas tilted his head back and caught the scent of impending victory on the rising wind. He'd waited sixteen years for the opportunity to exact revenge for the murder of his father and brother. Soon he would be able to bury his guilt for failing his family, and his hate for the man who, with a careless swipe of his sword, hadn't taken Nicholas's life in battle but had marked him as a coward, damning him to a life of shame. A bitter laugh caught in his throat. Was it possible to shed the hate winding through his veins, slicing away at his heart until he doubted he possessed one any longer? How could he hope to live through each day without the destructive emotion to feed on?

What would happen if he cast off the black garments of mourning? The daily reminder that his father's and brother's blood was on his hands? He should have saved them, he thought, feeling the familiar smoldering hold on his soul. Or at least died with them. But he had the chance now to claim revenge. Afterward he prayed he could look at his reflection without seeing the scars that lingered . . . both inside and out. Perhaps then he might do the impossible . . . look to the future.

Nicholas forced the thoughts behind his inner shield. He couldn't consider his future until he resolved his past. At any moment Christel Armstrong and her guards could emerge from the line of trees. Once he spotted them he'd signal for his men, positioned a short distance away, to join him.

The strange humming faded, making him more curious about its absence than its brief presence. Hades ceased fighting the reins, but his large body shuddered with tension. Nicholas scanned the countryside, spikes of anticipation running hot through his veins.

Chaotic gusts blew the knee-high ferns shielding a small brook. Gray clouds churned, obliterating the sun and vast blue sky. A faint stench of smoke clung to the air. The thick green grass and towering oaks darkened beneath the gloom. A vibration shook the earth as if a legion of horses raced across it. The sudden change in weather suited him, for it matched the black moment he expected ahead.

Clouds swirled, then parted, allowing a narrow stream of light to bathe the land with vibrant colors of spring. A wash of beauty among the darkness, he thought ruefully. His gaze focused on the distance, but a movement in the trees caught his attention.

A horse and rider emerged from the thicket. A man wearing tan britches and a black coat. Nicholas reached for the sword at his waist, but paused in pulling it free. Not a man, but a woman. At this distance he couldn't see her features clearly. The scant description he had of Christel Armstrong claimed her to be a beautiful woman, one who wouldn't be mistaken for a commoner. Her trademark lay in her fiery mane of red hair.

This woman had a tangled mess of it draped over her shoulders. It had to be her. But why was she alone? What had happened to her escort? From the tattered look of her, he guessed they had been attacked before reaching this point. He smiled dryly. So much the better.

'I'll save my fighting for your murdering father, dear lady.' Nicholas dropped his helmet's visor into place and spurred Hades into motion. With Christel Armstrong sitting like a frightened hare, capture would be both quick and unchallenging. The woman watched as he raced toward her. Her mouth opened in surprise.

Seconds passed, and the distance between them shortened before she kicked the mare into a run. Nicholas added pressure to Hades's sides. The stallion changed course and bore down on the sleek mare to cut her off. Excitement needled Nicholas's skin, his heart pumped blood like molten steel. He shouted a battle cry, and Hades responded, running faster, pushing harder to gain on their prey.

The woman glanced over her shoulder, her eyes widening at the sight of him close behind her. She hugged the mare's neck and urged her on. The chestnut sailed over a four-foot hedge and landed without breaking stride.

Hades followed, taking the jump easily, if not as gracefully as the mare. With each thrust of the stallion's powerful legs the distance between seeking revenge and having it shortened. Within moments she would be his. The mare would tire soon. Already her neck lathered, and her gait slowed.

Gaining, Nicholas edged beside Christel and grasped the reins. The woman slapped his gauntleted hand and fought for control. She jerked the mare's neck around, trying to pull away. Hades bumped the other horse and threw the mare off balance.

'Let go!' the woman shouted as they drew to a stop.

Nicholas laughed as a rush of power surged through him. 'Not after I have gone to so much trouble to capture you.'

'Capture me?' Her eyes narrowed with disbelief. 'Who are you?'

The mare pranced and fought his hold. Nicholas tightened his grip and drew his captive closer. The mare reached over and bit Hades's neck. The stallion snorted and reared. His sharp hooves struck out to attack, but Nicholas barked a command, and Hades dropped to the ground, his nostrils flaring with aggression.

'Why are you doing this?' The woman sat erect in her saddle, the ends of the reins still tight in her fist. Like shards of precious emeralds, her eyes pierced him with her anger.

'For the sweet taste of revenge, my lady.'

'Revenge? This is madness.' Her chest shuddered with each deep breath. Strands of hair blew across her face. She swiped them aside, then tugged on the reins. 'Let go of my horse.'

'Not until I have what I want.' Her bold behavior took him by surprise. But then she was Scots, he mused. He shouldn't be surprised by anything she did.

Her brows dipped with suspicion. 'And what might that be?'

'Your father's head on a stake would suffice.'

'My . . .' Her voice broke. Anger drained from her face, leaving a glazed, haunted look. Then the expression vanished. If Nicholas had had a conscience, the vulnerable pain in her eyes would have shamed him. But years ago he'd shed all traces of compassion – especially for anyone related to Laird Armstrong.

She jutted her chin out like a stubborn child, but bewilderment lingered, darkening her green eyes. The cool wind and her struggle to escape had tinted her smooth cheeks pink. Her full mouth parted as a tremor shook her lower lip. Mad curls, the shade of wine, gathered about her face and the strange bowl-shaped black hat she wore.

He thought back to the informant's description of Christel Armstrong. There could be no mistaking her. Despite the dirt smudging her face and clothes, there was nothing common about this comely woman. Regret dampened his hate, surprising him. If she weren't the daughter of the man he sought to kill, he could want a woman such as her. Beautiful, with the spirit of a fighter.

She had yet to show any fear, sitting square in her saddle, her head tilted in defiance and her emotions blazing in her eyes. Surely she understood her fate now lay in his hands?

26

He scanned her clothes and frowned. Why would Armstrong allow his daughter to dress as a man? As a disguise to evade capture, perhaps? His gaze dropped to her muddy leggings. A rip at her thigh revealed smooth, pale skin. His stomach clenched in response, but the long scratch on her leg, spotted with dried blood, cooled his loins. He made a mental note to have the leech see to her as soon as they reached camp. He couldn't risk her becoming ill from an infection. Not when she was so vital to his plans.

At the sound of approaching horses, Nicholas drew his sword from his scabbard. The Armstrong woman gasped. Using his knees, he turned Hades to face the riders. Kenric, followed by a dozen of Nicholas's men, galloped through the tall grass and stopped beside them. Creaking leather and the snort of horses stirred the air, but the men held silent, their gazes fixed on the woman.

'My lord,' Kenric said, and nodded in greeting. 'We became concerned when your signal did not arrive.'

'Yes, well.' Nicholas grinned behind his visor as he glanced at the woman. The color drained from her face as she gawked as his soldiers. 'There . . . there wasn't time,' he finished haltingly.

She raised her slender hand and pointed to his men.

Nicholas's gaze dropped to her pink lips. They were full, lush, and should have belonged to a temptress. An unexpected conflicting need sprang up inside him to learn what they felt like. He imagined them soft and giving. *But not with me.* Cursing himself, he ground out the vision. There would be nothing gentle between them. Ever. He would take, and she would learn to give.

'Who are you people?' she whispered. She reached out and touched his armor like a curious child. Her fingers grazed the iron covering his arm, then flinched back.

Nicholas frowned, growing more perplexed with the woman's behavior. What was wrong with her? Instead of being afraid that her enemy had captured her, she studied each man as if she'd never seen anyone in full armor before.

'What happened to her escort, my lord?' Jacobson, the captain of his army, inquired.

'From the looks of her, I'd say they were attacked. Her guards were either killed or they ran off.'

Nods and grunts of agreement sounded.

'Why is she dressed so?' Thomas, an archer, reached out to touch her coat. She slapped his hand.

Nicholas's gaze scanned the fitted black wool coat that hugged the curves of her body. Tight wheat-colored leggings molded to the slender lines of her thighs. Her black knee-high boots were strange in design, but appeared costly.

'How should I be dressed?' The woman's voice dripped with sarcasm. Her indolent gaze raked over his men. 'Like you? Grown men playing knights in shining armor?'

'Nay,' Nicholas growled, irritated by her mocking tone. 'Like a woman.' He'd been prepared for Christel Armstrong's fear, and had hardened himself in the event she resorted to tears. Yet curiosity and a spark of anger simmered in her eyes. He handed the mare's reins to Kenric and ordered, 'Gag and bind her. I want her quiet until we reach Gowan Castle.'

'Gowan Castle . . .?' she began.

Jacobson caught her hands to bind them.

'Stop that!' She pulled free and swung her fists, managing to slap Jacobson's helmet. With a surprised curse, the captain grabbed her wrists and bound them in front of her with a leather strap.

'You can't do . . .'

Jacobson tied a cloth around her mouth, muffling her.

Thomas nudged his horse beside hers. He removed his barbuta helmet, plucked the peculiar black hat from her head and plopped it on his own. She glared at the archer. If the woman had access to a dagger, Nicholas imagined Thomas would be writhing in a pool of his own blood.

Hiding a grin at her display of temper, Nicholas almost regretted having to ruin the woman before returning her to her father. He rather liked her spirit. Which surprised him. He should loathe her much as he did her father. He had vowed revenge, and what better way to have it than to take the one thing Bruce Armstrong prized most? The comely, *virginal* daughter that had every laird in Scotland vying for her hand. It would eat away at Armstrong's black heart knowing an Englishman had claimed her first.

A vision of Christel lying naked beneath Nicholas, a sheen of sweat glistening her slim body, filled his mind and stirred his blood. He expected she would fight instead of welcome him. So far she'd shown a brave front – did a fiery passion hide beneath her courage? His loins warmed, pulsed with the prospect of finding out.

Watching the sharp rise and fall of her chest, he felt the cold hand of disgust touch the back of his neck, guiding him to reality. Regardless of how his body responded to her, his actions would be driven by his vow to avenge his father and brother. Nothing else. He wouldn't be tempted by this Scottish baggage.

He met the woman's gaze and felt a jolt, as if she stared straight into his soul. An odd tightening squeezed his chest. Would his plans for her douse the fire that burned in her green eyes? Would she come to hate him as much as he had to hate her?

Nicholas clenched his jaw and turned away. He didn't know what would happen to her, and he'd be damned if he'd care.

Lauren couldn't breathe. Fury with the idiots who'd abducted her clogged her throat. The cloth stuffed and tied around her mouth tasted of sweat and grime and smothered her screams. Her wrists stung from the leather binding as she grasped the pommel and held on.

The leader had set a mad pace across the moors, heading away from Westbourne Castle. Her headache jarred her temples. Silently, she willed Jessy to fight the giant in silver armor holding her lead, but for once the flighty mare seemed content to follow.

Lauren glanced at the ground rushing beneath her in a blur of green and purple. She toyed with the idea of jumping, but discarded the thought. If she didn't kill herself in the fall, the men would probably stop to collect her. Especially if what the leader had said about releasing her were true. '*Not after I have gone to so much trouble to capture you.*' Capture her? For what possible reason?

She couldn't forget his bone-chilling response about wanting her father's head on a stake. What could he possibly have meant? And why did she have the strange feeling that he hadn't been kidding? Dazed at the bizarre situation, she couldn't decide if she should cry with fear or laugh at the absurdity of it all. Men dressed in armor! *Men dressed in armor and carrying swords!*

She studied the leader in black armor. She hadn't been able to see his face beneath the iron helmet, but the hatred blazing from his steel-blue eyes had frightened her. After catching Jessy, he'd drawn his blade from his scabbard with a hissing scrape to face the approaching men. She'd expected him to bellow another of his war cries and start slicing the other men down.

If she gave in to her imagination, she might believe the suits of armor at Westbourne Castle had come alive and were fulfilling her childhood fantasies. *And her nightmares.* She looked at the men riding beside her. Each wore heavy steel helmets, their visors lowered. All she could see of their faces were their eyes. Hard, cold and fixed on the horizon. Where were

31

they taking her? The leader had mentioned Gowan Castle. But there wasn't any such place.

Lauren caught her breath, recalling a spot several miles from Westbourne named the Ruins of Gowan – an old castle destroyed during a siege hundreds of years ago. Was that where they meant to take her?

She bit down on the gag and tried to think rationally. There had to be a reason the men who'd kidnapped her were dressed as medieval knights. *Kidnapped? By knights?* A small thread of hysteria filled her with the urge to laugh. There had to be another reason. Perhaps they were filming a movie? Rehearsing for a local re-enactment? Or maybe it was some sort of prank. Everyone in the area knew how much she loved anything regarding Westbourne's history.

The leader raised his gloved hand, slowing the horses as they topped a hill. When she reached his side, her breath strangled in her throat.

Hundreds of men covered the valley floor and encircled a small castle. Colorful flags on the watchtowers snapped in the warm breeze. The surrounding two-story curtain wall and main keep were made of rough limestone, and the smooth walls stood intact, free of any signs of aging. A place out of a fairy tale. *But that's impossible*, she thought as her stomach flipped with unease. Though they had ridden fast, they couldn't be more than a few miles from Westbourne. And she knew every castle, every ruin within fifty miles. Where had this place come from?

Her breath wheezed from her chest as she realized

32

there were no movie cameras, trucks or trailers parked nearby. Her hope shredded like flimsy paper and scattered to the wind.

The rattle of armor and shouted orders drifted up to them. The sharp blast of a trumpet sounded. Sunlight glinted off the iron-clad men as they hurried about forming organized rows, six men deep. She reached up to tug at the gag. The man called Jacobson clamped his hand over hers. Turning to the leader, she gave him what she hoped was a pleading look to remove the cloth.

After studying her with eyes that failed to mask a savage inner fire, he nodded. Jacobson untied the gag but left her hands bound.

She gulped a deep breath and pointed to the mass of people. 'What . . . what is this?'

The leader reached out, took her chin between his gloved fingers and turned her face to his. The spicy scent of man and horse reached her. She looked into the visor's black slit and resisted the urge to shiver. His eyes turned hard and chilling, as if he wasn't seeing her, but something past her.

'What are these men doing here?' she asked again, irritated that her voice sounded weak and vulnerable.

Hate rolled off his body in a vaporous wave. His gaze seared through her, singeing her with its warning. 'Seeking revenge.'

CHAPTER 3

'Revenge?' Lauren lifted her shoulders in irritation. 'Fine, you want revenge. Against who?'

The knight released his hold on her chin, but kept his face so close to hers that, she could feel his heat, smell his musky scent that unnerved her as much as his hostile stare. 'Against your father.'

'*My* father?' She brought her hands to her chest, sure he couldn't possibly mean what he'd said.

'Aye.'

'That's going to be a little difficult, since my father's dead.' The last words choked in her throat. A year hadn't been enough time to soften the devastating loss of her parents.

The knight lashed out and gripped her arm in a vicious hold. 'He was struck down while taking Gowan Castle?'

'No, he . . .'

'Then he still lives, but not for long.'

A part of her mind insisted this was some sort of game, one where she didn't know the rules. Except the malice radiating from her captor warned her that *he* thought this was all very real. He had to be insane. That had to be the answer. To control her fear, Lauren bit down on her lip, but she couldn't control a shiver that rippled beneath her skin. She struggled to pull free, but the barbarian tightened his hold. Gritting her teeth against the pain shooting through her arm, she said, 'My father died last year!'

'What kind of fool do you take me for?' The hard lines around his eyes deepened, as if he were smiling.

'The kind that would dress up in armor and play knight!'

'She 'as the sharp fangs of a viper, my lord.'

Lauren glared at Thomas, the young man who'd taken her hat.

'Aye, and the lying tongue of an Armstrong,' the leader added. 'Your father is not dead, but he soon shall be, my lady, and by my hand.'

Lauren held her hands up to stop the bantering. Seeing the way they trembled, she grasped the pommel. 'None of this makes any sense.'

He leaned close so she could see the flare of anger in his pitch-blue eyes, feel his fury snap in the air between them. Rivulets of sweat ran along his temples. His breath turned harsh and ragged. 'That is what I told myself the day your father butchered mine!'

She gaped at his absurd statement. Men and horses stirred impatiently around them. Jessy swished her long tail and caught Lauren's scratched thigh. The sting spread through her leg, grounding her in reality. Or insanity. She wasn't sure which.

35

'Take her away, Kenric,' he ordered. 'And guard her well.'

'Wait!' She twisted around as Kenric edged her horse away. 'I'm not finished talking to you yet!'

The leader ignored her and started down the hill. She watched him leave, realizing he sat in his saddle like an English oak. Sturdy, rugged and irritatingly silent. She wondered if he filled out the iron suit he wore, or was it padded? The arrogant jerk. Correction. Arrogant, *insane* jerk!

The armed soldiers didn't bother to hide their laughter as they rode past her. Below, men merged into a throng of iron, horses and weaponry. A scream of frustration swelled in the back of her throat. She fought it down, and looked at Kenric. Maybe she could persuade him to release her. He had to have more sense than the leader. With his visor raised, the man's coal-black eyes watched her with something resembling contempt. She sighed and realized he wouldn't be any help.

Her headache continued in a dull throb. She raised her hands to rub the spot, but the binding cut into her wrists. She twisted the thick leather. It didn't give. She lifted her arms toward Kenric.

'Not bloody likely,' he drawled.

Lowering her hands, she looked over the crowded field. 'What are they going to do?'

Ignoring her, Kenric tugged Jessy's reins and started down the hill. After a few minutes, he glanced at her. 'Lord Kenward shall have vengeance this day.'

Lord Kenward? Her mouth dropped open. Her

lungs burned when she fought to breathe. 'Lord
. . . did you say Lord Kenward?' A doubting laugh
escaped her, rising to an agitated pitch until she
clamped her mouth shut. *Dear God, I'm becoming
hysterical.* 'As in Lord Kenward of Westbourne Castle?'

Kenric nodded once, then spurred his mount. Jessy
pranced sideways, but the man's hold forced the mare
into a canter. What was going on? And where had
these guys come from?

As they rode through the lines of armed men, cheers
rose. She felt her cheeks tighten with the effort to
smile. Laughter and bawdy shouts about Lord Kenward's prisoner irked her temper, so she squared her
shoulders and returned their curious stares. *I'm Lord
Kenward's prisoner? But why?* No, wait. She shook her
head. Lord Kenward was dead, had been dead for over
four hundred years. She needed answers, and she
needed them before she started believing this war-
rior-revenge story.

Reaching the rear of the battle line, Kenric reined to
a stop in front of a black tent. Once dismounted, he
pulled her with a rough jerk from Jessy's back.
Standing on her own, Lauren felt her legs wobble
with exhaustion. She felt herself sagging to the
ground. Why was she so weak? They hadn't ridden
that far. Nerves? Or had being held hostage zapped her
strength?

Kenric hauled her upright and half dragged her
inside the tent. At his rough handling, her temper
flared. She didn't know what was going on, but she

37

wouldn't tolerate being forced where she didn't want to go any longer. She pulled her arm, and to her surprise he released her. She spun around and teetered off balance.

Righting herself before she fell onto her backside, she glared at him. 'I'm not staying here.' Through the tent opening, she saw Jessy being led away. 'Where are they taking my horse?' she demanded, lunging for the flap.

Kenric raised a large scarred hand and pointed at her. 'Stay.'

'I most certainly will not!' She tried to step around him, but her shaking knees threatened to crumble. Kenric moved in front of her, easily blocking her escape.

She stared at the polished armor covering the man's chest. Her muted reflection stared back, a tangled mass of red hair and a pale, blurry face. A stinging curse sprang to her lips, but before it reached air, trumpets sounded. 'What is that?'

When he stepped aside and allowed her to move to the edge of the tent she started to glance at him in surprise, but what she saw stopped her from moving, from breathing. For an instant even her heart seemed to hang motionless inside her chest.

From her position at the crest of the hill, she had a clear view of the slope below, filled with organized lines of men facing the castle.

Soldiers in chain-mail knelt in the first row with arrows cocked in their bows. In the next several lines men stood with swords drawn and shields strapped to their arms. Behind them, soldiers on horseback struggled to control their mounts. Young boys scurried about carrying shields and long spears to waiting men, then ran on, responding to the endless bellowing of orders that were lost in the cacophony of sounds.

Before she could ask a question, which she felt sure wouldn't receive an answer, an array of trumpets blasted again, startling her. Then she noticed men lined the parapet along the top of the castle wall. She squinted to see what they held in their hands, but couldn't make it out.

Tension quivered in the air, electrifying the sudden heavy silence that engulfed the valley. It made her think of a church service, when everyone stopped for a moment of silent prayer. She scanned the sea of armed soldiers covering the slope. Though the sun glinted brilliantly off their armor, one man stood out. Lord Kenward, covered from head to foot in black armor, astride a coal-black stallion, looked like a demon commanding from the gates of hell.

His horse pranced through the lines. Lauren watched the knight in black and couldn't believe the excited tingle spinning through her stomach. Who was he, and why was he pretending to be Lord Kenward? The bold set of his shoulders, the easy way he controlled his horse and the horde of men proved he was a leader. Or a lunatic. Still, she couldn't deny the awesome sight he made.

Lord Kenward, or whoever he was, raised his arm, his roaring battle cry piercing the air. The deep, savage call sent a shiver of panic over her skin. She stared in horror as the archers raised their bows and released arrows with a screaming hiss. She followed their flight.

'No, no. Oh, God, no.' Her chest burned from lack of air, but she couldn't draw a breath.

Arrows rained down on the men along the parapet. Agonized cries sounded, high-pitched and tortured. Chaos erupted. Wounded men fell from the curtain wall and dropped thirty feet. Arrows flew in both directions, toward the castle battlements and into the lines of men below her. She could no longer distinguish between battle cries and the bellows of pain and death. She clasped her fingertips over her ears, the bindings cutting into her skin.

Far below, to her right, a group of men gathered beneath a leather tarp stretched over a wagon. Grasping the sides, they pushed the cart toward the castle.

This isn't real. She kept repeating the words, but the arrows bouncing off the cured hide looked authentic. And deadly. One man fell to the ground with an arrow protruding from his chest. 'What . . . what are they doing?'

''Tis a battering ram.' When she gaped at him, Kenric added, 'Lord Wright does not wish his castle to be destroyed, else we would use the cannon.'

'Who is Lord Wright?' Lauren felt ridiculous asking questions when men where flinging weapons and dropping to the ground as if they were wounded. *They aren't hurt. They can't be. This has to be an act!*

Kenric clenched his square jaw. His eyes narrowed, and for the first time an emotion filled their jet-black

40

depths. Anger. Dark and lethal and directed at her. 'Ye know well Lord Wright is the rightful owner of Gowan Castle.'

But there isn't such a place! She looked across the hill. The main keep was half the size of Westbourne. The stone curtain wall and rectangular inner building were in beautiful condition with young trees planted in the bailey, as if they were no more than a few years old.

The steady drumming of men ramming the lowered portcullis added to the rioting sounds. The hollow rhythm merged with the pounding of her heart and warmed her blood. She pressed her hands to her knotting stomach and couldn't stop the bizarre thought that all of this might be real. But that was impossible. It had to be. A small tremor erupted in her limbs. She covered her mouth with her hands. 'I think I'm going to be sick.'

Kenric gripped her arm and urged her inside the tent. When she resisted, he ordered, 'You must rest. My lord does not wish you ill.'

She shook her head and swallowed. 'I just need some water.'

The giant frowned at her. Afraid he might force her inside, she turned to watch the battle. From the corner of her eye, she saw Kenric nod, then he ducked into the tent.

The violence in front of her had to be an illusion, but she couldn't look away. The loud drone of noise, the screams and pleading cries for help caught her in a mesmerizing trap. Horses danced and reared, sending up clouds of dust. Riders fought to keep their steeds from trampling the swordsmen, who seemed to be waiting for an opening in the castle's defense.

She searched the field until she found Lord Kenward. *He's not Lord Kenward. I don't know who he is, but he isn't the dead knight!* Amber sunlight glinted off his black armor, reaffirming her earlier opinion of him. He was more demon than man.

He controlled his horse without the use of his hands. Gripping a shield with one fist, he held his sword high overhead with the other. The stallion galloped through the swarm of men as the Black Knight bellowed commands.

The Black Knight? In her mind she could hear Edith's shrill voice explaining how Lord Kenward always wore black to mourn his dead father and brother. *No, no, no, it's not him!*

A piercing scream made her gasp. A young man without protective armor fell to the ground a hundred feet in front of her. The shaft of an arrow protruded from his leg. He writhed as if in agony. She tried to call out, only her lungs constricted. As she stumbled toward him the sharp cry from a wounded horse stopped her. She looked up just as the Black Knight and his stallion fell.

A cry tore from her throat. Torn between who to help first, she glanced at the man with the arrow wound. Another soldier had stopped to tend him. Turning, she raced across the field toward the downed knight, dodging men and skittish horses. Blurred objects whistled past her ears. Acrid smoke curled through the air and turned her stomach, making her want to gag.

She dropped to her knees beside the fallen horse. The Black Knight had worked himself free of the stallion's weight and knelt over him. She reached out and touched the man's arm to see if he had been hurt. A strange snap of energy made her jerk her bound hands back.

She rubbed her tingling fingers down her pants and looked to where the man's attention was fixed. An arrow pierced the horse's chest. Blood made his black coat shimmer. A trail of it pooled to the ground and stained the grass.

'They've shot him!' Lauren cried, anger and disbelief clamoring for a foothold in her mind. Her hands shook violently. She clenched them and looked at the knight. 'How could you let this happen?'

Through the visor's slit, the knight's eyes widened with surprise. 'What are you doing here?' Not waiting for an answer, he shouted over his shoulder, 'Kenric! Blast your soul!'

The horse whinnied and struggled to rise. She threw her weight on the stallion's neck. 'Make him stay down,' she cried over the battle roar.

'Still, Hades.'

'What kind of name is Hades?' she heard herself ask. Easing off the horse, she gently probed the wound.

'The name suits him.'

She ignored the leader's bitter tone. Warm, sticky blood covered her hands. She felt the life of the horse run between her fingers, felt each jumping pulse of his vein. The stallion's sides heaved with every breath. His eyes were wide and wild. When Lauren touched the arrow Hades pawed the air, knocking her sideways with his foreleg.

Cooing to ease the animal, she asked, 'How deep do you think the arrow went?'

He glanced at the wound, then back at her. His hard eyes creased with worry. 'A handbreadth, perhaps.'

Not bothering to ask how big a handbreadth was supposed to be, she said, 'I don't think it punctured his heart. From the slow bleeding, no large arteries were cut either.'

Rising to her knees, Lauren grasped the arrow's shaft with both hands. Her muscles tensed as she prepared to pull it free. 'Do you have any antiseptic?'

The knight stared at her, not answering. Kenric appeared and knelt at his side.

'Alcohol, whisky, wine? Anything I can use to clean this with.'

The Black Knight nodded to Kenric. 'Fetch a flask from the tent and take her with you.'

'Not until I'm done.'

Kenric reached for her.

'I can help him!' Determination shook through Lauren's arms. Helping animals was what she enjoyed, what she lived for. Since her parents' death, it was all she had left. She couldn't walk away from an injured one now.

The leader nodded his consent and Kenric turned and ran for the tent.

Lauren bowed her head, closed her eyes for a

moment. Her mind screamed that somehow she'd stepped into a bizarre dream. A nightmare that had shouting men, cries of pain, and the constant pounding of the battering ram against a thick, wooden door. But if this was a dream, would she be able to feel the warm blood smeared across her palms? Tears burned behind her closed lids. She dragged searing smoke into her lungs and choked.

Hearing the knight curse, she opened her eyes. He rose to his feet, hauling her up. 'I have no time for this. Dying men litter the ground, yet you worry over an animal.'

Lauren struggled against his hold. Her gaze darted around them. Dozens of men lay unmoving, scattered across the trampled grass like forgotten mannequins, twisted and broken. She heard a loud, constant ring and wondered if it was her, screaming. Then she realized it was the sound of her own mind trying to deny what it saw. 'They . . . they aren't dying!'

Kenric returned with the flask and handed it to the knight, who shoved her away. 'Only an Armstrong would prefer to save a horse over a dying Englishman.'

In one swift move, he knelt and jerked the arrow free. Hades flinched, but didn't move otherwise. Then the man poured the contents of the flask over the wound. With a shrill cry, the horse lurched to his feet.

Kenric took Lauren's arm and pulled her away as the Black Knight mounted the stallion's back.

'He's injured!' Enraged, she struggled futilely against the vise clamping her arm. 'You can't ride him.'

45

'He is a war horse.' Men surged around them, moving the line closer to the castle. 'Return to the tent, Kenric. Take care not to let her out of your sight again.'

When Kenric pulled her toward the tent, Lauren didn't resist, but looked over her shoulder to catch one last glimpse of the Black Knight. She stumbled in her gait. Glancing down, she cried out. She'd tripped over a man who had a bloody gash on his forehead. She bent to help him, but Kenric tightened his hold and refused to let her stop.

'That man needs help!' she cried. Kenric ignored her.

She searched for Lord Kenward but he had melded with a sea of armor, swords and horseflesh. The fading sun and swirling gray smoke made her wonder if the violent scene wasn't an illusion. Perhaps the choking smoke would thicken, obscure the sight, and she would awaken from a nightmare.

But the agonized cries, the bodies lying motionless around the field, the blood streaked across her palms and staining her clothes were all real. The edges of her vision dimmed and blurred. When Kenric led her into the tent and forced her to sit on a stool, one thought overwhelmed her mind.

It's real.

The purple-gold hues of dusk had long since faded to a cold, shadow-filled darkness. Crisp spring air bit into Lauren's body. Shivering, she brought up the collar of her coat and tried to huddle into herself. Her bottom ached from sitting on the hard stool. Her hands were numb from the tight bindings. And she was long past hungry, though she desperately needed a drink of water to rinse the gritty taste of smoke from her mouth. She doubted she'd ever be completely free of the bitter, acrid scent of burning wood, and Lord only knew what else.

No one had bothered to bring a lamp to the tent, so she sat in the dark, alone. Her mind sorted through ways to escape, but she felt certain Kenric would appear to stop her. She didn't know where they'd taken Jessy either, and she refused to leave without her mare.

As nightfall settled, torches had been lit outside and the deafening sounds of battle had stilled. The quiet unnerved her more than the sounds of war. Now she heard the tormented moans and pleas for help. One man cried for an end to his suffering, another begged for someone to remove the arrow from his side. Through it all came the soothing voice of a priest, giving last rites.

To escape the wretched sounds, she thought of her grandparents. She could imagine Morna pacing the quiet halls and wringing her thin hands. Grandpa Angus would be on the phone with the local police, demanding someone search for his missing grandchild. Lauren half expected a police car to pull up and rescue her from this bad dream.

Shadows played over the tent as people moved past. Each time Lauren tensed, wondering if it was the Black Knight returning. She didn't know which would be worse – seeing him again or remaining in this limbo of not knowing what he planned to do to her. Not wanting to think about either of those options, she focused on Hades. She ought to find the stallion and tend his wound.

Like an arrow aimed true, the knight's words came back to pierce her conscious. She pinched her lips to stifle a sarcastic laugh. *'Only an Armstrong would prefer to save a horse over a dying Englishman.'*

But she had tried to help. They hadn't let her. For what reason, though? And why had he called her an Armstrong? Was she supposed to play the evil Scots in this deadly game? More out of desperation than true belief, she decided the scene had been an act. The moans outside her tent seemed to rise in a painful note with her thoughts. She pressed her fingers over her ears to shut out the endless cries. No one could act this well for so long. It had to be real. *Those men really were suffering!*

Her gaze went to the tent opening. Where was the Black Knight, or Lord Kenward, or whoever he was? Now that the battle had ended she'd thought he would come see her. His prisoner. The one he'd gone to so much trouble to capture. But why? That question, above the others, circled her mind like a top spinning out of control.

Perhaps he was among the wounded? Even now a priest could be leaning over him . . . Lauren stopped the horrible image. She sat bone-stiff. How could she sit here while hurt men needed her help? She might not be a true physician, but she could make a difference.

'To hell with the leader's order,' she muttered. If Kenric tried to stop her, she'd make him regret it. Somehow.

Rising from the stool, she felt the blood flow into her cramped legs, stinging her calves with needling pain. She clenched her jaw to keep from moaning and limped across the small space. She moved the tent flap back and ducked through the opening.

Straightening, she came face to chest with black armor. She sucked in a gasp of cold air and tilted her head back. He'd removed his iron helmet and held it tucked in the crook of his arm. A torch burned behind him, casting shadows across his face, hiding his expression, but she sensed his anger. For some odd reason she wanted to squirm, like an errant child caught sneaking outside in the middle of the night. But he was alive and whole, and for some reason relief eased through her.

'Where are you going?' Though he demanded an answer, exhaustion weighed his tone.

The deep timbre of his voice made her spine tingle. Concern for him edged into her mind. She shoved it away. He'd brought this on himself. She refused to feel sorry for him. 'I thought I could help.'

'How generous,' he sneered. 'The only way you can help is by obeying my orders.'

He took a menacing step closer, and, though she hated to concede, she wanted him to explain what had happened today; beginning with her capture. She turned and entered the dark tent. Behind her, he ordered torches to be brought, then he followed her inside.

49

Torches? Why not a butane lamp or a flashlight?

Wanting as much distance as possible between them, she moved to the rear of the tent. A young boy, dressed in a gray tunic and brown leggings, brought in a torch and lit several candles fixed to poles imbedded in the ground. After hours of sitting in the dark, the bright light hurt her eyes. She looked away and blinked.

Footsteps and the clink of metal brought her head up. A man she hadn't seen before ducked into the tent. Numerous dents marred his silver armor, and huge rust spots covered his elbows and knees. She caught a smoldering look of rage in the stranger's light brown eyes before he turned to face the Black Knight.

'Ye cannot stop now, Nick!' the man in rusted silver demanded. 'Ye must scale the walls. Armstrong's men have been sorely wounded. If we move now we can gain my castle back.'

'My men have been wounded as well, Anthony. I will not risk losing half of them needlessly. 'Tis suicide to climb the walls.' The Black Knight drew off his gauntlets and dropped them onto a scarred table.

Lauren lifted her gaze to her captor's face. Her gasp startled both men.

'So, this is Armstrong's daughter,' the man named Anthony said, with such loathing that Lauren took a step backward. Her gaze darted to his face. His cold eyes raked over her, giving her the urge to find a shadow and hide.

But it was the face of the Black Knight that reclaimed her attention and kept her from moving.

50

She stared, shock robbing her of speech. He watched her in turn, his eyes dark, intent. There wasn't enough light for her to see their color, but she knew they were blue. A deep, smoldering blue that contained both rage and sadness.

'Lord Kenward?' Lauren whispered. *No! It can't be him.* But the likeness of this man to the one in the painting was uncanny. He had the same angled cheekbones, lean and rugged and brutally handsome. His lips were hard and sensuous, making her bite down on her own to stop them from quivering. And she knew his eyes as well as she knew her own.

She mentally shook herself and tried to look away. It had to be pure coincidence that the two men looked alike.

The ache behind her temples throbbed sharply. She raised her bound wrists to rub her head, but paused to stare at her hands. What about the armed soldiers, the horses, the battle? Those were impossible as well, but the blood staining her palms was proof they existed.

Drawn against her will, she moved to stand in front of the Black Knight. When she lifted her hands to him, he sucked in a breath as if he didn't want her touching him.

The world slowed and blurred around Lauren. She sensed his breath, the steady rhythm of his heart. How many times had she reached out to touch the painting, wishing the man were real, wanting to wipe the sadness from his eyes? Now, a man with Lord Kenward's eerie likeness stood before her. All she had to do was touch him.

Sweat and dirt smeared his face. His black hair lay matted against his head and bound at his nape. The scar! She couldn't see the scar.

Lauren sighed with relief. How could she have been so foolish as to think this man was Lord Kenward? As her anxiety waned, she reached with her bound hands and touched his face. He held still, his eyes hooded like a snake watching its prey.

The feel of his heated skin sent a jolt through her fingers. Swallowing hard, she smoothed away the dirt. She ran her fingers over his cheek and felt a jagged line. Her hands began to shake. She stared at him wide-eyed, denial squeezing her chest. 'You have a . . . a scar.'

He grabbed her wrists and hauled her against him, their faces inches apart. ''Tis a small reminder your father left me.' His hot breath stirred her hair and touched a dangerous emotion buried in her soul.

'You're Lord Kenward?' Lauren choked on her own words.

'I say, Nick,' Anthony chuckled from behind her, 'has the wench only now realized who captured her?'

'You can't be him.' She pushed against his chest. The solid feel of cold armor startled her senses. She struggled against him. She had to escape. The knight tightened his hold on her wrists and wrapped his arm around her waist, drawing her flush against him. Like a rabbit snared in a trap, she stilled and met his cloaked gaze. 'You can't be. It's impossible.'

She looked at his straight nose, his firm mouth, the unforgiving line of his jaw. Her gaze lowered to his chest. She splayed her hand over his steel coat and felt the life of the man within. She grazed the pads of her fingers over the lion raised on his hind legs, engraved into steel, then the words *Kenward, A Lion Rampant*. The same words that were on the sword's pommel. The same armor that stood guard beside the portrait at Westbourne Castle. But how?

'Aye, I am Nicholas Kenward, and you, dear lady, are my hostage.'

'No.' She shook her head, not willing to accept any of this as real despite the unbelievable proof. 'You're dead!'

His hold around her waist tightened, making her gasp. With a bitter laugh, he said, 'I'm sure your father regrets the day he left a twelve-year-old boy bleeding on the side of the road instead of slicing his heart.' He rubbed the scar with his thumb, his lips twisting into a cynical smile. Something vicious flared in his dark eyes. 'I assure you, madam, I am very much alive.'

The muscle in his jaw pulsed. His teeth clenched, then he closed his eyes and held still for a moment, until she felt the anger tightening his body ease. His hold on her waist relaxed. The corners of his mouth lifted into a rueful grin, but the effort didn't budge the corners of his eyes.

With a callused finger he stroked her cheek, then touched her lower lip. A dizzying current flowed through her, clouding her mind. Could he really be Lord Kenward? Logic screamed he wasn't, but something inside her wanted to believe he was the man in the portrait. The knight who had filled her childhood with fanciful dreams of undying love. But her realistic nature had always considered undying love as much a fantasy as meeting Lord Kenward in the flesh.

Someone cleared their throat and jarred her back to reality. She glanced over her shoulder. The other man had poured himself a drink and glared at her over the rim of the pewter cup. Facing Lord Kenward, she asked, 'Why do you keep talking about my father? I told you he's . . .'

'Do not attempt to protect your father, Christel.' His hands slid up her waist and held her arms in a light, but firm hold. She couldn't suppress a shiver. 'He seized English property. His bold move may well cost him his life when I reclaim it.'

Lauren stared at him, unable to make sense of anything he said. 'Who's Christel?'

'By the sword, Kenward! Entertain the wench another time.' The soldier slammed his cup on the table, sloshing red wine onto the battered wooden surface. 'We must pursue victory tonight!'

The solid pressure of Lord Kenward against her sent a strange calm through Lauren. Part of her resisted thinking of him by the dead lord's name, but she had to call him something. She turned and stared at the stranger across from her. 'Who are you?'

'Can you believe the audacity of this Scottish baggage?' the man bellowed. 'I am Lord Anthony Wright, rightful owner of Gowan Castle.'

'I see,' Lauren managed, not trying to hide her dislike for the arrogant man.

'Aye, and if by some chance Lord Kenward – ' he pointed a gloved finger at her '– fails to cut down your father, I shall raise arms and bend Armstrong to my will.'

'Bruce Armstrong is supposed to be my father?' Part of the puzzle settled into place. *They think I'm Christel Armstrong!* The urge to laugh and tell them of their mistake rose to her lips. Then it occurred to her. Perhaps they did mistake her for someone else, but that didn't explain why she was being held captive by men who were supposed to be dead outside a castle that didn't exist.

She turned back and looked into Lord Kenward's shadowed blue eyes. The sadness she'd imagined seeing in the portrait was cloaked behind an icy blue veil. But, still, she couldn't deny they were the same. How could it be the same, unless he really was . . .?

'Nicholas? My God, it is you,' she whispered. A dizzying light spun through her mind, making her sway toward him. 'But how?'

'By the rod, Kenward, the woman is daft. First she knows not who ye are, then she stares at ye as if you're Saint Killian in the flesh!'

Lauren gasped for air and stared at Nicholas. *I'm in another time!* She couldn't deny it any longer. The proof stood before her, clad in armor and looking at her with burning, reproachful eyes. A muscle twitched in his jaw; his brow creased in a frown.

His scowl deepened as she held his gaze. She knew she must look like a halfwit, but she couldn't stop staring. He released her, and her knees melted. Cursing, he scooped her into his arms and carried her to a makeshift bed of thick quilts and furs.

'I know ye plan to ruin the wench by beddin' her, Nick, but another time, perhaps?' Lord Wright wailed. 'I demand ye send your men over the walls.'

'Fetch the leech, Anthony,' Nicholas ordered, and knelt to study the cut on her thigh. She felt his gaze burn into her bare skin where the material had ripped.

'But . . .'

Nicholas glanced over his shoulder and ordered, 'Now.'

Once Lord Wright had left, Nicholas faced her. Their gazes met, intensifying the surreal warmth gathering around her. *Nicholas*. Afraid to breathe, Lauren raised her hands. She wanted to touch the scar, reassure herself that the man was real, that she wasn't dreaming.

'Why do you stare like a bewildered child?' he barked.

His tone startled her out of her daze. Her hand was an inch from his face, but she could feel heat radiating from him. He gripped her wrist and held her fingers away.

'Are you still curious about my scar?'

Lauren shook her head, whispered, 'I'm more confused than anything else.' She wanted to laugh at the understatement. She was both curious and confused as to how she had gotten here. But she wouldn't put the question to Lord Nicholas Kenward, fearing he might think her insane. Given time, she would learn what had happened, then she would find her way back home.

'There is little to be confused about, Lady Christel.'
He drew a small dagger from his waist and cut the
bindings around her wrists. When the leather straps
fell away her skin stung, but she hardly felt it. He
picked up a mazer filled with water and cleaned her leg
with a damp cloth. 'You are my hostage. I shall ransom
you to your father when the time is right.'

Biting down on her lower lip, she tried to ignore the
fact that he was touching her. She refused to acknowledge how sensitive her skin now seemed, or the way a
fine tingle traveled an imaginary path up her thigh and
across her body. There were more important things to
consider. Like what would Nicholas do when he
discovered she wasn't Armstrong's daughter? If she
tried to tell him the truth, he wouldn't believe her. Just
like before. Feeling safe in her disguise for the moment, she decided to keep quiet about her identity.
Surely she'd find a way to escape by morning. In the
meantime, she could get to know him.

'What if my father doesn't pay the ransom?' He bent
his head to study her wound. Light from a flickering
candle danced over the blue-black length of his hair.
She curled her fingers into fists to keep from running
them through the dark, tangled satin. He touched her
skin with the pad of his finger, startling her as threads
of heat wove through her leg. She stiffened, a small
gasp catching in the back of her throat.

He looked up, their gazes locking. The constant
anger that lived in his eyes shifted into something
resembling shock. Had he sensed what she felt? Good
Lord, she hoped not. She wasn't exactly sure what

she'd experienced, but it had been powerful, and unlike anything she'd ever felt before. She understood the reason for her reaction to him, though. She was talking to a man who'd lived in her dreams. Who wouldn't react? His response to her wouldn't be so noble. There was no telling where such dangerous feelings could lead. And things were confusing enough already.

'Laird Armstrong will pay well for the return of his virginal daughter.'

An alarm sounded at the harshness of his voice. The hateful words matched the renewed fury in his eyes. She didn't like the way he'd said 'virginal,' either, as if that was somehow a mark against her.

'But what if he doesn't?' she asked, not really wanting an answer.

'Then payment shall be up to you.'

CHAPTER 4

Alone in the tent, Lauren lay still on the bed of animal pelts and blankets. Her eyes wide in the darkness, she steepled her hands over her chest and listened. A melody of snores and moans blended with the quiet outside. After long hours of tense waiting, the muscles in her neck and back ached. The stinging in her wrists, where they'd been bound, had faded to a constant throb. A crackle from a nearby campfire startled her. Her heart pounded against her ribs and echoed in her ears. She blew out a breath and forced herself to relax.

So far her patience had paid off. Gradually the wounded had been tended; the healthy had bedded down. If she guessed right, dawn was an hour or so away. If she wanted to escape, now was the time. Only one small detail kept her from moving.

Where was Nicholas Kenward?

After informing her she'd be responsible for her own ransom, he'd left, his face set in anger, his fists clenched at his sides. Some deep emotion she hadn't understood had rolled off him in waves. She'd stared at the tent flap, wondering what he'd meant. That same thought troubled her now. She told herself not to worry about it. She was leaving. *Let the real Christel Armstrong deal with it*. But her mind wouldn't let go of the puzzle.

She recalled Lord Wright's sneering voice. '*I know ye plan to ruin the wench by beddin' her . . .*'

And Nicholas had used the term 'virginal daughter' in a derogatory sense. She envisioned his hostile glare, the mad pulse in his jaw. But his eyes had been filled with something else. Determination? Regret? Disgust? She didn't know which.

Lauren sat upright on the bed and stared into the darkness. Did he plan to force himself on Christel Armstrong before returning her to her father? Her mouth gaped in outrage. Was that part of his plan for revenge?

'How could he?' The man in the portrait wouldn't seduce a woman with the intention of ruining her! Not *her* Black Knight. Her mind reeling, she pushed the warm furs off her legs and stood. She had to find Jessy and leave.

She accepted the fact she was in another time, though she had no idea how or why. She'd witnessed men die in a barbaric battle. She'd met the knight who had filled her childhood dreams. Now her virginity – no, Christel Armstrong's virginity – was to be used as a pawn in a political game. The outrageousness of it all almost made her laugh.

While she *was* a virgin, it wasn't by choice but by default. During her sophomore year of college she'd dated Bryan Libberman, a junior. Wanting to shed her reputation for being distant and uptight, and learn what all the fuss was about, she'd come close to making love with him. It had begun as an incredibly awkward event, one she'd regretted as soon as it had started. She'd felt like a salmon tossed onto a riverbank, flopping around and gasping for air. Before it had gone too far she had called an end to it and, thankfully, had never seen Bryan again.

But she'd never dreamt that by saving her virginity she might be raped by an English lord in the sixteenth century. And all in the name of revenge.

Stealing to the tent opening, she eased the flap back and peered outside. Smoldering fires dotted the country-side like bright stars dropped from heaven. Dying embers cast enough light for her to see men scattered across the ground. She prayed they slept soundly. A faint breeze stirred the smell of smoke. Despite the occasional cough and dream-filled mutterings, all remained quiet. She didn't question her luck when there was no sign of Lord Kenward or Kenric. It was either now or never, and she didn't want to be around when the sun rose on Gowan Castle.

Stepping into the night air, she turned left, the way they'd taken Jessy, and inched her way toward the end of the tent. She hoped they'd tied the mare nearby. Her stomach clenched with a peculiar mixture of fear and excitement. Sweat bathed her palms.

As she rounded the tent, a gust of wind caught her unbound hair and swirled it around her. She raked it from her face and continued in the darkness. Lauren clamped her lips together when her breath rasped in her ears. She stepped further into the shadows to skirt a small fire and the sleeping men surrounding it. A soft nicker made her pause. Squinting her eyes, she made out the dark shapes of several horses.

Relief eased the tension in her shoulders, but the knot in her stomach stayed firm. She still had to find Jessy and leave camp without being heard. Crossing the last few feet, she whispered to the horses. She wove her way through the small herd, searching for the chestnut mare with a white star on her forehead.

The mare lifted her head and nickered softly in greeting. Realizing it was Jessy, she gave the horse a quick hug and urged the mare away from the pack. Jessy stumbled. Glancing down, Lauren saw the rope that hobbled the horses together.

She clamped her jaw tight. She supposed it would've been too convenient to find her horse saddled and ready to go. Kneeling, she grasped the coarse rope and fumbled in the dark to free the knot. With each passing second her heart pounded harder. Sweat trickled down her temples, her hair stuck to her face and eyes.

A ripple of panic flowed through her veins. She'd come too far in her escape to let anything stop her now. She didn't need a saddle and bridle to ride Jessy away from this nightmare. If need be, she would drag the mare away from the camp by her mane, then ride her bareback. She forced herself to believe that once she was gone they wouldn't come after her. After all, they had a battle to fight. A castle to destroy. Surely that had to be more important than one woman's virginity!

The knot slipped free. Lauren rose and pushed against Jessy's neck, guiding her away from the other horses.

'Where are you going?'

Lauren spun around and smothered a scream with her hand. Lord Kenward stood directly behind her. How had he done that? She hadn't heard a thing.

Her heart thundered in her ears. Gasping for breath, she felt cool air dry what spit she had left. Frantic and terrified, she struck him in the chest. Her fist bounced off him; pain shot up her fingers.

'Blast the saints in heaven,' she muttered through clenched teeth, and shook her hand to ease its throbbing.

'Curse them well, lady, for they will not aid in your escape.'

She gave thanks that shadows concealed his eyes. Imagining his angry glare was enough to jolt her. She inched back and reached behind her for Jessy. 'I won't stay here.'

Just as her fingers brushed the mare's coat Lord Kenward reached out, caught her by the waist and hauled her against him. He squeezed tight, cutting off her breath. She fisted his shirt in her hands to keep from crying out.

'You will stay,' he whispered, and splayed his hand possessively across her back, pressing her against his immovable length. The solid feel of his thighs was like a slap in the face, leaving her feeling exposed, liking it and hating it all at the same time.

She stiffened in defense. 'Why? So you can rape Bruce Armstrong's daughter?' She leveled him with a challenging stare, though she doubted he could see it.

His chest shook with a villainous laugh. The vibration sent goosebumps over her skin. He ran a finger along her jaw. 'Perhaps I will not have to rape you.'

'You arrogant . . . I'm disappointed in you, Lord Kenward. You're not at all what I imagined.'

She struggled, but he caught her wrists and locked them behind her back. He bent slightly and his face, a dark mask in the shadows, hovered inches above hers. The crazy notion that he intended to kiss her sent her mind into a frantic spin. She arched away from him, but he pursued. When he finally pulled back, an inappropriate combination of relief and disappointment pulsed through her.

'And you are too spirited and outspoken for your own good.'

As quickly as he'd captured her, he released her, then he bent to hobble Jessy's legs. Lauren glanced around for a weapon, something to hit him over the head with, stun him, but she couldn't see anything in the dark. A desperate inner voice told her to run. The coherent side of her knew he would catch her, that was if she didn't trip over a patch of bramble and break her neck first. But rationality had no foot-hold in her mind.

She turned and darted through the darkness in a blind run. A muffled curse sounded behind her. She pushed faster, her ragged breath covering any warning of pursuit. Campfires dotted the ground to her left, so

64

she turned in the opposite direction toward the shadows. A steel vise closed around her waist, snatching her off the ground.

'Let me go!'

His warm breath sent shivers down her spine. 'I have had enough of your foolish attempts to escape me, Lady Christel.'

She kicked her legs in a futile attempt to break free. She pushed his arm, but couldn't budge his crushing hold on her waist. A spasm of pain shot through her sides. She knew her ribs would crack if he didn't let go of her soon. In a raspy voice lacking air, she asked, 'What would you say if I told you I wasn't Lady Christel?'

He headed toward the camp, carrying her on his hip like a bag of groceries. 'I would suggest you save your lies. You are my hostage. I'll not release you.'

'You've made a mistake,' she insisted.

'Aye, in not trussing you up like a swine to slaughter.'

Lauren went limp with defeat in his arm, resting her head against his shoulder. 'You're hurting me.'

'If I release you, will you do as you are told?'

The question, gently put, made her wonder if she hadn't erred in thinking Lord Kenward would resort to seducing an innocent woman for revenge. 'Am I supposed to make this easy for you?'

With his face bent close to her, she sensed his grin. Apprehension made her hold her breath. With a new kind of panic she wondered if he was right, that he wouldn't have to go to the trouble of seducing her.

He, after all, was her fantasy knight. Except now he was a living, breathing man and not a conjured dream. She was feeling things, thinking things that were impossible . . . or ought to be. She shook her head, not understanding her own mind. She didn't want a relationship with a real man *or* a dream. A real man would undoubtedly mean risk and heartache. She'd been doing fine on her own, and she didn't plan on changing. So, how was she supposed to relate to a man conjured from her imagination? And keep her heart and sanity intact? She hadn't a clue.

She had to escape, but she couldn't if he tied her up. 'I won't run away again,' she lied.

He set her down and turned her to him. The first amber rays of sunlight broke across the distant bluff. The faint glow revealed his doubting smirk, a look that said trusting her would be like trusting the devil not to lead the innocent astray.

'You won't tie me up again, will you?'

'I would be a fool not to.' He gripped her arm in a less than bruising hold and started toward the tent.

Lauren tried an encouraging smile, but he refused to look at her. She pursed her lips in thought, then said, 'Kenric could watch me.'

He grunted.

She glanced around for help. What she needed was a diversion to keep him from taking her to the tent. 'How is Hades's wound?'

He shot her a glance, then shook his head in exasperation.

As he pulled her along, men stirred from their

66

pallets to stare after them. Whispers accompanied the curious glances and approving nods. She searched their dirt-streaked faces for any trace of compassion. Would any of them help her escape? The gleam in their eyes told her their loyalty lay with Nicholas Kenward, and not with the Scottish enemy's daughter. Except she wasn't the enemy!

Growing desperate, she rounded on Nicholas and clasped his arm. Hard muscles flexed against her palms, swaying her thinking. 'I'm trained in healing animals. Please let me look at Hades.' She heard the panic in her voice and cringed.

His gaze moved over her face in a slow study before settling on her lips and lingering there for a moment. As if shocked, or angered, his eyes flew up to meet hers. 'There is no need for your help. The leech put a poultice on the wound.'

Lauren couldn't help but shudder. Last night the frightening excuse for a doctor had come to tend the cut on her leg. She'd sent him away, refusing to let him touch her. 'That man doesn't know the first thing about healing. He tried to put mud on my cut!'

'It was most likely a herbal salve.' With his hands resting on his hips, Nicholas muttered a curse and looked away. He clenched his jaw in an irritated gesture she was quickly becoming familiar with. She wondered if he had this reaction with everyone – or only her? 'I have no time for this.'

When he urged her forward, Lauren cried, 'Wait!'

'Enough of your diversions.' He bent and caught her stomach with his shoulder, heaving her up.

A shocked cry tore from her, then she couldn't breathe at all. Cheers and ribald calls rose from the men who hurried to flank the path and watch her being carried off. Humiliated, she beat her fists against Nicholas's back. 'Put me down!'

The arm secured around her legs tightened. Then she felt his large hand on her thigh. Heat crept up her leg, horrifying her further. His massive shoulders shook, as if he were laughing. Grasping his black tunic, Lauren buried her face in the wool and tried not to envision the spectacle he was making of her. She failed. Anger rose up her throat until she thought she would choke. Tears burned her eyes, but she'd be damned if she'd let them fall.

Before Nicholas set the woman down, he struggled to wipe the grin from his face. He had disgraced her enough by carrying her like a string of snared pigeons. A small voice of reason suggested he apologize. Granted, she was his hostage, but he didn't want her angry; he wanted her willing. But she had tried to escape him. He shouldn't apologize to her; he should punish her. Severely. The instant her feet touched the ground, he regretted letting go of her at all.

With both hands, she shoved against his chest. Even caught off guard, her attack couldn't budge him, which only seemed to enrage her further. Fury glowed like twin emerald daggers in her eyes. Her pink-tinged cheeks darkened to complement the beautiful shade of her hair: russet with a touch of gold. The same color as a perfect English sunset. God, the woman was a hellion. Did nothing frighten her? Nicholas stared at her in amazement and took note of things he'd missed before.

She stood with her trim legs planted apart. Dirt and dried blood smeared her tan leggings, but that didn't deter him from appreciating the way they molded against her. Her clothes were highly indecent, but there was nothing to be done about that now. He hadn't thought to pack a gown for a siege. He would, however, have to make a point to keep her out of sight of his men.

She propped her hands on her hips, her long fingers kneading her small waist in agitation. They probably itched to strangle his neck, Nicholas mused. Resisting the urge to grin, a display he rarely indulged in, he slid his gaze on an upward path. Her chest heaved within the fitted black coat. The white shirt collar that poked through enhanced the pale elegance of her slender neck. Her lush mouth clenched with indignation, giving her jaw a stubborn line.

Over the past day he'd witnessed her wide-eyed confusion, seen her pale with fright, and now she trembled with rage. Irritated by his interest in her, Nicholas wondered what she would look like if she smiled. He imagined her eyes softening to the color of polished jade.

Aware of how dangerous such thoughts could be, he willed them away and searched for the anger that had sustained him most of his life. As hard as he fought to retain his rancor, he couldn't seem to hold onto it.

He ought to hate her.

His enemy.

But he didn't, and for that he cursed himself. Why couldn't he punish her with the cruelty her father was so gifted at wielding? *Because she is innocent of her father's crimes.*

'How dare you!'

Nicholas stared at her, momentarily at a loss to understand her outburst.

'Hoisting me up on your shoulder like I was . . . was . . .'

'A prisoner who tried to escape?' he finished for her.

She snapped her mouth shut and buried her hands in her hair, pulling the tangled mess away from her face. The feminine gesture revealed her struggle for patience. Watching her, he felt his own patience and the purpose of his mission slipping away, while a new and passionate urge took its place.

He tried to quell the lustful ache. He didn't have time to deal with her the way he wanted to, but the heat gathering in his loins caught like a newly kindled fire. All he needed was to add more fuel and he'd follow through with his vow to ruin her. With his imagination fanning the idea, he took a step toward her.

She retreated, and tensed like a doe cornered by a hungry wolf. 'Don't come any closer.'

'Oh, I intend to come much closer, Christel.'

She glanced nervously to the side, then ran her tongue over her lower lip. She didn't cower in fear as he'd expected, but held her ground and searched for a way out. Her courage both surprised and intrigued him. It would make taming her an even greater pleasure. Perhaps she wouldn't want to return to her father when he was done with her. That would be the ultimate, devastating blow to Armstrong.

Nicholas reached out and cupped her neck, stroking her clenched jaw with his thumb. After catching her trying to escape he had touched her in much the same way. Her softness had startled him then. Now it intrigued him. When he'd devised the plan to ruin Laird Armstrong's daughter, he hadn't thought he would enjoy it. He hadn't expected to want her. But he did. He wanted to see how far he could push her, tempt her into giving herself freely.

She clasped his wrist, tried to pry his hand away. 'Please, don't,' she pleaded in a shaken whisper.

'Look at me, Christel.'

'I'm *not* Christel.'

He lifted a brow, tightening his hold on her chin.

'I'm not intimidated by you, either.'

'You should be.' He resisted the urge to show her why, releasing her instead.

She slipped away from him, rubbing her jaw as she paced the small space.

Watching her nervous actions convinced Nicholas she was searching for another way to escape. She could look all she wanted, he mused. He had her now, and he wouldn't let her go.

Sounds of men readying their armor filtered into the tent. Jacobson's commanding voice rose above it, giving orders to take positions. With another long day of siege ahead of them, he needed to end this conversation. But before he tied and gagged the woman he wanted to make sure she knew how hopeless her situation was.

'*Are* you afraid of me, Christel?' As he poured two goblets of watered wine, she rolled her eyes heavenward.

'No, I'm not afraid of you.' She swiped a strand of hair off her forehead and continued to pace.

'Most people are,' he said, his voice a lethal thread. 'And with good reason.' He offered her one of the cups. She stopped and stared at it, as if he'd filled it with poison. Nicholas hid a scowl by taking a sip from her goblet.

'Well, I'm the exception.' She snatched the wine from his hand and turned away.

'So it would seem.' Placing his cup on the table, he took a silent step toward her. He grazed his knuckles down the tangled length of her hair. She stiffened, and glanced over her shoulder.

'Don't you have a castle to destroy?' she asked.

'Aye, that I do. But first – ' he clasped her arm and turned her to face him '– tell me why you do not fear me.'

Her gaze traveled over his face, lingering on his scar before dropping to his lips. The wariness shadowing her eyes softened as she whispered, 'Because you're Nicholas Kenward, and I know you won't harm me.'

Her misplaced faith in him momentarily stunned him. 'That is where you are wrong, Christel,' he said, with a venom he didn't completely feel. A small tremor erupted in her body, and his hand absorbed it.

'You would take your revenge against an innocent woman?'

'Only if she were an Armstrong!' Her question was too pointed, too jarring. He didn't want to interrogate his methods or their rightness. He had a vow of revenge to fulfil. Until then nothing else mattered. Not the future of his own life and certainly not hers.

He pulled her roughly into his arms. Her goblet tumbled to the floor, its blood-red liquid seeping into the dirt.

Her hands came up and pushed against his chest, but she couldn't stop him from claiming her mouth in a hungry, punishing kiss. He slanted his head to capture all of her, show her a glimpse of what was to come. Her lips parted on a gasp. He took advantage and thrust his tongue inside her warmth.

She tensed in his arms, her fists clenching his tunic. She ceased her struggles, held still as if unsure of what to do. He couldn't believe she would give up or accept him so easily. He waited for her cries for mercy, her tears, perhaps even her trembling withdrawal into submission. His hands roamed in a greedy search over her body; grazing her breasts, sliding down her waist, her back, lower. He touched to frighten her, but found he couldn't stop.

His body came to life with a vicious roar. Heat pulsed with his blood, pounding in his mind, tempting him with feelings he couldn't feel. He didn't want this. He wanted her to know the hate that coiled like a living thing inside him. It was there, waiting beneath the surface to strike out. But it didn't. The absence of rage puzzled him as much as it frustrated him.

He stopped his assault on her mouth, but didn't pull away. Her lips stayed close to his. The tremor in her breath wasn't from fear, he realized, but from the first wave of desire. She leaned into him, pressed her lips to his. Nicholas closed his eyes, drew in a breath, filled his lungs with her scent; horses, soap and something female.

She didn't respond with the innocence of a virgin, he reasoned, nor did she kiss with experience. Instead, she met him with curiosity, caution and not a shred of trepidation. Against his will, he probed the liquid sweetness of her mouth.

Slower this time, he slid his hands beneath her hair, then followed the curve of her body from shoulder to waist, feeling things he'd missed before: the firmness of her back, her small waist, the tight muscles of her thighs.

He nipped her bottom lip with his teeth, then pulled a searing kiss from her. A moan escaped her and wrapped his need in a tight hold. *God, how could she taste so good? How could he want her so much?*

The thought stunned him. He opened his eyes to see hers closed, with thick, dark brown lashes shadowing her cheeks. No! It wasn't her but vengeance that caused fire to race with his blood. She belonged to him, to do with as he pleased. To use and ruin and ultimately cast aside. He had to control his emotions, or risk confusing his loathing for a sentiment that didn't exist.

Nicholas broke the kiss and held her at arm's length. Her lids fluttered open to reveal something he didn't want to see: glazed pools of green, dreamy and wanting. She stared at him for a long moment, then blinked, awe filling her gaze. A faint smile touched her kiss-swollen lips.

'You don't kiss like a painting.' She released her hold on his tunic and touched her mouth.

'What did you say?'

Surprise widened her eyes. She took a step back and propped her hands on her hips. With her shoulders squared, she said with little conviction, 'Don't ever kiss me again.'

'You, Lady Christel, are in the sore habit of telling me what I can and cannot do.' Nicholas moved so close to her she had to crane her neck to look at him. When he caught her chin, the bravery glowing in her eyes dimmed to wariness. 'I shall take great pleasure in breaking you of that habit.'

She opened her mouth, but snapped it shut.

'Were you going to say something?'

With a forced smile, she said, 'I have nothing to say to you.'

He chucked her under the chin and turned to leave. 'Good, you are learning already. And by the way,' he added with a malicious grin, 'I intend to do much more than kiss you when I return.'

Ducking out of the tent, he heard her mutter a strange oath and stomp her foot.

He signaled to Kenric and scanned the valley below. Jacobson had prepared the horde of soldiers that had rallied at Nicholas's request. Dressed in full armor, they only waited for word to begin the siege.

Something inside the tent crashed. Nicholas grinned. The siege would end today. On the morrow he would take his hostage home to Westbourne Castle and claim the sweetest revenge of all.

Christel Armstrong.

CHAPTER 5

Lauren tugged at the bindings around her wrists and cursed Nicholas Kenward for an idiot. If she could manage to free herself, she'd gladly stab the infuriating knight with his own bloody sword.

The sounds of shouting men and endless war cries sawed across her nerves, making her feel anxious, irrational and on the verge of tears. She had to escape. It didn't matter that she was in another time. She couldn't continue listening to the wails of dying men and do nothing. Earlier she'd worked the gag around her mouth free, but Kenric had refused to respond to a single question. When she'd called him a dimwit, he'd stared at her with his black, emotionless eyes.

A battle cry, louder than before, and with the promise of victory, rose in a deafening wave. Lauren stood, ignoring Kenric when he moved to stand beside her. As she opened the tent flap an explosion rocked her off balance. Kenric caught her as she fell. Jerking herself free, she darted out of the tent and froze.

The constant drumming of the battering ram

against the portcullis stopped. The men beneath the tarp pushed the wagon away from the castle. The swordsmen and archers moved back as well. A black cloud of smoke rose in the air, then dissipated with a gust of warm wind.

She spotted Nicholas riding Hades, not far below her, in the sea of men. He raised his sword, then sliced it through the air and bellowed a command. The cannon beside him exploded to life. A second later portions of the castle wall crumbled. The Scottish soldiers stationed there fell to their deaths, buried beneath the debris.

'No!' Lauren screamed, horrified. She raced toward Nicholas. She had to stop him from destroying the castle and hurting the men. Kenric caught her and hauled her off the ground, his arm tight around her waist. 'Let me go, damn you!'

She kicked her legs and struggled futilely. Kenric turned back to the tent. 'Stop, wait! Please, I have to talk to Nicholas.'

When he ignored her, Lauren turned her head and bit his bare upper arm until she tasted blood in her mouth. He grunted and flinched, dropping her to the ground.

Lauren scrambled to her feet. Tears clogged her throat and burned her eyes. Kenric gripped her arm. '*Nicholas!*'

Her cry resounded through the valley. Soldiers turned in her direction. Nicholas faced her, his body rigid with tension. He raised the visor of his helmet, but she couldn't see his face clearly. She tugged against Kenric's hold. For some unknown reason he released her, but stayed by her side.

With her wrists tied, she ran with a stumbling gait through the swarm of soldiers. They moved out of her path, their curious stares following her. Reaching Nicholas, she gripped his leg. The steel armor over his thigh was as cold and hard as his expression.

She grasped Nicholas's arm, the unbending armor sending a tremor through her. 'You can't do this. Please, I'm begging you, don't kill any more innocent people.'

A nerve twitched at his temple. Hades pranced with impatience and knocked her aside.

'Have you given this speech to your father?' Nicholas asked with malice. 'He is the one who exceeds in killing the innocent.'

'I told you, he's not my father!'

'I am weary of your lies.' He raised his sword. A man with black soot covering his face held a torch over the cannon's fuse.

'No!' Lauren pleaded. 'Okay, okay, let's say I am Christel Armstrong. Take your revenge out on me.'

He stared at her, his brows drawn together in an angry frown. 'You would sacrifice yourself to save your father?'

'I would if it meant ending this nightmare.' A tremor shook her body. She gulped a breath and held his intense gaze. She wondered what he meant by 'sacrifice.' Was she supposed to give up her life for people she didn't know? She clenched his arm tighter, wishing she knew him better. But she had to believe

79

he wouldn't hurt her, no matter who he thought she was.

'It is very noble of you, Lady Christel. But it is your father who must pay for his crimes.' Pulling his arm free, he waved to Kenric. 'Take her away.'

Lauren dodged Kenric's grasp just as the cannon detonated, rumbling its deafening roar across the valley. 'If you aren't going to end this, then let me go,' she demanded over the clamor, taking a step back as Kenric advanced on her.

'Why? So you can return to die with your people?' Nicholas scowled. 'I think not.'

She heard the lethal agitation in his voice, knew she'd tested his patience, but she didn't care. 'No, so I can leave. I won't watch you murder those people!'

'It is odd to hear an Armstrong speak so passionately against murder.'

'I'm not an Arm . . .' Kenric grabbed her arm and pulled her toward the tent. She fought and dug in her heels. She kicked Kenric time and again, but he didn't seem to feel it.

'Return to the tent, Christel,' Nicholas called. 'Or I shall carry you there myself and finish what we started!'

The cannon exploded again, washing out his men's laughter. Lauren flinched and tried to shut out the crashing rocks and shrill screams. She opened her eyes and glared at Lord Nicholas Kenward. The Black Knight. The man of her dreams. The man she was growing to hate.

* * *

A group of small pipits fluttered overhead and filled the air with their sweet, melodious chatter. Lauren glanced at them, but couldn't find it within herself to appreciate their charm. They were the first birds she'd seen in two days. Probably the first to brave returning to the valley now that the cannonfire had ceased.

That was if she didn't count the buzzards flying over the ruins of Gowan Castle.

Jessy stomped her foot and took a step. Kenric tightened his hold on her reins. The thoroughbred obeyed the silent command and stood quietly next to his horse. Lauren held still, anger trembling through her body at being as helpless as her mare.

She stared at the grassy slope, littered with broken arrows, pieces of discarded clothing and useless armor, still not believing the destruction. The quaint, beautiful castle, with its colorful flags waving from the four turrets, lay in a tumble of shattered stone. A fire smoldered where a kitchen garden had been. Smoke and clouds of dust still hovered like a blanket of death over the rubble and the bodies buried beneath.

How could he have done it? How could a man hate so much? Over the years, Lauren had thought she understood Nicholas's vow to avenge the murder of his father and brother. Her own parents had been killed by a drunk driver. She'd been devastated, then outraged at the man who had taken their lives. But murder? To what end? It would not have brought back her parents, just as it wouldn't bring back Nicholas's family.

She couldn't imagine living with such hate. It had to eat away at his soul. Once he claimed his revenge, what would be left of him? An empty man? A man without a cause, without a life?

She refused to acknowledge the similarities between her life and his. She might have retreated to the isolated moors of England with her veterinary practice, but she hadn't gone after the man responsible for killing her family and ruining her life. Because it hadn't been ruined. She'd made the most of it by believing she was stronger for living through it.

No, they were nothing alike. During the past year she'd simply avoided risking her heart in a relationship. Life was safer that way. Though she admitted being lonely at times, she led a fairly contented existence. Nicholas couldn't boast the same, she mused. Anger ruled his life, leaving a residue of sadness. She'd seen the shadows in his eyes, ghosts, she imagined, haunting his every thought. Did his demons follow him into his dreams? The answer had to be yes. Nothing else would account for his malicious actions.

Though he hadn't been completely evil. His treatment of her had been rough at first, but she'd caught glimpses of a gentler side when he'd cleaned her wounded leg, then again when he'd kissed her.

Though his kiss had been brutal at first, it had turned slow and hungry. And incredibly wonderful. As much as she tried, she couldn't forget the moment, nor the feel of his mouth on hers. Hard and possessing.

The kiss had reached inside her, disturbed her safe little world.

His powerful effect on her hadn't surprised her, though her reaction frightened her more than the man. How could she be furious with him, for the loss of life and the destruction of the castle, yet want to feel his lips on hers again?

She hadn't been so lost in the kiss that she hadn't sensed his own surprise. Had he been shocked that she'd responded to him? Or startled that he'd enjoyed kissing her? Lauren rubbed her eyes and sighed. Things were far too confusing. The workings of Nicholas Kenward's mind didn't matter. She had to concentrate on escaping. And soon. Now that the castle was destroyed, the soldiers were making preparations to return home.

Home. Westbourne Castle. A part of her wanted to see what it looked like in the sixteenth century. But she knew the longer she stayed the more embroiled she'd become in Nicholas's life.

As if thinking of him had conjuring powers, Nicholas appeared before her. Seeing him clad in lighter chain-mail and riding Hades at an easy gallop sent a warm thrill through her limbs, sensitizing her as if she had downed a glass of wine. He had removed his helmet, and held it propped against his leg. His hair escaped the leather strap at his nape and flew behind him like black silk against the sun.

Regardless of her rage at what he had done, she couldn't deny the calming, unnerving effect he had on her. An effect that could prove dangerous if she didn't leave soon. Unconsciously, she reached for the reins, but Kenric's sideways glance made her pause.

Beside Nicholas, Lord Wright rode a dappled gray stallion. As the two horses stopped beside her their armor rattled, but not loud enough to drown Lord Wright's whining voice.

'You turned my castle tae rubble, and the blasted Scot wasn't even there!'

Lauren raised a brow and looked at Nicholas, his expression clouded in anger. 'What happened?'

'Your father was not within the castle,' he replied with contempt.

She let the assumption of her father pass. She had tried to tell him the truth, and he wouldn't listen. Let him think what he wanted.

'He escaped during the night,' Lord Wright sneered, as if it were her fault, 'and sacrificed his men to stay and fight.' Lord Wright turned his mount and looked at the sight where his castle had once stood. 'And for what? There is nothing left but destruction.'

The sorrow in Wright's voice tempted Lauren to feel pity for him. But for some reason she couldn't muster enough emotion for the arrogant fop.

'We shall rebuild it, Anthony,' Nicholas offered.

'No, you won't,' Lauren said, and stifled a curse, appalled that she'd hinted about the future.

'What say you?' Lord Wright turned a frown of suspicion on her.

Both men stared at her – Lord Wright with unguarded hatred, Nicholas with open curiosity. She cleared her throat, her mind racing to cover her slip. 'I said you won't rebuild it.'

'Why would you say such a thing, Christel?' Nicholas asked.

Lauren shrugged and tried to look away, but couldn't. There wasn't a trace of the cruel barbarian she'd thought him to be for attacking the castle. Regret marked the frown pulling at his mouth. The ghosts she'd imagined haunted his steel-blue eyes. 'I just know you won't. It'll probably be called the Ruins of Gowan.'

'What are you, some kind of witch that can tell the future?' Lord Wright demanded.

Stunned, Lauren felt her mouth drop open. Well aware of the dreadful things that could happen to her if she were accused of witchcraft, she realized she had to be more careful. 'Of course not,' she managed. 'It's just my opinion. I imagine it's too risky and expensive to rebuild your home so close to the Scottish border.'

'I think we should put her to the stake and be done with her, Nick.' A wicked grin was curving Lord Wright's thin mouth.

Nicholas tensed, and Hades pressed forward to stand between Jessy and Lord Wright's horse. To Lauren's dismay, the mare nuzzled Hades' neck. 'She is for me to deal with, Anthony. No one else.'

Lord Wright studied Nicholas with wary pale brown eyes. 'So be it, Nick. You deserve your revenge. I shall claim mine on her father another day.' With that, he reined his gray stallion around and spurred it into a run across the littered field.

The instant Lord Wright disappeared from sight, the tension stringing her body taut fled, making her shoulders slump with relief. 'I don't like that man,' she said, not meaning to voice her thoughts out loud.

'He has reasons for his anger.'

'And you have yours?'

His burning gaze held her still. 'Aye.' He took Jessy's reins from Kenric and headed for a well-worn path leading south.

'Where are we going?'

'To my home.'

Hades stepped into a gallop. Jessy resisted the tug on the reins, dancing sideways, but finally gave in and followed.

'Westbourne Castle?' When he didn't respond, Lauren gripped the mare's sides with her knees. A cold sweat broke out over her body. Her hands grew slick as she gripped the saddle's pommel.

She would see the castle in its original state. She didn't know if the prospect should excite or terrify her. Would it be more beautiful than in her time, or crowded with foul-smelling people and spoiled with refuse?

Unease roiled inside her. She didn't want to see it. Didn't want to know the people who lived there. She had to escape. Four, perhaps five miles to the east lay the copse of oak trees. Deep within, a hidden cave held the answer to sending her home. After replaying the events of two days before, she knew the cave had brought her here.

Perhaps it had been the Gaelic words she'd spoken,

or maybe the storm had caused her to travel back in time. Or a combination of both. She didn't know or care. The one thing she knew for certain was that she had to return to the cave if she ever wanted to go home again.

Home. The word made her flinch. She didn't really have one to speak of. Hadn't had one for the past year. She'd still been in college when her parents died. Since then she had simply existed from day to day. Floating from one class to another, unconsciously shutting out her friends. When she'd realized what she'd done, she knew she needed to change her life. So she'd moved to England.

She glanced at Nicholas's broad back. Confined in his rigid stance was the strength of a warrior. A man who would protect all he held dear, regardless of the price it cost him. A man with a home and a legion of men who respected him enough to follow him into battle.

Was there a man like him in her own time? If so, she hadn't found him. Even if she did, she wouldn't risk loving him. A man with Nicholas's capacity for hate, who would jeopardize his life in the name of vengeance, would surely be killed . . .

'Oh, my God!' Her gasp for air caused those around her to stop and stare. Nicholas reined in his horse and pulled Jessy beside him.

'Christel, what is it?' Lines of concern deepened along his brow and at the corners of his eyes.

Lauren stared him, her heart pounding a wild beat in her throat. *He's going to die!*

Oh, God, not Nicholas! She'd always known of his violent death. How many times had she heard Edith recount the tale of an arrow piercing his armor during a siege by the Scots? Hundreds? Thousands? But he had been a portrait then. A romantic portrayal of a man who had lived and died hundreds of years before her. A dream.

But this man was alive, radiating energy and power. She looked into his eyes, saw his concern. An inherent strength defined the line of his square jaw and chin. Even the scar along his cheek couldn't detract from his handsomeness. This beautiful man wasn't a dream, but a reality. Hate drove him, his will to live bled into others by evidence of the men who followed him. Could a single arrow truly have the power to end such a life?

An icy knot formed in her stomach. She'd only known him for two days, yet she couldn't imagine him still and lifeless.

'Christel, tell me what is wrong.' Nicholas captured the side of her face in his palm. His thumb grazed her cheek and caught the tears flowing down it. Tears she hadn't been aware of.

She drew in a breath, but could only manage a whisper, 'You're going to die.'

Sympathy fled his eyes. Chilling emptiness took its place. 'I am sorry to disappoint you.'

When he released her, Lauren caught his wrist between her bound hands and held his palm against her wet face. 'Forget your revenge against Armstrong, Nicholas. He's going to come back and kill you.'

The contempt in his gaze faded to confusion. 'You sound as if you care.'

'Well, I . . . I do.' The admission stunned her. She couldn't allow herself to care too deeply. Surviving her parents' death had been difficult enough. She knew it was selfish, but she didn't want to endure living through another loss. Yet her reasoning couldn't stop her from wanting to throw herself against him and feel the weight of his arms around her. Or stop the need to hear him reassure her everything would be all right.

He leaned close to her, his lips inches away, his intent gaze warming her. 'You are very good, Christel. I almost believe you.'

Lauren blinked, confused. 'What do you mean?'

'This ploy of tears and concern will not sway me to release you.'

'This isn't a ploy!' When he drew his hand away, a chill ran over her skin, making her shiver. 'Damn you . . .'

'I already am, madam.'

'Nicholas, listen to me.' The stubborn fool ignored her. Her voice shook on a hysterical note, but she couldn't control it. 'I'm telling you the truth.' She grabbed his arm. 'Cut me loose.'

He raised a brow in suspicion. 'I think not.'

'Why? Are you afraid of one Armstrong woman?'

Challenged, he let his mouth pull into a grin. Lauren couldn't drag her eyes from the sight. When he leaned close, her breath quickened with anticipation. His gaze slipped to her mouth and held. Would he kiss her? Here, in front of his men? God, she hoped not. She'd probably wilt right off Jessy's back.

The sounds of horses stomping their hooves and swishing their tails blended with a few discreet coughs and whispers from the men. She tried to turn away, but the feel of Nicholas's breath against her cheek, the scent of man, leather and sweat held her immobile.

Then he leaned back.

Lauren stared at him, feeling a poignant sense of loss. Disgruntled by the possibility of being attracted to the man instead of the myth, she closed her eyes and tried to shake the feeling. She couldn't risk caring about him, not in the physical sense at least. Raising her hands to move her hair back, she paused and opened her eyes. He'd cut her bindings.

Nicholas took one of her hands in his and studied the chafed area around her wrists. Her once white skin was now red and swollen. In reality, it looked worse than it felt.

'Does this pain you?' He rubbed his thumb over her palm

His concern made her throat close. She shrugged her shoulders as an answer.

'See that the cuts do not become infected.'

Lauren pursed her lips, perturbed. Was he concerned for her health or did he simply not want his hostage damaged?

'Give me the reins,' she snapped, and was as surprised as Nicholas to hear the irritation in her voice.

'Why?' His mouth quirked in amusement.

'Because I don't care to be led.'

He studied her, as if trying to discern her emotions. Good luck, Lauren thought. She couldn't figure them out herself. One moment she was madder than hell at the Englishman. The next, it was all she could do to not collapse into a fit of tears. Now she felt put out. She yanked her hair from her face in an effort to calm down.

'I can't escape, Nicholas. I'm surrounded by soldiers and we already know Hades can outrun Jessy.' That admission pricked her ire even further. For the past two years Jessy had won multiple races at Kingmoor, giving her the title of the swiftest thoroughbred in the county.

So how had Hades, who was larger and heavier, beat Jessy? Lauren hadn't a clue. But then Jessy hadn't acted herself since going inside the cave.

'Do not make me regret this, Christel.' A stern frown pulled at his mouth as he draped the reins over the mare's neck, but she had the notion it was forced, either for her sake or his men's.

For the moment she conceded that any attempt to escape would be futile. The opportunity would present itself, though, and when it did she would grasp it. Until then she'd stick by Nicholas's side and convince him to call off his fight with Bruce Armstrong.

She straightened her spine with determination and nudged Jessy alongside Hades. When her leg brushed Nicholas's, she looked at him. He didn't spare her a glance, but kept his gaze focused on the surrounding countryside.

Lauren clenched her teeth and made a vow of her own. Whether Nicholas Kenward liked it or not, before she left his time she was going to save his worthless life.

CHAPTER 6

'Great Scot!' Lauren cried, and stared at the vision on the knoll. Whatever she'd expected to find at Westbourne Castle, this wasn't it.

'You are on English soil, Lady Christel,' Nicholas commented dryly. 'I suggest you keep that in mind when you speak.'

Lauren didn't spare him a glance. She couldn't take her eyes from the enormous, rough stone curtain wall that encircled the castle. In the future, in her own time, only crumbled remnants of the wall remained, and a visitors' parking lot of pale gray concrete replaced the rows of rough wood buildings and the lousy marketplace now crowding the lower bailey.

'You look as if you have seen this place before.'

The intensity of Nicholas's gaze pulled her from her reverie. She swallowed back the sudden sense of loss, her thoughts struggling between appreciating the magnificence before her and accepting it wouldn't survive the ravages of time.

To see Westbourne Castle alive, bustling with activity, the way it was meant to be, made her chest

93

ache with a longing to be a part of it. She wanted to see it all, taste it all. Learn what it was like for these people in this time. Without thought, she reached out and clasped Nicholas's arm. Hard muscles tensed beneath her palm. Smiling, she turned to him. 'It's beautiful.'

Jessy's ears perked forward, as if she realized where they were. Snorting, the mare tugged the reins.

'Control your mount, Lady Christel,' Nicholas warned.

The thoroughbred's eagerness spread into Lauren. With a challenging grin, she said, 'I'll race you.'

She caught his disapproving scowl seconds before she leaned over the mare's neck. Jessy responded by lunging into a full gallop. Above the beat of hooves against dirt, Lauren heard Nicholas bellow a curse. The clang of armor and a thunderous battle cry from his men made her shiver with excitement, and a little fear.

She glanced over her shoulder and gaped at the sight behind her. With Nicholas in the lead, his entire troop of men raced after her, the eager look of hunting prey on their faces. Just before she reached the entrance to the lower bailey, she reined the mare to a stop and whirled around to face the oncoming army. She couldn't help but laugh, thrilled that Hades had not been able to catch Jessy this time.

By the time Hades slid to a stop beside the mare, Nicholas couldn't decide whether he should strangle the woman for her mischief or laugh with her. As much as it irked him, the gleam shimmering in her green eyes tempted him to smile. An unwelcomed effect she continually had on him.

The wild ride had flushed her cheeks to a becoming rose. Alive with tangles, her russet-colored hair surrounded her oval face like a fiery halo. Lord help him, he wanted to kiss her again. Right here in front of his men. And not as punishment.

'Were you thinking to escape me, Lady Christel?' Nicholas asked, his voice strangely thick.

Laughing, she shook her head so the sun caught gold streaks in her hair. 'Escape inside *your* castle? I don't think so.' As her gaze traveled over the curtain wall, an odd seriousness settled over her. 'I was just anxious to see it.'

Baffled by her statement, as well as her lack of fear, he asked, 'You wish to see my home?'

She nodded and glanced at him long enough for him to see the melancholy in her eyes. He sensed a longing in her, which confused him even more than her lack of fear.

Turning away, she urged her mount forward and passed through the gate. Nicholas watched, bewildered, as she paused beside the curtain wall to run her hand over the chiseled stone. What was she about?

The simply dressed castle inhabitants paused to stare, their gazes darting between the strange woman and Nicholas. A young girl in a wool dress, stained from working in the dye vat, came forward with a handful of pink wildflowers. Christel bent to accept the offering and murmured something Nicholas could not make out. When she straightened, the frown had vanished, replaced by a startlingly warm smile. When the child's mother hurriedly shooed the girl away, Christel's faint smile remained.

Nicholas tried to imagine how his people viewed Christel Armstrong. Even the immovable Kenric glanced at him, the soldier's dark brows raised in question. His enemy's daughter, dressed in filthy, blood-stained leggings, rode astride like a man, her slim shoulders back and her body relaxed. She was a puzzle. She was his hostage. He'd expected her to cower in fear of him and his people, not greet them as if she were a welcomed guest.

Jacobson cleared his throat and nodded toward the castle's main keep, breaking Nicholas's thoughts. 'My lord.'

Following Jacobson's gaze, Nicholas spotted his mother on the castle steps. Her hands were clenched together at her waist. Even with the distance separating them, he could imagine her slight frame trembling with her long-burning hate. Beside her stood his sister, Elise. Tall and slender, and past the marriageable age of eighteen, Elise fidgeted with the jeweled girdle hanging about her hips, her eyes narrowed in disapproval.

Time to present his prisoner to his mother, he realized. A sudden trepidation gripped him. He prayed his mother would not create a scene by losing control. Her ravings were nothing new to anyone at Westbourne, but he didn't wish to deal with her at present. He took the mare's reins and, reaching the landing, he dismounted and greeted his mother with a kiss on her wrinkled cheek.

Lady Kenward's sharp gray eyes never met his, but cut to his hostage. As a boy, Nicholas had always compared his mother's eyes to that of a dove, gentle and compassionate, until hatred for the Scots had turned them to cold, unforgiving steel.

'Is that the girl?' his mother asked in a tight whisper.

'Aye, Lady Christel Armstrong.'

His mother gave a slight nod of satisfaction, her mouth thinning into a grim line. 'Put her in the oubliette.'

Elise gasped. 'Mother, you cannot!'

Christel's startled gaze flew to his. A visible shiver tore through her. Where he hadn't been able to instill fear in his prisoner, his mother had easily done so with a few harsh words. For a reason he couldn't ascertain, he wanted to reassure Christel.

Clenching his hands into fists, he cursed himself for his own weakness. He refused to allow her pleas or frightened looks to sway him from his duty. His original plan had been to lock her away for a time so she would understand her position in his home. He wouldn't change his mind now. Stepping around the mare, he took hold of her waist to help her down. She pulled back, resisting him.

'You aren't going to put me in the dungeon, are you?'

Nicholas's insides twisted. 'Dungeon' was a kind word for where he intended to put her. The oubliette was no more than a small dirt hole beneath the dungeon floor. A trap door provided what little air reached the cramped space. But then little was needed. There was only room enough for the prisoner to lie in one position, flat on his back.

Her soft hands trembled when she gripped his. 'Nicholas, please. Tell me you aren't going to put me in the dungeon.'

He tightened his hold on her waist and lifted her off her mount, registering her slight weight. She slid her hands up his arms, gripping his tunic.

'Put me in the East Tower or in the stables – I don't care. Just not . . . Please don't do this.' Her voice faded, and she stared at the castle door, unable to finish.

Angry with himself for even listening to her pleas, he clenched his jaw. He motioned to Kenric, who took Christel by the arm and urged her toward the keep.

She twisted, trying to break free. 'I won't go!' She stomped her heel on Kenric's foot, but he only flinched in surprise. She reached around and tried to bite his arm, but he stopped her. Growling dangerously low, he spun her around, grabbed her by the waist and hauled her off the ground.

She glared at Nicholas, her mouth trembling in anger and unshed tears brightening her eyes. Her chest heaved as she fought for breath.

'Take her . . .' Nicholas began, but his mother interrupted him.

'Nicholas, I insist she be put in the oubliette.'

He stared at his mother. A buzz of warring voices filled his head. He couldn't believe his own uncertainty in the matter. The woman belonged in the dungeon. She was his prisoner and deserved to be treated as such. So why did he hesitate?

Nodding to Kenric, he clenched his jaw and ordered, 'Take her.'

'No!' Christel beat against Kenric's arms. Her green eyes went wild with panic. 'You can't do this.'

The soldiers and other folk watching the scene whispered among themselves. His sister, Elise, stepped forward, twisting the ropes of her girdle into knots. 'Perhaps you could . . .'

'This does not concern you, daughter,' Lady Kenward snapped. 'Return to your room.'

Elise straightened her stance. Her mouth set into a stubborn line, but she obeyed her mother and left the courtyard.

'You may take her now, Kenric,' his mother said in a flat, unimpassioned tone.

Christel stared at Nicholas, disbelief dulling her eyes. 'Put me down, Kenric.' She swallowed hard, and her mouth trembled. 'I can walk.'

Once lowered, she straightened her black, tattered jacket and entered the castle, her steps slow and hesitant. Nicholas followed, but paused at the door. Clenching and unclenching his hands at his sides, he watched her lead the way and turn down the corridor to the dungeons. At the archway, she stopped and glanced over her shoulder at him. She pierced him with a look he knew he'd never forget; raw hurt mixed with vivid fear.

He tried to shake the doubt chilling his blood and coiling his gut, but couldn't. Stifling an oath, he ran a hand over his mouth. He must be growing soft to be feeling anything besides satisfaction. This was what he wanted, what he'd planned for: Christel Armstrong at his mercy. And her father soon to follow.

Perhaps claiming revenge against a woman had caused the bitterness that lingered in his mouth? Whatever the reason, he had to ignore it. He'd waited too long to change his mind now. When Christel disappeared around the corner, he drew a deep breath and wondered how she knew the way to the dungeons. She'd never been here before, yet, as he recalled the pleasure visible on her face when she'd seen the castle walls, it'd seemed as if she'd seen it before . . . or was coming home.

'You have done well, Nicholas,' his mother said, the glow of victory shining in her pale eyes. 'I want her shut away. She must be punished.'

Nicholas glanced at his mother, surprised that he had forgotten her presence during the last few minutes. Seeing the contorted curve of her mouth, the deep lines creasing her eyes, he realized her hatred for the Scottish clan Armstrong had aged her beyond her years. With tired acceptance, he knew it had done the same to him.

'The oubliette may be too harsh a punishment, Mother.'

''Tis what she deserves,' she hissed so no one else could hear. 'I will not allow you to release her.'

'As Lord of Westbourne Castle,' Nicholas began, suddenly weary, 'it is for me to decide her punishment.'

'And I am your mother. I want her spirit broken as mine was the day your father was murdered!'

'The foul air will do more than break her spirit. It will mar her with disease.'

With an age-spotted hand, Lady Kenward tilted his face to hers. 'Would you care if this were to happen?'

'I have plans for her, Mother.'

'Such as?'

He stiffened when Kenric reappeared, his ruddy face visibly paled. The older soldier crossed the room toward Nicholas, his eyes averted, the dungeon keys clenched in his hand.

''Tis none of your concern,' he answered tightly.

'Take care, my son. Do not forget who she is.'

Nicholas lowered his gaze to the floor and squinted, as if that would aid him in seeing through the layers of rush and stone and into the dungeon. A chill wrapped around his body as he imagined the frightened red-head lying on the sodden earth, unable to move in the impossibly black pit. Over the past two days, she'd proved she possessed a wealth of courage. She would need it all, and more, to see her though the hell he had put her in.

He met his mother's somber frown and replied, his voice hollow, 'There is little chance of my forgetting Lady Armstrong.'

Lauren gasped thin, damp air. Harsh, grated sounds echoed around her. Cold. Her blood raced cold through her veins, leaving icy trails beneath her skin. Lying flat on wet earth, she fisted her hands against her chest and trembled violently. She stared, wide-eyed, at the blackness, knew the roof of her

101

prison was inches above her. She'd seen it as Kenric lowered the trap door into place. Clamping her mouth shut, she sealed the screams clawing her throat.

A sob pushed through her body. She tried to stop it, but couldn't. The ragged cry vibrated inside her, jarring her, making her cry harder. Hot tears slid down her temples and into her hair.

'Oh, God,' she whispered. 'Let me out. Please.' Not the dungeon . . . anywhere but here . . . *please*!

How could Nicholas do this to her? The man of her dreams, the knight she'd believed to possess honor and courage? That man wouldn't have done this, locked her away in the one place that terrified her most. A place where she could die. She'd begged Nicholas – *begged*. And he'd looked straight through her as if she were already dead.

Lauren raised her hands to cover her face and quiet the wrenching sobs. Her elbows brushed the ceiling, knocking dirt loose. Clumps fell on her chest and stomach. She screamed, a choking sound, knowing she'd be buried alive. She reached above her, searching for the trap door. More dirt fell on her face and into her mouth.

Coughing, she spit out pieces of grit. She had to get out, had to, but couldn't move. The ceiling might cave in. She'd be buried alive. No one would know . . . or save her.

No, no, she couldn't panic. Relax, please relax. She had to calm down, think rationally to survive. And she would. She had to. She couldn't die, not like this.

Cold seeped up from the floor and slipped into her body. The black walls closed around her, suffocating her. She imagined them moving in, touching her, crushing her. There wasn't enough air. Oh, God, there wasn't enough. Fear stabbed like needle-sharp pricks in her mind.

Her breath turned to shredded gasps, filling her lungs with the scent of sweat and terror. Her body shook in spastic waves, draining her energy, making her limbs weak and aching. She closed her eyes and tried to envision something else. Tears slipped down her sides of her face and clogged her throat.

In her mind, she pictured herself riding Jessy through a heathered field. She imagined tilting her face toward the bright blue sky, the gentle breeze that moved the clouds overhead brought the crisp scent of spring. Of decay. Death.

Black shadows crowded the edge of her vision. She willed the fear back. She'd get out of this. Somehow she'd get free. The shadows moved in, swallowing her vision of blue sky and fields of green grass. *Nicholas! Don't leave me here.* He couldn't be so heartless. She had to believe.

Gradually, the tightness in her chest eased, but her limbs shook in a constant tremor. Her breathing slowed, and caught on tired sobs. Her eyes grew heavy and burned from her tears. The vision dimmed in her mind. She let it go and sank into the safety of sleep.

★ ★ ★

Lauren woke with a start. Her eyes flew open and searched the black void for light. Where was she? Seconds passed before she remembered. The dungeon. No, this wasn't the dungeon. If she had been put in the room above, she would be able to see and move, not be trapped in a prison worse than hell.

She wondered what had awakened her. She didn't hear anything. How long had she slept? An hour? A day? She had no way of knowing. The torchlight in the dungeon above couldn't penetrate her tomb. Lauren shivered and cursed herself for using such a horrible word. She was in a pit, a dark hole, not a tomb for the dead!

A ruthless shiver gripped her. She was cold, so cold. Her wet clothes clung to her limbs, holding her down like an invisible hand. A nightmare from her childhood returned in haunting detail. She'd roamed the castle halls, but had always avoided the dark, foul-smelling dungeon. She'd been afraid of finding the decayed bones of men who had been shut away and left to die. She had imagined their cries for help, echoing through the walls, falling on deaf ears.

Now she was a prisoner, living out her worst fear.

A faint scrape caught her attention. She strained and heard the muted sound of dripping water. Vibrations from above worked their way down to her. Pieces of dirt drifted onto her face. She recoiled and coughed to clear her throat. Someone was up there.

Her body tensed. She wanted to scream and tear at the ceiling until she found the door, but she didn't dare move. She clenched her hands and stared at the black space above her, praying it would open.

She heard a shuffling, then the faint rattle of metal. Tears rolled from her eyes, and she cried silently. Waiting. Waiting.

'Please, someone be there,' she whispered. She wanted to scream and beg, but somehow knew it wouldn't do any good. They had put her here for a reason. Her pleas wouldn't save her.

A tired creak rent the air, then the trap door lifted, sending a spray of dirt over her. Lauren flinched, turned her face away as bright yellow light pierced her eyes. Blinking against the white pain stabbing her head, she looked up. Nicholas and Kenric were kneeling above her.

'Take her other arm, Kenric.' Nicholas's voice was a low whisper, but it flooded her with hope.

When they reached for her, she raised her cramped arms to them, gripped the sleeves of their tunics. They lifted her out of the pit. Kenric released her, and her knees gave way under her weight.

As she slid to the ground Nicholas caught her against him, lifting her in his arms. Lauren wrapped hers around his neck, squeezing him, afraid he might change his mind and return her to the hole. If he tried, she swore he'd be coming with her.

When he headed for the stairs, tears of relief pressed against her eyes and heated her cheeks. She was free. Nicholas had let her out. She fisted her hand and hit his chest with all the strength she had left.

'I hate you, Nicholas,' she choked, and buried her face against his neck, unable to stop the tears.

His hold on her tightened, and he rubbed his chin against her hair.

Through the hammering of her heart, she thought she heard him whisper, 'Forgive me.'

Through the arrow loops in the circular tower room, Lauren watched the merchants, four stories below in the lower bailey, pack up their wares and close their shops. To her left, the falconer collected a pair of hawks from their wooden perches set in the sun and returned them to the dark safety of the mews.

She closed her eyes against the scene that, in a strange way, seemed too normal, too peaceful, in light of everything she had been through. She ran her hand through her hair, cringing when she felt clumps of dirt and matted tangles.

She turned, her gaze combing the rough gray walls, the planked floor and the short stool that served as her one piece of furniture. She assumed the pile of withered hay in the corner was to be her bed. Her body began to itch as she thought about the creatures who'd probably set up house in the straw.

An empty laugh caught in her chest. Why worry about a few bugs? She wasn't in the oubliette. That was all that mattered.

A metal click had her facing the door. Her heart, which had been thudding a tired beat, picked up its pace. She knew it would be Nicholas returning. He'd said he would. That thought did make her laugh. The man had locked her in hell. Why should she believe anything he said?

The door swung open, and two women hurried inside. Without a word, they began cleaning the sparse room, but Lauren barely noticed. Her gaze swerved as Nicholas filled the doorway. Dressed in a clean black tunic and leggings, he stood with his arms crossed over his broad chest. She searched his face, but the harsh planes of his cheeks and brow were cloaked in shadows. His eyes were reflections of black pools, unrelenting, unrevealing.

Every nerve in her body tensed. When he ducked through the portal and entered the room, she took an involuntary step back and came up against the wall. His towering height and the wide breadth of his shoulders consumed the small space, making her feel powerless, and hating it.

'Is there anything you need?' he asked, his tone cool, detached.

She thought about asking for her freedom, but realized how futile that would be. 'I suppose it would be pushing my luck to ask for a real bed.'

His dark brow quirked in surprise. 'Bedding is expensive and not wasted on prisoners.'

'Wasted?' she repeated, and clenched her jaw. Being able to stand and breath fresh air gave her a spurt of courage. She folded her arms across her waist, refusing to cower. She wouldn't spout her mouth off, though, and risk him returning her to the oubliette. She wasn't a fool. 'Then how about a bath?'

His gaze took a slow path over body. Lauren fought the urge to turn and hide from his inspection. Her clothes were torn and wet. She was filthy, stained and smelled like the sewer he'd locked her in. She tilted her chin with defiance. *Let him look.*

'I believe a bath would be in order. And some proper clothing.'

When he turned to leave, she reached out and caught his arm. 'Nicholas . . .'

One of the serving women gasped. Lauren glanced over her shoulder and saw the woman's brown eyes wide with shock and her mouth gaping open. Not sure what had caused the servant's reaction, she released Nicholas's arm and cleared her throat. 'There is one more thing.'

With his hands clasped behind his back, he stepped within a foot of her. Towering above her, he leaned forward, giving her the precarious feeling he was a hawk reaching out to snatch its prey. 'What is it you wish?'

'Are you going to keep me locked in here?'

The cold detachment in his eyes wavered with something she thought might be regret . . . or it could have been annoyance. 'I will not put you in the oubliette again.'

She swallowed and looked away from his intense gaze. Something in his eyes, the rough timbre of his voice, made her want to say thank you. Was she crazy? *Thank* the man for not returning her to that black hole? She should be screaming at him for putting her there in the first place.

'Is there anything else?' he asked.

'Will I be allowed to walk the grounds?' Since she'd

come this far, she might as well push him until he said no.

'Is there something you wish to see?'

Yes! A cave about five miles from here. 'I'll go crazy in here with nothing to do.'

His eyes narrowed, turned cobalt blue. The same shade as storm-brewing clouds. 'I shall consider it.'

He turned to leave, and she fought the rise of panic that clenched her throat. She was in the East tower, where there was light and fresh air, not shut away in the bowels of the dungeon. For now, she'd be grateful for that.

As he pulled the door closed behind him, he glanced over his shoulder. 'Sleep well, my lady.'

Nicholas leaned against the back of the high seat, vaguely aware of the debate ensuing between Lord Wright, who sat to his right, and his mother, who sat on his left. He lifted his tankard of freshly brewed ale, the finest batch the ale-wife had produced so far this year, and took a deep draught.

He held the tangy liquid in his mouth before letting it slide down his throat. The cool drink spread a warm flush in his stomach and helped ease the tension coiled in his limbs. Only he would need more than ale if he wanted to numb the guilt embedded in his mind. Guilt he found difficult to believe. He'd rejected the notion at first, but when it had persisted he realized he had to accept the abhorred emotion for what it was. And he had to accept the truth; he hadn't liked the image of Christel locked away, alone, in the oubliette.

He stared at his tankard, trying to focus on its contents instead of listening to the argument battling around him, or considering its cause.

The woman. Christel Armstrong. Everything seemed to revolve around her.

Who would have thought that by capturing her he would have created so much strife in his own home? Yet by seeking revenge he had brought the devil into his own lair. Except the evil he had envisioned all these years hadn't possessed the haunting green eyes of a she-cat, or the fiery mane that enticed a man to lose his soul in its silkiness.

Perhaps that was the evil.

Her beauty. The illusion of vulnerability which lured a man to forgetting his own mind.

It had happened to him when he kissed her.

Her response to him had taken him aback, weakening the goal that drove his life. On the return trip to Westbourne he had purposely distanced himself from her, needing to understand her appeal so he could use it to achieve his own end.

Nicholas gritted his teeth and tried to block the memory of shocked terror in Christel's eyes when he had given the order to lock her in the oubliette. With a curse, he downed his ale and welcomed the burning in his throat.

But it didn't dull his conscience's demand to atone for the ill he had done to her. She wanted permission to walk the castle grounds. *Probably to seek a way to escape.* He rubbed his hand along his beard-roughened jaw. There would be no escape for Christel Armstrong. She belonged to him. But he would allow her a small measure of freedom if it meant gaining her trust.

Nicholas frowned, wondering why it mattered to him that she trust him. His plan had been to capture her, break her spirit, bed her, then return her to her father in disgrace. Trust had nothing to do with his plans. Yet he didn't want to take her by force. He wanted her to come to him freely. Desire him. Wouldn't that make her shame all the greater?

His thoughts drifted to the moment he'd freed her from the dungeon and left her in the East tower. She hadn't been afraid of him. Wary, yes, and visibly shaken. She'd claimed she hated him, but he knew she didn't. Something about her eyes, the way they searched his, looked inside and made him question himself, hinted that she saw more in him than was there.

He shook his head. Her lack of fear had perplexed as well as intrigued him since the moment he had captured her. Perhaps she hadn't the sense to be frightened, he mused. Grunting at the unlikelihood, he noticed a brief pause in the continuing argument between his mother and Lord Wright.

No, Christel Armstrong was far more intelligent than any woman he had ever known. She'd faced him, newly freed from the pit, ragged and filthy, and tried to bargain with him. He wanted to know what fueled her bold independence. Surely the Scottish blood coursing through her veins wasn't the cause. There wasn't a single man in the entire Armstrong clan with an ounce of the tenacity she possessed.

'What say you, Nick?' Lord Wright demanded, drawing Nicholas's attention by waving a jeweled hand between his face and the pewter tankard. 'Is the woman a witch?'

Nicholas thought about the woman and resisted the urge to grin. Christel *was* a witch, but not the sacrilegious kind. Her type knew how to trap a man's heart with a sensuous smile or a daring glance. Fortunately for him, he didn't possess a heart for her to trap. 'She is a woman, Anthony, nothing more.'

'A woman who spouts knowledge of the future!' Anthony's wail caused a hush to fall over the room. The soldiers crowding the tables in the hall stilled, their food and drinks forgotten as they waited for Nicholas's response to their guest's outburst.

'Not a prediction, Anthony, but common sense. The woman spoke truthfully when she said it would be too expensive, not to mention foolhardy, to rebuild so near the Scottish border.'

'What do you suggest I do? Give up my lands? Hand over everything I own to Laird Armstrong?'

'To do so, Nicholas,' his mother interrupted in a warning tone, 'would only bring those wretched Scots closer to us.'

Nicholas glanced at his mother, knowing she spoke the truth. If Laird Armstrong were allowed to claim Lord Wright's property, the Scotsman would use that gain to push further south and invade Kenward land. If the people entrusted to Nicholas weren't killed by

Scottish reivers, they would be driven away once their crops were destroyed, their livestock stolen and their homes burnt to the ground.

He had seen it happen before, and knew it could happen again.

But it wouldn't.

Sixteen years ago he hadn't had Bruce Armstrong's daughter tucked away in his tower to ensure his people's safety. He did now, and he planned to use her. But first he had to settle Lord Wright's dilemma. Glancing at the foppish lord, who preferred the safety of fashionably ruffled shirts and silk trunk hose to iron-plate armour, Nicholas said, 'I suggest you go to London and petition the King for the necessary army and funds to rebuild.'

'As you said yourself, Nick, 'twould be foolish to remain so close to Scottish borders.' Lord Wright picked up a ravaged bone from his plate and tossed it to a dog lying a few feet away. Impervious to the glare Lady Kenward sent him, he dipped his fingers in a bowl of lemon water.

'Perhaps you could barter your land.'

'Exchange it with the King's property? Would he do it?' Lord Wright asked, the bushy curve of his brow lifting with the possibilities.

Nicholas shrugged and turned his attention back to his empty mug. He motioned for a serving woman to refill it. When Lord Anthony rose to take his leave, Nicholas nodded absently at the man's parting words, his mind already working through the mounting issues at hand.

He prayed King Henry would exchange lands with Lord Wright instead of sending an army to protect the border. He might hate the Scots, but he didn't wish to fight a war against them all. Just one would do.

And he planned to begin that war. Tomorrow.

CHAPTER 7

Bleak, gray morning light brought Lauren upright on her straw bed just as the door to her tower room swung open. The two women who had cleaned her room the day before entered, carrying a small wooden tub and a bundle of material. Sparing her a wary glance, they left, but returned a moment later with buckets of steaming water.

Without muttering a word, they filled the tub and closed the door behind them. The lock grated into place, but Lauren didn't care. A bath. A hot, wonderful, much-needed bath. She stripped out of her filthy clothes and tossed them to the side.

She stepped into the tub and sank into liquid heat. Having to tuck her knees beneath her chin to fit, she sat back and moaned, welcoming the chance to soak away the grime that was a constant reminder of her time in the black pit. She sighed as warmth soothed her aches and relieved some of her exhaustion from having lain awake all night. Once darkness had settled, the confines of her tower room had pressed against her, bringing back the choking fear of the dungeon.

No matter how hard she'd tried, she hadn't been able to control the returning waves of anxiety.

As the water began to cool, Lauren washed her body with a rough bar of soap smelling of violets. She rose from the tub and dried off with a towel one of the women had left, then bent over the edge of the tub and washed her hair.

Satisfied she was as clean as she was likely to get, she slipped into a coarse wool chemise of grayish white, then a plain brown overdress. She stretched her arms behind her and fumbled with the laces of her gown. Her shoulders strained until they burned, but still she couldn't manage to tie a knot. She dropped her arms and rolled her head from side to side, easing the pain pinching her neck.

Sinking onto the stool, she leaned against the wall and combed her hair with a heavy, metal comb. Freeing a mountain of knots, she wondered what would happen to her today. Anything would be better than the day before. In a tired gesture, she ran her hand over her face, thinking she could hardly wait.

When the dress slipped off her shoulder, it crossed her mind that she might have it on backwards. A weary smile pulled at her mouth as she remembered Edith, the expert on life in historic times. Edith should have been the one to go back in time. The wiry tour guide would have been quite at home, with her knowledge of customs, clothing, the preparation of food and battle strategy. Unfortunately, Lauren had limited her own studies to the castle's hiding places and a certain mesmerizing portrait.

She shook her head and tried to clear her mind of all thoughts concerning Nicholas Kenward. Her emotions trembled between total outrage for his locking her beneath the dungeon and crushing disappointment.

So far, the man of her dreams had proven to be vastly different from the real thing. He harbored a lust for vengeance that would eventually kill him, he'd destroyed a castle and hundreds of lives, and his treatment of her had been anything but gallant. She struggled to understand this Nicholas, whose tough outer shell protected him from the harsh world he lived in.

But was there a gentler side? Or had the death of his father and brother destroyed his ability for compassion? He *had* rescued her from the pit, but had it been out of kindness or was it part of his grand scheme for revenge? To wear her down then gain her trust? Keep her off guard for the next bit of torture he had planned for her?

Yet she couldn't forget, or discount, the tight, possessive way he'd held her when he'd freed her. She should hate him – Lord knows she had every reason to – but something stopped her from reaching that hard level. She remembered the erratic beat of his pulse when he'd carried her. Sensed his concern for her.

Or had she imagined it because she wanted to believe there was good in him? And his whispered, *'Forgive me?'* Was she trying to convince herself he regretted punishing her so severely?

Lauren closed her eyes and rubbed the dull ache spreading in her temples. She had to stop thinking about the Black Knight. Her emotions were too volatile, too confusing where he was concerned.

The raspy scratch of metal against metal drew her attention. An instant later the oak door swung open with a reluctant squeak. Thomas, the young archer, stood on the threshold with his chest puffed up like a cocky rooster. Her black felt hat was perched on his head, reminding her of an organ grinder's monkey. She felt a half-hearted grin slip over her face as she imagined Thomas tipping the hat in hopes of receiving a shiny coin.

Somehow the right side of the hat had been singed, as if it had been grazed with fire. Lauren wondered if he'd had it on at the time. Brown curls peeking from beneath the brim did seem shorter on the right than those on the left.

'You are to come with me, my lady,' Thomas announced.

Exhaustion made it impossible to take the young man's dire tone seriously. 'To where, Thomas?'

'I am to escort ye to break your fast in the hall, then ye are allowed a brief walk in the bailey.'

'You're kidding.'

Thomas's brow pulled into a frown beneath the felt brim. 'I jest not, my lady.'

'Well, then, let's go.' She pushed herself from the stool with stiff, jerky movements.

'Lord and Lady Kenward await ye in the hall.'

'Terrific,' Lauren managed, and grimaced as she

crossed the room. She really didn't want to see Nicholas right now. At least, not until she'd sorted out her conflicting emotions. And she definitely didn't want to see his mother.

A breath of cold air down her back reminded her she wasn't quite ready to greet her hosts. She stopped beside the archer and turned her back to him. 'Do me a favor, Thomas, and lace me up.'

She heard an audible gasp then a series of thuds. Glancing over her shoulder, she saw Thomas lying flat on his stomach. Apparently, he'd turned around so quickly he'd tripped over his feet and landed face-first on the floor.

'Thomas, are you . . .?' Before she could finish, he scrambled to his feet, his face flushed apple-red. He bowed his head and darted down the hall. 'Where are you going?'

He skidded to a halt at the top of the spiral staircase. 'Ye need assistance.'

Lauren lifted the wool skirt that was a tad too long and walked toward him. 'For heaven's sake, all I need is for you to tie a knot.'

Thomas turned away, refusing to meet her gaze in the darkened corridor. 'I cannot do such a thing. 'Tis not proper.'

'It's not like I'm baring any body parts . . .' The young man's gulp for air stopped her from finishing. Her mouth twitched with the urge to laugh. 'Never mind,' she managed, 'I'll find someone else.'

Brushing past him, she sped down the winding staircase that was as dark and musty as it was in her time. She led the way through the corridors until she reached the balcony that overlooked the main hall. From her safe perch she studied Nicholas, who sat between two women. One she recognized as his mother, the woman who'd demanded Lauren be sentenced to the death pit below the dungeon floor. Lady Kenward sat arrow-straight, her fingers tapping an agitated rhythm on the table.

Lauren didn't know who the other woman was. She recalled seeing her the previous day, but her attention had been solely on staying out of shackles. Perhaps the woman was Nicholas's wife.

Her heart lurched, and her mouth turned dry with the thought. From her vantage point, she could tell the young woman was tall, slender and strikingly beautiful. Lauren's skin prickled with a flash of heat. Jealousy? she wondered. Not likely. She merely pitied the woman for being married to such a jerk.

Sensing Thomas's nervous fidgeting, Lauren descended the stairs and crossed the room before losing her nerve. She longed to study the ornate tapestries lining the walls and the beautiful longbow and shield hanging over the fireplace, but she didn't stop until she reached Nicholas's side.

She stood there, her hands clasped together in front of her, and waited for him to acknowledge her. Finally, he leaned against the back of his chair and faced her. 'Good morning, Nic . . .' Her ability to speak faltered when she saw the warm glint in his dark blue eyes.

'Good morrow, Lady Christel.' With a wave of his

hand, he indicated the chair beside the young woman. 'Please join us.'

Lauren eyed him suspiciously. He hadn't spoken to her in a tone that resembled kindness since capturing her. What was he up to now? With her guard up, she forced a sweet smile. 'Thank you, Nicholas. But first, I need to ask a favor.'

'Of course, if I am able to grant it.'

She wanted to grunt in response. Where had this agreeable side of him been yesterday? Perhaps, she reasoned, he's trying to make up for what he did. Moving closer, so her skirts brushed his arm, she turned her back to him, whispering over her shoulder, 'Lace me up.'

Lauren expected a shocked response similar to Thomas's. She didn't know why she was trying to provoke a reaction out of these people. It was foolish. Risky. Downright idiotic. But something drove her to prove she wouldn't cower in fear. She'd always been one to stand on her own, buck the system. If that was what was driving her to behave rashly now . . . well, heaven help her. She tensed at the stunned silence. Had she made a colossal mistake? A goblet thudded on the table, rolled, then landed on the floor with a crash that echoed throughout the room.

'Nicholas! I forbid you to touch that wanton.'

Lauren had expected Nicholas's wife to protest, but the venomous voice belonged to his mother, Lady Kenward. The younger woman watched the scene, a mixture of shock and excitement in her brilliant blue eyes. Eyes remarkably like Nicholas's.

Feeling a tug at her back, Lauren glanced over her shoulder and met the man's challenging gaze. From the corner of her eye she saw Lady Kenward's icy glare. The older woman's thin lips disappeared into a straight line, but she said nothing more.

Nicholas's hands worked quickly, but his eyes never left Lauren's. A flush burned her cheeks and spread downward, awakening every nerve along the way.

How could such a simple act make her feel so wicked? Especially since she should slap the man's face instead of appreciating its rugged strength. She should hate him, yet she didn't. Damn it all.

His blue eyes darkened with some mysterious emotion. He clenched his jaw and drew in a breath, his nostrils flaring like a lion on the prowl. He gripped her waist, and for a heated second, her mind spun in a crazy loop. Then he gave her a gentle push toward the chair, startling her back to the moment.

She took her seat on the other side of his wife and concentrated on steadying her nerves.

'I trust you slept well, Lady Christel,' his wife asked. His *beautiful* wife, she noted.

Lauren gritted her teeth and looked into large blue eyes surrounded by incredibly thick velvet lashes. The woman's black hair hung clear to her waist; a jewel-studded knit cap covered the crown of her head. She wore a dove-gray gown with gold embroidery trimming the squared neckline and full, draping sleeves.

The young woman held herself painfully erect, making Lauren realize how pitiful she must appear as she slouched against her chair. She struggled to an upright position, but found it too tiring to maintain. She couldn't compete with the young Lady Kenward, and she refused to try. 'Actually, I didn't sleep at all. I asked your husband for a bed, but he refused.'

Laughter danced like brilliant stars in the woman's eyes. She turned her elegantly coiffed head to Nicholas, then back to Lauren. A throaty giggle escaped her. 'Nicholas is not my husband. He is my brother. I am Elise.'

Lauren's heart skipped a beat, and her breath hung in her chest. 'Oh,' she managed and cleared her throat. 'That accounts for the resemblance.'

'We both take after our father.'

Lauren looked past the woman to the man. Nicholas took a drink from his cup. Over the rim, his gaze snared hers with a probing look that made her pulse race. To her horror, she felt a blush rise in her cheeks. 'Your father must have been a handsome man.'

Nicholas lowered his cup in a startled move. His brow arched with a silent question. The side of his mouth lifted with a taunting grin.

Her blush turned to an outright fire. Of all the stupid things she could have said, she had complimented him. Her stomach fluttering with nerves, she reached for her cup. She'd never felt so unsettled before. How was she supposed to act anyway? Nothing in her experience had ever prepared her for coming face to face with a fantasy . . . however tainted that fantasy might be. Achingly aware that her hand trembled, she took a deep drink and gagged. Something close to acid scorched her throat. She spit the bitter liquid into the goblet just as a coughing fit seized her.

She caught the drops that ran down her chin with the back of her hand, and turned to look at the three people staring at her. 'What is this?' she asked in a raspy voice.

'Wine,' Nicholas answered, frowning.

Lauren tilted the tankard and looked inside at the murky liquid. 'Are you sure?'

Elise patted Lauren on the back. 'Perhaps you would prefer watered wine.'

Lauren shivered at the prospect of drinking the wine in any state. 'Plain water would be fine.' She lifted a hand and stopped the servant who had whisked her cup away. 'Boil it first, if you don't mind.'

Other servants came forward and placed trenches of glazed carrots, peas with onions and large loaves of bread before them. The wonderful smells made her mouth water and reminded her she'd only had cheese, bread and thick warm milk for dinner the previous evening. Lauren pointed to a bowl filled with something black and shiny. 'What is that?'

Elise pierced the food with a two-pronged fork and laid it in Lauren's plate. 'Boiled eel.'

Lauren pressed her hand to her mouth. The hungry rumble in her stomach turned sour. 'I think I'll pass.'

'By the rod, Nicholas, 'tis intolerable to have her at my table,' Lady Kenward sneered. 'Look at her. She turns her nose at the food we offer. I'll venture 'tis far better than any she has seen in Scotland.'

'Mother,' Nicholas warned.

'I will not have it, my son!' Lady Kenward tossed her wadded napkin on the table and stood, her fists clenched at her sides. 'I demand you return her to the oubliette.'

Nicholas rose and faced his mother. Lauren stiffened, terrified he might do as Lady Kenward ordered, regardless that he'd promised he wouldn't. She gripped the table and looked toward the open door, gauging the distance and the odds for escape.

Elise clasped her hand and held it in a reassuring hold. The young woman's warm smile sparked a bud of hope in Lauren that perhaps this wouldn't be a repeat of yesterday. The reason as to why Elise had chosen to befriend her instead of hate her like her mother eluded Lauren. But she'd take what allies she could find.

'Do not attempt to gainsay me on this issue, Mother.'

Issue? I'm an issue? His choice of words made Lauren frown with annoyance. She was a person, dammit, not dirt collected under someone's feet. She was extremely tired of being the bad guy. But she knew no one would believe any differently.

'Then you have made your choice.' Lady Kenward clasped her hands together until her knuckles turned white. She drew her shoulders back and glared at Lauren. 'I shall sup in my room until you tire of this wench and the air has been cleansed.'

Unexpected tears blurred Lauren's vision. She looked away before anyone could see how deeply Lady Kenward's hatred affected her. She knew better than to take the woman's embittered words to heart. They weren't really directed at her, but at someone she was supposed to be. Still, she'd never been the focus of so much consuming hate.

She kept her eyes averted and listened as Lady Kenward left the hall. Feeling a gentle squeeze on her hand, she looked up. Lauren's gaze slid from Elise's frown to Nicholas's shuttered stare. He'd clasped his hands behind his back, and the line of his jaw flexed as if he worked some demon from it. His blue eyes were cool, emotionless, with no trace of his earlier warmth.

Lauren wondered what it had cost him to defy his mother. Would he eventually give in to the woman's anger and lock her away? She shifted in her chair and pulled her hand from Elise's. The open space of the hall seemed to close around her. The air was lacking. She had to leave, now. Placing her napkin on her wooden plate, covering the slimy eel, she rose.

'Please stay and eat, Lady Christel,' Elise urged.

Lauren met Nicholas's gaze. Was he as detached from his feelings as his cold expression suggested? A helpless tremble erupted inside her. She shook her head, trying to deny the obvious answer. But if he was so cold, why did he defy his mother? 'I'm not hungry,' she whispered.

She stepped away from the table and bumped into Thomas. He grabbed her arm, but after a signal from Nicholas, he released her.

'I'll be in the bailey,' she said, aware of the exhausted quiver in her voice. She needed to be out-doors. She wanted to feel the wind on her face, see the sky, whether it was a brilliant blue or hidden behind heavy gray clouds.

Then, maybe she'd control the roller coaster her emotions were riding on. Especially the fear. She couldn't stand the way her heart constricted or the way her limbs went numb each time she envisioned being returned to the oubliette.

He'd said he wouldn't confine her like that again. She had to believe him, had to. Because she had no other choice.

Nicholas clenched his jaw at the haunted look dulling Christel's eyes. With her arms wrapped around her stomach and her chin tilted back, she turned and left the hall. Cursing, he moved away from the table to pace and think, only his sister's voice intruded on his thoughts.

''Tis shameful, Nicholas,' Elise said, rising to face him.

'On what matter do you speak?'

She nodded toward the door. 'Lady Christel, of course.'

'The lady does not concern you.'

'Ha! What if it were me the Scots had captured?' she challenged.

'They will never have the opportunity, little sister.'

'I am not so little.'

'Yes, I know,' Nicholas said, in a scolding tone he found himself using more often with his sister. 'And because of your refusal to marry, you will likely become an old maid.'

She harrumphed, but didn't stomp off like she usually did. 'What if the Scots were to capture me? Would you want them to lock me away in an appalling dungeon the way you did Lady Christel?'

'Of course not,' he growled, not liking the way the conversation prodded his conscience. 'But I released her.'

'Aye, you did.' A mischievous grin replaced her frown and lightened her eyes. 'Why, I wonder?'

The muscles along Nicholas's back tensed. His reasons weren't an issue he wanted to discuss.

Elise tapped a finger against her chin and stared at the ceiling as if she were contemplating some great question. A beguiling smile transformed her face. 'I think you let her out because you like her.'

Nicholas knew he should leave the room rather than banter nonsense with his sister. He stared at the empty doorway. The urge to go outside and see what Christel was about made him take a step forward. He halted and drew himself up.

What did he plan to do? Follow the woman? There were more pressing issues requiring his attention. Like planning the next stage of revenge against Laird Armstrong. Changing direction, he headed for his private solar, calling out to anyone who cared to listen, 'My only concern regarding Lady Christel is that she remain my prisoner. Nothing more.'

Doubt over his own statement crept into his mind and planted a seed. He envisioned her green eyes, alight with laughter, after she had raced toward his castle. Then her stunned disbelief when he had ordered her confined below. He hadn't known what to expect when he permitted her to join them to break her fast. Anger, perhaps, even fear, though he had given his word he wouldn't return her to the dungeon. But he hadn't expected a saucy challenge to lace her gown.

Would the woman never cease to surprise him?

Climbing the stairs to his solar, he remembered holding her waist between his palms. Small, with a gentle curve to her hips. He hadn't wanted to release her. Only his mother's presence had stopped him from drawing Christel onto his lap.

Since the moment he'd captured her, he'd felt an odd tension between them. He had attributed it to their situation. His need for revenge. Now, he wasn't so sure. A fine thread connected them. Invisible, undefinable, but still there. What did he intend to do about it? Break the tie? Or bind it, make it stronger?

Nicholas examined the strange feelings, turning them over in his mind, analyzing each one. The woman intrigued him to the point of distraction. He'd regretted the order to imprison her the moment he'd given it. He could admit that now. During the time she'd been in the dungeon, he had paced and bellowed orders until no one would come near him.

Even after pulling her from the hole and carrying her to the tower, it had taken the rest of the night for the turmoil in his mind to ease. The woman was definitely a distraction, unwittingly drawing him away from his goal. Or had she beguiled him on purpose, hoping he'd became obsessed with her?

Perhaps she was a witch, as Lord Wright suggested. Slyly casting a spell over everyone at Westbourne Castle. A sorceress who had trapped him within her powers. Or was she merely a woman whose beauty and courage made him want to believe there was more to living than hate and revenge?

Finding no answers, he cursed to the empty room. How could he put a name to his feelings for her? He'd never felt anything like them before.

CHAPTER 8

Nicholas sat at the imposing oak desk that had belonged to his father. Its straight lines and carved paneling had been an extension of his father's stalwart authority over everything he ruled. Piercing marks and gashes from the careless handling of swords scarred the wood, added to its strength and character.

A particular dent distracted Nicholas from his ledger. He rubbed his finger along the jagged groove and recalled the day he and his brother had entered the forbidden solar. Nicholas had been ten years old at the time. His brother, James, twelve.

Their secret mission had been to retrieve a pair of matching swords from the wall above their father's desk so they could practice their fighting skills with the other soldiers. They had not known the weight of the swords would be more than their own. James had dropped the first sword, scarring the desk and frightening both boys into fleeing. Their father had found them, hours later, hiding in the stables. As punishment, they'd had to muck out horse stalls, a lowly, humiliating job for the lord's sons. Nicholas leaned

131

back in his chair and stared out the bay window, a slight grin pulling at his mouth, remembering how he and James had ended up dueling with rakes instead of completing their chores.

As he watched the castle folk go about their work, pushing carts and herding animals, the memory of his brother faded, but not the easiness of a happier time. He frowned. How long had it been since he'd remembered James without feeling the rage of his death? Nicholas waited for the familiar anger to return.

He watched a pair of pipits race across the courtyard in a sporadic flight of follow-the-leader. Seconds ticked by, then minutes, and still no bitter heat burned his stomach and tightened his chest. Did this lack of fury mean anything? Had he lost his need for revenge? No, never! Yet he couldn't rekindle the hot, cutting emotion that had chased him like a demon through the years.

Rubbing the tension from his face, Nicholas rose to stand by the window. Was he losing his ability to control his emotions, bring the hate to the surface when he needed it? Or had he carried this legacy of revenge for too long, as Elise constantly accused him of doing? But how could he forget? His father and brother had died, murdered on the side of the road, and he had lived. That single fact had left him with a dark, guilt-ridden soul. Since that bloody day he'd wished countless times that he had died with them, but that was a cowardly wish. His punishment for not saving them was to live each day, unable to escape the truth.

The troubling thoughts shifted to the back of his mind as he spotted Christel in the bailey. The sun, set high in the sky, caught the fire in her hair as it swayed carelessly against her back. She stopped to talk to woman who had a heavy bundle of firewood strapped to her shoulders.

The older woman shook her head and tried to back away, but Christel stopped her and motioned to Thomas. The archer folded his arms across his chest, refusing to move.

Nicholas rubbed his chin, wondering what his beautiful prisoner was up to. Christel propped her hands on her hips and stomped her foot. Nicholas laughed out loud. The unfamiliar sound startled him into turning around to ensure no one had heard.

Looking back out the window, he grinned as Thomas placed the older woman's burden onto his own back and took it toward the kitchen, *leaving Christel unguarded*. Nicholas growled a curse. So, helping the old woman had been a ploy. He should have known she would try to escape again. He had been a fool to trust her with only one guard.

As he raced down the stairs he collided with the laundress, nearly knocking her over. He ran through the hall and ignored his mother's shrill questions. Pushing open the heavy oak door, he paused on the landing when bright sunlight pierced his eyes. He blinked, waited impatiently for his sight to clear.

Then he saw her. She stood where he'd last seen her, in the middle of the courtyard talking with the old woman. Several other women, their eyes wide with curiosity, had drawn near to listen.

Nicholas's heart pounded against his chest. His breath rasped in his ears. Clamping his jaws tight, he willed both to a normal level. He watched the easy way Christel moved her hands when she spoke. Though he couldn't hear her, she seemed to be opening herself up so the other women would join her.

She swiped at loose strands of hair floating about her face, then pulled the entire mass over one shoulder in a gesture so vulnerable Nicholas's mouth went dry and his pulse turned to a slow, heavy beat. Even in her ugly loose-fitting gown, he couldn't take his eyes off her. Her lush curves and slender hands. Soft hands, as he recalled. He imagined the air between them crackling with the effects of a summer storm.

With slow, deliberate steps he came up behind her and stopped. She tensed, lowered her arms and turned to face him. Her eyes brightened when they met his. He saw something flicker in their green depths. Hope? Relief? He couldn't tell. It hadn't been fear. He realized he never wanted to see that emotion dim her eyes again.

Her hair was still pulled away from her face, draped over her breast like layered silk, and his blood drummed through his fingers with the urge to touch it. Hell, he wanted to bury his face in it.

Her mouth parted as if she had something to say. He stared at her lips, full and pink. He'd never wanted to kiss a woman so badly in his life. The one kiss they'd shared seemed like a distant memory. And that kiss had been hard and reckless, like everything else in his life.

No, next time would be different. He wanted her, but with a urgency that had little to do with his vow for revenge. And it had to be soon. Any plans he'd had for a slow seduction languished in the back of his mind. He'd take her first, then seduce her.

'It's not time to go back inside, is it?' Her hesitant tone drew him out of his reverie.

She stared at him, anxiety pulling her brow into a frown. Nicholas was amazed at the way her feelings reflected in her eyes. They shifted from light to dark as quickly, and as unexpectedly, as an English wind. 'There is no need to return as yet.'

'Good.' Her frown disappeared, and she touched his bare forearm. The muscles tensed in response. 'I . . . I . . .' She drew a deep breath and stared at his arm. Pulling her hand back, she hid it in the folds of her skirt. 'There's something I want to discuss with you.'

'I hesitate to guess what that might be.'

She gave him an exasperated look, then motioned for the woman she'd been talking with to come closer. Nicholas knew the woman to be one of the kitchen servants, but he hardly recognized her humped form without a bundle of dried sticks strapped to her back. For some reason he knew this conversation with Christel was not going to bode well for him. The thought almost made him grin.

'Do you know Glynis, Nicholas?'

'Of course. She has worked in the kitchen for years.'

'No,' Christel corrected patiently. 'She has had the duty of collecting firewood for years.'

Nicholas stared at her, sure he'd missed the point she was trying to make. When she propped her hands on her hips, he responded by folding his arms across his chest.

'Her job should be given to a younger person. Like those boys over there.' Christel pointed to three lads sitting beneath a sapling oak with assorted armor scattered about them. 'They're only polishing armor. I'm sure they could be given a more strenuous duty.'

He quirked a brow at her. 'Have you ever polished armor?'

'That's not the point.'

'But it is,' he countered. 'It is a tedious job that requires a great deal of . . .' He paused when her gaze lowered, fixating on his mouth. She leaned closer, as if pulled by the invisible thread he knew existed between them. If it weren't for the crowd gathering around them, he'd pull her closer for a more intimate perusal.

He glanced at the older woman, who seemed fascinated by their exchange, and nodded. 'Go about your work, Glynis.'

'But – ' Christel interrupted.

'I will consider changing her duties,' he added, before she could argue. He heard Glynis leave, but everything else had ceased to exist except for the gratitude shining in Christel's eyes. Odd, he thought, that a prisoner should care about the trials of a peasant. Odder still was the pleasure he felt in giving her what she asked. This wasn't at all how their relationship should be proceeding. But he didn't feel inclined to change it at the moment.

She wrapped her hand around his arm and turned to walk. He fell in step and wondered if she had manipulated him. It didn't matter, he decided. He'd gladly dismiss Glynis from her duties for a year to feel Christel's hand on his skin. But he intended for her to touch much more than his arm. A slow burn warmed his blood and settled between his hips.

He clenched his hands and tried to redirect his thoughts. 'Did you enjoy your walk?'

'Very much,' she said, smiling as she took in the activity around them. 'I never imagined it would be anything like this.'

Nicholas stopped. Why would she have imagined his home at all? He surveyed the grounds. Everything appeared normal. A number of servants worked the garden. Men unloaded a new supply of salt from an ox cart. Throughout the bailey people were busy with their day's work. Nothing unusual.

He glanced back at her. 'Does something seem strange?'

Her laughter caught him off guard. After what he had done to her yesterday, he hadn't thought he would hear her laugh again.

'Oh, Nicholas,' she sighed, 'if you only knew.'

Covering her hand with his, he urged her to face him. 'Tell me.'

She shrugged her shoulders. 'I hadn't expected it to take so many people to run a castle.'

'But what of your father's? Surely it is similar.'

A doubtful frown shadowed her eyes. She lifted her gaze to his, and for an instant he thought she could see inside him. Several times she opened her mouth to speak, then snapped it shut. Finally she said with a huff, 'My name is not Christel Armstrong and my father doesn't own a castle. In fact . . .'

'Come now, Christel.' Nicholas ran his finger along the stubborn tilt of her jaw, irritated that she was trying, once again, to convince him he had the wrong woman. His annoyance waned when he saw the frustration clouding her eyes. Her desperation to escape him filled him with the urge to secure her to his world. An insane thought, he knew. She was his enemy's daughter. His pawn, to use in his game of revenge. Somehow that thought didn't make him feel any better.

'My name isn't Christel,' she insisted, squaring her shoulders as if challenging him to defy her. 'It's Lauren Ferguson.'

'Of Clan Ferguson?' When she rolled her eyes heavenward, Nicholas crossed his arms and waited for her to continue her ruse.

'I don't belong to a clan,' she said with exaggerated calm. 'It's just plain Ferguson.'

'And what part of Scotland do you come from, Lauren Ferguson?'

For some odd reason she seemed taken back. The stiffness in her back relaxed. The sparkling flame in her eyes dimmed to a tranquil wonder. Then she shook her head as if to clear some mental fog. 'I . . . it doesn't matter where I'm from.'

'But it does. If I have captured the wrong woman, it would be my duty to return you to your family.'

'You would let me go?' she asked, in too hopeful a voice for his liking.

'Aye,' he managed with his jaw clenched. 'But only if I had the wrong woman.' He wrapped a handful of her hair around his hand. Cool silk, the color of fire. 'But we both know I have the right one.'

Yanking her hair from his grasp, she glared at him. 'You are the most stubborn man I've ever met. I swear you wouldn't know the truth if I hit you over the head with it!' She paced in front of him, mumbling odd phrases to herself. Something about 'dimwit' and not knowing which way was up. Finally she turned to him. 'What do you plan to do to me?' she demanded. 'You said you were going to ransom me, but when?'

She bit down on her lower lip. The worried gesture baffled him. Did she *not* want him to return her to her father? Or did she simply want to know how much time she had before he sent her back in disgrace?

Unwilling to answer her question, he reached out and ran his thumb down the side of her cheek. An act he found himself repeating whenever he had the chance. The worry lines at her brow deepened, as if her thoughts were elsewhere. She turned her face into his palm, a motion that both startled and pleased him. She raised a soft, slender hand to his wrist, but he

139

didn't think she was aware of her action. Her eyes scanned the curtain walls surrounding the bailey as if to memorize them. *Or search for a way out.* He ground his teeth.

Her cheek warmed against his palm. He slid his hand down, cupped her neck. Her eyes fluttered closed, and her breathing changed to shallow intakes of air. Then she flinched and jumped back.

She stared at him with eyes as green as the moors at dusk. Sultry, yet cautious. 'I want to check on Jessy. Where is she?'

'Who is Jessy?'

'My horse.'

Nicholas set his jaw. She *had* been looking for a way to escape, and she planned to take her horse with her. He hated to disappoint her, but escape would be impossible. Still, she could see the mare if it helped her think otherwise. He nodded toward a row of buildings at the far side of the bailey. 'She is in the stables.'

She gave him a weak smile, but didn't relax her stance. Taking her elbow, he nodded greetings to the villagers they passed, but his thoughts remained on the woman at his side. He should be irritated that she would try to flee, but he found himself admiring the strength of her determination instead.

Entering the stables, they paused until their eyes adjusted to the dim light. He inhaled the familiar smells of horses, sweat and hay. Light seeping through cracks in the walls caught dust motes clinging to the air, making the dark space hazy.

Hades looked at them from his stall and nickered a low greeting. Nicholas placed his hand at the small of Christel's back. She stiffened when he urged her toward the stallion.

'I don't care to see your horse. Where's Jessy?'

'Are you afraid of Hades?' he asked.

She bristled at his words, but before she could respond, the mare poked her head out of her stall and stared at them with wide, nervous eyes.

'You put her next to your horse?'

'Aye, I think they are well suited.'

'Yeah, like a match and gasoline.'

Nicholas frowned. 'What is a match and gasoline?'

Christel's dress tightened across her chest as she drew a deep, agitated breath. 'It's the explosion that's going to happen if you keep them together.'

'I plan to mate them.'

'Over my dead body!'

Nicholas let his gaze roam the length of her, starting with her stiletto-sharp eyes. Her arms were folded beneath her breasts, pushing them to swell above the ruffled chemise. He stared at the expanse of pale skin, imagining her softness beneath the dull wool gown. Clenching his jaw, he lowered his eyes and saw she tapped the tip of her slippered foot impatiently against the dirt floor.

Blood pulsed through his veins, heating his skin with a need he'd come to associate with this woman. She'd threatened he would have to cross her dead body before allowing him to mate the mare with Hades. The only way Nicholas wanted to see her body was beneath him, naked and slick with the rush of desire.

'They are a perfect match.' He reached out and caught a strand of her hair. He tugged gently, so she had to move closer. 'With his strength and her sleek lines . . .' He ran the silky curl across her cheek and down her face. 'They would create a beautiful foal.'

The anger receded from her eyes. She tilted her head back and stared at him. 'Hades will kill her.'

'No, he wants her too much to hurt her.'

Christel's mouth parted on a soft gasp. He drew the tip of her hair over her lower lip and down the pale curve of her throat.

'Don't do this to me,' she whispered.

'I have done nothing.' Nicholas leaned toward her, expecting her to pull away. Her eyes silently pleaded for him to stop, but the slight quiver in her breath, the way she raised her hands and held onto his tunic, told him otherwise. 'Yet.'

He gripped her waist, drew her against him, then covered her mouth with his. Her soft lips burned into his, driving him to deepen the kiss. Her body trembled as he took her in small doses, tasting and stroking and nipping.

Her eyes slipped closed as she tentatively responded to him. A frown marred her brow, as if she were tempted by desire but knew she shouldn't be, not with her father's enemy.

Brushing his lips against hers, he urged her mouth open. With a soft cry, she gave him what he wanted, leaning the length of her body against his. His tongue plunged in and explored the warmth of her mouth. God, she was honey-sweet. He grazed her teeth, drawing a shiver from her.

She slid her arms around his neck, raised herself against him. Growling low in his chest, he kissed her hard, thought he might have bruised her, but he couldn't stop. His pulse-beat surged hot through his mind. He couldn't see, couldn't think. He could only focus on her taste, the feel of her tongue against his, and the need for more.

He left her mouth and kissed his way down the column of her throat. She leaned her head back, her breath catching when he bit her tender flesh. Burying her hands in his hair, she held him to her.

Nicholas supported her back with one hand, cupped her bottom with the other. He pressed her against the ridge of his core, damning the clothes between them, wanting to feel the silkiness of her skin. A shudder tore through him. God, he wanted her. It didn't matter that they stood in the stables where anyone could find them.

He cupped her breast, squeezed, and heard a moan deep in her throat. Without a stiffened bodice, he could feel her lush fullness through the thin material. One thought raced through his mind. Christel fit him perfectly.

Lauren tensed. A flare of pleasure and pain sped from her breast to her belly. It pooled low, making her muscles clench, her body ache. She held Nicholas's head between her hands. His satiny hair curled around her fingers and palms, tickling them with raw sensation.

His lips grazed her skin; he nipped her shoulder with his teeth, making the ache between her legs coil into a tighter knot. She'd never known anything so erotic, so demanding.

Was this what it felt like to make love? She'd never imagined it to be this powerful. Her thoughts flamed with the solid feel of his body against hers. His musky scent enveloped her like a seductive cloak. Heaven help her, she couldn't withstand more. Yet she didn't want it to stop. It was insanity to want him, she knew, but it didn't seem to matter.

Nicholas whispered something against her ear.

Lauren blinked her eyes open. 'What did you say?'

She studied the thick wood beams framing the ceiling, trying to regain control of her senses. A lark flew over her and settled in a nest tucked in a dark corner.

He pulled back slightly, and she saw the dark hunger in his eyes. It mirrored everything she felt, everything except the return of reality.

'I want you, Christel.'

'That's what I thought you said.' He took her hand and pulled her toward the door. Lauren jerked free, startling him, and wrapped her arms around her stomach. A trembling erupted in her body. She avoided looking into his eyes, not wanting to see the desire that would be there. She wanted him enough. All of him. But she couldn't go through with it.

She already cared what would happen to him. If she made love to him, simple, unattached caring would be impossible. She might need him. Needing him meant exposing herself, risking pain and loss. She wasn't ready for that. Very little of her heart was left undamaged after her parents' death. She could admit that now . . . now that she was faced with losing the rest of it. And what she had, she had to protect.

'What is wrong?' he asked, reaching out to her.

'Don't!' Lauren held up her hand and took a step back. 'Don't touch me.'

His jaw clenched. 'Why should I not touch you?'

'I can't let this go any further.'

'You think you have a choice?'

She straightened, her cheeks burning with disbelief. 'You'd force me?'

He grazed his finger over the swell of her breast. A blue flame of desire smoldered in his eyes. 'I would not have to.'

Lauren knocked his hand away. 'Stop that.'

He chuckled, a deep rumbling sound that, to her dismay, whittled away her meager defense. 'Do not fight me, Christel.'

Lifting her skirts, she turned and headed deeper into the stables. She hadn't a clue where she was going. She just needed distance. And air. There seemed to be a lack of it in the huge barn. She passed several empty stalls, hoping to find an exit at the other end. She knew Nicholas was behind her, stalking her like a wolf after a lone deer. If he pounced, she'd be helpless against his attack. Worse yet, she might not bother trying to fight if he touched her again. She had to escape him. Somehow. She had to.

Just then she heard a muffled cry. She stopped, tilting her head to listen. It came again, from the last stall to her left. It sounded like a baby's cry, faint and weak. She opened the gate and stepped inside. She scanned the trampled hay, but saw nothing. When Nicholas came up behind her, she tried to ignore him. She closed her eyes. How could she possibly ignore the man when her body was so finely tuned to his?

'Were you thinking to make love in the barn?' he whispered against her ear. 'I had thought to take you to my chamber. However . . .'

She shuddered and glared at him over her shoulder. 'I thought I heard a baby crying.'

The mischievous light fled his eyes and he stepped past her. He searched the stall, then knelt in the far corner where the hay was stacked deep. ''Tis not a babe.' He glanced at her. 'Come and see.'

Reaching his side, she saw the amber-colored cat, lying on her side. The cat raised her head and looked at them with glassy brown eyes. She opened her mouth to meow, but no sound came out.

'She is birthing her kittens,' Nicholas said, and rose to leave.

Lauren took his place. 'No, she isn't. She's dying. Look.' She felt along the cat's sides. 'The babies are stuck.'

Nicholas grunted. 'A pity, but there is nothing to be done.'

Lauren stiffened her back and turned to face him,

146

ready to call him an insensitive lout. When her eyes met his, she saw a flicker of compassion. Her hands began to tremble. Too much had happened in the last few minutes. To her dismay, she still wanted to kiss him. She wanted to slap him, too, though she wasn't sure why. And she had to help the mother cat give birth to her kittens.

Somewhere in the chaos of her mind, she thanked the small animal for creating this distraction. Who knew what would have happened if she'd had more time to consider making love to Nicholas?

'Get some water and a towel, please.'

'For what reason?'

She found the tiny paws of the first kitten. Wrapping the dry edge of her chemise around them, she pulled gently. 'I'll need to bathe the babies. The mother is too tired.'

A full minute passed before she heard Nicholas leave. He returned just as the first kitten emerged. Nicholas knelt beside Lauren, watching as she dipped a cloth in the water and cleaned the wet brown bundle. 'Isn't he adorable?'

'It looks like a rat.' Despite his words, he reached out and ran his thumb over the kitten's head.

She watched his large fingers against the tiny kitten, taken aback by his gentleness. Sometime during the last few minutes an easy comfort had settled between them. Raising her head, she caught his gaze. The desire that had raged in their blue depths had softened. A slight grin pulled at his mouth.

'Why, Nicholas,' she teased, smiling at him and

147

feeling a strange warmth flutter down to her toes, 'I think I've found the gentle side of you.'

His grin vanished, and his eyes widened with indignation. His hand hovered over the kitten's head for an instant before he pulled it away. She wanted to laugh at his sudden change. But she supposed he didn't consider her statement a compliment. After all he wasn't a nineties man, in touch with his inner self. To hide her amusement, she tucked the kitten against the mother's warm body and prepared to help with the next delivery, all the while feeling Nicholas's disturbing gaze on her back.

By the time all five kittens were born, washed and nestled against their mother, Lauren's hands were shaking. Not because of the silent man standing guard behind her, but from the lack of food. Thankfully, the horn for dinner had just sounded. Rising, she leaned one hand against the stall for support and rubbed the tension from her lower back with the other.

Feeling Nicholas's hand on her arm, she glanced at him, saw the unasked question in his eyes. 'I'm fine. Just a little stiff.'

He nodded as he led her out of the stables and into the busy courtyard. 'You are good with animals.'

Lauren sighed, not minding his possessive hold on her waist. She realized the danger of it, but was too tired and hungry to do anything about it. 'I've been trained to take care of them.'

He gave her a puzzled look, but said nothing as they entered the castle. He guided her toward the dais and gave her the seat next to his, the one his sister had

148

occupied that morning. Lauren eyed him warily, but sat down. He turned and left to speak with one of the servants.

Curious as to what he was about, her thoughts were interrupted by a swoosh of material. Lauren looked to her right and found Elise seated next to her. 'I'm in your chair, Elise. I'll switch with you.' She started to rise, but the younger woman laid her hand on Lauren's arm and stopped her.

''Tis all right. This is where Nicholas wants you.'

Lauren studied the beautiful woman, expecting to see resentment in her dark blue eyes. She only saw a flicker of amusement. 'Isn't there some rule about being above the salt, or something?'

'Yes, of course there is.' Elise's eyes crinkled with a curious look as she placed her napkin in her lap.

'I'm surprised he wants me to sit at the table, what with your mother mad, and all.'

Elise's gaze turned soft and dreamy, a look Lauren refused to translate. 'He honors you greatly.'

'I'm his prisoner.'

The young woman just smiled, then turned to the trenchers of wonderful-smelling food before them. Lauren forgot all about table settings and being a prisoner, and helped herself to the boiled potatoes, warm bread and a huge portion of the meat pie. To top it all off, she ladled a big scoop of plums, sprinkled with sugar, onto her plate.

She looked for a fork, but only found a spoon. To her embarrassment, her stomach growled, loudly. With a spoonful of meat pie halfway to her mouth, she paused, feeling Nicholas's gaze on her. Slanting her eyes to the left, she saw he sat in his chair, watching her. 'Aren't you hungry?' she asked, resisting the urge to squirm in her seat.

His eyes turned dark and moody. 'Aye.'

The smooth texture of his voice felt like a caress over her bare body. Lauren clenched her spoon and turned to Elise, declaring it safer to talk to the young woman. Taking a bite of her pie, Lauren closed her eyes and moaned with pleasure. She'd never tasted anything so wonderful. A mixture of tender meat, potatoes and herbs she couldn't identify. Sighing with delight, she ate in silence.

By the time she'd finished the last sugared plum, Lauren felt her shoulders droop with fatigue. The amber glow of fading sunlight softened the room. She wanted to raise her arms and stretch, but settled for patting her mouth with her napkin. When the urge to yawn overwhelmed her, she rose from her chair. 'I think I'll go up now.'

Nicholas leaned against the back of his chair. A glint of promise warmed his eyes. 'Rest well, my lady.'

Lauren turned and headed up the stairs, with Thomas close on her heels. When she started her climb up the spiraled staircase, her calves began to burn. With no railing to hold onto, she used the coarse stone wall to keep her balance. As her steps slowed, she tried to interpret Nicholas's expression. His eyes had been intense, mischievous, as if he knew something she didn't.

She kneaded the sore muscles in her neck with her

fingers. It was useless to try and second guess him. The only time she had been sure of his thoughts and motives had been when he'd kissed her. He'd wanted her. That thought made her stop and stare into the dimly lit passageway.

'Is something amiss, my lady?' Thomas asked from behind her.

Jumping at the sound of the young man's voice, she glanced over her shoulder. 'No, nothing's wrong.'

By the time she reached the tower door, Lauren was more than ready to collapse on her straw bed and go to sleep, the strain of the past few days finally catching up with her. Nothing could possibly keep her awake now. Not her makeshift bed, nor the thought of the bugs that might be living in it.

Thomas opened the door and stood aside to let her pass. She walked inside and froze, her jaw dropping, her breath locked in her throat. Her straw bedding was gone! In its place sat a bed frame of elegantly carved oak. Over the thick mattress and crisp white sheets lay a dark green blanket with a gold embroidered lion in the center. He was raised on his hind legs and his mouth was opened in a silent roar. Several goose-down pillows had been fluffed and propped against the headboard.

'Who . . .? What . . .?' Lauren's heart thudded against her chest. She turned to Thomas. A flush rose up the young man's neck.

"Tis from Lord Kenward,' he explained. 'I shall be in the hall should you be in need of anything.'

The door closed and the lock clicked into place.

Lauren stood rooted to the floor, her body a tight fist of nerves. She envisioned the parting look Nicholas had given her. The glint of promise in his eyes, the way his mouth had curved into a grin all spoke of his plans for her. She understood that now.

She had worried he might try to seduce her. With a hysterical laugh she realized he wasn't trying, he was *doing*. The bed, which would fit two comfortably, was proof.

Would that be so bad?

Lauren buried her hands in her hair. Was she crazy? Of course that would be bad. It would be worse than bad, it would be dangerous. She couldn't control her body or her thoughts when he touched her. If she made love to him, what would happen to her heart? Eventually it would break, shatter into hundreds of tiny pieces. She couldn't let that happen. But could she stop him?

She had to try. But how? With what weapon? A physical challenge would be foolish. Reasoning with him would be a waste of breath. In her mind, she envisioned a beast on the prowl. Predatory. Hungry. For revenge? Or for the woman? She knew the answer. Nicholas Kenward's only passion was to fulfil the vow that consumed his life.

But what about her? Lauren Ferguson?

She steepled her fingers together and held them to her lips, prayer-style. She paced in front of the bed, studying it, afraid to give in and sit on it. How would she protect herself against him? When she had imagined him to be the knight of her dreams she'd been

152

safe, in control. Now she was at his mercy. Only she knew he wouldn't hurt her. Not physically.

No, he would seduce her, create a longing in her that would burn deeper than any cut or bruise. His kiss in the stables was proof of his power over her. She hadn't been able to resist him, though her mind had screamed, demanded that she run.

Lauren brushed cold fingers over her lips and remembered the hard feel of his, the wild sensations that had shot through her soul. She curled her hand into a fist as the image evoked an aching need in her body.

This can't happen! I won't let it. She pushed her fist into her stomach until pain dulled the memory. Her limbs shook as she sank onto the bed. She laid down on the blanket and rested her head on a pillow. A heavy weight settled in her body, making her moan at the pleasure-pain pulsing through her.

Her eyes grew heavy, but she fought sleep. She had to stay in control. And she had to escape, which meant walking a fine line with Nicholas. Somehow she had to keep his trust without encouraging him.

Escape. Conflicting emotions battled inside her tired mind. Could she leave without first ensuring he wouldn't die in battle? If he refused to believe she was not Christel Armstrong, how would she convince him he was going to be mortally wounded during a siege? Especially if she was not here to prevent it?

Lauren reached for another pillow, crushed it against her chest and curled her body into a ball.

Hopeless tears stung her closed eyes. There was no guarantee she could save him, even if she stayed here.

Giving herself over to sleep, one last thought followed her. She couldn't live with the pain of watching him die.

Not after knowing him.

CHAPTER 9

'Oh, you are still abed!'

Lauren blinked open her sleep-heavy eyes. Elise stood at the foot of the bed, her cheeks flushed and her much-too-bright gaze wide with abashment. 'Yes, I'm still in bed,' Lauren said, her voice thick from hours of deep and thankfully dreamless sleep. 'And I don't plan on getting up.'

'But half the day is gone.'

Lauren pulled a pillow over her head and muttered into it, 'I don't recall having any plans today.'

'Oh, come now.' The mattress sank as Elise settled on the bed. ''Tis a beautiful day. You must come outside with me.'

Lauren didn't move, and after a moment she felt a tap on her shoulder.

'I have brought you something,' Elise said in a coaxing tone.

Peeking around the side of the pillow, Lauren lifted her head and squinted against the thin stream of hazy light washing her small room. She looked down and saw a beautiful midnight-blue gown draped across her legs. Impulsively, she reached out and fingered the soft, heavy satin.

''Tis one of mine,' Elise said. 'I believe it will fit you, though.'

'Why?' She couldn't fathom why Elise would be so kind to her. There had to be a catch, though from the beginning the young woman hadn't displayed any of the hostility the rest of her family felt toward her.

'It is unseemly, if you ask me, for my brother to have dressed you as a servant.' Elise stood, crossed her arms over her modest chest and paced the short distance from the bed to the wall. 'You are a laird's daughter, after all. You should be treated accordingly.'

'Does Nicholas know you're here?'

Elise's full mouth quirked into a rueful grin. Her eyes sparkled with a secret. 'My brother will not mind once he sees you.'

Just the thought of seeing Nicholas created a cloying warmth in the feminine part of Lauren's body, startling her. It worked its way through her limbs, igniting sensitive nerves along the way. She eyed the dress, its tapered sleeves, the low, square-cut neckline and tailored waist. How would she look in such a gown? Would Nicholas even notice?

She tried to kill the thought, but her dormant, womanly side wanted to know what it felt like to have a man look at her, really, really look at her and appreciate what he saw.

Haunted by the burning hunger in Nicholas's eyes when he'd kissed her the day before, she lifted the dress, held it to her and shuddered. Did she honestly think she could step into the lion's den and expect the beast to look and not devour her? And what about her resolve to stop the growing attraction she felt for him?

The tap on her shoulder kept her from answering her own questions. Elise leaned over her, her brow dipped into a worried line. 'Are you well, Lady Christel?'

'I'm fine,' Lauren said, not at all sure that was true. Reluctantly, she handed the bundle of blue satin to Elise. 'I just don't think wearing this would be a good idea.'

Elise straightened and pursed her lips into a stubborn frown. 'You are still angry with him, aren't you?'

Lauren rested her elbows on bent knees. She rubbed the sleep from her face with her hands and tried to define her feelings for Nicholas. Anger, attraction, outrage, desire. A virtual yo-yo of emotions. 'I don't know how I feel about him. But wearing that dress might confuse matters.'

'Hmm. May I tell you something about my brother?'

Positive she didn't want to know anything more about Nicholas Kenward, but too curious to voice her objections, Lauren peeked through the slits of her fingers.

'My brother harbors a deep hatred for the Armstrongs.'

'Tell me something I don't know.'

'Yes, well, he still aches over my father's and brother's deaths. I think he feels he should have saved them that day, or at least died trying.'

Lauren imagined a young boy of twelve standing up to an enemy, then blaming himself when he failed. Her heart constricted for the boy. She swiped a strand of tangled red hair from her face, unable to block the sad picture from her mind. 'I'm surprised you don't share his feelings.'

Elise shrugged and looked out the narrow arrow loop in the stone wall. Grayish light flowing in defined her elegant profile, but couldn't ease the disquiet shifting in her eyes. 'I was but a babe when they died. I have no memory of them. My brother clings to vengeance because of guilt, my mother because she cannot accept the loss of her husband. She had to blame someone. As for myself, I see no point in spending my life with hate as my only passion.'

She turned and stared pointedly at Lauren. 'He put you in the oubliette with the intention of punishing you for your father's crimes. Only, I believe it was he who suffered.'

'Excuse me?' Lauren choked. 'If you think being buried beneath the dungeon was a picnic, think again.'

'I am not explaining myself very well.' Elise twisted her hands together and paced the room, her crimson velvet skirt rustling with each step and sweeping small dust clouds into the air. 'I have never seen Nicholas behave the way he did when you were confined.'

'What did he do?' Lauren cringed inwardly. She should cover her ears and not listen to any more. The last thing she needed was to be concerned about Nicholas's emotional state.

'At first, nothing. He stood in the hall, staring at the floor with his fists clenched. Then he began to yell.'

The nerves along Lauren's spine came alive with a sensitive tingle too intense to ignore. Her hands began to perspire. She rubbed them against her coarse brown skirt, now wrinkled from having slept in it.

'It's not like Nicholas to bellow orders. He prides himself on his control over his emotions. That was when I knew something was amiss.'

'I don't think I want to hear this, Elise.'

'After a short time,' the young woman continued, 'he began to pace, each time stopping at the entrance to the dungeon. Mother confronted him. They argued bitterly, I can tell you.'

Lauren swung her legs off the bed and propped her hands on the edge. 'Why are you telling me this?'

Elise sat beside her, her young woman's eyes shadowed with a knowledge exceeding her years. She opened her mouth to say something, but paused. Shrugging with an innocence Lauren didn't buy, she said, 'I just thought you should know.'

'Now – ' Elise smiled and jumped up from the bed '– 'tis time for the midday meal. Everyone has gathered downstairs and are awaiting us.'

Lauren gave her a cynical look. 'Even your mother?'

Elise paused as she bent over the bed, her hands hovering over the rich gown. Slicing Lauren a conspiratorial grin, she said, 'Well, almost everyone.'

Lauren stood at the top of the stairs, sure her feet had rooted themselves to the floor. She couldn't move.

Hell, she could hardly breathe. Even Elise's persistent nudge at her back couldn't make her take a step.

In addition to the soft light filtering through the mullion windows along the front of the castle, dozens of torches had been lit. Servants in plain, earth-toned tunics maneuvered through groups of men, placing trenchers of food on long, wooden tables.

The men – guests, she assumed, since she'd never seen them before – wore a colorful array of fitted waistcoats, some of which sported ruffles, fluffy sleeves with slashes and elegant embroidery. Several wore tight-fitting hose with short, puffy skirts that gathered around their thighs. Caps with foot-long plumes, knee-high leather boots and enormous codpieces added flair to their gaudy costumes.

Amidst the chaos of color and frump, Nicholas rose from his seat at the dais and turned to face her, spotting her as if he had sensed her presence. Against the sea of color, his solid black waist-length doublet and tight leggings made him seem larger, bolder and mysteriously feral. Lauren released an unsteady breath.

With his hair pulled away from his face and tied at his nape, his blue eyes became twin pools of smoldering invitation. Silently, he beckoned her to join him. When she didn't move, his gaze lowered to touch every inch of her. Her body tightened in response, startling her with its intensity.

So, this is what it feels like to be looked at . . . her mouth turned dry . . . *and devoured.* She glanced down at her dress to make sure she was wearing Elise's blue gown and not a strip of plastic wrap.

'We cannot stand here all day, Lady Christel,' Elise whispered.

'Oh, I don't know,' Lauren mused. 'It seems safer up here.'

Elise laughed softly. 'Aye, you might be right. It appears the entire county has arrived to meet you.'

The urge to groan was smothered by a rising wave of anger. 'He's putting me on display? Like a caught pig?'

Pulling on Lauren's arm, Elise said, 'Come now, 'twill not be so bad. They are merely curious.'

With no choice but to follow, Lauren clenched her skirt in her fists and lifted the material so she wouldn't trip over it. Glaring at Nicholas, she paused on the last step. Every pair of male eyes turned and fastened on her. Silence clamped down over the room.

Her anger shifted to unease. Nicholas walked toward her, his steps slow and calculated. His hands were clasped behind his back. He stopped before her with his legs planted a foot apart, his shoulders squared and his hooded gaze locked with hers. She tried to swallow the dry lump of dust in her throat, but it wouldn't budge.

'I suggest, my lady,' Nicholas said in a low rumble, 'that you lower your skirts, lest it is your wish to bare your legs to all in the room.'

Startled, Lauren looked down and discovered, in her nervousness, she had raised her clenched fists and skirts to her chest, exposing her stocking-covered legs from the knees down. She willed her hands to release the satin, then smoothed out the wrinkles, unable to look up and meet Nicholas's gaze.

For heaven's sake, she grumbled to herself. She was completely covered except for her hands, her face and a small patch of her chest. So why was she embarrassed?

'This gown suits you.' He stepped closer, his eyes lowering to absorb her body, pausing at the low neckline of her bodice.

She tried to think of something witty to say, but had to struggle to breathe. She settled for ignoring his statement.

'I trust you slept well?' he whispered, his voice smooth.

Warm tingles sprinkled across her skin as he watched her. She didn't want to think about the bed, not now, when his intense gaze had the power to unnerve her. 'Fine, thank you.'

Nicholas clasped her elbow in his palm and guided her to the table, giving her the seat beside his. She tried to move down to the next seat, but his hold on her tightened and his glower told her she'd have to suffer sitting by him through the meal.

Taking her place, she returned the roomful of stares. Her earlier irritation at being displayed like a new species of wild animal returned. She clenched her jaw to keep from saying something she might regret, and met each curious stare with a disapproving one of her own.

When Nicholas sat beside her, the men took their own seats. It was then she realized introductions weren't going to be made.

'Are these men here to see me?' she asked, unable to conceal her annoyance.

He leaned toward her and rested his elbow on the arm of her chair. 'Aye, they were anxious to meet the daughter of the infamous Bruce Armstrong.'

With a defiant grin, she said, 'They've made a wasted trip, then, since I'm not his daughter.'

Nicholas ran his finger along the back of her hand, which she clasped in her lap so tight her nails dug into her skin. 'I will have no more of this foolishness, Christel.'

Though his tone could have been mistaken for a caress, she'd heard the unmistakable warning behind it. Lauren ran her tongue over dry lips. The way his rough finger grazed her skin made it impossible to heed the warning. For some insane reason that had nothing to do with escape she wanted him to know who she really was. 'It's the truth, and my name isn't Christel.'

Nicholas leaned back against his chair and studied her, rubbing his thumb against his clean-shaven jaw. Lauren shivered, as if he'd run the callused pad down her spine.

'I suppose you wish me to call you Lauren?'

The sound of her name jolted her. His rough voice had deepened, as if she were the only person in the room. 'I . . . well, yes. It is my name.'

The slow, rakish pull of his mouth reached his eyes, turning them to spheres of warmth. The scar on his right cheek flexed and darkened, making her want to reach out and touch it.

'Perhaps I should call you Lauren,' he said after a moment. 'The name suits you. It is strong and stub-

163

born, like the woman. Unlike Christel, which has a graceful, lilting quality.'

Lauren felt her mouth drop open. She snapped it shut, then muttered, 'I can be as graceful as the next person if you'd stop locking me away and treating me like a prisoner.'

His eyes clouded to black and his voice lowered. 'How should I treat you?'

A seductive rush sped through her. She wouldn't begin to touch that. She straightened her spine and forced her attention to the clicking voices filling the hall. Rows of men were seated at the tables in front of her, picnic-style. Ignoring Nicholas's disturbing presence and his insolent chuckle, she compared the guests to a gathering of arrogant roosters, all perched on a fence with their hair curled and waxed. They alternately bobbed their heads toward her, then whispered among themselves, as if they viewed her as the wolf who'd snuck into their midst.

When a bowl was passed to her, Lauren glanced to her right, expecting to see Elise. A laugh popped out of her when she saw Lord Anthony Wright beside her, wearing a purple doublet with enormous puffed sleeves covered with slashes and gold embroidery. Jewels studded his waistcoat and a waist-length cape of soft black fur draped from his shoulders. A matching purple velvet cap with a tawdry plume was perched at a smart tilt on his blond head.

Seeing her reaction, Lord Wright leaned away from her, his hands fidgeting over the surface of the table. 'I say, is something amiss with my attire?'

164

'Not if you're trying to impress a peacock.' She let her gaze rake over him, not quite able to suppress a grin. 'That is some outfit, Lord Wright.'

'Perhaps you should eat,' Nicholas interrupted.

Lauren turned at the sharpness in his voice. The gleam in his eyes had hardened to irritation. Perhaps he was tired of wearing solid black, and wanted to wear flamboyant clothes like the cackle of men filling the room.

She studied the tailored fit of Nicholas's jacket, buttoned to his neck, and the black sleeves that didn't need puffing to give his arms the illusion of muscle. An abundance of them played and flexed beneath the soft wool fabric each time he moved. The more she looked, the more she hoped he wouldn't give in to fashion trends. She rather liked him the way he was.

Not until she raised her eyes and found him watching her did she realize she'd been ogling him. A blush seared her neck and cheeks. She looked away and stuffed a piece of bread in her mouth, determined to ignore his silent, ardent stare.

She ladled food onto her plate, not sure what some of it was, but too consumed with her own discomfort to care. How unlike her to prefer the dark and dangerous man instead of the gentler, more controllable one. *Don't lie to yourself, Lauren. Lord Nicholas Kenward is exactly your type of man. In fact, he's the only man you've ever dreamed about!*

Lauren sighed in disgust. When everyone stopped talking and turned to her, she shoved a spoonful of food into her mouth. The heavy, slightly bitter taste and mushy texture caught her off guard. She suppressed a gag. She wanted to spit the food out but couldn't, not with a roomful of strangers watching her. Closing her eyes, she concentrated on swallowing without chewing. The second it went down, she shuddered and reached for her goblet. With it halfway to her mouth she paused and looked at Nicholas.

''Tis water,' he assured her.

She wanted to slap his amused expression off his face, but the sour roil of her stomach demanded her immediate attention. Once she was sure the food would stay down, she kept her focus on her plate, eating only what she recognized.

When the last of the empty trenchers were carried away by servants, Lauren's only thought was to escape the rude stares and contemptuous whispers. She rose to leave, but a flick of Nicholas's wrist made her sit again. He caught her hand in his and raised it to his mouth, but he didn't kiss her as she'd expected. And, in all honesty, half hoped.

He held her hand an inch from his lips, so close his warm breath brushed her skin. Heat swept through her arm and joined the skittering pulse in her body. Her dress suddenly felt two sizes too small. She couldn't breathe, could hardly think with the liquid buzz spinning through her mind. 'I . . . I'd like to go outside.'

Rising, he drew her to her feet. He placed his arm at the small of her back and led her toward the door. 'Perhaps you would care to go riding?'

Lauren stopped and faced him. Though her body

was in a riot of sensation, she wondered if this was a test to see if she would try to escape. She knew Jessy could outrun Hades. The stallion had caught the mare the first time, but Lauren attributed that to what had happened inside the cave. Whether a test or not, she had to take advantage of any opportunity given her. 'I'd love to.'

But could she leave? Just ride away from him, knowing what she did about his life and death?

Nicholas turned to a young boy and gave orders for the horses to be made ready. She studied Nicholas's profile: sensuous power and ageless strength. A face she knew so well, and had known for so long. An alarm buzzed in her mind. Her heart gave a wild, anxious beat as a thought suddenly occurred to her. She turned and headed for a hallway leading to the castle's east wing. She knew without looking that Nicholas was behind her, his silent steps gaining on her.

She lifted her gown and hurried her pace. Her heart thudded against her chest, quick and hard. Her mouth turned dry, her palms sweaty. She rounded a corner and ran down the hallway, stopping halfway, her breath ragged against the silence of the empty corridor.

She stared at the bare stone wall where Nicholas's portrait should have been hanging. She didn't know why she felt driven to see it. It wouldn't change her situation. Or make it any more real. She knew she was in the sixteenth century, and that Nicholas was alive. Alive and breathing and awakening a part of her like a spring rain awakens the hidden seeds in the desert, giving them life and purpose. But for how long? How long would he live?

'Christel?'

The sound of his voice affected her like a physical touch. A rush of heat swept away the desperation clinging to her soul. She wrapped her arms across her stomach to fight the need to turn to him. She wanted him to hold her, soothe her fears the way she had imagined he would when she was younger.

'Where's the portrait?' she finally asked.

He shifted so he faced her. 'What portrait do you speak of?'

'Yours.'

Confusion shadowed his eyes. 'There is none of me.'

'No?' Lauren frowned. She ran her hand across her brow in an attempt to organize her thoughts. 'Nicholas, what year is it?'

His frown deepened, and he looked as perplexed as she felt. ''Tis the year of our Lord, 1530.'

'1530? Oh, my God!' She paced in front of him, chewing on her lower lip. She had no idea what month the battle that claimed his life would take place. Only the year. 1530. It was now the end of April. Perhaps there was as much as eight months before it would occur. Eight months!

She couldn't stay here that long. Spend months getting to know him, growing closer, caring for him, only to leave. And he wanted her in his bed. What about that temptation? God help her, how much will power was she supposed to possess?

Pressing her hands to her cheeks, she stopped.

There was something else, something missing. Then she realized.

Rounding on him, she asked, 'Are you married?'

His frown shifted to a scowl, and his eyes turned as hard and emotionless as two blue stones. 'No, I have not taken a wife.'

'No?'

'No.'

'Are you sure?' When his mouth lifted in a sneer, she pressed her hand to her forehead. 'What am I saying? Of course you're sure. Is there any chance you might be marrying someone soon?'

He answered with a barely audible growl. She propped her hands on her hips and tried to think. There was no painting, he wasn't married with a baby on the way, and the prospects of it happening in the near future were slim. Were these pieces missing because of her presence? Had she in some way changed history?

Then she remembered he was supposed to marry an outsider, a foreigner. Christel! Of course. He must have married Bruce Armstrong's daughter. That would explain why Armstrong had laid siege to Westbourne Castle in 1530 – to reclaim his daughter. But would Christel have led Nicholas's men in a battle against her own father? Perhaps, if she had loved her husband enough.

If only there had been a record of his wife's name she could be sure. At best, she was guessing. But it all made sense, she reasoned. Only he hadn't captured Christel. Would that mean the battle would never take place and Nicholas's life wouldn't be threatened?

'What a mess.' Lauren buried her face in her hands as questions without answers bombarded her mind.

'Because there is no portrait and I have no wife?' Nicholas lowered her wrists and drew her flush against him.

'No. Yes. Oh, I don't know if I've made things worse or better.' She rested her forehead against his solid chest and sighed when his arms closed around her.

'I don't understand, Christel.'

'I know.' She squeezed her eyes closed. 'Neither do I.'

They stayed that way for long, quiet minutes. She didn't move except to turn her head so she could hear the strong, steady beat of his heart. She let her thoughts float with his clean, masculine scent.

He stroked her back until her insides calmed. She pressed one hand against his chest, the other she slid around his waist. The safety of his arms, his strength, amazed her. She'd never known anything like it before. Doubted she ever would again.

Nicholas tilted her chin with his finger, raising her face to his. She blinked her eyes open, saw him bending toward her. The instant his lips touched hers, her lids dropped closed again. He grazed her mouth with gentle, feathery touches. So soft, so tender, her breath turned warm and husky. Tears filled her eyes.

'Nicholas,' she whispered, not surprised his name sounded like a plea.

'Shh, let me love you.' His mouth closed over

hers, taking and teaching. He urged her to open. When she did, his tongue slid inside and dissolved her ability to stand. Reason faded into nothing. All she could do was feel and taste and drown in a flood of sensation.

His hand brushed the arch of her neck, her shoulder, moving down to her side where he cupped her ribs, his palm pressing against the edge of her breast. Heat flared and spread. 'Please . . .'

'*Nicholas!*'

Hearing the screeching female voice, Nicholas' arms tightened around her. He broke the kiss and straightened to stare over Lauren's head, toward the end of the hallway. Not trusting her legs to support her, she kept her grip on his doublet, but followed his icy gaze.

'Mother,' he said, in a voice as devoid of emotion as his expression.

'How dare you touch this harlot? This wretched piece of filth! And in my own home!'

'Mother, this does not concern you.'

'Everything about you concerns me, son. I will not have you defile yourself with the likes of *her*.'

Lauren had the overwhelming urge to move behind Nicholas's back and hide. Lady Kenward's small, withered body visibly shook. Her pale blue eyes were glazed with rage.

'I will remind you, Mother, I am lord here. I shall do as I wish.' He sighed, adding in a softer tone, 'Return to your chamber. I will speak to you later.'

Anger darkened Lady Kenward's wrinkled face,

making her appear more haggard and beaten than a woman of her years ought to be. She turned to leave, but not before slicing Lauren with a cutting glare.

'I apologize for her,' he said as his mother disappeared around a corner. 'She has not been the same since my father's death.'

'Sixteen years is a long time to carry a grudge,' Lauren muttered, unable to shake the unease of Lady Kenward's loathing.

'It is more than a simple grudge.'

'I know,' she said, feeling an endless frustration gather inside her. 'It's about revenge and wearing black and wasting your own life until you've evened the score with Armstrong. Did you ever consider you might be killed in the process? That, no matter what happens, your father and brother can't come back to life?

'Dead is dead, Nicholas,' she said, her voice breaking with the effort to hold back hot tears. 'Nothing can change that. But you can think about the people who love you and spare them from suffering another loss.'

Pulling out of his arms, she hurried down the corridor. She couldn't look at him without hearing Edith's shrill voice recounting his death. She pressed her hand to her mouth to seal off the sob tightening her throat. She wouldn't care about him. She wouldn't. Nothing in the world would make her fall in love with him, then watch him die.

Lauren didn't want to cry, but the tears came anyway. She ran through the hall, ignoring the curious stares, and out into the dull afternoon light. She paused and swayed on the castle steps, thinking how easy it was to lie to herself.

God help her. She already loved him.

By the time Nicholas caught up with her, Lauren had successfully harnessed her emotions, but she couldn't meet his gaze. When he tried to take her arm she moved out of reach, not trusting herself enough to let him touch her.

As they crossed the bailey she occupied her mind with the activity buzzing around her; a young boy herding a small flock of sheep, women gathered around a peddler, arguing over the price of colorful ribbons. She passed wagons loaded with barrels and sacks of grain. A small group of men, teenage boys, really, were honing their sword skills in a mock battle.

The array of sights and clashing sounds filling the bailey soothed her nerves. The tension along her back eased and she smiled at the people she passed. It occurred to her that the castle was like a well-organized company. Everyone had their place, their duties to perform. From all appearances, it seemed like a tightly knit group, a family, a place to belong.

Lauren stopped when she experienced a wave of understanding. She turned in a circle, scanning the busy grounds. Unlike the castle of her time, which was barren of life, this castle pulsed with the heartbeat of the people who made this their home.

A place to belong. She didn't have a place to belong anymore. Any roots she'd had were cut the day her parents died. This place, with its primitive way of life, called to her. She felt it like a soft, steady beat that grew in strength each day. She closed her eyes and drew a deep breath, filling her lungs with clean earth, the scent of hay and the heavy smell of animals. At that moment, she realized this world could seduce her if she let it. *If she let it*.

A touch on her arm made her open her eyes and meet Nicholas's questioning gaze. His slight frown pulled at the scar on his cheek. She raised her hand to touch it, but caught herself. She crossed her arms and stepped back, putting meager distance between them. Remembering they were supposed to go riding, she asked, 'So, where are the horses?'

At that moment, a stable boy emerged from the barn with two horses in tow. Neither of them Jessy. Alarmed, Lauren turned to Nicholas. 'Where's my horse?'

'You will ride this mare.' Nicholas took her arm and led her to the left side of the dappled gray.

'I'd prefer to ride Jessy.'

'I'm sure you would,' he said with a half-grin.

'That's a side-saddle.' She tried to pull free, but he gripped her waist and, in an effortless move, set her on top of the horse. 'I can't ride this way.'

With a much too familiar touch, he hooked her leg around the high pommel. 'Only peasant women ride astride like a man.'

As Nicholas swung himself onto Hades's back, Lauren muttered, 'Well, it *is* the practical way to ride.'

She didn't examine the relief she felt at having her opportunity to escape snatched away. It would have been too dangerous, she reasoned. If Nicholas had caught her, she'd risk being returned to the oubliette.

Struggling to keep her balance on the side-saddle, she followed him through the bailey, past the guarded entrance and relaxed with the freedom of being on horseback. Nicholas might have suspected her plan to escape on Jessy, but it didn't matter. She let herself admit she wasn't ready to leave yet. Soon. A few more days. But not yet.

'Where are we going?' She nudged the mare alongside Hades.

'Where would you like to go?'

Lauren looked at the windswept meadow, awash with purple heather and white spring flowers. For as far as she could see, deep, swaying grass covered the ground like rich green velvet. 'Let's race to Hadrian's Wall.'

His laughter startled a grin out of her. 'And risk losing you to a band of Scottish reivers?' He reached out and ran his finger along her jaw, then touched her lower lip. 'I know of another place.'

Content to follow, Lauren lost herself to the rolling countryside and the quiet presence of the man beside her. White cotton clouds rolled across the sky and blocked the sun, turning the breeze cool and welcoming. After riding for a time in comfortable silence, she realized where he was taking her.

In the future, an aging copse of oak trees harbored a modest glen and a small pond. It was a favorite place for teenagers to meet in private and do what teenagers do. Lauren stared at the towering oaks standing guard around the secluded hideaway, seemingly unchanged. She wondered if these were the same trees as in her time, or were these the grandparents of a generation yet to come?

As the mare picked her way around twisted tree trunks and beneath a canopy of branches heavy with green leaves, Lauren became acutely aware of Nicholas's presence . . . and their isolation. She felt his eyes on her back as strongly as if he were sitting in the saddle behind her.

She called herself a fool for having worn the blue satin gown. She'd captured Nicholas's attention, and now she was walking straight into the lion's den. No fight, no fuss, no mess. She wondered if she'd receive a quick, painless death, then sighed, knowing that wouldn't be the case. If Nicholas tried to seduce her here, beneath the shelter of silent oaks, she would most likely die from pleasure. His kisses had rendered her unable to stand on her own. What would happen if he did something more?

At the edge of the glen, she reined the mare to a halt. Nicholas dismounted, then came to help her down. After hobbling the horses, he took a blanket from his saddle and led her to the pond. Spreading the blanket beneath a shade tree, he motioned for her to sit, but he remained standing.

After a few quiet moments, he said, 'I used to come here when I was a boy.'

'It's beautiful.' Lauren tried to imagine what Nicholas had been like before the death of his father. Had he smiled? Teased? Laughed?

'My brother and I would sneak away from our lessons and come here to practise with our swords.'

'You had *real* swords?'

Nicholas chuckled. 'No, we were too young. My father had a matching pair of wooden ones made for us. But they were real enough for us to learn how to joust.'

'Ah, just another day of young boys knocking each other off a horse with blunt instruments,' Lauren said with mixed disbelief and sarcasm. When he didn't comment, she asked, 'So, who won?'

Nicholas stared across the lake, his eyes hooded as if he were watching two boys learning to become men. He smiled then, but it was a lonely smile, one that made Lauren's heart ache.

He turned and sat beside her, one knee drawn up with his arm resting on it. 'My brother usually won, he being larger and stronger than me.'

She clasped his hand. 'You miss him, don't you?' She knew it was a ridiculous question. He wore his pain like a badge. But if he talked about his loss, perhaps she could persuade him to end his need for revenge.

He gave a slight nod. Sadness deepened his eyes to a haunting blue.

An impulse, so strong it caught her off guard, made her lean forward and brush her lips across his scar. Nicholas stiffened, but didn't pull away. Neither did she. She was so close she couldn't see his entire face, not even his eyes. She could smell his musky scent, feel the heat rising from his skin, see the vein at his temple pulse in a mad beat.

She wanted to hold his face between her hands, feel the rough stubble of his beard and the firm skin beneath. She wanted to kiss his scar again, then move to his eyes, his nose, his lips.

She'd never wanted anything so badly in her life.

The strength of her conflicting need frightened her. It went against her warnings about caring for him. She leaned away to see his eyes, then wished she hadn't. They burned like hot blue flames of passion, searing into her soul, marking her, his for life.

He caught her hand, drew it to his mouth. Pressing a kiss to her palm, he then held it against his face. 'I want you.'

She stared at his lips, wanting to feel them on her. Yearning shivered through her. She shook her head, trying to deny the growing ache. 'I can't do this.'

'Why do you fight me?'

A silent cry tore through her mind. She didn't *want* to fight him. She *had* to. 'I'm the wrong one, Nicholas. Don't you see? I'm not supposed to be here.'

'I know no such thing. I can see it in your eyes. Your body burns for me.'

She trembled as if invisible fingers had grazed her bare skin. 'No.'

'Admit what you feel for me.'

Lauren tried to scoot away. He reached out and cupped her neck in his hand. His palm caressed her skin, flooding her with warmth. His fingers slid into her hair, sending tingles over her scalp to dissolve down her back.

'I want you,' he whispered.

'No.' Though she managed to say the word, it held no meaning, no conviction.

'You will come to me.'

'I can't.'

'But you will.' He leaned forward and brushed her lips with a promise. Lauren closed her eyes to savor the feel of him, but he pulled away. 'When you are ready, you will come to me. And it shall be soon.'

Nicholas rose and walked toward the pond. A wash of golden sunlight filtered through the trees and surrounded him in a gentle glow, easing his hardness, helping her see him for the man he was. She *felt* more than saw the strength of his stance, the safety of his powerful arms.

She tried to look away, but couldn't. She tried to deny his declaration that she would go to him of her own free will. By doing so, he would not be the one to seduce and take. She would be the one to give.

Heaven help her if she let that happen. There would be no going back. She would be bound to this time, this land and to this man.

She closed her eyes, spilling hot tears down her face. Clenching her fists in her lap, she fought against the part of her that wanted to live and thrive in Nicholas's world . . . *forever*.

CHAPTER 10

Lauren leaned over the huge dog – a levrier, Nicholas had called it. Similar to a greyhound, only larger, his coarse, stone-gray coat was matted with dirt and littered with bits of grass and twigs. Though he didn't whimper in pain, he took short, quick breaths. Large brown eyes watched her as she ran her hands over his sides and legs.

'What happened to him?' she asked.

Nicholas knelt beside her, scratched the dog's head and received a wet lick across his palm. 'The stag he cornered on this morning's hunt turned on him. Kicked him in the side.'

'Ouch,' Lauren commented absently, her attention focused on the animal. When she pressed a spot on the dog's chest, he flinched and yelped in response. 'Nothing's broken, a few cracked ribs, though. Hand me my basket, would you?'

He handed her the straw-woven basket. 'You should allow the huntsman to tend him.'

'Why? This is what I like to do.' She drew out several long pieces of cloth. Glancing at Nicholas, she

180

caught her breath as he reached out to brush loose strands of hair from her face. She held still as he tucked them behind her ear, then trailed his fingers along her jaw.

They stared at each other, the air between them alive with strained desire, the dog at her side forgotten.

'How long do you intend to resist me?' he asked.

Two weeks had passed since he'd stated he would wait for her to come to him. During that time he'd shown more patience than she'd given him credit for. His fingers grazed her bare neck, igniting sensitive nerves hidden there. The rough pad of his thumb drew slow circles over her collarbone. Lauren's breathing turned shallow. Her mind spun as if she'd drunk a glass of wine in a single swallow.

'Tell me you want me,' he urged.

She opened her mouth, but no sound emerged.

He leaned toward her, his mouth closing in on hers. Need smoldered in the blue flame of his eyes. She shivered, wanting to give him what he asked, but she couldn't move, couldn't say the words.

'Tell me,' he whispered, his breath caressing her face.

Damn it, Nicholas, kiss me!

She moved toward him, but he kept the slight space between them, teasing her with the promise of his kiss. Frustration heightened her need. God, how could he do this to her? Push her past all boundaries, make her want him when she shouldn't. She had been administering aid to a wounded animal. But one heated look from Nicholas and her thoughts were ashes, allowing images to filter in of making love to him on the stable floor.

'Nicholas, please . . .'

The dog whimpered, and the sound of footsteps wove through her fixation on his mouth. Not until Nicholas pulled away did she realize Thomas stood behind them, fidgeting and looking quite anxious.

'What is it, Thomas?' Nicholas glanced over his shoulder at the young man and withdrew his hand from her neck, placing it over the fist she clenched in her lap, covering her with his heat.

''Tis a dispute with the miller, my lord. 'E's been accused of cheating while weighing the grain, 'e has.'

Nicholas nodded, dismissed Thomas, and turned back to her.

'Do arguments like that happen often?' she asked as her heart began to make a slow recovery.

Ignoring her question, he brushed her lips with his. 'I will not wait for you much longer.' Then he was gone.

Lauren closed her eyes and sighed. The kiss had been a tease, a frustrating, irritating tease. She dropped her head back and sighed. *Lord, help me. I want that man.*

The dog whimpered again. She turned her attention to it, thankful that she had something besides the Black Knight to occupy her mind.

An hour later, Lauren stepped from the dark shelter of the stables and squinted against the bright afternoon sun. The scent of hay, and the heady smell of animal fur clung to her coarse brown dress.

Shifting the basket containing an assortment of herbs, salves and bandages she'd scavenged onto her left arm, she shielded her eyes with her right hand until they adjusted to the light. A contented sigh escaped her as she took in the now familiar sounds and activity.

The bailey was busy as usual. Shouts from competing peddlers mingled with the raspy voice of the laundress. The plump, good-natured woman had positioned her washtub near the well, her arms elbow-deep in dirty, sudsy water. A group of laughing children darted past Lauren, playing a game of Blind Man's Buff.

It was just past noon and lunch wouldn't be served for another half-hour. She thought about going to the miller's shack to see what the dispute was about. But seeing Nicholas again so soon after her nerves had played volleyball changed her mind. She decided to stroll through the market instead.

Since the day Nicholas had taken her to the pond and pushed her defenses to their limit, he'd given her the freedom to wander the bailey. She wasn't so naïve as to think there wasn't a guard watching her. There just wasn't one on the heel of her every step.

Nicholas still locked her in the tower each night, but he hadn't come to her room as she'd expected. So far he'd kept his word about waiting for her to come to him. And, to her ire, she felt her resolve slipping away with each day.

Damn his black heart! He made her want the one thing she couldn't let herself have. But what she wanted most. *No, no, no! Good Lord, Lauren. How many times do you have to remind yourself!*

She knew she should make a plan, some attempt to return to her own time, but for the past weeks she'd repeatedly found a reason to delay. A new lamb was being born, a horse suffered from colic. Groaning, she forced herself to be honest. They hadn't been the real reasons she'd stayed.

It had been Nicholas. Wanting to know him, see him, be near him. She had willingly walked into the trap she'd been afraid of falling into; staying as long as possible and risking her heart in the process.

To force all thoughts of Nicholas behind a mental door, she quickened her steps, pounding the earth until her teeth jarred. She took in the sights and smells. The pungent odor of freshly caught fish reached her first, making her nose wrinkle. As Lauren moved on and watched a peddler hawk clay pots, metal spoons and wooden trenchers, a wary tingle snaked down her back. She stiffened and glanced around, curious about the silent alarm ringing in her mind. For two weeks she had felt safe within the stone walls, confident that Nicholas would let nothing happen to her.

So why the unsettled feeling now?

Through the milling crowd, she saw nothing unusual. No evil faces, no one rushing toward her bearing a weapon. Still the feeling persisted, as if she were being watched, but not by Thomas or Kenric, or even Jacobson. This was someone else.

The hair at her nape prickled with unease. She rubbed her neck and turned away from the vendor. Working her way through the crowd, she stopped several times to look behind her, but saw nothing strange. Giving it up to an overactive imagination, she turned back toward the castle.

A man stood directly in her path. She slapped her hand over her mouth, capturing her startled scream. He wore a simple tunic of gray wool and black leggings. A lion crest on his shirt and the sword sheathed at his side identified him as a soldier. One of Nicholas's.

He bowed. 'Forgive me for startling you, my lady.'

Lauren could only nod and will her heart out of her throat and back into her chest.

'You are to come with me.'

She gripped her basket and retreated a step. 'To where?'

'Please, my lady, come with me.' He stepped aside and motioned toward the stone wall beyond the stables.

'Did Nicholas send you to get me?'

'Aye.' The man glanced at the castle, then back to her.

Though a trace of reluctance lingered in her mind, she followed him. Once they passed the stables he grasped her arm and quickened his pace. He glanced behind him several times, his free hand holding the hilt of his sword.

Lauren pulled back, but he jerked her forward. She dropped her basket. Her heart thudded against her

185

chest. She opened her mouth to scream, and he stopped long enough to whisper, 'Utter one word, my lady, and ye shall regret it.'

When he started forward again, Lauren looked behind her, praying someone would notice what was happening and alert Nicholas. The path behind her was empty. Her skin turned cold.

Reaching the wall, he stopped and pressed her against its jagged surface. She gasped, panting in fear. What did he mean to do to her? Rape her? Kill her? Hide her body behind a patch of weeds for someone to find?

The horrible image made her shiver. If he meant to kill her, she wouldn't go down quietly. She'd scream her bloody head off. She drew a deep breath, but the soldier clamped his hand over her mouth, suffocating her. She gagged, but he didn't ease his hold.

Instead he jerked her from the wall, led her around a corner she hadn't noticed before, then down a flight of stone steps. Within seconds darkness engulfed them. She clawed her nails at the hand he pressed over her mouth. He released her and swore. She gasped a breath and choked on the stagnant, decaying air. Her stomach roiled and heaved. She turned toward her abductor, thinking it'd serve him right if she threw up on him.

Just when she thought she would lose her stomach, he opened a door and a cool breeze washed over her, lifting the stench away. He drew her up to the threshold. Lauren looked down and swayed when she saw the twenty-foot drop to the ground beyond the castle wall.

186

'What is going on here?' she demanded. Ignoring her, he picked up a coiled rope ladder from the floor and tossed it out.

'Where's Nicholas? Does he know you're doing this?'

The soldier refused to answer or to meet her gaze. He pointed to the ladder. 'Climb down.'

'Why?'

The soldier shifted his weight from foot to foot. She sensed his unease, and when he spoke she heard the distress in his voice. 'I have my orders, my lady. You must climb down.'

Something was wrong. Terribly wrong. The last thing she should do was obey him. Somehow she needed to stall. 'Why can't I leave the castle through the front gate?'

He didn't answer.

'Nicholas doesn't know about this, does he?'

'You must go. Now!'

Lauren looked into the dark tunnel behind her. Even if she managed to reach the stairs, the soldier would catch her before she made it to the bailey. She considered refusing to climb down the dangerous rope ladder, but her abductor seemed so determined to complete his duty she thought he might decide to push her out the door if she didn't go on her own.

With her limbs trembling and her heart in her throat, she sat on the rough stone floor and caught the rope with her foot. The man held her arms as she worked her way around and began her descent. A third of the way down she paused to look up and ask what she was supposed to do once she reached the bottom. The soldier had vanished and the door was shut, leaving her only one option. Down.

Gripping the rope with sweaty hands, she struggled to find a foothold and prayed the woven ladder would hold her weight. She concentrated on each step, each rung. Sweat beaded on her brow despite the cool breeze. It ran down her face and into her eyes, stinging them, blurring her vision.

The wind pulled her hair. Curls clung to her face, blinding her, but she didn't dare release the rope to move them. When she reached the bottom, Lauren held onto the ladder and leaned against the castle wall. She closed her eyes and tried to slow her breathing.

Hearing a soft nicker, her eyes flew open. 'Jessy!'

Saddled with English riding gear, the mare stood patiently a few feet away. The bridle with its reins looped around a post was hers, too. Purchased at a local tack shop no more than a year ago.

Lauren glanced to the side, then above her, sure there were archers poised with arrows locked in their bows, waiting for her to make a move. She saw no one. A breeze whispered against her, cooling the sweat on her brow.

Who had organized this? Who wanted her to escape? It couldn't be Nicholas. He had made it clear he wouldn't let her go. Even if he had changed his mind, he wouldn't free her this way.

Chewing on her lower lip, her gaze shifted from the thick stone walls to the leather reins. Here was her chance to escape. It was being handed to her, free and easy. That was if she didn't get an arrow in the back first. And she highly suspected that might happen.

But from whom? Who would want her gone? An answer formed in her mind, but she discarded it, not willing to believe it.

Lauren gripped the ladder and considered climbing back up. She stopped herself. What was she doing? She was throwing her chance to escape away, and why? Because of Nicholas. She released the thick rope and stepped back. Indecision turned to panic, and that to somber reality. She couldn't stay. She'd already delayed finding a way out for too long.

She had to return to her own time, her own life. Faced with the harsh decision, she knew she had to leave, now, while she had the chance. Nicholas had been patient with her. But his tolerance was growing thin. As was hers. How much longer would she be able to resist him? Not long, she suspected. She wasn't sure she wanted to anymore. What would happen to her then? What would happen if she acted on her feelings? She knew. They would both be hurt in the end.

Taking the reins, Lauren moved without thought and mounted Jessy. She hesitated in turning the mare around. Despite everything, she wanted to leave a message for Nicholas. She didn't want to disappear this way, without a word, vanishing into thin air, never to be seen or heard from again. She could imagine the devastation she'd feel if he disappeared from her life without a trace. Unshed tears stung her eyes. There was nothing she could do.

She had no choice. She had to go, and she had to go now.

Nicholas pulled his gaze from the doorway to stare at the empty chair beside him. Agitation gathered in his limbs as he waited. He didn't like to wait. He had done too much of it during his life. Waiting for revenge. Waiting to be free of the bonds that tied him to the past. Waiting to begin his life . . . *with Christel*.

The startling conviction of that thought made him reach for his goblet of wine. His second in the past thirty minutes. He ignored the trenchers of food, not caring if they grew cold, and locked his gaze on the door once again. He held his cup in a loose grip, though he wanted to crush it in his hand. Where was she?

The bell for the midday meal had sounded almost an hour ago. A few minutes late himself, from dealing with the miller, he had expected to find Christel waiting for him at the dais, as she had every day since he had given her the freedom to roam the castle.

At first her absence had startled him, now it had his blood flowing hot and his mind brewing with dark questions. Was she injured? Lying somewhere needing help, needing him? Or had she tried to escape?

Though he allowed her to wander the grounds without a guard at her side, there had always been a man or two following her at a discreet distance. So what had happened? He'd sent Thomas in search of Vernon, the soldier in charge of watching Christel that morning. As yet, neither had returned with news.

'Is something wrong, son?'

Nicholas glanced at his mother, surprised by her appearance at the table, her first since the morning she had demanded he return Christel to the oubliette. His mother's presence sent a thread of relief through him. Perhaps her hatred had softened toward the Scottish woman. He prayed it was so.

'I'm sure all is well,' Elise said, though Nicholas detected a trace of doubt in his sister's voice.

He turned to her and saw she chewed on the nail of her index finger, a sure sign she was worried. He thought she'd broken that habit years ago. Clasping her hand, he lowered it to the table.

Frowning, she looked at him. 'I am sure she wouldn't try to escape.'

'Escape?' His mother folded her hands across her waist and tilted her chin.

Nicholas ignored her. 'What makes you so sure?' he asked Elise, wanting to believe his sister.

She lifted her shoulders in a hesitant shrug. 'She seems to be content, almost happy here.'

Lady Kenward grumbled behind him. 'Of course she was content. You allowed her the run of the castle.'

Nicholas took a drink of wine to shield his thoughts from both Elise and his mother. The last few days had passed like a dream for him, surreal, easy, only disturbed by the occasional reminder that Christel was his prisoner. He had difficulty thinking of her as his hostage.

Each day the barrier that separated their lives, English versus Scottish, withered away. Like

191

Hadrian's Wall, built centuries ago by the Roman Empire to protect their lands, was now crumbling, worn away by the constant, changing wind.

Each time he looked at Christel he failed to see her Scottish blood. Instead, he saw her as a woman. A woman he wanted. A dangerous thing to do, he knew. But something about her, some indefinable quality, drew him to seek her out, look at her, speak with her, and wait for the moment she gave in to the attraction that bound them together.

It would happen soon. Tonight, perhaps. He would not accept her reasons to delay any longer. She wanted him, but was afraid. He would reassure her she had nothing to fear with him.

The sound of running feet drew his attention to the door. Thomas raced across the hall, his youthful face flushed, his brown eyes wide with alarm.

'My lord.' Thomas panted as he slid to a stop before the table. 'I cannot find Vernon anywhere, and no one has seen him for the past hour.'

Nicholas rose. 'What about Lady Christel?'

The boy swallowed to catch his breath. 'She's gone, sire.'

Elise gasped. His mother remained silent.

The nerves along Nicholas's spine hardened with anger. His blood chilled and ceased to flow. He shoved a breath from his lungs. 'Explain yourself.'

'The mare, Lady Christel's mare, is missing from the stables. As is her strange saddle and bridle,' Thomas said in a rush. 'And I found this,' he added, but Nicholas barely heard him.

He stared at the basket Thomas held in his out-stretched hand. Nicholas knew without looking that it contained the medicines Christel used to treat the animals. He rarely saw her without it.

No. He staggered backward in disbelief. Clenching his hands, he fed his shock with anger, letting it grow to take over everything else. *She's gone!* He didn't want to believe it. Over the past few days he would have staked his future that she cared for him. Obviously he'd made a faulty bet.

In a strangely calm voice, he said, 'Go to the stables, Thomas, and have Hades prepared.'

'Aye, my lord.'

As Thomas ran from the hall, Nicholas crossed the room and retrieved his sword from the table beside the hearth. As he strapped it around his waist, he knew he wouldn't catch her. She had an hour's head start. Even without the advantage, the sleek chestnut mare would have outrun any horse he owned. He didn't stand a chance of finding her again.

He turned to discover his mother behind him, her withered face set with determination.

'Let her go, son,' she said tightly. 'We are far better off without her.'

Glaring his mother into silence, he moved around her and headed for the door. With each step, a smothering weight engulfed him, filled him with an emptiness he'd never known. It settled around his heart and waited until he gave it a name.

Despair.

For a few brief days he'd caught a glimpse of what contentment could be. Now he'd lost it.

He'd lost her.

Cresting a hill, Lauren spotted the dense weald of oaks that sheltered the cave. She reined Jessy to a halt. The mare's sides heaved with each breath, but she pawed the ground, anxious to move on. Lauren reached down and patted the horse's sweaty neck. She'd pushed Jessy at a hard run most of the way, wanting to stay far ahead of the group of men following her. Since they had yet to appear on the horizon, she had a moment to rest.

Once leaving the castle, she'd barely covered a mile before she'd spotted five soldiers in hard pursuit behind her. Though she knew she had to escape, her heart had demanded she stop to see if it was Nicholas coming for her. As the men came into view, she scanned each one. By the way they held themselves, the shape of their bodies, she knew none were Nicholas. Her disappointment surprised her, but reality wouldn't allow her to linger over it.

The soldiers took orders from someone, just like the man who had forced her down the rope ladder. She had to believe that whoever had orchestrated this had no intention of letting her escape. They planned to hunt her down like an escaped criminal. Did they have orders to return her to the castle, draped over a saddle with an arrow protruding from her back? Or did they plan to leave her where she fell for the night scavengers to find?

Anger joined the chaos in her mind. She was leaving Nicholas, yet she didn't want to. Now she'd been forced to make a decision about returning to her own time, the truth had become obvious. But how could she stay? There was more than Nicholas's life at stake now. There was her own. Someone wanted her gone. Dead and gone. And all because they thought she was a Scottish laird's daughter.

'Oh, Nicholas,' she whispered as the five soldiers on horseback drew closer. She had no more time to waste; she had to make her decision, now. She turned and faced the woods. Inside the dark expanse of green shadows and quiet timber lay the door to her world. Edith giving tours at Westbourne Castle, her grandparents searching for new discoveries and acting like lovesick teenagers. And her own life as a veterinarian.

Jessy fought the reins, trying to enter the shelter of trees. Lauren caught a sob in her throat as she glanced behind her. The soldiers were gaining on her, five hundred yards away at most.

With each passing second, her chances for escape diminished. Yet she couldn't move. She couldn't force herself to enter the woods and return to her own time.

The breath in her lungs suspended as she finally understood her hesitation. If she found the cave, she wouldn't be returning to her own time, she'd be leaving Nicholas. Everything she had ever searched for, ever wanted was here.

A home, a family and the only man she had ever dared to dream about. The one man she loved.

A shout and the pounding of hooves brought

Lauren around. When she saw how close she'd let the soldiers come, she jerked back on the reins, causing Jessy to rear. She kicked the mare into a run and headed for the woods. She had no other choice. If she tried to return to the castle, they would simply cut her off.

Slipping through the first row of trees, Lauren let Jessy make her way through the brush until it became so thick they had to slow to a frantic walk. After a few minutes, Lauren urged the mare to the right, hoping to circle back and escape the woods while the men searched for her in the jungle of oaks and vines.

Cold sweat bathed her body. She picked her way through the foliage, playing a life and death game of hide-and-seek. She leaned over the mare's neck, prayed they blended with the forest's shadows. For the first time she was thankful for the simple brown dress she wore.

Muted shouts echoed beneath the canopy of trees, making her think her pursuers were everywhere, surrounding her, waiting for the moment she stepped into their path. Her breath shuddered from her chest. Nearing what she hoped was the way out, she nudged Jessy faster. Shouts rang out behind her, louder, closer. Then, 'There she is!' pushed her fear to the surface.

Lauren kicked the mare hard and gripped Jessy's neck to shield herself from the branches clawing at them. Sharp limbs pulled at her hair, ripped her dress, beat against her legs.

Panic clenched her throat. She wanted to cry, but

refused to. She had to think. The brush behind her rustled and snapped as if a herd of elephants were stampeding toward her. She didn't turn around. Didn't want to see how close the soldiers were with their arrows. Jessy stumbled over a log, nearly pitched Lauren from the saddle. Clinging to the mare with her legs, Lauren struggled to regain her seat.

'Come on, girl,' she pleaded, anticipating the hot sting of an arrow piercing her back.

Just when she was certain she was lost, Jessy plowed through the last of the brush. Brilliant sunlight pierced Lauren's eyes; a cool wind slapped against her face. She tilted her head toward the sun and would have laughed if she hadn't heard the other horses emerge from the forest. She glanced behind her as all five riders whipped their mounts into a run. Lauren lay against Jessy's neck. 'Come on, girl. *Please.*'

The mare responded with an outpour of strength. Her strides grew longer, her breathing deeper. They covered the rolling terrain at a speed Lauren had never taken before.

Lather coated Jessy's neck. Lauren knew she was pushing the horse beyond her limits, but the mare gave, seeming to know their lives were at stake. She could only hope that if Jessy tired, so would the war horses behind her.

But she was afraid that wouldn't happen. Jessy had been bred for speed. War horses were built for strength and endurance. The beasts might fall behind, but they would never stop.

Jessy's pace slowed, but she kept a safe distance

between them. As they neared a four-foot hedge, Lauren held the pommel with both hands. She felt the mare's muscles tense and quiver as they sailed over it. Jessy floundered in her landing. Lauren lurched forward, caught the mare's neck and struggled back into the saddle.

Lauren wiped the tears blurring her eyes and urged Jessy on. 'You can do it, baby. Only two more miles at most.' Her voice choked and she could do nothing more than hold on. And pray.

The chestnut pressed harder. Soon she spotted the white stone castle appearing on the horizon. Nicholas would be there, waiting for her. She could imagine his frown of concern, and would kiss him for it. Jessy stumbled, but regained her step. Her home drew closer. So close. She'd never seen anything so beautiful. Lauren began to believe they might make it.

Then a brush of wind grazed her cheek as an arrow flew by.

CHAPTER 11

Sitting astride Hades, Nicholas scanned the country-side for any sign, the slightest movement. The stallion fought the bit, stomping the ground despite Nicholas's repeated commands to remain still. The animal's restlessness bled into his own. He needed to keep moving. To find Christel. But the fresh trail they followed made no sense.

'Are you positive, Kenric?' Nicholas asked.

'Aye, sire.' Kenric rose from where he knelt by the tracks. 'Five horses, perhaps six, made these marks only a short time ago. One is her mare. Her horseshoe is different to those our blacksmith makes.'

'And the others?' Nicholas asked.

'Come from Westbourne Castle.'

Nicholas pressed his knees against Hades's sides. The stallion sprang into a run, leaving Kenric and his half-dozen men behind. Questions raced through Nicholas's mind, beating against his temples with the same thudding pitch as the animal's hooves pounding the earth.

How had Christel escaped? No one had seen her

pass through the gate, which meant someone had helped her. Someone who lived within his own walls. But who? He forced the questions back. Answers would have to wait.

He followed her trail, still confused about the direction she had taken. She was heading for the forest of oaks where he had first found her, not toward Scotland and her father.

Within minutes Nicholas slowed Hades, not believing his eyes. Christel was bent over her mare's neck, racing toward him. Anger had pushed him to find her, punish her for escaping from him. Seeing her heading toward him, relief doused his fury. He'd spared little hope of finding her again, and now that he had . . . Nicholas frowned as the distance narrowed between them.

White lather coated the mare's neck and flanks. The chestnut's long strides were strained and awkward. Five riders closed in on the mare. Five soldiers. His. Had they helped her escape . . . or were they running her down, trying to capture her? And if so, why was she racing toward the castle?

Nicholas tightened his knees. Hades surged beneath him, covering the distance in ground-eating strides.

Christel saw him. She glanced behind her, then sat up, one arm outstretched toward him. The wind whipped her red hair behind her. Terror twisted her pale face. She screamed his name. The cry sliced through him like a steel blade, cold and painful.

Nicholas watched as if he were in a dream, a sick nightmare, where his body was bound and he couldn't move, couldn't reach out in time. The soldiers gained on her. One drew an arrow and secured it to his bow. Nicholas shouted for him to stop. The arrow took flight.

Still too far to reach her, he watched as the weapon arced through the air, finding its mark. Christel's body stiffened. Her head dropped back; her mouth opened in a silent scream. Then she relaxed and slid from the saddle, landing with a soft thud, rolling to a stop in deep heather and tall grass.

The mare, sides heaving, changed direction and returned to her mistress, nudging Christel with her muzzle.

Nicholas jumped from his saddle before Hades came to a stop. He shoved the mare aside and knelt beside Christel. She lay on her side, her arms stretched above her, shielding her face. A broken arrow shaft protruded from her shoulder.

His hands shaking, he lowered her arm and brushed her hair from her face. 'Christel, answer me!' She didn't respond. His throat clenched with burning fear. 'Damn you.' His voice broke to a whisper, 'Do not die.'

She didn't move. Didn't open her beautiful green eyes.

He felt her neck for a pulse. A faint beat throbbed against his finger. He drew a cautious breath, ran his hand over her face. Her skin was so soft, so cold. So still. She wouldn't look at him!

Horses rode up beside him. He glanced up to see Kenric and the other men he'd left behind. Teeth clenched, he ordered, 'Seize those men. Return them to the castle.'

Kenric nodded and spun his mount away. The others followed, all except Thomas. The young archer dismounted and knelt beside him. 'Let me help, my lord.'

'No,' he snapped, not wanting anyone to touch her. 'I'll take her. You lead the mare back to the castle and see she is cared for.'

Nicholas held his breath and worked his arm under Christel's body, afraid he might make her injury worse. So afraid. Blood drenched her back and shoulder. A trail of red streaked along her neck and chest. Drying specks marred her deathly pale cheek.

With his other arm beneath her legs, he cradled her against his chest. He paused, peering down at her to see if he'd hurt her. She didn't make a sound. Her breathing remained shallow, labored. He mounted Hades and settled her in the saddle before him, her body flush with his, her cold face pressed against his neck.

Reaching inside his saddlebag, he pulled out an extra shirt he kept there and wrapped it around her bleeding wound. As Hades began the slow walk home, a cold tremor began in Nicholas's soul. He held her frail body tight against him, afraid if he let her go a horrible emptiness would claim him. Engulf him. Consume what little was left of his world.

He pressed his lips against her forehead. 'Please, love,' he pleaded, the words barely crawling out of his throat. Tears he'd never before shed pressed against his eyes. 'Please don't die.'

A throbbing ache pulled Lauren from her deep sleep. She resisted, but the pain flared, bright and hot in her right shoulder, searing its way down her side. Her lungs were dry, raw. Her entire life hurt. So cold. She shivered despite the fire burning inside her and the heavy weight of blankets pressing her down.

It only took seconds, but she recalled what had happened. Her escape, the soldiers, her decision to stay. A horrible moment resulting in a grueling, biting pain. And then nothing. If the soldiers had caught up with her, where was she now?

Slowly, she pried her eyes open. In the dim light she saw a wood-paneled ceiling, rich and polished. She lowered her gaze to the elegantly carved bedposts, to the dark blue bedspread. Then she recalled the moment before she was wounded. Nicholas had been there.

She considered tilting her head back, sure there would be a lion rampant engraved on the headboard, but decided the pain that movement would cause wasn't worth her finding out.

Turning her head, she disregarded the ache when she saw Nicholas slouched in a chair beside the window. Early rays of sunlight haloed his bent head in amber. She smiled, watched him sleep, thinking she'd never seen him so unguarded, so vulnerable.

Or so beautiful. During her desperate ride she'd been so afraid she'd never see him again.

Simply lying in bed hurt, she didn't dare move, but she had the overwhelming urge to touch him, hold him to her. She must have made a sound because he sat up, fully alert, his eyes on her.

Trying to smile, she asked, 'Did you notice the number of the bus that hit me?'

He frowned and sat on the bed beside her. Combing her hair off her forehead with his fingers, he said, 'It was the ground you hit. Hush, do not speak.'

He lifted a tankard from the side table with one hand and eased her head up with the other. Horribly thirsty, Lauren took a deep swallow, then choked, cringing at the same time. The pain in her back flared to life. Gasping, she closed her eyes and waited for the fire to dim. 'What is that?'

'Calendula, to break your fever.'

Having no idea what calendula was, she looked into the cup. Yellow-orange petals floated in the murky liquid. Flowers. They couldn't hurt her, could they? She tilted her head and drank.

When the tankard was empty, he set it aside, then studied her, his expression solemn. 'You tried to escape.'

She wanted to know how he felt about that. Was he angry, disappointed, relieved? His voice reflected nothing. His expression conveyed even less. Pulling her hand from beneath the blanket, she touched the scar on his beard-roughened cheek. 'I was coming back.'

A muscle pulsed in his jaw. 'For what reason?'

'For you.'

Hesitancy and doubt shifted behind his eyes. She sensed he struggled to deny her words. She was Scottish, he English. He should hate her because of who he thought she was. But she felt certain he cared about her in a way that had nothing to do with revenge.

'I've made my decision, Nicholas. I tried to leave, but I couldn't. I'm afraid you're stuck with me. I'm not going back.' She knew he'd think she was referring to Scotland. It didn't matter. She would explain where she came from . . . somehow.

'What of your father?'

'We'll deal with that later.'

He leaned over her, his upper body shielding hers. Arrogance glittered like sapphires in his eyes. 'I knew you would come to me, but I had not thought you would be wounded.'

'Ah,' she moaned as he nuzzled her neck. 'You don't want me now that I'm damaged goods.'

He pulled back and cupped her face between his hands, grazed her cheeks with his thumbs. 'Oh, I want you, lady. I have waited for you . . .'

'Two whole weeks.'

He shook his head and brushed her lips with his. 'I have waited for you forever, Christel.'

Tears filled her eyes. She wanted to tell him she wasn't Christel. She was Lauren. But his mouth was on hers. His lips were kissing, touching every part of her face, her eyes, her cheeks, her tears, the base of her throat. She was drowning in the feel and taste of him. Not even the pain, spreading down her back like hot lead, could interfere with the longing that grew inside her.

She laced her fingers through his hair. The urge to tell him she loved him pressed against her chest. She held the words back. Now wasn't the time. When he knew the truth about her, then she would reveal her heart.

He sighed and rose from the bed. 'You must rest now.'

The thought of being alone sent chills of panic through her. She glanced at the door. 'Stay with me, please.'

He bent to kiss her brow. 'There are things I must attend to. I shall return later.'

'But . . .' She hesitated, not sure how she should voice her fear. 'Who were the men chasing me? Were they your soldiers?'

His jaw hardened. 'Aye.'

'I take it you didn't order them to help me escape.'

'Not likely,' he growled, but his eyes caressed her face.

'Then who?' She had her own suspicions, but bit down on her lip, compelled to keep them to herself.

He sighed in frustration and looked away. 'I know not as yet. One man escaped, two were killed when Kenric tried to capture them. The other two were injured and refuse to speak. But I swear to you, I will find out and they will be punished.'

'They followed someone's orders.'

He nodded. 'I know. But I am their lord, and they defied me.'

Lauren hated seeing him so troubled, especially because of her. 'I'm sorry for all this.'

He glanced at her, a startled look on his face. She knew it sounded ridiculous for her to apologize. She was his prisoner. She'd been given the opportunity to escape and had taken it. Had almost died because of it.

He took her hand and kissed her palm, staring at her with open curiosity and something else, something she'd couldn't identify . . . caring, perhaps.

'Will you ever cease to amaze me?'

She sighed and smiled, her eyes growing heavy. 'I'm saving the biggest surprise for last.'

CHAPTER 12

She had made up her mind.

Lauren paced the length of the room, *Nicholas's room*, as she came to terms with her decision. She'd already set the plan in motion. Elise had seen to every detail for her. There was no going back. Still, she couldn't help but wonder if she was making a mistake.

'You can leave now, Glynis.'

'But, my lady, should ye not rest a while?' The servant hovered over an assortment of jars containing herbs and salves.

Lauren tried not to growl with impatience. Ever since she'd been wounded, Glynis had given up her new job of mending clothes to be Lauren's personal maid. For the past week Lauren had lain in bed, her shoulder slowly healing as Glynis forced tankards of bitter-tasting medicine down her throat and layered thick, smelly paste on her wound. She appreciated the older woman's loyalty, but could do without it tonight.

'I'm fine, Glynis.' She took the woman's arm and led her to the door. 'I'll see you in the morning.'

'I shall return later and 'elp ye prepare for bed.'

Lauren smoothed the skirt of her borrowed forest-green silk gown. 'That won't be necessary. I'll manage by myself.'

As Glynis closed the door behind her, Lauren unconsciously, rolled her shoulder and winced as the last bit of pain resurfaced. She had to give primitive medicines credit. She had healed at a remarkable rate, without the aid of antibiotics.

But it wasn't her injury that had her so anxious she couldn't sit still. It was Nicholas. Though he had come to see her every day, he'd become distant. He never came near the bed, but stood in the middle of the room and left after a few minutes. Not at all the same man who had kissed her witless, then declared he had waited for her forever.

Had he changed his mind? Had he only hinted he cared about her because she'd been in danger? And now that the threat was over, had he come to his senses? Doubts pressed on her mind. If the answer to any of those questions were 'yes' her decision to stay would be for nothing.

And she didn't think she could live with that.

She glanced at the fire blazing in the hearth, then at the table and two chairs sitting beside it. Elise had assured Lauren the dishes prepared for tonight were Nicholas's favorites: fresh herring pie, flavored with ginger, pepper and cinnamon; honey-glazed apples sprinkled with almonds; baked carrots; bread and cheese. A pitcher of wine and two goblets completed the setting.

Now all she needed was the man.

The horn announcing dinner had sounded ten minutes ago. She paused by the window and stared out into the bailey without seeing it. What would she do if he didn't come? Track him down? Beg, push or plead for him to come with her? She sighed. She'd do anything to get more than a few polite minutes with him.

'You should be abed.'

Lauren spun around at the sound of Nicholas's voice, her skirts rustling in the otherwise quiet room. Her heart and breath collided in her chest. He stood at the threshold, his hand on the door as if he intended to make a quick retreat. Dressed in solid black, with a jeweled belt clasped around his waist, his towering body filled the portal. His eyes were shuttered from emotion, his body rigid with harsh control.

With her hands clasped together at her waist, she moved toward him. 'I'm feeling much better. Could you come in, Nicholas?'

He took a step, then hesitated. His gaze slid from her to the table set for two. His jaw clenched; a pulse beat against his temple. When he didn't take another step, she gripped her sweaty hands tighter to keep from reaching for him. 'I thought perhaps . . . well, would you . . .?' She propped her hands on her hips and managed not to wince from the pain. 'Blast it, Nicholas, do you want to have dinner with me, or not?'

She half expected him to decline her 'invitation' and leave. She tried not the let the pensive set of his eyes bother her. When he didn't move, hope teetered in her direction.

'There are guests in the hall . . .' he began.

Her stomach lurched. 'Please stay.' She went to the table, poured a cup of wine and held it out to him. She willed herself not to smile as his emotionless mask turned into a scowl, but he closed the door and crossed the room.

Taking the goblet, he took a drink, his cool gaze locking with hers. 'You are not yet recovered. I should leave you to rest.'

Annoyed at his indifferent tone when her nerves were coiled so tight she thought she might explode, she snapped, 'I'm fine!'

'And in good spirits, I see,' he returned dryly.

She blinked, then smiled. 'I'm sorry. It's just that I've been locked in here by myself for days and, well, you . . .' she lowered her gaze, suddenly uneasy '. . . you've been so distant lately.'

'You have been ill.'

'Stab wounds aren't contagious.'

He arched his brow and his mouth twitched as if it wanted to smile. He raised his cup to take a drink.

'I've missed you, Nicholas,' she finally whispered.

The cup halted halfway to his lips, his gaze darkening, holding hers.

'I came back for you,' she added. 'Did I make a mistake?' Silence stretched across the room. *He doesn't want me!* An icy tightness pressed against her chest. Her ears rang with a silent denial. She turned away and walked toward the window, refusing to let him see her cry. 'Perhaps you should return to your guests.'

She heard a clink as he set his cup of wine on the

table. Closing her eyes, she waited to hear the door open and close behind him. What would she do now that he had refused her? Find another way to leave? God, she didn't know if she could.

His arm came around her waist and drew her back against him. She gasped and trembled all at once. Her nerves dissolved to water. She rested her head against his shoulder as tears seeped from beneath her closed lids.

He bent and kissed her wet cheek. 'Are your tears for me also?'

'Oh, Nicholas.' Lauren turned and pressed her face against his neck. She caught a sob as his arms wrapped around her. She splayed her hands over his chest, feeling hard muscles through his tunic, his heat, the steady beat of his heart.

At once, her senses were overwhelmed. The feel of him along the length of her. The enveloping scent of musk and man. She rubbed her cheek against his clean-shaven jaw, then pressed her forehead to his lips. She raised her face, and he kissed her closed eyes.

'Look at me.'

She did. The fire in the hearth burned behind him, angling shadows over his face. She felt more than saw the smoldering blue of his eyes. 'Make love to me, Nicholas.'

He drew a deep breath that shuddered against her palms. 'Do you know what you are asking?'

She nodded.

'Your father . . .'

'I don't want to talk about that,' she interrupted.

'You are my enemy,' he insisted.

'No, I'm not.'

He cupped her face between his hands and studied her. Desperate for his kiss, she leaned into him until their lips were a breath apart. Still, he waited.

'Nicholas,' she said, her voice low and throaty. 'We were meant to be together.' She clenched his tunic in her fists and waited.

Then his lips touched hers, light and searching. She slid her arms around his neck and rose to meet him. His kiss hardened, turning urgent, more demanding each time he claimed her mouth.

Their breath turned hot, sweet, filling the air with the scent of desire. He kissed the line of her jaw, then his tongue feathered down her sensitive neck. He nipped and bit, then loved her tender skin. She moaned helplessly as a whirlwind of tingling light swept through her.

He mastered her body with a roaming, provocative touch. A current, alive with sensation, flowed from his hands to her back, her ribs, the underside of her breasts. She arched back as his palms crept up and cupped the weight of her. His thumbs grazed the green silk covering her nipples. Twisting sparks sped through her chest and landed low in her belly.

Her blood pulsed, spreading the ache to her limbs. It thrummed a heavy rhythm, making her want to do things, feel things she'd never thought possible. Along with the passion came frustration.

She wanted more.

She wanted Nicholas.

All of him, touching her, filling her.

She reached for his belt, fumbling and cursing, until with a whispered 'please', she managed to unbuckle it. He chuckled as she dropped it to the floor then struggled to lift his tunic over his head. Discarding it, she sucked in a breath.

He was hard muscle and tanned skin. Strength and beauty rolled into one. She turned him toward the fire. Crisp black hair dusted his chest. She ran her fingers through it, her stomach tightening as dark curls tickled her palm. She grazed her hands over his shoulders, down to his ribs, feeling healed scars of past battles. Instead of marring his flesh they decorated him, like badges of honor.

She pulled lose the black ribbon holding his hair and combed the heavy mass with her fingers. A sheet of ebony satin fell forward, shadowing his eyes, making them mysterious, dangerously sensuous. 'Do you know how long I've wanted to do this? Touch your hair.'

Grinning, he moved behind her, lifted her loose hair and draped it over her shoulder. The heavy weight pressed against her breast like a seductive blanket. Without touching her body, he kissed the vein along her neck, grazing it with his teeth, until she squirmed. She reached back for him, needing to feel him, but the movement sent a flash of pain down her back. She gasped and lowered her arms.

'Slowly, love,' Nicholas whispered against her ear. 'There is no need to hurry.'

The pain in her shoulder combined with the agony

burning deep in her body forced a moan past her lips. 'I've never wanted anything so much, Nicholas. It hurts.'

'Aye, I know.' His breath was raw and grated against her neck.

She felt a tug on the back of her gown as he unfastened the row of tiny buttons. A kiss of cool air caressed her back. She shivered when his hands slipped inside, cupped her waist. His long fingers kneaded her stomach, pulled coiled muscles, winding them tighter with pleasure-pain.

Her gown slipped from her shoulders, billowed to the floor. He pulled her back against him, and the hard length of his arousal pressed against her. His harsh, ragged breath brushed her throat as he reached around and untied her chemise. Her breasts tingled, swelled with anticipation. She gripped his upper arms.

His fingers trailed over her satin-covered breasts, pulling the material taut over her nipples. He traced the hardened tips. Lauren squirmed, cried out, begged him to hold her.

'Not yet,' he said, though his voice sounded strained. 'I want to touch you.'

'Then do it!' she pleaded.

His hands moved slowly down her stomach and stopped at the source of her ache. He trailed lazy circles over her ridge and his hard fingers rubbed the soft satin of her chemise against her, teasing her, shattering her control.

She tried to turn and face him, end the torture. He

215

stopped her with an arm around her waist. 'I want to see you, love.'

Dropping her head back against his shoulder, she said in an agonized moan, 'You want to kill me.'

His deep chuckle vibrated against her back. Then the chemise grazed her arms and slipped down her hips. His large, rough hands touched her bare stomach, her thighs, then moved back up. She held her breath waiting, needing.

He cupped the heavy underside of her breasts, lifting her, holding her gently. Her breath caught with a gasp. She arched against his hands and breathed his name, drowning in sensations as he stroked and played and loved her.

Taking her hardened nipples between his fingers and thumbs, he pulled. White fire roared down her stomach.

She reached up and gripped the back of his neck, urging his head to hers. She kissed him, hard and deep, her tongue plunging past his lips. She soared on the exotic taste of him: wine, male and desire.

His hand grazed down her belly. She moaned into his mouth. Then he claimed her, firmly, between her legs. She tensed and gasped and pushed against his palm.

'Shh,' he said, and began to kiss her again. His lips were on her eyes, her face, her neck. One hand cupped her breasts, the other seared her core, making her burn brighter, hotter.

'Relax against me,' he told her. 'I'm going to take you to heaven.'

Heaven? It felt like hell, this burning, consuming need that pulsed through her veins. How could it end? How long could she survive it?

He stroked between her legs, soothed, stirred and built the pressure inside her. She shifted against him, then something changed. Her body set a rhythm, and she rocked against his hold. Clenching his arms, she dropped her head back and moaned his name over and over, begging release.

Begging for the explosion building inside her. A surge swept her up, held her suspended in a dark cloud, then the fury burst into shattering stars. Lauren gasped. Her body pulsed as waves of crystalline light washed over her, caressing, loving, fulfilling every corner of her mind. A lush numbness settled over her. Trembling, she sagged against Nicholas.

He tightened his hand on her, preparing her for another peek at heaven. She stopped him. 'I don't think I can survive another one.'

He laughed and nuzzled her neck. 'Was it so bad?'

She sighed and brushed a kiss across the base of his jaw. 'I've always wondered what heaven looked like. Now I know.'

'No,' Nicholas said, and lifted her in his arms. He carried her to his bed and laid her across it. 'You have only had a glimpse. It is time for you to see it all.'

Lauren stretched leisurely, feeling content, if not completely sated. Heat shimmered over her skin, her blood pulsed at sensitive spots along her body. She kicked off her slippers and watched Nicholas remove his boots and trunk hose. What she saw made her sit up.

The black hair covering his chest narrowed at his waist. There it extended to his powerful legs like a dark mist. From the hips down his skin was pale, untouched by the sun. The contrast was startling, bold and erotic.

Her eyes were drawn to his erection, hard and thick, and so very male. It pulsed in the air. 'Is it supposed to do that?'

He laughed softly, though his voice held an edge of pain. 'And more.'

Her breath shook. Just looking at him made her skin hot, her insides melt.

'Are you afraid?' he asked.

She forced her gaze to meet his. 'No.'

'It will hurt the first time.'

'So I've heard.'

He knelt on the bed, then leaned over her, forcing her to lie on the mattress. He lowered himself. Her body tensed, her breath turned shallow, waiting for his touch.

The coarse hair on his chest brushed her nipples. Before she could react, he pressed himself against her, covering her. A riot of sensations assaulted her mind: the cool bedspread against her back, Nicholas's body, firm and raging with heat, enveloping her front.

She touched every part of him she could reach with her hands, ran her legs along the length of his, learning and loving their shape.

His hands and lips explored her body without patience. His kisses turned frantic, almost desperate. He lifted her breasts, then alternately took them into his mouth. He lavished her with his lips, his tongue. Taking the pebbled tip into his mouth, he pulled, tightening the invisible cord that ran the length of her.

She writhed beneath him, wanting to escape the torture yet not wanting it to end. His hand followed the line of fire down her stomach and captured her in a possessive hold. She cried out from the shock of it.

Nicholas caught her cries with his mouth, absorbed the explosion that shook her. Christel's pure response wove through his mind, blinding him with a sensual grip. He felt possessive, protective. He wanted to push her to greater heights, make her feel the impossible, then follow along with her.

His mind spun, dizzy from the intoxicating scent of her, all female, fresh and beautiful. He wanted her, needed her. This woman touched a part of his soul he'd thought long dead. Hell, a part he'd never known existed.

She gripped his shoulders, her nails digging into his flesh. She writhed against him, moaned his name. The throaty sound sent his blood rushing through his veins. Arching her hips, she pressed against his erection. His breath hissed through clenched teeth.

Holding her smooth waist, he urged her to be still. 'Love, you must slow down.'

She shook her head and tears slipped from her eyes. She tried to pull him to her. 'Please, Nicholas, don't make me wait any longer.' She lifted her head and kissed him feverishly, desperately.

'I feel empty, so empty it burns,' she pleaded in a raw whisper.

Blood pumped like fire through Nicholas's veins. He couldn't control his desire for this woman. She wanted him, and, God help him, he wanted her as much. Everything she felt burned within him as well. Only one thing would end it, make them whole. When he claimed her, she would be his. She would complete his world as he would complete hers.

Nicholas centered himself between her legs. She watched him, her eyes as dark and haunting as a forest in moonlight. She slid one leg up to rest on his hip, opening herself to him. His mind fogged with the pain of anticipation. The tip of his erection brushed against her. Her mouth parted and she shifted her body. He pushed, gritting his teeth as she stretched to receive him.

Liquid heat surrounded him, consumed him. It seeped into his body, flowed with the pulse of his blood. He buried himself until he met her maidenhead. He moved inside her, readying her for the pain. 'Christel . . .'

'Lauren,' she breathed huskily. 'Call me Lauren.'

He pushed through the barrier. She sucked in a gasp, and her eyes squeezed shut. His breathing ragged, Nicholas rested his forehead against hers and waited, holding still, feeling as if he might die if he waited too long.

Christel's hands threaded through his hair, pulling his mouth to hers. She moved against him, slowly, testing, her legs squeezing his waist. A hungry growl escaped his chest. He moved inside her in an unhurried, painful rhythm. He fought the need to drive into her hard and find his release. With any other woman he would have. Not with Christel. He had promised her a glimpse of heaven, and he meant to take her there. Because he wanted to see it as well.

Her hands clenched his shoulders. He pulled back to see her face. 'Love me, Nicholas.'

The whispered words thundered through his heart. His blood surged, and with it he buried himself in glory. She met his frantic rhythm. He gritted his teeth and fought for control. He gave and soared, but still held back.

Finally she tensed. Her breath caught as she strained against him. She called out his name, sending him beyond control. He drove into her, giving her what she needed, what he needed. He poured his life into her, emptying himself, yet filling his soul with something new and beautiful.

Sensual tremors passed through his body, fading to cherished peace. He held her close, not wanting to let her go. Afraid he might crush her, he pulled back slightly.

Her arms locked around his neck. 'No, don't leave me.'

Nicholas felt himself harden again as her warm body tightened around him. Nestling deeper inside her, he said, ''Tis too soon for you. You will be sore come morning.'

'Hold me,' she whispered and kissed his jaw.

He wanted to do more than hold her; he wanted to love her until the sun rose. He wanted to hear the throaty sound of his name as she clung to him. Afterward, he wanted to feel her in his arms as they settled down to sleep, comforted in knowing she would be there when he awoke so he could love her all over again.

His thoughts stunned him. He would have dismissed any other woman by now. These feelings for Christel were so foreign his first instinct was to push them away. He cared for her when he shouldn't. And what of his plan for revenge?

Now that he had taken her, it was time to negotiate a ransom with her father.

His gut tensed as he remembered his duty. How could he let her go? How could he use her as if she were no more than a bartering tool? His heart twisted with an ache he knew he would never recover from. There was no choice. Regardless of what he might feel for her, or want from her, he had to return her to her father.

'Nicholas, what's wrong?' She stroked his face, watching him, concern clouding her eyes.

He couldn't respond. Fury and desperation raced through his mind. He held her gaze and drove into her with possessive force. She frowned in confusion, but the lines marring her brow gave way, and she joined his reckless pace. He knew he might hurt her, but he couldn't stop. Thoughts of her gone from his life filled him with a need to claim her, hold her to him.

Driving inside her, he heard the words she'd whispered over and over, '*Love me Nicholas*'. The litany closed around his heart. He buried himself deeper, trying to bury the ache of longing as well.

He couldn't do it.

He wanted her. Forever.

God help him, he wanted her.

CHAPTER 13

Nicholas stared at the ledger until his eyes stung. Blinking, he shoved the book across the desk and tossed aside the feather quill. He couldn't concentrate. Hadn't been able to think beyond a certain red-haired woman for the past week.

Only the demands of ruling the castle and questioning the two men who had assisted in Christel's escape had kept him from spending every moment with her. He scowled as he thought of the two soldiers, now prisoners, held below in the dungeon.

Every day for the past two weeks he had interrogated them, but they refused to name the person who had given the order to kill Christel. Even opening their backs with a whip had produced no additional information. So he had lived with the daily fear that someone was still free with the intent to harm her. But who? His mind turned that single phrase over and over, never lighting on an answer.

Frustrated, he leaned back in his chair and rubbed his brow in a tired gesture as another problem surfaced in his mind. Yesterday he had vowed to make the trip to Armstrong's castle, across the border in Scotland, to deliver the ransom demand for his daughter. But lying in bed this morning, with Christel safely asleep in his arms, he'd watched the sun rise, reach into his room to touch her pale cheeks, and had delayed the trip . . . again.

Kissing her soft hair, he'd promised himself just one more day. He wanted one more day with her.

Only one more day, or one more week, or year, would never be enough, and he knew it. The idea of simply never releasing her had occurred to him, but he'd discarded it. Christel seemed content to be with him now, but in time she would want to return home, to her father and her people. He could, of course, refuse, but what would that do to the bond between them?

His thoughts drifted from the problem of what to do with the woman to the woman herself. She had not returned to the tower after the first night they'd made love, but had remained in his room, with him. She'd shown no signs of embarrassment at the arrangement. In fact, she had slipped into the role of wife, at least where lovemaking was concerned, with unabashed zeal.

His own parents had had separate sleeping quarters for as long as Nicholas could recall. And they had never kissed in public. As for Christel, it didn't seem to matter where they were. If she saw him during the day, she made a point of speaking to him, touching him. And she never left his side without first kissing him.

Strange how he had become accustomed to her display of affection.

It had taken several days for Nicholas to realize not everyone was as pleased with his relationship with Christel as he was.

Lady Kenward had railed at him, demanding he stop his sinful relations with Christel. When he had tried to reason with her, it had only made her more irrational. So he'd quit trying. Elise had clicked her tongue and scolded as much as she could about the way he treated Christel. As much as his sister liked their Scottish prisoner, Elise didn't think it proper that he put her in the position of leman.

He scowled at the thought. He didn't think of Christel as his mistress, but as his . . . what? Prisoner didn't seem right anymore. Lover? Nicholas shook his head, not liking the temporary ring to the word. If none of those, then what was she to him? *Life mate.*

The thought startled him. He sat upright and frowned. Reason told him to reject the idea of the Scottish woman becoming anything more than what she was. But he couldn't. He wanted her. As his wife.

He laughed out loud and hit his palm on the desk. *His wife.*

He quickly worked out the details of how he would go about making Christel the true mistress of Westbourne Castle. There would be problems, of that he had no doubt, but nothing he couldn't handle. What was more, the dissension between their two families would come to an end. He could finally bury the axe of revenge. And not with a sword in Armstrong's back, but with a ring on his daughter's finger.

Nicholas smiled into the empty solar, but his smile faded when a horrible wail echoed from the hall outside his office. He started to rise to investigate, but Glynis rushed into the room.

He hardly recognized the woman without a bundle of firewood strapped to her back. Her brown fuzzy hair no longer floated like dried willows about her face, but was pulled into a tidy knot at the back of her neck. Christel's self-appointed, and extremely devoted, lady's maid now had tears streaming down her haggard face and wailed about something beyond his understanding.

'Glynis, come now, what is wrong?' Rising from his chair, he pulled a handkerchief from his pocket and held it out. The hysterical woman refused it and used her sleeve instead.

Between sobs, she answered, 'My lord, I beg your pardon, but she is doing it again! Pray 'elp me lady. 'Twill be the death of her yet!'

Sudden fear had Nicholas around the desk, grasping the woman's arms. His chest constricted, making it almost impossible to breathe. Forcing himself not to shake Glynis, he demanded, 'What happened? What has Christel done?'

'She's taking another bath!' Glynis cried into his chest. ''Tis the fourth one she's 'ad this week!'

Nicholas stared at the woman. It took an endless moment for the dark images building in his mind to recede. Once they did, and he could draw a true

227

breath, he released her and stepped away. Rubbing a hand over his face, he couldn't decide if he should laugh with relief or bellow at the old woman for scaring precious years off his life.

Christel hadn't escaped. It drummed through his mind like a litany.

He could understand Glynis's concern, though. Christel's affection for bathing was as unusual as it was erotic. He stifled a groan as he envisioned her immersed in a tub, her pale skin glistening with beads of water. His blood warmed and pulsed with need, a condition he seemed to be in more often than not lately. He headed out of the room, calling over his shoulder, 'Do not worry, Glynis, I shall save your mistress.'

Steam rose in luscious waves, turning the tiny room she'd claimed as her own bath into a sauna. Off the kitchen, and within calling distance of more hot water, Lauren had found her own private piece of heaven. Having pinned up her hair haphazardly, she settled into a tub twice the size of the first one she'd used in the tower. A sigh turned into a throaty laugh as heat seeped into her skin.

She leaned against the padded edge and closed her eyes. A niggle of guilt wormed its way into her mind at all the trouble she'd put the staff through to prepare her bath. She'd tried to do it herself, but Glynis had refused to let Lauren lift a finger.

Feeling spoiled and pampered, she let her mind wander, and, as always, her thoughts settled on

Nicholas. Her blood thrummed a steady beat that made the bath water feel warmer than before. She stirred, sloshing water over the sides, and tried to find a more comfortable position.

She found it incredible how much her life, her dreams, had changed since the first night she'd made love to Nicholas. She'd been in heaven, floating on a cloud ever since. Occasionally reality tried to creep in, but she forced it away, wanting to cherish her moment of happiness. Or perhaps it was 'ignorant bliss' she wanted to hang on to.

She resented having to face the problems that still existed. Like convincing him who she really was. But she would have to . . . eventually. She didn't want to spoil Nicholas's happiness either. The man who'd lived most of his life behind an emotionless mask had begun to emerge. He smiled and laughed more often now, and loved her with an urgency that frightened her at times.

The first night they'd made love had given her a glimpse of how wonderful their life together could be. Yet there were times she sensed his frantic need to possess her. He took her with desperation, as if each moment were their last. At those times she wanted to ask him what was wrong, but fear stopped her. Fear that he still considered her a prisoner and would send her away.

'Is there room for one more?'

Her eyes flew open at the deep-timbred voice. Her troubled thoughts vanished with the rising steam. She laughed, a low, throaty sound that sounded seductive to her own ears. 'We could probably work something out,' she said, wishing the bath *were* large enough for the both of them.

He leaned against the closed door and crossed his arms in a relaxed stance. 'Glynis is convinced your numerous baths will be the death of you.'

'A misconception on her part, I assure you. Bathing is quite healthy.' Lauren ran her hand through the water, creating ripples, purposefully distorting Nicholas's view of her naked body.

His nostrils flared as he came away from the door and knelt beside her. His kiss was savage, hungry. It left her no time to breathe, or think. When he broke the kiss and pulled away, they were both shaking. 'Enjoy your bath, love. It may be a few days before you have the opportunity for another.' His hand slid into the water and cupped her breast.

'What do you mean?' she asked, and moaned when his hand moved to give attention to her other breast. Desire swam to the spot where he touched, filling her so she arched into him.

With a reluctant sigh, he rose and stepped to the door.

Missing him, Lauren sat up. 'Where are you going?'

His gaze seemed to smolder when it slipped to her exposed chest. Her skin tingled in response. Modesty insisted she cover herself, but she wanted his eyes on her. Damn, she wanted more than his eyes. He stood there, hesitant, one hand on the door, his attention fixed on her.

'Nicholas,' she said, and let the rest of her plea hang unspoken in the air.

'I must speak with the carpenter,' he said. A muscle leapt in his jaw. 'And there are other things I must see to if we are to leave in the morning.'

'Leave?' Her stomach clenched with a spasm of alarm.

'Aye, we leave for Armstrong's hold at dawn.'

'No! Oh, God, no.' Lauren bolted from the tub, dripping water onto the floor. She grabbed Nicholas's tunic. 'We can't go there. There's no need.' Through her panic, she registered his hands on her wet back, urging her toward him, soaking his clothes.

'There is a need, Christel.'

'He won't pay a ransom for me because I'm . . .'

'I will not be asking for one.'

Lauren stared at him. Had he decided to just hand her over to Bruce Armstrong? Had he only been toying with her, making the Scottish laird's daughter love him so he could toss her aside? Did he really care so little about her?

She searched his blue eyes. Lust simmered below the surface. But she saw confidence there as well. And his mouth was curved in a beautiful grin that, more than once, had made her heart flutter like a butterfly trapped inside her chest.

No, he couldn't be so heartless. She backed out of his hold and a chill swept down the front of her where his body had warmed hers. 'You can't take me to Armstrong. If you don't want me here, then let me leave on my own.'

231

His smile vanished, and his eyes bored into hers. Pulling her against him, he growled, 'You will go nowhere without me.'

'But you're sending me to Armstrong's castle.'

His brow dipped into a questioning frown. 'Why do you refer to your father as "Armstrong"?'

'Nicholas!' She hit his chest with her fists. 'Answer me. Do you intend to leave me there?'

'Of course not.'

'Then why go?'

His grin returned, and an incredible light filled his eyes. 'To arrange our marriage.'

'Our . . .' Lauren covered her gaping mouth with her hands and turned away. 'No, oh, God, this can't be happening.' She paced the small room, her mind frantically searching for a way to stop a disaster. When she finally turned to face Nicholas, he wasn't listening to her, he was watching her.

His eyes were shadowed pools of blue. His hands were fisted, his jaw clenched. Each breath he took stretched his black tunic tight across his chest.

Lauren snatched up a towel and wrapped it around her.

'A bit late for modesty, love,' he said quietly, and took a step forward.

She held out her hand and took a step in retreat. 'You can't make love to me now. There is something I have to tell you first.'

He stopped and raised his gaze to meet hers, though she doubted he was actually listening to her. That

232

same look of possession that overcame him at times had returned. From experience, she knew she only had a few minutes before she gave in to his demanding hunger. 'I've told you this before, and you didn't believe me, but now you have to.'

'What are you speaking of?'

'You can't take me to Armstrong to ask permission to marry me because I'm not his daughter.'

For the first time in weeks, Nicholas scowled at her. She cringed inwardly and took another step back.

'Are you so ashamed to have bedded me you would lie to escape confronting your father? Does your dishonor run so deep?'

'No,' she insisted, shocked he would come to such a terrible conclusion. She knew that had been his plan in the beginning, but she'd thought they had worked past all that. 'I'm telling you the truth.'

In one startling move, he closed the distance between them. Grasping the towel, he flung it aside and hauled her to him, kissing her hard at the same time.

Lauren tried to fight him. Really tried. She had to make him believe her. If Nicholas rode onto Armstrong's land without the laird's daughter for protection, they would all be in danger. She pushed against his shoulders, but he held her tighter. His jeweled belt dug into her stomach. His mouth closed over hers, punishing, bruising, possessing.

She tasted tears. They had to be hers, but she wasn't aware she was crying. She stopped fighting and clung to him instead, desperate to end his fury. He reached between them, unclasped his belt, dropped it to the floor.

'Nicholas, please listen to me.'

'No more lies, Christel. You may be ashamed of what you feel for me, but it will not always be so.'

She wanted to tell him she wasn't ashamed, but he was kissing her again. He cupped her breast with one hand, the other slipped between her legs, stroking, readying her though she didn't need him to. She felt strangely vulnerable, as if she were suspended on a precipice. Afraid to let go. Afraid she'd fly away and never land again.

Gripping her waist and lifting her, he told her to wrap her legs around him. She hadn't realized he'd moved his clothes aside until she looked down.

He drove into her in one hard thrust. Her head dropped back. She wanted to cry out, but only managed a throaty moan. Her volatile emotions exploded into a climax, shocking her, leaving her gasping for air.

He pushed into her again and again, burying his face against her neck, and shuddered with his release. Lauren raised his face and held it between her hands. She kissed his closed eyes, his temple, the jagged scar, until their breathing returned to normal.

Minutes passed before he finally lowered her, but he didn't let her move away. She tried to think of something to say. But what was there? *Thank you, that was wonderful* just didn't seem right. And *By the way, you just made love to a woman from the twentieth century* would certainly earn her a glare. In the end, Nicholas said it for her.

'You belong with me,' he whispered, pressing his lips to her brow.

'It's where I intend to stay. And . . .' she ran her fingers over the worry lines on his forehead '. . . I'm *not* ashamed of you.'

'Then no more talk of you not being an Armstrong.'

She sighed, resigned to the fact that he wouldn't believe her. 'I suppose there is only one way to prove it to you.'

Nicholas might have chosen not to believe her, but, she reasoned, he would certainly listen when Bruce Armstrong informed him he'd captured the wrong woman. She prayed Nicholas took the news well.

He shook his head but didn't say anything more, apparently not willing to discuss it further.

'Nicholas, there is a favor I need to ask of you, though.'

'If I can grant it, I will.'

'Don't take me to Armstrong's castle.' *Wherever that might be*, she wanted to add. 'Send a messenger to have him meet us at Hadrian's Wall.'

'You do not wish to see your homeland again?'

She ignored his question. 'And bring an army with you.'

His jaw dropped, then snapped shut. She didn't blame him if he thought her request bizarre. How often did a daughter need protection from her own father?

'You would have me arrange a marriage with an army at my back?'

'If it means saving your life, I would.'

'Jesu, woman, you are a puzzle.'

Lauren hugged him to her. 'Perhaps, but not for much longer.'

CHAPTER 14

It was a nightmare, a living, breathing terror that she could reach out and touch. Lauren wanted to close her eyes, but knew that wouldn't make the horrible vision go away. She had to face it, and hopefully put it behind her.

A cowardly tremor swept through her.

Jessy stomped her foot and tugged on the reins, and for once Lauren was inclined to let the mare have her way. They both wanted to escape. Jessy from the possessive bites Hades kept trying to take out of her neck, and Lauren from the two armies that had gathered to discuss *her* future.

When she'd first seen the vast number of West-bourne men gather behind her, all wearing light chain-mail with doublets bearing a lion's crest, she'd become dizzy. Shouts from Jacobson as he'd organized his men had meshed with the clang of metal from swords, shields and armor. Mounted knights headed the throng. Behind them, two hundred or so archers waited on foot, and drawing up the rear were dozens of wagons loaded with heaven knew what.

When she'd insisted Nicholas bring an army, she hadn't dreamt he would take her quite so literally. But now that she saw the size of Bruce Armstrong's force, three hundred men at least, she welcomed the extra protection.

Still, if Nicholas hadn't kept her at his side, she would have headed for the thicket of oaks and the hidden cave. As it was, she'd tried to reason with him during the trip, talk him out of this fool's mission before it was too late. His warm smile had told her he was humoring her by listening, but the hard set of his eyes had meant he couldn't be persuaded to change his mind. Spinning in a tumult of worry and fear, she gave up trying.

'Are you frightened, Christel?'

Lauren glanced to her right at Elise. Nicholas had forbidden his sister to accompany them, and Lauren had told the young woman it would be too dangerous for her to come along. But, as Lauren had come to learn, Elise had a mind of her own, one which had proved to be as stubborn as her brother's.

At the moment, an excited flush brightened Elise's beautiful face. Her sable hair had been tucked beneath a silver cowl studded with rubies. Lauren hadn't managed anything quite so elegant. Her hands had shaken so badly this morning she'd only tied a silk scarf around her unruly red curls.

Elise sat tense in her side-saddle, her dove-gray dress draped elegantly across her legs. Her blue eyes, a shadow of her brother's, glittered as she absorbed the view of the massive army stationed across Hadrian's Wall.

Lauren followed the younger woman's gaze and did a quick comparison. The Scottish soldiers reminded her more of an angry mob than an army. Whether on foot or on ponies, they were armed with various swords, spears and axes, all glinting dangerously in the afternoon sun. Most wore kilts or thick leggings, and shirts with no protective armor. Lauren prayed the meeting wouldn't come to blows. Though she'd been told Armstrong's men were ruthless fighters, they wouldn't stand a chance against Nicholas's well-armed and armor-clad soldiers.

'You should have stayed behind, Elise,' Lauren said, struggling to control the fear knotted inside her. 'There's no telling what might happen when we finally meet Armstrong.'

Both Nicholas and Elise turned to her with matching frowns. Lauren avoided them both and kept her sight trained straight ahead . . . on the two men riding along toward the wall that divided England from Scotland.

'What a strange thing to say, Christel,' Elise said. 'You sound as if you have never met Laird Armstrong before.'

'I haven't! For the last time,' Lauren said, thoroughly exasperated, 'I am not Christel Armstrong!'

The force of Nicholas's gaze made her turn to him. His eyes quietly assessed her. Then she noticed the wariness in his features, the fine wrinkles at the corners of his eyes, the firm set of his mouth. Did he expect her to plead with him to release her? Or perhaps he still thought she was ashamed to face her 'father' after giving herself to an Englishman? Or could she possibly be getting through to him?

Lord, she was tired of second-guessing. She just wanted an end to her rioting nerves. Resigned to seeing this through to the end, she said, 'Well, Nicholas, what do we do now?'

'Your father awaits us at the wall.'

'He's not my –'

Nicholas glared at her. She snapped her mouth shut and shrugged. She'd had to try one last time.

His gloved hand touched her cheek, startling her into facing him. 'Should you regret this . . .'

Lauren clasped his hand and shook her head to stop him. 'I can promise you one thing, Nicholas. No matter what happens today, I'm staying with you.'

'Do you mean this?'

'Yes.'

His breathtaking smile sent a trail of warmth through her. If she could have reached over without falling out of her side-saddle she would have kissed him.

Releasing her, he motioned for her to follow him. The instant Jessy fell in step with Hades, helpless fear trembled through Lauren's body. Nausea roiled her stomach. She clamped her midsection with one hand, the other she pressed to her mouth.

She wished she knew how Bruce Armstrong would react. Would he be furious when he learned Nicholas had tried to capture his daughter, regardless that he had failed? Or would he laugh at Nicholas, thinking him a fool? She couldn't decide which would be worse. Or perhaps Armstrong would insist they not waste a nice afternoon and just battle each other since they had gathered together.

She made a small, frightened noise, thinking these people might fight, and possibly lose their lives, because of her.

'Are you ill?'

She could only shake her head at Nicholas's question. What did she care how the Scotsman would react? It was Nicholas's response to learning the truth that terrified her. Would he be furious with her? Enough to want to send her away?

'Did I mention how beautiful you look this morning?' he asked, his voice warm and intimate, as if he were oblivious to their surroundings.

Lauren managed a smile when she really wanted to cry. 'I love you, Nicholas.'

Her admission startled her as much as it did him. His expression stilled, his eyes protected behind shields of blue.

'Nicholas, is the one on the right Laird Armstrong?'

Nicholas and Lauren turned to Elise, both unaware she had followed them to the wall.

'Wait with the men, Elise,' Nicholas ordered.

She didn't look at her brother. 'I want to see the man who killed Father and James,' she said tightly, then gasped and looked at Lauren. 'I do not mean to offend you, Christel. But I have heard so much about this man I am . . . well . . .'

'Curious,' Lauren finished for her. 'I understand, but since he's not my father I can hardly be offended.'

Elise sighed, shook her head without comment, and turned her attention back to the two men ahead. Lauren wanted to scream in frustration. Elise had been told about her claim that she wasn't an Armstrong, but the younger woman didn't believe her any more than Nicholas did.

When the horses stopped, Lauren kept her gaze lowered. She considered pinching herself, forcing herself to wake up, anything so as not to believe this was really happening. Elise's gasp brought Lauren's head up. The young woman sat motionless, her face pale and eyes wide.

'Lord Kenward, what is this about? Your missive claimed it concerned me daughter.'

Lauren's attention snapped to the older man she assumed to be Laird Armstrong. His burly size appeared even larger wrapped in a green and blue plaid kilt, the end of it draped over his broad shoulder and fastened with a gold brooch. Faded red hair, tangled and streaked with gray, fell to his shoulders. A scowl etched across his weathered face, and his harsh green eyes were focused entirely on Nicholas.

Nicholas turned to her, and in that moment she saw his confusion and unasked question. Why hadn't Armstrong addressed her? She chewed on her bottom lip and looked away.

Her gaze fell on the younger man beside the laird, who bore a striking resemblance to Bruce Armstrong.

242

His son, perhaps. The simple way he held his powerful body conveyed an ability to lead. His squared jaw and straight nose added to his air of confidence. She imagined his vivid green eyes could nail a person in place. And those eyes were locked on Elise.

Lauren glanced at Nicholas's sister, and saw she stared at the young Scot. Her once pale cheeks were now flushed. Her deep blue eyes were wide and a bit frightened.

'I have decided to end the war between us, Armstrong,' Nicholas said, his voice decisive and calm.

Lauren's heart twisted. She couldn't breathe, knowing the incredible bond that had developed between them would change irrevocably within the next few minutes.

'What makes ye think I want the feud tae end?' the Laird demanded.

'What 'ave ye in mind, Kenward?' This came from the younger man.

'A union of our families.' When the laird's face reddened in fury, Nicholas added, 'I intend to marry your daughter, Lady Christel.'

The laird howled, 'I'll see ye dead and buried first, Englishman! She's safe in Kelso Abbey, and that is where she shall stay until I choose a husband for her meself.'

Nicholas turned to Lauren, his eyes narrowed, his mouth set in a firm line. Feeling her life spinning out of control, she gripped the saddle's pommel. The horrible tightness in her chest nearly kept her from whispering, 'I tried to tell you.'

'Father, perhaps what Kenward suggests . . .'

'Quiet, Ronan, I would not defile your sister in such a way.'

In a tone so void of emotion it frightened her, Nicholas asked, 'This woman is not your daughter?'

Both Scotsmen turned to Lauren. Ronan studied her, his brow narrowed in bafflement. But she saw none of the hatred that hardened his father's eyes. An eruption of bitter laughter made her tighten Jessy's reins, causing the mare to retreat several steps before Nicholas stopped her.

'You thought this woman my Christel?' Armstrong sneered. 'She's a comely wench, aye, but she's no Armstrong!'

Lauren straightened her spine, disliking the man more each time he opened his mouth.

'Did she tell ye she was my daughter?'

Nicholas's jaw flexed in a way she recognized as he tried to contain his anger. 'No.'

'Then why would you have thought . . .?' Armstrong stopped mid-sentence, his critical gaze sweeping over Lauren. 'Did 'e capture ye, gel?'

Having the Scotsman's full attention focused on her robbed Lauren of the pitiful amount of courage she had left. She couldn't respond.

'A blind man can tell ye are Scots. And Kenward thought ye my own lass.' The laird's leaf-green eyes turned as sharp and piercing as a blade. To Nicholas, he said, 'Ye thought ye'd captured my daughter, did ye, Kenward? Tae hold her ransom over me!'

Nicholas's features remained harsh, immobile. His

natural tan darkened as he controlled the anger and humiliation she knew he had to be feeling.

'I did not come with a ransom demand,' Nicholas said, 'but an offer to end the rift between us.'

'You offered a truce when you thought ye held my daughter as bait!' Armstrong raged. 'For that ye shall pay, Englishman!'

Lauren stared at Nicholas, silently urging him to say something in his defense. True, he had captured her, thinking she was the Laird's daughter, but he hadn't demanded a ransom. He had offered peace instead. Why didn't he say something? Exasperated with the entire mess, Lauren said, 'Laird Armstrong, I'm sure . . .'

'Quiet!'

Lauren halted, shocked by Nicholas's sharp demand.

'I dinnae know your true intent, Kenward,' Ronan said evenly, 'but the woman is obviously Scots. Let me return her to her people.'

Nicholas pulled the reins from Lauren's grip. She clasped his wrist, terrified he might hand her over to them. He ignored her and answered, 'She stays with me.'

''Tis not the end of this, Kenward,' Armstrong warned. 'First ye destroy Gowan Castle . . .'

'Which did not belong to you, Armstrong,' Nicholas interrupted, his tone deadly. 'I sought to return it to its rightful owner.'

'And what of your attempt to capture me daughter? Ye think I shall forget it? Nay, ye shall suffer, Kenward, and suffer greatly.'

'Would you care to test your threats now, Arm-strong?'

Lauren tightened her grip on Nicholas's arm. She had never seen anything to compare with the cold rage claiming him now. She had to stop him before the Scotsman accepted the challenge.

Laird Armstrong laughed out loud, a vicious shout that chilled Lauren's soul. 'I think not. The odds are not to my liking this day. But we shall meet again, and soon. That I vow.'

Before Nicholas turned their mounts away, Lauren caught the hard look Ronan gave Elise. She imagined sparks arcing between the two of them. But she didn't have time to wonder about it.

Nicholas spurred his horse, and they returned to his waiting men with Armstrong's final words ringing out behind them. 'Should ye tire of the wench, let me know, Kenward. I'll give ye a fair price for her.'

Nicholas didn't slow their mounts upon reaching his men. Soldiers rushed to move out of their path, some dropping their shields in their haste. When the horses broke through the last of the line, Nicholas pushed Hades into a run, forcing Jessy to follow. Within minutes, his men and Elise were far behind them.

Lauren clung to the pommel to keep from falling off the side-saddle and killing herself. 'Nicholas, please,' she called. 'Slow down!'

He pulled Hades to an abrupt halt, startling Jessy into fighting against his hold on the reins. They'd stopped on the crest of a hill. Below them, two armies were disbanding and going their separate ways.

The horses' sides heaved, as did Nicholas's. His jaw was clenched and his eyes were as hard as shards of ice and just as cold. She reached out to touch him, but his cutting look stopped her.

'Who are you?' he asked in a deadly whisper.

Now was the time for her to tell the truth, only she didn't know where or how to begin. Not with him looking as if he'd rather strangle her than listen to her. 'I'm the same woman I was yesterday.'

He gripped her face in his hand and drew her close to him.

'Do not mince words with me! What is your name?'

'Lauren Ferguson.'

He released her abruptly, staring at her as if he had never seen her before. 'From Clan Ferguson?'

'No – well, yes, I suppose I must be related to them in some way.' Lauren squeezed her eyes closed, not able to look at the confusion and anger straining his face. Opening her eyes, she stared into the distance, where the copse of oaks was barely visible. 'I'm not from here, but from another time.'

'What nonsense is this, Chris –?' He stared at her, his eyes troubled, as if he realized he had just lost something of precious value. 'Lauren.'

Taking Jessy's reins from him, she said, 'I'll show you.'

In tense silence they rode to the grove of dense oaks and tangled brush. She hadn't been able to look at Nicholas, afraid she'd lose her thin grip on her control. She refused to cry or show any other signs of weakness. Since the day she'd decided to stay, she had known this moment would come. She'd avoided thinking of it over the past two weeks to delay considering how Nicholas would handle it.

She couldn't begin to imagine his reaction. Out of desperation, she'd clung to the chance he might believe her. But in reality she knew he'd think her crazy.

At the edge of the forest, she reined Jessy to a halt. There wasn't a sound. Anticipation swelled in the air. Trees stood tall and quiet, as if they were listening. And waiting. She shuddered and turned to Nicholas.

'This is where I found you,' he said. 'And this is where you were heading when you escaped.'

She nodded.

'Are you saying you live in these woods?'

'No, but they're how I got here.' That earned her a puzzled frown. 'Follow me and I'll show you.'

She urged Jessy into the woods, and this time the mare went without balking. Lauren didn't turn to see if Nicholas followed; she could feel his eyes on her back, studying her. She imagined she could hear the silent questions plaguing his mind.

A few minutes into the grove Lauren reined Jessy to a stop, unsure of what direction to take. There was no path to follow. When she'd left the cave, she hadn't paid attention to any landmarks, but had let the mare find her own way out.

'Is something wrong?' Nicholas asked.

'I'm not sure where the cave is.' She studied the thick, ancient trees surrounding them. Milky light drifted through the canopy of leaves, creating shadows that distorted her judgment. All remained still, not even the chirping of nesting birds stirred the silence.

'I am not aware of a cave in this forest,' Nicholas commented doubtfully.

'Well, there is one,' she muttered, and urged the mare to continue.

She pushed deeper into the woods, skirting dense brush and ducking low-hanging branches, searching for the granite overhang that shielded the cave from view. When she could no longer avoid being scraped by sharp limbs, she stopped the mare and dismounted. Nicholas followed without speaking. He didn't have to. She could feel his thoughts, his doubts, his confusion.

Looking back at him, she tried to smile for reassurance, but the tense set of his jaw, the lethal coolness of his eyes made the smile fade from her face. 'We'll have to walk from here.'

His eyes scanned the forest as if he expected her to lead him into a trap. She couldn't blame him. Turning away, she led Jessy through the brush, but stopped a second later when her gown caught on a thorny bush. Working the dress free, she gathered the layers of blue satin and draped it over one arm.

'What are you doing?' he demanded.

'I'm ruining my dress.' She glanced back and saw his eyes were focused on her legs.

'Do you know where you are going . . . Lauren?'

Her heart stilled at hearing her name. 'Not exactly.'

'It isn't wise to become lost in these woods.'

Annoyed, she pursed her lips. 'I'm not lost. I just haven't found where I'm going yet.' She turned back around and her heart lurched against her chest. The cave was to her left, partially covered with thick, clinging vines. 'There it is!'

She hurried forward, tugging the mare behind her. When she reached the cave, she dropped the reins. Nicholas stopped beside her and ducked his head to peer inside.

'There are markings on the walls.'

'Yes, I know,' she whispered. She took his hand and led him to the back wall of the shallow cavern. She knelt on the ground so her shadow wouldn't fall on the carved words. Nicholas joined her, his eyes fastened on the ancient pictures. In a move almost identical to hers a month before, he ran his fingers over the drawings, then traced each word.

'It is Gaelic.'

'Do you know what it means?' she asked, watching his reaction.

He frowned in concentration, then read, "'*Co Sambith beir Arianrhod . . .*'"

Lauren clamped her hand over his mouth. He turned to her, his eyes narrowed. 'Don't say it out loud.' When she was sure he wouldn't, she lowered her hand.

'Why?'

Chewing on her bottom lip, she plunged in with the truth. 'I'm afraid it might send me back to my time. And I don't know what it would do to you.'

At his baffled expression, she clasped his hand and drew him down to the ground. 'What I'm going to tell you will sound absurd, but it's the truth.'

He gave a curt nod for her to continue.

'I'm not from this time. My home, my world, is over four hundred years in the future.'

He sneered and started to rise, but she continued in a desperate rush. 'I'm not making this up. Please, hear me out.'

Reluctantly, he sank to the floor. His jaw clenched as he ran his free hand over it. 'You expect me to believe a tale of you coming from the future?'

'It's crazy, isn't it? I didn't believe it myself at first. It took seeing men die and witnessing a castle being destroyed for it to finally sink in. And meeting you, of course.' She tilted her head and looked at the picture of the woman with red hair in silhouette. 'It's this cave. Somehow it sent me here.'

Not wanting to, but unable to stop herself, she reached out and touched the ancient words. 'I was riding Jessy when a storm came out of nowhere. I brought her inside this cave to escape the rain. That's when I discovered these carvings. After I read them out loud, I heard a strange noise that sounded like music, but it wasn't. It pulsed . . .' She stopped when Nicholas drew up, tensed. 'What is it?'

'The day I captured you . . .' He paused, as if reluctant to continue.

'What did you see?'

He shook his head. 'Nothing. But I heard something, like what you described.'

Excited that he might believe her, her heart doubled its beat. His frown deepened. 'It proves nothing.'

She ran her hand through her hair in frustration. 'I don't have any proof to give you except myself.' She straightened and looked at the mouth of the cave. 'And Jessy.' Staring at Nicholas, she asked, 'Have you ever seen a horse like her before?'

Nicholas scowled at her, obviously not wanting to answer.

'Or her saddle? Or the clothes I was wearing when you found me?'

He remained stubborn and kept his jaw clenched tight.

Lauren struggled to be patient, give him time to accept. How could she expect Nicholas to believe such a fantastic story when she couldn't prove it? If their situations were reversed, she wouldn't believe it either. Actually, she was lucky he hadn't accused her of being a witch and ordered her burned at the stake.

'Do you think I would make up something like this?' she asked.

A granite shield dropped into place, protecting his emotions. 'Since I do not know you, Lauren, I don't know what you would do.'

She sighed and had to look away when tears blurred her eyes. 'I'm the same woman, Nicholas, only now you know me by a different name. My real name.'

'You say you are from the future. Can you foresee it?'

Worrying her bottom lip, she debated how much

252

she should tell him. It wasn't as if she remembered dates and places of wars during this time period. Her knowledge of this era centered around Nicholas himself.

'I know Gowan Castle won't be rebuilt.'

'That is common sense. It would be foolhardy to rebuild it.'

She dropped her gaze and stared at her hand gripping his. Her knuckles had turned white, she held onto him so hard. 'I know you will marry someone and have a child.'

He stiffened and his grip tightened until she winced. 'Who?'

She shook her head, feeling miserable, hurting so much she thought an invisible hand had reached inside her and struggled to rip out her heart. 'I don't know her name. It was never recorded.'

'Then how do you know I marry?'

The tears that had stung her eyes slipped free. She quickly wiped them away. 'There is a legend about you.'

A pleased gleam appeared in his eyes. 'Pray continue.'

Her heart pounded against her chest. 'Nicholas, I don't . . .' She rose and headed to the entrance of the cave. How could she tell him he was supposed to die? Should she even tell him? If she did, and history changed, what would happen to her own time? She ran her hand over her brow. What if she had already interfered with history? If he had been meant to marry Christel, she'd ruined that the first day she'd arrived here. And that meant he might live, eventually marry, have children. His family line wouldn't end with him.

A gentle touch on her shoulder urged her to turn around. She tilted her head and looked into eyes that had the power to see inside her soul.

'What about this legend?' he asked calmly.

'Bruce Armstrong attacked Westbourne Castle in 1530.' As she began the story she could imagine Edith's high-pitched voice retelling the tale.

'He would not dare!'

'Well, he did. I mean, he will. During the battle . . .' her breath caught on a quiet sob as she finished '. . . you were struck by an arrow. It pierced your armor.'

'I was killed?'

Lauren nodded, tears flowing freely down her face.

He wiped her wet cheeks with his thumbs. 'I am not happy to hear this, but why would my death make me a legend?'

'Your wife, your pregnant wife, encouraged your men to continue. They won the battle and saved the castle.'

Nicholas's mouth pulled in a arrogant grin, one brow arched in approval.

'But your wife disappeared afterward. She was never heard from again and the Kenward line ended.'

His eyes widened in surprise, then narrowed in anger. 'How could you create such a story?'

'I'm not making this up.' He withdrew his hand and turned from her. But he didn't walk away as she feared he might. 'In my time there is a painting of you that hangs in Westbourne Castle. When tours are given . . .'

He glanced over his shoulder at her. 'Who owns my home?'

'No one. Well, that's not true. The National Trust takes care of it.' When he started to sneer again she explained, 'Through the years castles began to fall into ruin. They became too expensive for their owners to maintain. Instead of losing a valuable part of England's history, the National Trust was formed, and it cares for the castles, raising money by letting people visit them.'

He nodded solemnly, as if accepting his way of life would not survive. 'What about this painting?'

'That's how I knew who you were. I grew up looking at your portrait, dreaming about you, wondering what you were like.' She gave a disheartened laugh. 'I never expected to meet you.' *Or fall in love with you.*

'You must have regretted hearing of me at all when I placed you in the oubliette.'

Lauren moved to stand in front of him. She wanted to wrap her arms around his neck and kiss him until he kissed her back. More than anything she needed him to hold her, quietly reassure her that he loved her. But she didn't touch him. 'Does this mean you believe me?'

He studied her for a long moment, so long she thought she would have to repeat the question. 'I don't know. It is hard to believe you would create such a story. But it's a story that is impossible to believe.'

'But . . .' His finger on her lips stopped her.

'Give me time, Lauren. I have just learned the woman I wanted to marry is not the woman I thought she was, but something entirely different.'

He guided her out of the cave and to the horses that were waiting patiently. Lauren frowned, surprised the two weren't nipping at each other like they usually did. When Nicholas clasped her waist to help her mount, she stopped him. Now that they were out of the cave, she felt it safe to ask what the Gaelic words meant.

Nicholas looked inside the dimly lit cave, then back to her. His eyes turned a smoky blue. 'It is a strange verse.'

'Can you interpret it?' she whispered.

'Aye.' His voice lowered, as if he too were afraid someone beside her would hear. '"Whoever brings forth Arianrhod shall rip the womb of time, spilling its blood into yesterday."'

The blood drained from Lauren's head. She stared at him, the verse ringing in her ears. A cold shiver passed through her heart. *What have I done?*

CHAPTER 15

'I demand it, Lauren!'

Lauren flinched, wishing she could do what Nicholas wanted. More than anything she wanted to give in, to say yes. But she couldn't. Not with the words in the cave etched in her mind and her heart.

Whoever brings forth Arianrhod shall rip the womb of time, spilling its blood into yesterday.

Had she ripped open time? She shuddered, knowing the answer to be yes. She only prayed the blood spilled wouldn't be Nicholas's. 'I can't.'

She dared a glance at him. Anger darkened his eyes to blue fire, and his jaw clenched with rigid hardness. His chest heaved as if he were in a battle for his life.

He moved from behind his desk and made his way toward her. 'For three weeks I have been patient with you. But no more. You will become my wife.'

Gripping the edge of her chair to keep from going to him, she said, 'You know why I can't marry you.'

He paced in front of her, his burning gaze never leaving her. 'Because I am to marry Christel Armstrong? In the cave you said you did not know who I was to wed. You may be wrong.'

'It's the only thing that makes sense.' She gave him a pleading look. 'You were supposed to capture Christel that day, not me. If I hadn't interfered, you would have married her and would have had a child on the way by now.'

He stopped and gripped her chin, forcing her to look at him. 'Perhaps I already do.'

Blood rushed through Lauren's ears, making her dizzy. When she opened her mouth to respond, her chest tightened with a pressure so fierce she couldn't speak. The possibility of being pregnant with Nicholas's child had occupied her mind as much as giving in to the temptation to marry him. She wanted both so much she didn't think she could live with the pain of having neither.

When she didn't answer, he took her hands and drew her from the chair. His palm pressed against her flat stomach and his fingers kneaded her through the layers of her pale yellow gown.

'You have not had your monthly flow,' he said, kissing her temple. 'I believe the day I captured a red-haired Scotswoman I captured the woman meant to be my wife.'

His hands slid up to cup her waist and gently draw her to him. She leaned against him, feeling her resistance melt with each kiss he placed on her closed eyes, the tip of her nose, her chin and corners of her lips.

'Say yes, Lauren,' he whispered.

She wanted to say yes, desperately wanted to reach out and grab what happiness she could. But she held back, knowing it wasn't rightfully hers to take, but possibly another woman's.

The day she had escaped she'd made her decision to stay with him. But she soon realized it was a decision she might have to change. If she couldn't be his wife, at least she could ensure he would not die in a battle with Armstrong.

She shook her bent head against Nicholas's chest. 'I can't.'

He tensed, his hold on her waist turning into a vise before he released her and moved to the door. Standing with his hands clenched, his body rigid, he asked, 'Do you remember the first time I made love to you?'

'Don't do this to me, Nicholas,' she pleaded, on the verge of crumbling.

'Damn it, Lauren! Do you remember?'

Swallowing a breath to fight back waves of tears, she nodded.

'Do you recall what you said to me?'

When she didn't respond, he told her, 'You said, "We were meant to be together." I believed you then. I believe you still. And I will not rest until you believe it as well.'

After Nicholas left, Lauren sank into the chair. Her body ached with the need to cry, but she refused to give in to another bout of tears. She needed a clear mind and rational thoughts, but images of the frustration in Nicholas's eyes haunted her.

He wanted to marry her, regardless that she wasn't a

Scottish laird's daughter, or even a woman who would bring land and wealth to his holdings, which was so important in his time. Hell, he couldn't even verify who she really was or if she was crazy.

But what if he was right? What if she *had* been meant to come back in time and he *was* supposed to marry her?

Lauren considered the unlikely possibility, wishing with all her heart that it were true. Could she marry Nicholas and risk changing the future? Would marrying him save his life or end it? And, if she didn't marry him when she was supposed to, that would change history as well.

The endless questions sent her mind spiraling out of control. She gripped her head and closed her eyes. When the sickening unease faded she opened them. She couldn't continue this way. They were both suffering and it had to stop. She had to make a decision, one she prayed she wouldn't regret.

Pushing up from the chair, she left Nicholas's private solar and went in search of him.

'Where is he, Elise?' Lauren asked for the third time as the younger woman fussed with non-existent wrinkles on her pale green day dress.

'I believe he left with Jacobson to visit the tenants,' Elise answered, and pursed her lips.

'Are you sure?'

Elise averted her gaze to the window of her bed chamber. Sunlight poured through the clear panes to wash the ornate tapestries along the walls. 'Oh, yes, I'm sure.'

Lauren crossed her arms over her chest and tried to keep her voice even. 'That's odd, because I spoke with Jacobson on the tilting field a few moments ago and he said Nicholas had gone hunting with Kenric.'

'Well, then, I must have been mistaken,' Elise said with a relieved sigh. 'He is with Kenric.'

'Except Kenric insisted Nicholas was instructing Thomas and several other archers and could not be disturbed.'

Grimacing, Elise said, 'It would seem my brother has been busy this day.'

Lauren tapped her foot with impatience. 'Especially since Thomas was in the hall and told me . . .'

'Oh, all right!' Elise sprang out of her chair and turned to Lauren with an exasperated frown. 'Nicholas does not wish to be found at the moment.'

'Then why didn't someone just say so instead of lying to me?'

'They didn't tell you a falsehood to hurt you, Lauren. 'Tis that Nicholas does not wish *you* to find him.'

The bottom fell out of her stomach. 'Is he that mad at me?'

Elise's eyes softened to a soulful blue. She crossed the room and clasped Lauren's hands. 'He is not angry with you.'

Lauren frowned, remembering the way Nicholas had stormed from the solar. 'Yes, he is, Elise.'

The young woman conceded with a shrug. 'All

right, he is angry, but that is not the reason he does not wish to see you.'

After spending an hour searching for Nicholas, only to learn he didn't want her to find him, her frustration turned to panic. 'Tell me where he is. Now!'

'But he . . .'

'I have to talk to him.' Fighting to control the sudden fear that she had pushed him too far, she said with more calm, 'It's important or I wouldn't insist.'

'Very well,' Elise said with the enthusiasm of a person sentenced to cleaning out the garderobe. 'He is in the East tower.'

'The tower? Why?'

'That you will have to discover for yourself.' Turning away, Elise strode to the door, muttering, 'I think it would be a fine time for a ride. And I think I shall take Jacobson, Kenric and Thomas with me.'

As soon as the younger woman disappeared around the corner, Lauren's thoughts shifted to the tower room. What could have driven Nicholas to hide in a room meant for prisoners? *It's the one place I wouldn't have thought to look for him.* She moaned and pressed her hand to her brow. 'Good heaven, what have I done now?'

Lifting her skirts, she ran from the room and down the long, imposing hallway. She took a short cut up a little-used staircase to the third floor. A few wall brackets held candles to light the dark, narrow corridors. By the time she reached the spiraled stairs leading to the tower, her breath echoed against the cold stone walls.

262

At the heavy oak door she paused to listen. The sound of her pounding heart and the rush of blood in her ears drowned everything else out. Gripping the metal handle, she pushed and the door swung open. She took one step inside the small room and froze, her breath leaving in a loud gush.

The small, wiry man in front of her flinched and turned to face her. He pursed his thin lips into a scolding frown, then raised his fist and pointed the tip of a brown stick at her.

'What is this?' the man whined in a flowing French accent. 'I left specific instructions not to be disturbed. I cannot complete my work if I am to be interrupted every few moments.'

Lauren registered the man's complaints but she couldn't respond. Her eyes were locked on the canvas behind him, a canvas with a nearly completed painting of Nicholas. Her mouth dropped open and she couldn't draw a breath. Her limbs went numb. She felt herself sink to the floor, a pile of yellow satin billowing up around her.

Strong hands gripped her arms. Dazed, she looked to the side and into a pair of deep blue eyes narrowed with concern.

'You are ill, Lauren?' Nicholas asked, his voice harsh with worry.

'It's your portrait,' she whispered. She shivered as waves of emotion poured through her, disbelief being only one of them.

Nicholas absently grazed the base of her neck with his thumb. A faint smile touched his mouth. 'It was meant to be a wedding gift. I see you do not care for it.'

On the verge of tears, her lips trembled. She pressed a hand to her mouth. 'I love it.'

The small man she'd first seen grunted with disgust. 'She loves it! *Mademoiselle*, what is to love? Monsieur Kenward is most difficult. Look at what he insisted I paint.' He stepped aside so light from the narrow window washed the painting.

''Tis bad enough I must paint in this horrible little room without proper lighting,' the artist wailed. 'But my lord insisted I paint this . . . this . . .' the man flailed his hands toward the portrait '. . . this scowl! He would not even permit me to remove the scar.'

Lauren sat upright. 'Well, of course not!' Softer, she added, 'It's a part of him.'

Turning to Nicholas, she ran the tip of her finger along the two-inch wound, then reached over to kiss it, cherishing the heat of his flesh against her lips. Looking into his eyes, she searched for a hint of his feelings but found them guarded. 'He wouldn't be who he is without it.'

Some deep emotion stirred within him, darkening his eyes to black.

Facing the artist, she asked, 'When did you paint this, Monsieur . . .?'

The small man swept into a bow. 'De Chocques, *mademoiselle*, Sigar de Chocques.'

'Monsieur de Chocques, when did you paint Lord Kenward's face?'

'Why, just this morning. I insisted we wait until my lord was in a better disposition, but he would hear

264

none of it.' De Chocques shook his head and frowned with disgust.

Feeling Nicholas start to rise, Lauren reached for his arm and silently urged him to wait. She studied the portrait as Nicholas asked Sigar to leave. After the door closed, she asked, 'You came here after our argument?'

'Aye,' he said, his tone flat.

'And you were angry with me when he painted this,' she said, as more of a statement than a question.

'Very.'

A shaky smile touched her mouth, and hot tears pressed against her eyes. 'I always wondered what you were thinking when this was painted. Why you looked so angry, so lost, almost lonely.'

His hand rested on her shoulder, drawing her gaze to him. He studied her with a wary frown. 'What do you mean?'

'It's the same painting.'

His hold on her tightened, and she tried not to wince from the pain.

Paling, he asked, 'The one you searched for in the hall?'

Lauren nodded. 'Yes, it's exactly the same.'

She could see the doubt in his eyes, see his struggle to accept, if not truly believe what she said. 'I'm sorry I spoiled your surprise.'

He looked away and released her. 'It does not matter.'

Knowing she'd hurt him, she vowed to change things. If anyone deserved happiness in their life, it

265

was Nicholas. He had lost so much already. 'It does matter. I love surprises.'

He rose and moved to stand beside the portrait. 'Since there will be no wedding, there is no need for a gift.'

Clamping her lips together to keep from laughing, she struggled with her skirts and pushed herself to her feet. She met his hooded gaze and quelled the urge to kiss the hard line of his mouth. 'I say there is a need.'

'I am not marrying another woman,' he snapped.

'You'd better not.'

His frown softened. 'What are you saying?'

'I'm saying . . .' Lauren pressed her lips together, her earlier giddiness sobering. The need to cry tears of joy for them both threatened to overwhelm her. 'I'm saying I love you. And more than anything in this world I want to marry you.'

Nicholas didn't grab her and swing her about the room the way she'd needed and expected him to. He held still, studying her, his face an unreadable mask. Forever the soldier. 'Why have you changed your mind?'

Lauren wanted to curse his control. 'I thought about what you said earlier today – that I might be the one you were supposed to marry. Even if I'm not, I believe we're worth the risk. Though it means I might change history. Finding you here with the painting . . .' She paused to look at his likeness and felt a rush of relief that she was doing the right thing.

'Your expression is the same as in my time.' When he didn't respond she grasped his hands, desperate to

266

make him understand. 'Don't you see? You are scowling because you had a fight with me. With me!' she laughed. 'I'm meant to be here. I am meant to be your wife and have your baby.'

She stopped and closed her eyes, forcing away the knowledge of what would eventually happen to Nicholas if she couldn't stop the siege. Just because part of the legend came true, it didn't mean it all had to, she reasoned.

He gathered her to him and she dissolved in his arms, melded with his body, his soul. A veil of security and contentment slipped over her, but fell short of cloaking the fear, deep inside her, that she couldn't make it last.

'I do not understand you,' he whispered against her hair, then pulled away to look at her. 'But it doesn't matter. If you agree to become my wife, nothing else is important.'

'I agree.'

He tilted her chin so her mouth was inches from his. 'Then I am truly the happiest man in all England.'

His mouth closed over hers, claiming her, kissing her so deeply, so completely, it touched every sensitive nerve inside her body. Her senses came alive, aching for his body to join hers, to soar with hers to their private place.

'Nicholas,' she whispered between kisses. She pulled the ribbon from his hair and buried her hands in black silk. She touched him, held onto him, urged him closer. It wasn't close enough.

To finally be free of the doubts that had weighed her

mind and heart all these weeks was like stepping into sunshine for the very first time. She felt wonderfully free, and ready to take the life Nicholas offered.

She lowered her hands and fumbled with his belt. 'Make love to me.'

He nipped the sensitive skin along her neck and chuckled, his warm breath feathering over her shoulder. 'Monsieur de Chocques is waiting in the hall.'

Lauren laughed, the sound a mixture of frustration and happiness. 'I can be quiet.'

His hand closed over hers before she had the belt free. 'You? Quiet? I think not.'

Before she could argue, he was kissing her again. A possession that pulled her heart to the surface made her mind spin with the intoxicating scent and taste of him. And beneath it all was the promise to sweep her away, if not now, then soon.

When he finally ended the kiss, she dropped her forehead against his chest. Her blood flowed hot and heavy through her limbs, as if she were drugged. Sensation, intense with hunger, pooled between her thighs.

She had made love to Nicholas countless times over the past month, but had never felt such an urgent need for completion as she did now. She shook with it, felt drained and elated by it. This moment marked a new beginning for them. A new life.

He cupped her face in his hands. His deep blue eyes, so often harsh and cold, were soft and so warm her body responded with a silent cry of longing.

'Soon, love.'

'Oh, Nicholas.' She wrapped her arms around his shoulders and buried her face against his neck. 'I love you so much. So very much.'

His hands slid up her sides until his palms cupped the edges of her breasts. A flame erupted, making her gasp. She felt herself swell against his touch, her bodice tightening across her chest. His thumbs grazed over her nipples, sending a staggering jolt down her body. She gasped and pushed against his chest, breaking free. 'You're teasing me. That's not fair.'

A devilish grin, one she'd never seen before, spread across his face. 'I just wanted to make sure you still wanted me.'

Smiling in return, she let her gaze drift down his body, settling on his erection. 'Two can play that game.'

His hands fisted and his body tensed. Raising her gaze, she saw his smile vanish. His eyes darkened with a possessive, devouring look that made her take several steps back. She raised her hand to stop his approach. 'Don't come any closer, Nicholas.'

'You play with fire, madam.'

'You started it.' Though she knew she shouldn't, she couldn't help laughing. She manoeuvered behind the painting but he followed, trapping her in a corner. 'I didn't even touch you.'

'You don't have to,' he answered in a seductive growl.

'Okay, I give. You win. Now stop this.' She knew

they couldn't make love on the tower room floor, not with the painter waiting for them, but every fiber in her body tingled, urging her to do just that. Trying to sound serious, she added, 'Monsieur Sigar de Chocques is outside. He can hear us.' She ruined her authoritative tone by giggling through the last part of her speech.

With nowhere to go, she flattened herself against the wall.

Nicholas braced his arms on either side of her. 'I am going to allow de Chocques in now,' he said with cool control. 'Can you behave?'

'You'll terrify him with that scowl on your face.'

'If he sees me smiling, he'll want to repaint the portrait.'

Lauren huffed. 'Never. It's perfect the way it is.'

'I'm glad you think so.' With a wicked grin he leaned down to kiss her.

Lauren pressed her palms against his shoulders. When his lips met hers, she lightly raked her nails down his chest to his stomach, feeling his muscles contract in response. He sucked in a breath and pulled back. She ducked beneath his arm and lunged for the door. She jerked it open, startling the French painter who sat on the stairs with his chin propped on his palm.

In a breathless voice, she said, 'You may come in now, *monsieur*. Lord Kenward is ready to continue.' After the small man hurried into the room, she turned to face Nicholas. He stood rigid, his shoulders back. Jet-black hair framed his face and settled against his heaving chest.

She glanced at the portrait, then back to her soon-to-be husband. Though Nicholas was scowling at her and his stance reflected a man prepared for war, his eyes were far different from the painting. Now they were a hot blue fire instead of cold, empty ice.

She met his gaze, her heart hurting with the amount of love she felt for him. Silently, she mouthed the words *I love you*.

The move was barely perceptible, but he nodded his assent. Smiling, feeling happier than she probably had a right to feel, she left the room so Sigar de Chocques could complete the portrait she already loved.

CHAPTER 16

Lauren waited outside the massive door. She wasn't prepared for this. Didn't think she ever would be. But she had to do it. Now, if she wanted a future with Nicholas. And she did, more than anything.

She smoothed the skirt and fitted bodice of her cream satin and lace gown. Fine gold embroidery adorned the square neckline and the cuffs of her tapered sleeves. A breathtaking girdle of pearls and sapphires hugged her waist, the front tassels almost reaching the floor. She'd never felt so elegant, or so beautiful.

Her wedding dress.

Only it wasn't her wedding. *Yet.*

She reached up to brush away her hair, but caught herself. Elise had spent an hour pinning Lauren's mass of hair on top of her head, then had artfully arranged a strand of pearls through it. The final result was stunning, and she didn't want to ruin it.

Drawing a deep breath that did little to soothe her nerves, Lauren knocked on the door. Seconds ticked by like days before a young maid named Clara opened the heavy oak door.

'I'm here to see Lady Kenward,' Lauren said, amazed she could speak at all for the thudding in her chest.

Clara's light gray eyes widened with fright before she glanced behind her. 'Oh, my lady. Mistress Kenward is not well.'

'I only need a few minutes of her time. Please tell her I'm here.'

The young maid hesitated a moment, then winced as she closed the door in Lauren's face.

She stared at the dark oak paneling, wondering what she should do now. Just walk in and announce herself? She certainly wasn't going to leave without speaking her mind. She reached for the metal doorhandle, but it was snatched from her hand.

Clara stared at her, grim-faced, as she opened the door wide and allowed Lauren to enter. 'My lady awaits you in her private solar.'

Lauren nodded and entered her soon-to-be mother-in-law's enormous room. Heavily carved chairs were placed throughout the room with no particular theme in mind. Exquisite tapestries lined the walls, and yards of violet silk hung from the bedposts of a large, elegantly carved bed. The room was beautiful, appealing, and so unlike the woman they belonged to. Searching for the private solar, Lauren spotted an open door to her left and headed for it.

The smaller room was filled with the same heavy oak furniture and ornate rugs. But her attention centered on Lady Kenward, who sat on a bench seat at a panel of windows. The older woman looked wasted, shriveled in her severe black wool dress, and startlingly out of place in the elegant room. Like a shadow amid color.

'Lady Kenward,' Lauren began, willing her voice to remain calm. 'It's time we talked.'

Lady Kenward ignored her and stared out the window. Unexpected pity invaded Lauren's hold on anger. The older woman had filled her life with hatred when she should have appreciated the things she did have: a son and daughter she could be proud of, a beautiful home.

At that instant Lauren's troubled conscience spoke to her. How would she react if something happened to Nicholas? Would she grieve, then move on with her life, or become buried in anguish?

Reaching for the back of a chair, she swayed off balance. She closed her eyes, waited for the dizziness to pass, praying she would never have to deal with that kind of pain. She would do everything within her power to prevent Nicholas's death. The more she thought about it, the more she believed she was in this time, possessing knowledge of the future, for a reason. A future that was meant to be changed.

She opened her eyes and found Lady Kenward's gaze fastened on her, sharp and intense, unlike her frail body.

'I have nothing to say to you,' Lady Kenward said.

'Your son is getting married today. He wants you there.'

274

Lady Kenward turned to face the window.

'I don't ask for my sake or your own, but for Nicholas's. He deserves to be happy.' Lauren hated the pleading tone in her voice, but she didn't want to be the cause of the rift between Nicholas and his mother.

Once Lady Kenward had been informed Lauren wasn't Laird Armstrong's daughter everyone had thought the older woman would soften her attitude toward Lauren. To everyone's surprise, she had only become more hateful.

'I will not condone my son's marriage to you,' she said, her thin mouth twisting with disdain.

'But I'm not Armstrong's daughter,' Lauren argued. 'You have no reason . . .'

Lady Kenward bolted from the bench, her small body trembling. Lauren took a startled step back. 'You are nobody! Do you hear? Nobody! Nothing! Except a harlot who wormed her way into my son's bed and convinced him to marry her.' She turned away. 'You are dismissed. I never wish to lay eyes on your worthless soul again.'

All traces of pity fled Lauren's mind. 'Nicholas still hasn't discovered who tried to have me killed.'

Lady Kenward said nothing, but her back stiffened.

'I know who was responsible.' Lauren had hoped she wouldn't have to confront Lady Kenward about this, especially not today, but she didn't have much choice. 'I haven't shared my suspicions with Nicholas. Nor do I want to. But I won't stand by and allow you to ruin our lives. I'm warning you, never try anything like that again.'

The old woman spun around to face her. 'Do you dare suggest I had something to do with your escape?'

'Who else would the guards be trying to protect with their lives?' Lauren asked.

'My son would not believe such a lie!'

'Perhaps not.' Lauren turned and headed for the door, but stopped at the threshold. 'I don't intend to tell Nicholas, but I know you were behind it.'

'You are a lying witch as well as a whore!'

Lauren sighed, exhausted from the strain of controlling her temper. 'I didn't come here to accuse you or to fight with you, Lady Kenward. I came because I want there to be peace between us, for Nicholas's sake. We both love him. And I'm going to do everything within my power to make him happy.'

Lady Kenward's eyes glazed with contempt. Lauren turned and left, leaving screaming silence behind her.

CHAPTER 17

With Father Bryan standing beside him at the head of the chapel, Nicholas scanned the crowded room for the one face he was growing desperate to see. He'd wanted to go in search of her, but Elise had stopped him, insisting he couldn't see Lauren until the ceremony. Some foolishness about being surprised.

He didn't want any surprises today. He wanted Lauren by his side so Father Bryan could say the words that would bind them together for life. Only then would the persistent fear that Lauren would somehow vanish from him be eased. He couldn't put an exact reason to his fear – perhaps her tale of being from another time, or the worry he saw in her eyes when she thought he wasn't looking caused his unrest.

He had been prepared to marry her the day she had agreed to, but Lauren and Elise had insisted on waiting a week. Elise had wanted to make it a grand celebration, and Nicholas hadn't the heart to deny her. So he'd waited, grudgingly so, but now the moment was here and his bride was late.

Nicholas glanced at his sister, who had turned to watch the back of the room, nervously knotting her handkerchief in her hands. The seat beside Elise was empty. The place his mother should have taken but refused. The weight of failure pressed against him. Nothing he'd said to his mother about his marriage to Lauren had made a difference. He didn't know how to reach her anymore, or if it was possible to get past her hate. A hate he had helped fuel.

His mother had become hysterical upon learning Lauren wasn't Christel Armstrong. She'd insisted Nicholas either send her away or kill her, then capture the real Christel. Nicholas had refused. When he'd met with Laird Armstrong, Nicholas had been sincere when he'd offered the Scotsman a truce. That the woman he wanted to marry wasn't the laird's daughter didn't matter to Nicholas now. For the first time in his life he had visions of a future. He wanted to see what those visions held.

But his refusing to pursue his revenge against Armstrong had only enraged his mother more. Nicholas worried she might be losing her mind, might even harm herself with her ravings. She no longer thought rationally, but then neither had he, he admitted with brutal honesty, when his only purpose in life had been to exact revenge.

Then he had captured Lauren, treated her in the worst possible way, but she had come to love him despite the cruelty he'd done to her. That she had any feelings for him at all still stunned him. He hadn't thought himself worthy of someone's love, had never

278

considered it necessary. Now he couldn't imagine living without it.

A rustle of commotion and startled gasps drew his attention to the door of the chapel. Nicholas sucked in a breath, not believing his eyes.

Lauren stood in the portal, like a shimmering apparition of cream and gold. A vision so beautiful, so ethereal, he wondered if he hadn't created her from a dream, a wish for something so precious to truly be his. Her jewel-green eyes locked with his. She smiled as if he were the only man in the room, as if they shared some special secret between them.

As she started down the aisle, Nicholas moved to meet her halfway. He took her free hand so her palm rested against his, then curled his fingers around her wrist. He kissed the back of her hand, lingering over the soft, cool feel of her. 'You are beautiful.'

Her eyes deepened, warmed with shifting emerald light. Tears glistened at their corners. Her lips trembled with a nervous smile. 'So are you.'

The compliment made his chest swell unexpectedly. During the week before the wedding he'd had a doublet of sapphire-blue velvet made. He still wore black hose and boots, but he had decided it was time to make a change, break from his dark past.

'What is this?' he asked, indicating the bouquet of roses and baby's breath she held in her other hand.

She gave him a curious grin. 'It's traditional for the bride to carry flowers.'

With his hand at the small of her back, he led her to

the altar where Father Bryan awaited them, his heavy, ivory-inlaid Bible open in his hands.

The priest began the ceremony. Nicholas heard his name, then Lauren's. He even heard his own voice repeating the vows, yet he did so on a subconscious level. He couldn't take his eyes from the woman at his side. Her flame-red hair was wrapped in loose curls and laced with a string of pearls, and, as usual, free of any headdress. He prayed she never covered it. But it was all he could do to keep his hands from burying themselves in the blaze of silk.

When he repeated the words 'till death us do part', he felt her tense. He squeezed her to him, wanting to ease her mind and her belief that he would die in a siege.

Then, without hesitation, with her voice growing stronger with each word, she repeated her vows.

Nicholas faced Father Bryan as the priest took a box from a clerk and blessed the rings. Nicholas took the enameled case and presented it to Lauren. She gasped. The color drained from her face. The bouquet of roses fell to the floor.

'What is it, love?' he asked, concerned that her wound hadn't healed as he had thought.

Trembling, she ran her fingers over the painted surface, lingering over the woman with flowing red hair sitting in a field of heather, then moved to the young girl who held out a handful of the purple flowers. 'It's the same case. The one Grandma found in the dungeon.'

A wary tingle touched the back of Nicholas's neck.

She looked up at him, tears brimming in her eyes. 'Is this for me?'

'Aye, as a wedding gift. It holds . . .'

'I know what's inside.'

He frowned at her. 'How could you?'

'It's a gold ring with a lion raised on his hind legs. Your family insignia surrounds it. *Kenward, A Lion Rampant.*'

The priest sucked in a breath, but Nicholas couldn't look away from the brilliant shine in Lauren's eyes or the excited flush on her cheeks. Nor could he believe she had described the contents of the case in such detail.

'Have you seen this before?' Nicholas whispered.

She glanced at the priest, who now held the Bible pressed to his chest and stared at her, his face twisted with distress. Biting her lip, she answered, 'Once.'

Unsettled by her admission, Nicholas lifted the lid. 'I pray it fits.'

On a breath, she whispered, 'It does.'

He removed the ring and handed the box to the cleric. As Nicholas said the last of his vows, he slid the ring on her finger. It fit perfectly.

The rest of the ceremony passed in a blur, with Nicholas trying to ease his distress with reason. Lauren must have seen the jewelry case and the ring while the craftsman was making it. Or perhaps someone had told her of it. He didn't believe, couldn't believe that she had seen it in another time, as she claimed to have seen his portrait.

He didn't believe her story about coming from the

281

future because that was all it was, a story. He hadn't cared or given much thought as to why she would make up such a tale, either. It didn't matter. He loved her and wanted her for his wife, regardless of who she was or where she came from.

When Father Bryan announced it time for the kiss that would bond them, all Nicholas's troubling thoughts vanished. *His wife!*

She faced him, her hands resting on his chest. All the love he felt for this woman was reflected in her eyes. He gripped her waist in a gentle hold and bent to give her a chaste kiss. Anything more he couldn't handle.

Her hand slid to his neck, urging him to deepen the kiss. With a growl, he gathered her in his arms and crushed her mouth with his. The kiss turned deep and long, and utterly soul-shattering, leaving him burning for more.

She pulled away and eyed him mischievously. 'Nicholas, we're in church.'

'You have turned into a temptress, I think.'

'I'm just making sure you still want me.'

A low chuckle escaped him as he nuzzled her neck. Then he turned to face the watchful crowd. A young woman moved forward and retrieved the flowers Lauren had dropped, handing them to her.

Nicholas laced his fingers through his wife's and raised their joined hands for all to see. 'This day has been long in coming. Never did I believe I would be fortunate enough to take a wife, let alone one that would mean so much to me. Hear me now, for my wife is the new mistress of Westbourne Castle. Lady Kenward's voice is my own. Her wish is my wish. You now serve her as you do me, with loyalty and good faith!'

A few voices rose with enthusiastic cheers, then silence abruptly fell over the chapel.

Nicholas looked at his wife. Anxiety pulled at the corners of her eyes. He knew what she thought. He'd heard it as well.

His people were not happy.

The celebration to honor the wedded couple reached its peak by nightfall. The iron chandeliers had been lowered and lit. Rushlights along the stone walls were burning, as were the twin candelabra on the dais.

Nicholas watched the revelers, his most trusted soldiers and neighboring lords among them, with a mixture of satisfaction and irritation. After hearing the dispirited cheer of his people in response to his wedding, he had wanted to demand that each of them beg his wife's forgiveness. Lauren's pleading glance had stopped him. That and her whispered understanding that she was a stranger to them, not to mention Scottish. His people simply needed time to come to know her. He had been amazed that she hadn't been affronted by their insult. He certainly had.

Now everyone laughed at the jugglers and acrobats. They danced as musicians strolled through the room. Most had come to congratulate him and kiss Lauren's hand. Despite the wine-induced revelry, he had detected wariness in more than one person's eyes as they came to meet their new mistress.

Nicholas rubbed his jaw, contemplating how to ease his people's obvious distrust of his wife.

'It's your wedding and you're frowning already. Not a good sign,' Lauren teased.

Rescued from his dark thoughts, Nicholas took up his wife's hand and kissed her wedding ring. Meeting her questioning gaze, he said. 'There is an inscription in your ring.'

'Yes, I know.'

Nicholas felt his smile fade from his face. 'How could you? Have you removed it?'

'Not since you placed it there,' she said, her voice still in the rowdy room.

His gut tightened. He didn't want to ask, but had to. 'What do you think it says?'

'"*My love, my life I give you. N.*"'

He stared at her, his mind racing for an explanation. She winced. 'You're squeezing my hand.'

'Who told you about the jewelry case and ring? The craftsman?'

Her eyes shifted with the volatility of storm clouds. She pulled her hand free. 'You don't believe I come from the future, do you?'

Nicholas ran his hand over his hair in exasperation. He didn't want to have this conversation. Where his wife came from was an issue he didn't wish to address, not now anyway. 'How can I? It is a tale impossible to believe.'

She grunted. The corner of her mouth lifted in a

rueful grin. 'I would have agreed with you whole-heartedly a few months ago.' Her eyes widened and she stared at him with something close to wonder. 'You married me even though you think I made it up?'

Nicholas leaned toward her and slid his hand across her stomach to cup the side of her waist. At that moment he would have gladly given up his lands and his title to be alone with his wife. He brushed her lips with his. 'I would have married you had you said you were Satan's daughter.'

After a deep, hungry kiss, she pulled away and turned to the crowded room. Her kiss-induced flush faded along with her smile. He followed her gaze and stiffened. Over half the guests had stopped their dancing and laughing to watch Nicholas and his wife.

In a shaky whisper, Lauren said, 'From the looks on their faces, I'd say they think you *have* married the devil's daughter.'

Nicholas wanted to disagree, but couldn't. He clenched his jaw in frustrated anger. He couldn't tolerate his people's distrust of his wife, nor could he demand their respect. But something had to be done.

Feeling her grow tense beside him, he stifled a curse. This was their wedding night, and he refused to allow his people's suspicious nature to ruin it. Standing, he pulled her to her feet. 'Come, it's time we retired.'

'Isn't it rude to leave before your guests?'

With his finger, he touched the corner of her mouth where a frown pulled at it. 'It is customary for the bride and groom to depart first. Only then do the guests feel they can take their leave.' Leading her to the stairs, he added, 'Besides, I have a wedding gift still to give you.'

'Another one? You're going to spoil me at this rate.'

As they neared the door to his bedchamber, he whispered against her ear, 'Actually, this gift is for us both to enjoy.'

She shivered as he pushed open the door. Entering his room, she made it halfway to the bed, then stopped to look around. When she spotted her 'gift' before the fire she laughed, a seductive, throaty sound that made every nerve in his body respond.

He reached her side and slid his arms around her waist, bending to kiss the satiny skin along her neck. 'Have you seen this gift before?'

Her laugh turned into a moan. 'No, never.'

'Do you like it?' Lightly, he bit the curve of her shoulder.

'I . . .' She melted in his arms. 'I love it. What made you think of it?'

He unfastened the row of tiny pearl buttons along her back, then eased her dress and chemise from her shoulders, letting them drop to the floor with a soft rustle. He bent and pulled off her cream slippers, then her pale silk stockings. The simple act almost killed him. He wanted to pull her to the floor and take her, quick and hard. But he forced the urge away, wanting to savor the anticipation.

It had been a week since he had last made love to her. Now that she was his wife, he wanted this night to be special for them both.

Lifting her in his arms, he carried her to the fireplace and lowered her into the bathtub he had had especially made for two. Rectangular in design, it was wide enough for them both to fit comfortably and long enough for him to fully recline. Steam, and the scent of lavender, rose from the hot water.

As Lauren settled against the padded edge with a moan, Nicholas removed his clothes, tossing them to the floor in his haste. He stepped into the tub and sat next to her, his muscles responding as hot water enveloped and soothed him. Drawing her into the crook of his arm, he laid her head on his shoulder.

'This is heaven. So relaxing.' She draped her leg across his arousal.

Nicholas gritted his teeth, fought for a steady breath. She shifted, and her breasts, wet and silky smooth, pressed against his side. His erection tightened painfully. 'Woman, be still.'

She lifted her head to look at him, her eyelids heavy and seductive. 'You don't sound like you're enjoying this.'

'I am trying my best.'

With a sly smile, she kissed him, then ran her tongue over his bottom lip. 'Perhaps I'm crowding you. I'll move a little bit.'

She slid her leg over his waist and shifted until she straddled his hips. When she settled her weight on him, Nicholas gripped the sides of the tub and sucked a breath through his teeth. 'Lauren . . .'

'You don't act as if you like our new bathtub, Nicholas.'

Her flawless, creamy skin glistened wet in the firelight. Dark nipples, pebble-hard against the cool air, taunted him into taking them into his mouth. As he stared at her, her breasts seemed to grow fuller, more lush. His mouth watered, knowing what she would taste like. 'On the contrary, wife, I may never allow you to bathe without me.'

He drew her against him and took her mouth in a hungry, impatient kiss. The tips of her nipples pressed into his chest. Her velvet core encased him, held him immobile like an agonizingly erotic glove. He stroked the sides of her breasts. She moved against him, sending shards of pleasure-pain through his body. His hands drifted to her buttocks and tried to urge her up so he could enter her. His body demanded it; his mind could think of nothing else.

She resisted and pulled away, her breath as strained as his, but her expression had changed from seductress to serious, hinting at a trace of sadness. She drew the tips of her fingers over his face, as if to memorize what she saw. They lingered over his scar.

'I have a wedding gift for you.' Her eyes darkened with a desperation he didn't understand.

'Can it not wait? I rather like you where you are.'

She gave him a small, secretive grin. 'I don't have to get up.'

'Then by all means, where is my gift?'

'In a way, you're already holding it.'

Nicholas frowned, puzzled. 'What do you mean?'

'I'm pregnant,' she said quietly, as if afraid to hear the words out loud.

'You're . . .' Nicholas couldn't finish, couldn't breathe. His mind went numb with her words, words he had never imagined he would live long enough or be fortunate enough to hear. He'd never allowed himself to look to a future with a wife and family. Now he had both. What had he done in his life to deserve such gifts? To his fear, he couldn't think of anything.

'Pregnant,' she finished for him. 'You know – with child, a bun in the oven, quickening, or whatever it is you call it in this time.'

She tried to make light of it, but Nicholas saw the threat of tears in her eyes. The flare of mindless joy he'd experienced quickly became concern. 'Are you not pleased about this child, Lauren?'

With a forlorn look, she shook her head. A tear slipped down her face. 'Other than being your wife, I can't think of anything more wonderful than having your baby.'

He sighed, relieving the anxiety gripping his stomach. 'Then these are tears of joy?'

Her bottom lip trembled. 'I'm afraid.'

'Of what?' He held her face between his hands, kissed her brow, the corners of her eyes, tasting the salt of her tears. 'Whatever frightens you, let it go. I shall protect you, Lauren, always.'

She shook her head and sat up. 'I'm not afraid for me. It's you!' She drew in a shuddering breath. 'Everything about the legend is coming true. You have married an outlander that your people don't trust, and now I'm pregnant.'

'That still proves nothing.'

She studied him, the fear in her green eyes fading in the wake of determination. 'Okay, you don't have to believe me. But I'm going to ask something of you and I want you to promise you'll do it.'

'If I can, you know I will.'

'If . . .' her cheeks flushed with resolve and a tremor sped through her body '. . . if I am right and Armstrong does attack Westbourne, you have to promise you'll do whatever necessary not to be hurt.'

'Lauren, there is no way I can promise such a thing,' he said truthfully, though he wished he could tell her otherwise.

'Give me your word, Nicholas.'

'What would you have me do?'

She sighed, exasperated. 'I don't know. Stay in the back where arrows can't reach you. Wear more armor, strap shields around your body! Anything, just promise me!'

He pulled her stiff body to him, hating the fear in her eyes and desperate to soothe it. 'Shh, love, I give you my word. I shall do whatever is within my power to avoid being harmed.' Though he made the promise, he knew if her prediction came true he would have no choice but to be in the thick of battle. He could never allow his men to fight while he watched from a safe distance. Besides, her prediction wouldn't come true. Laird Armstrong would not dare attack Westbourne Castle.

'That's all I'll ever ask of you, Nicholas.'

'That is all? I have found women never cease asking for something.' He smiled, trying to lighten her distress.

'Anything of importance, that is,' she qualified, her mouth curving with a coy grin.

'As I recall,' he said, as his hand slipped between them to cup her full breasts, 'we were discussing your being with child.'

She moved so both his hands could have access to her. He squeezed her, lifting the weight of her. She closed her eyes and tilted her hips in response. His erection, which had softened when she'd become upset, flared with a burst of power, taking his breath away.

'Are you happy about my pregnancy?'

'Wife, I am more than pleased. I can hardly believe I have done anything worthy enough to deserve both you and a son of my own.'

'It's going to be a girl,' she said as she rocked against him, sloshing water over the sides.

He gripped her waist, lifted her, then lowered her over his shaft. In the cooling water, her heat surrounded him, flowed into him. Fire and ice. He didn't want to think beyond their pleasure. 'If this is more of your legend, I will hear no more of it.'

She moved on him slowly, as if she were dancing to music only she could hear. 'It's the truth. The legend says we'll have a girl first.'

'Lauren,' he warned, and sucked in his breath when she changed her rhythm.

'We're supposed to name her Aurora.'

His smirk made her laugh.

'I know, it's not the name I would have picked either. What do you think about . . .?'

'Enough!' He dipped his hand into the water and found her core with his thumb. Stroking, delving deeper into her, he pushed her to the brink of climax. Her breathing turned to shallow gulps of air. 'I have made you a promise, Lauren, now I want one in return.'

When she didn't answer, he stopped moving his thumb. Her lids fluttered open to reveal the glazed urgency building inside. 'Nicholas, please . . .'

'I want your promise never to mention the legend again.'

She shook her head. 'Can't we talk about this later?'

'If you cannot give your word, I will have to do something quite rash.'

'Like what? Return me to be oubliette? You wouldn't.' She rubbed his chest with her hands, her nails raking sensually across his skin.

'No, I would not, but I would do this.' Though it almost killed him to do it, he lifted her off him and started to rise from the tub.

She caught his arm. 'This is sexual blackmail!'

'Aye. Though it is not what I want.'

'Neither do I.'

'Then give me your word.'

Her jaw clenched as she fought with indecision. 'Oh, all right. I promise not to bring it up again.'

He rose and drew her against him. Lifting her in his arms, he stepped from the tub, then knelt on the fur covers before the fire. She stretched out, her creamy, damp body framed by layers of soft black fur. He removed the pins from her hair, freeing flame-red curls, letting them spill about her shoulders in a blaze of passion. He buried his face against her neck, inhaled her clean, womanly scent.

'I never knew a man could go insane from his wedding night. I don't think I have ever wanted anything as much as I want you.' He gritted his teeth, not believing he'd revealed feelings he was hardly aware of. Feelings that still frightened and overwhelmed him.

He loved this woman. He could admit that to himself when he lay awake at night, staring into the dark. But to give voice to the powerful emotion tore at a vulnerable part of him. He'd learned at a young age what it was like to love too much then lose that love. It had led to years of darkness, isolation. He didn't ever want to return to that place.

He wanted to tell her he loved her. Knew she wanted to hear the words. But they burned in his throat, building to a dangerous flame. He looked into her eyes, saw her deep current of love, knew she waited, waited. He couldn't do it. Not yet. He'd lived his life shielding all emotions. He couldn't tell her of his feelings, but he could show her.

He covered her body with his, and her legs gripped his hips, squeezing him, urging him closer. He found her, burying himself in a single thrust. Her intoxicating scent surrounded him, pulled him as nothing else ever had. Taking deep, burning breaths, Nicholas held still, afraid it would be over too soon. He heard her mindless whisper that she loved him. The words were kindling to flame, bursting inside him.

He moved inside her, his rhythm slow, his eyes closed, using his sense of touch to explore her tight heat. His body strained against the controlled pace. Sweat coated his skin. Hers glistened a flushed rose in the dancing firelight.

Shaking, he pulled himself from her body, returned with slow, lingering stokes, never burying himself, barely penetrating the edge of her. She whimpered at the teasing action, her hands gripping his shoulders, her hips lifting in search of him.

'Please, Nicholas, love me.' She clung to his neck and kissed him, her tongue forging his mouth with the same rhythm as he claimed her body.

Shuddering, he buried himself deeper. Then again and again. His body shook as he repeatedly touched the sweetest part of her soul. Sweat dripped into his eyes. He clenched his teeth, waiting for the moment his wife grew tense with the beginning of her release.

Lifting her hips, she met him. Her hands gripped his buttocks, holding him against her. Nicholas raised himself on his arms and dropped his head back. His sight turned red, then black as he fought back the explosive pressure of his climax. He heard his wife's feminine gasp, looked down and saw her eyes were glazed. His name shook from her lips.

Blood rushed through his veins, exploding in his mind. He drove into her, clenching his jaw and tightening his body. His breath burst from his chest. He shuddered as his release swept over him in waves that were dazzling bright and so intense he thought they might never end, prayed they would never end.

As the fog of passion gradually cleared, he found his wife watching him, her eyes soft and dreamy. A sated smile curved her pink mouth.

'Have you something to say, wife?'

She snuggled against him with a throaty laugh. 'Are you looking for a compliment?'

Nicholas pulled free and rose. He lifted Lauren in his arms and strode to the bed. 'I need no compliments. All I need do is look at your face to know you are happy.'

He laid her on the bed and she scooted over and held the covers back so he could climb in beside her. Once settled, with his arms around her and her head on his chest, she yawned and stretched. 'I am happy, Nicholas. Happier than I've ever been.'

He stared at the firelight dancing on the tapestry-covered walls and paneled ceiling. He alternately stroked his wife's soft, thick hair, then moved to her silky waist. A waist still small and trim.

Lauren twisted around so her back was to him. He shifted so the front of his body followed her curves. His hand sought her flat stomach. He covered her smooth skin, trying to imagine the child nestled within the safety of his wife's body.

A girl-child, according to Lauren. Aurora. Nicholas smiled into the fading light. For the first time in his dark life he had everything he wanted; a tentative peace along the Scottish border, a wife he adored more with each passing day, and now a child. *His child.*

A chill grazed his skin and he hugged Lauren tighter, afraid something so wonderful couldn't possibly last.

CHAPTER 18

Kneeling on the ground, Lauren shivered against the cold and drew her cloak around her thickening body. A sudden breeze picked up a layer of dirt and swept it into her face. She dropped her shears and turned against the wind. It was nearing the end of November, and, with the threat of frost, Elise had insisted on collecting the remaining herbs from the garden before they were ruined.

Knowing next to nothing about gardening, Lauren's first response had been to grumble, but then she remembered how thankful she was for Elise's knowledge of running the castle. The day after her wedding, five months ago, Elise had tried to hand over the keys to the pantry, as well as the staggering responsibilities of running the keep, to the new mistress of Westbourne Castle. Lauren had shoved them right back at her sister-in-law.

What did she know about organizing the slaughter and curing of pigs to see them through the long winter months? Or how to inventory the pantry and order supplies by the ton? It took so many people to run the castle, she couldn't begin to keep track of who did what. When she'd relayed her lack of knowledge to Elise, the young woman had stared at her in astonishment, questions poised on the tip of her tongue.

But, whatever Elise had wanted to ask, she had kept it to herself. Taking Lauren under her wing, Elise had begun the arduous task of training her.

Everyone knew Lauren was not Laird Armstrong's daughter, but their knowledge of her ended there. Nicholas hadn't deemed it necessary to give his people any sort of explanation about where his wife had come from. He hadn't even pressed her for a story more plausible than the one about the cave. So rumors and suspicions had begun to fly.

One story regaled that she was a Scottish highland princess, the sole survivor of a clan wiped out by victorious English soldiers. The other tale had not been so sympathetic. Supposedly, Lauren was a changeling whose sole purpose in life was to kill innocent English villagers while they slept.

Nicholas had been furious when he'd heard the stories, but powerless to stop them. So Lauren had made it her task to meet and befriend his people. It had been a slow, painstaking process, one that oftentimes had pushed her close to tears. To add fuel to the flame, there was his mother, Lady Kenward, to deal with. The woman still wouldn't acknowledge Lauren as her daughter-in-law. She refused to speak to Lauren, though she joined the family at meals, turning them into strained and miserable affairs.

Lauren's heart ached through each one, knowing

she had caused a rift between Nicholas and his mother that might never be bridged. Though he insisted he wasn't concerned, that his mother would come to accept her in time, Lauren knew Lady Kenward's hostile feelings weren't likely to change. Once, after the wedding, Lauren had tried to resolve the disharmony between them by calling a truce. The older woman had looked straight through Lauren, as if she wasn't there, then turned and left the room.

Glancing toward the gate leading to the lower bailey, Lauren saw Thomas leaning against the stone wall as he kept an eye on her. Her bodyguard. Ever since she had recovered from her wound, Nicholas had insisted someone be with her at all times. It had infuriated her at first, but he had assured her he didn't believe she would try to leave him again. The extra measure was for her safety.

Nicholas still had no clue as to who had orchestrated her escape, and Lauren didn't plan to tell him. She doubted Lady Kenward would attempt to have her killed again, but there where times, like when Nicholas was gone for days visiting tenants, when she welcomed the extra protection.

The baby shifted and kicked Lauren hard in the side, as if to interrupt her mother's burdensome thoughts. She leaned back and rubbed her stomach, hoping it would soothe her daughter back to sleep.

'Are you tired, Lauren?' Elise asked. The younger woman knelt on the ground two rows away, relieving a marjoram plant of its leaves.

'No,' Lauren sighed. 'The baby's restless is all.'

Elise's dark blue eyes warmed with longing. She rose and came to sit by her. 'Is she moving now?'

When Lauren had told Elise the baby would be a girl, her sister-in-law hadn't thought it unusual that a mother would know the gender of her child. At a sudden, well-placed kick, Lauren grunted, then laughed. She reached for Elise's hand and drew it beneath her cloak, settling it on her rounded stomach.

They held still for a moment, and when the baby finally moved Elise's eyes widened with wonderment. 'It must be a wonderful thing, to feel a life growing inside you.'

Lauren smiled, wanting to ease the yearning she heard in Elise's voice. 'It is. You'll have your own someday.'

Elise pulled back, her forlorn gaze on the stone-gray castle walls. 'Sometimes I wonder.' Shifting her eyes back to Lauren, she said, 'I am nearly beyond an acceptable marrying age.'

Lauren frowned at the beautiful woman whose coal-black hair enhanced her dark, secretive eyes and creamy, flawless skin. 'Nonsense! How old could you possibly be?'

'Eighteen.' She bent her head as if the fact were a burden. ''Tis my own doing, though.'

When Lauren lifted her brow in silent question, her sister-in-law added, 'I refused to marry the men Nicholas chose for me.'

'They weren't your type?'

Elise huffed in disgust. 'Most were old enough to be

my father and portly to boot.' The young woman shuddered.

So did Lauren at the image of this gorgeous girl being married to an old coot. In defense of her husband, she said, 'I'm sure Nicholas meant well.'

Elise rolled her big blue eyes. 'His only requirements were that the man be wealthy and titled.'

'In these times, it is important.'

'I have sufficient dower lands to bring into a marriage. I accept that I may not love my husband at first, but I at least want a mate who has qualities I could grow to love.'

Lauren held the woman's fisted hands. 'Is there someone in particular you have in mind?'

Once tense with frustration, Elise's features now crumbled with distress. Tears brimmed in her eyes, and her mouth trembled.

Startled by the sudden change, Lauren said, 'It can't be that bad. Tell me who it is. Are you in love with this man?'

Elise threw her hands up in despair. 'Yes! No! Oh, I don't know. I don't even know him. But . . .' Her voice softened with confusion. 'But I feel as if I do. Does that sound insane?'

Biting back a smile, Lauren thought how insane she was to fall in love with a painting, then with the man himself. 'No, it isn't crazy at all. Tell me who it is. Perhaps I can help.'

A bitter laugh escaped her sister-in-law. 'No one can help with this. It is impossible.'

'Maybe not. Come on, Elise, spill it.'

The young woman quirked her brow at Lauren's choice of words. Then she bit her bottom lip and grimaced. 'Ronan Armstrong.'

Dazed, and sure she hadn't heard right, Lauren felt her mouth drop open. 'Is there perhaps another Ronan Armstrong I'm not aware of?'

A low, pitiful sound rose from Elise as she shook her head.

'Oh, heavens. Of all the men you have to choose from, you fall in love with Bruce Armstrong's son?'

Pressing her hand to her mouth, the young woman shoved herself from the ground and started toward the keep. Lauren tried to follow, but as she pushed herself up, she wobbled off balance and landed on her backside with a startled cry. Instantly, her sister-in-law was at her side, helping her to her feet.

Expecting to have to deal with Elise's tears, Lauren was puzzled when she saw anger flush the woman's face.

'I would not have you speak of this to Nicholas.'

'Why not? He may be able to work something out. If it's what you truly want.'

'No, he would be furious. And if Mother should ever hear of it . . .' She broke off the rest of the statement and shook her head, as if to wipe out the image. 'Besides, I never claimed to love him. It was the way he looked at me when we were at Hadrian's Wall.'

'Like he wanted you.' Lauren recalled the way Ronan's gaze had riveted to Elise, intense and fiercely possessive.

'And hated me, all in the same instant.'

302

Lauren laid her hand on the young woman's arm, wanting to reassure her but knowing there was little chance for Elise and Ronan to ever meet again. 'I'm sorry.'

'Thank you for listening.' With a quick hug, she added, 'I'm so glad you're here. I have never had a sister before. I wonder how I managed to survive so long without you.'

'What is this?'

Both women jumped at Nicholas's cajoling voice. Lauren turned to see him give a subtle nod, dismissing Thomas from his post. With a shaky laugh, she stepped toward her husband, hugging him when he opened his arms to her. 'Just girl-talk.'

He eyed her suspiciously, but let the matter drop. 'You look tired, love. You should be resting.'

Lauren bit her tongue and smiled. She'd heard those two sentences a thousand times during her pregnancy. If he had his wish, she would be sitting before a fire with her feet propped up and a handful of servants waiting on her.

She could admit to herself that she was slightly terrified of going through childbirth without modern medicines and doctors, but treating her like a child wasn't going to help matters. 'And how has your day been?'

He kissed her forehead and chuckled. 'Humor a besotted husband and come inside for a while. I'll challenge you to a game of chess before supper.'

Turning toward the door to the castle, Lauren muttered, 'This should be quick.' After Nicholas had taught her the game, she'd discovered she had no head for strategy, at least none that would compete with her husband.

Lauren stopped and turned to Elise. 'Are you coming?'

A wistful smile touched the young woman's face as she watched them. 'You go ahead. I will finish here.'

Before Lauren could argue, Elise knelt and resumed her task of clipping herbs, only she cut the stalks with such vengeance Lauren couldn't help wondering if Elise wasn't trying to exorcise the vision of a certain Scottish laird's son.

Later that night, Lauren lay beside the naked length of her husband. She watched the fire he'd lit, losing herself in the golden flames that curled and danced in the air. The fire provided the only light in the room, starting bright and hot at the source then fading as it reached the far corners of the room, casting comforting shadows in their private little world.

Nicholas's callused hands rubbed her back, as he'd lovingly done almost every night for the past month, easing the aches that had settled in her body after a day of trailing after Elise, seeing to the never-ending list of chores. She thought of the young woman and the hopeless plight of her sharing her life with the one man who had finally stirred her heart.

Hopeless? Was there such a thing? She had only to look at herself to know that anything was possible. She had been half in love with a man in a painting a few months ago, and here she was now, married and carrying his child and living in the sixteenth century.

She rolled onto her back. Nicholas's hand slid onto her swollen stomach. She had the uncomfortable urge to cover herself. Once she'd started to show she had tried to disguise her body, shield him from having to look at the odd bulge of her stomach, the heavy weight of her breasts. Even her feet were swollen, and, to her, a horrible sight. But Nicholas would have none of it, insisting, 'I would know my wife's body, especially when she carries my child.'

So she endured the nightly inspection of her body with his eyes and hands. She smiled, not able to complain. His 'inspection' usually turned to something warm and intimate. Beautiful in a natural way.

When Nicholas made love to her now, he was slow and gentle, as if they had all the time in the world and nothing more important to do than to see to each other's pleasures.

She studied her husband's face, caught in dark angles by the firelight. His lids were half lowered as he watched the path his hand took over the tight surface of her skin. The lines of his jaw and sensuous lips were relaxed, a state he was in more often than not these days. Looking at him, realizing how lucky she was to have him, she wished the same for his sister. Elise had lived most of her life in a household strained by revenge and loss. She deserved to marry the man of her choice.

'Nicholas?'

'Hmm?'

'Do you think England will have some sort of peace with Scotland anytime soon?' She realized the stupidity of her question as soon as it left her mouth. Even in her own time animosity lingered between the two countries, and there hadn't been a war between them for two hundred years.

His cynical frown only confirmed her thoughts. 'Not likely.'

'But can't we negotiate some sort of peace among the English and Scottish border lords?'

'What is this about, love?' His hand moved up her stomach and cupped her breasts. The heat of his palm sent an unexpected tingle to spread through her body like fingers of lightning. 'Are you still concerned about Armstrong?'

'No – yes.' She licked her dry lips. 'No.' *Liar*. A day didn't pass that she didn't worry about the Scottish laird, but her concerns were dulled as blood thrummed through her mind in warm, pulsing beats.

He kissed the sensitive vein along her neck, chuckling. A throaty, seductive sound that made her body flush and her insides warm. She wanted to tell Nicholas about Elise's feelings for Ronan, then remembered her sister-in-law's wishes that Lauren not mention it. The sensation of her husband's fingers grazing across her nipples turned the last of her thoughts to ashes.

She tilted her head and found his mouth. She breathed him in, his scent, his taste, until her head swam and she thought she might drown. Nicholas stopped the erotic, frustrating tease of her breasts and glided his hand over her stomach, then slowly down to the part of her that had a low-burning ache. He paused, his fingers trailing circles just above the line of her hair.

The way he touched her body, used her protruding shape to arouse her, should have embarrassed her. It didn't. She felt things, experienced things, as if Nicholas knew what she needed at that exact moment.

Her desire built, creating a pulse-beat at her core that made her lift her hips in search of his hand. When his palm and fingers covered her, the tightening ache within her calmed for an instant, as if her body had breathed a sigh of relief.

Lauren closed her eyes and relaxed, focusing on the warm flow that stole through her body. Nicholas pressed his palm against her and a spark flared and spread. Then another. She sucked in a breath, moved against him, kicking the covers from her legs. Cool air bathed her hot skin, adding to the flood of sensations.

'Easy, love,' Nicholas whispered as he bent to stroke her hardened nipple with his tongue.

Easy! Nothing could be easy when he touched her like this. And she told him so. He only raised his head and gave her a wickedly satisfied grin.

His fingers parted her flesh and delved deeper inside her, stroking, pressing, twisting her into a coil of pleasure. Her body clenched and strained for release.

Lauren pushed herself into the bed, her head thrown back. 'Nic . . .!' He caught her cry with his mouth, absorbing it and her shudders as she soared over the edge and floated in a dark, safe void.

307

Soft cries broke from deep within her throat. 'I love you, Nicholas,' she whispered between shallow breaths. Expressing feelings she'd been so terrified of before came easily now. They were like the air she breathed, the food she ate – she needed her love for Nicholas to survive.

'I know.' Despite his smile, frustration shadowed his eyes.

Lauren waited for him to say the words. When they didn't come, she closed her eyes. Not once had he admitted he loved her, though she knew he did. It was in his actions, in his eyes when he looked at her, in the way he cared for her, as if she were a precious gift he was afraid of losing. That was enough, she reminded herself. She didn't *need* to hear the words.

Nicholas kissed her neck, her shoulder, working his way to her breasts while he stroked her calming body into a fevered pitch once more. Feeling empty, wanting him inside her, she turned onto her side and pressed her back against his chest.

'You are impatient tonight,' he said as he slipped his arm beneath her neck, then clasped her breast in his hand, lifting and molding its heavy weight. His other hand stayed between her legs, as if reluctant to release her.

The tip of his hardened shaft touched her. He pressed against her, then drew away. His hand squeezed her tighter.

'Nicholas, please, don't tease me.'

She felt the muscles of his arms and chest tense. Holding her to him, he drove inside. She dropped her head against his shoulder. His jaw brushed her hair, and his breath turned ragged and strained in her ear.

They'd found this position, him entering her from behind, because of her swollen stomach. But the sensations were so intense, so explosive, she didn't know if she would ever give it up. With Nicholas's hard frame pressed against her back his hands were free to roam, to clasp and explore her breasts, her sides, her core.

Her release came with a sudden burst. Her body, so tightly wound, uncoiled like a cat stretching out beneath the hot rays of sunlight. She could swear she heard herself purr.

She closed her eyes and moved with her husband as he strained toward his own climax. His breathing shifted, turning harsh, as if the air burned his lungs. She opened her eyes to watch his body. His long leg was draped across hers. His muscles flexed beneath skin. She ran her hand across his lean hip, hot and slick with sweat, then down to his hard thigh.

'Lauren,' he moaned, his voice deep and husky.

She turned her head. His mouth closed over hers, devouring, sucking, pulling. He drove into her harder, trembling with each thrust. Finally, he threw his head back, his teeth clenched. She tightened her hold on his leg and watched his body strain as he emptied himself into her.

Corded muscles stood out against his tanned neck. His arms flexed around her. His entire body went taut, poised as if he were in pain. Then he relaxed. The lines etching his face softened. His tight hold on her eased. He wrapped his body around hers, pulling her against him as if trying to make her a permanent part of himself.

Lauren burrowed into him, feeling safe and small and cherished. Nicholas kissed the side of her face, the curve of her jaw, then moved to the valley between her neck and shoulder. He ran his hand down her arm then laced his fingers with hers, curling them, holding them tight.

'I don't think I shall ever tire of this.'

Lauren resisted the urge to poke his ribs with her elbow. 'I should hope not.'

His beard-roughened face grazed her cheek when he smiled.

'That isn't the kind of statement I can deal well with in my condition.'

'Are you worried I will ease my lust elsewhere, wife?' he asked, amusement lifting his brow.

'The thought might have crossed my mind. It's hard to think of myself as attractive when I'm as round as I am tall.' To prove her point she shifted in his arms to face him. Nicholas grunted and scooted back a little, to make room for her stomach. 'See what I mean?'

He kissed the tip of her nose. 'You are beautiful.'

'To another walrus, maybe.'

Laughing, Nicholas reached down and pulled the covers up around them. He drew her into his arms so her head rested on his chest. She entwined her legs with his as he kissed her temple. 'I . . .' he began.

Lauren looked at him, hoping she might finally hear the words that her mind knew didn't need to be said but her heart ached to hear.

Silent longing darkened his blue eyes to black. 'You are everything that is beautiful, Lauren.'

She tucked her head beneath his chin and smiled. They weren't the words she'd hoped to hear, but they were close enough.

CHAPTER 19

A loud crash and muffled oaths startled Lauren into rising halfway out of her chair. The warning cluck of Glynis's tongue reminded her of her promise not to move until Nicholas returned. Sitting beside her before the fire in the main hall, Glynis paused in mending a pair of wool hose to give Lauren a disapproving shake of her head.

'I was just going to see if Thomas needed any help,' Lauren said as she sank back into her seat.

The old woman narrowed her thinning gray brows. 'I been tell'n ye, Lady Elise can handle the preparations witho' your 'elp, my lady.'

'Walking is good exercise.' When Glynis made a tsk-tsk-tsk noise, Lauren gripped the arms of her chair in frustration, her mangled needlepoint forgotten in her lap.

'Lord Kenward, 'e gave me specific instructions. Ye are to rest if ye want to attend the Yuletide celebration.

Lauren relaxed against her chair with an exasperated huff. She eyed the woman she'd saved from the chore of collecting firewood, thinking Glynis should show some loyalty toward her. Instead, her maid had turned into Nicholas's guard dog, making sure Lauren didn't walk, lift or move without his permission.

She had repeatedly argued with her husband that she was *only* seven months pregnant, a condition that thousands of women dealt with everyday. But he refused to relent. Today he had threatened to lock her in their bedchamber if she moved from her chair in the hall.

She felt far removed from the woman she'd been a few months ago. That Lauren had been strong enough to see herself through the heartache of losing her parents, then starting her own veterinary practice. She might not have been happy, but she'd been independent.

But, she added with a tender grin, she had gladly given up that life for one where she had to learn how to be a mistress of a castle, a wife to a man who had turned into a mother hen, and soon she would become a mother herself.

Images of Nicholas, her powerful, hard-as-stone husband, as he'd been this morning wavered in her mind. Settling her in a chair by the fire, a worried frown had narrowed his eyes and pulled at his mouth. The vision lingered, softening her irritation at being treated like a helpless child. His illogical fear for her had her emotions flipping from amusement to furious to everything in between. Yet his concern was also endearing. Her frustration teetered with the urge to laugh. She gave in to it, her shoulders shaking.

'Are ye well, my lady?' Glynis asked, lowering her mending to pat Lauren's arm.

She gripped the old woman's weather-roughened hand and squeezed affectionately. 'I'm fine, Glynis. But I think I'm suffering from cabin fever. I have too much free time to think.'

Sobering, she looked into the fire's steady flames. She had yet to pin down the reason for Nicholas's overprotectiveness, and he refused to discuss the subject. If anyone should be frightened and cautious, it should be her. With each advancing day of her pregnancy, her fear rose another notch.

It was the nights she feared the most, when she couldn't escape Edith's voice. '. . . *Lord Kenward died that night, but his wife, heavy with their first child, lifted her husband's sword in anguished fury . . .*'

Lauren forced her thoughts behind a mental door and slammed it shut. She wouldn't think about that. It wouldn't happen. It couldn't. Life had been peaceful, almost perfect during the past months. Yet as she struggled to convince herself that history wouldn't repeat itself she remembered Laird Armstrong's rough voice bellowing, '. . . *ye shall suffer, Kenward, and suffer greatly! . . . we shall meet again, and soon. That I vow!*'

Lauren rose and moved to a stool close to the fire, desperate to ease the sudden chill clinging to her heart.

The celebration quickly rose to a joyous cacophony of tenants and castle folk alike, drinking the Kenward ale and helping themselves to roasted beef that had been cooking on the spits since the previous night.

Catching the spicy scent of cooked food, Lauren's stomach growled, a loud, savage sound. Nicholas grinned and stole a small meat pie from a vendor and gave it to her with a wink. With one hand wrapped around his muscled arm, she sighed and ate the rich pastry, sharing bites with her husband.

Following him through the bailey, she nodded to people she'd met, receiving smiles and words of thanks in return. Lauren wanted to believe they were sincere, but she still sensed a hesitancy from them. Today, she refused to let it affect her.

Nicholas stopped next to a group of his men-at-arms. 'How goes it, Jacobson?'

The older soldier lowered his tankard of ale and scanned the curtain wall. Lauren followed his gaze. Guards with bows strapped over their shoulders were stationed at certain intervals, but most were watching the festivities in the bailey. 'All's quiet, my lord. As it 'as been for months now. Not so much as a burned cottage to disturb the peace.'

Lauren shifted her gaze to Jacobson. 'You sound as if you're disappointed.'

'Aye, mum, peace is good for the villagers and farmers, but too much of it makes an old soldier like me nervous. Makes me wonder what the Scots are up to.'

Lauren resisted the urge to wring her hands. She knew all too well how Jacobson felt. What was Armstrong doing right now? Was he plotting some sort of revenge, or had he forgotten his threats against Nicholas? Those relentless, unanswered questions prevented the tranquil life she'd found from being completely perfect.

'All will be well, Jacobson,' Nicholas said in a surly tone.

Glancing at her husband, Lauren saw his warning frown directed at the older soldier. Everyone fell into an uneasy silence, making her suspicious. Before she could question them, Nicholas took her arm and led her toward a table where tankards of ale were set out. He retrieved one for himself and found a cup of milk for her.

'What was all that about?' she asked.

His hold on her arm tightened. 'Nothing. Jacobson tends to overreact at times. You are to pay him no mind.'

Had her nerves not tightened at that instant, Lauren would have laughed at his presumptuous order. 'Is that so?' She stopped and stared at him. 'You know something, don't you?'

He returned her gaze for a full minute before kissing her. 'Come, there is something I wish to show you.'

Lauren followed, knowing he was avoiding her question. And, God help her, she let him. She didn't really want to know if it was something bad. Didn't want to think about what might happen to them in the near future. She shook her head, thinking it odd that she now considered the past her future. Besides, if it had something to do with Armstrong, Nicholas would tell her.

He led her to the farthest corner of the large bailey where a huge crowd had gathered. Skirting then, she

316

clasped her hands over her mouth and gaped at the temporary jousting field. She followed her husband up a short flight of stairs to the raised dais and took her seat.

With a hand pressed to her chest, she absorbed the incredible pageantry below. Several tents flanked the crowd. Their bright fabrics created an array of color; red, blue and green stripes set the festive mood. Horses, covered from head to tail with decorative colored cloth, pranced and snorted, seeming as eager to begin the competition as the knights nearby. Wearing thick, cumbersome armor that glinted like silver fire in the sun, the soldiers wore surcoats that matched their stallions' trappings.

Other young boys struggled beneath the weight of blunt-tipped lances and heavy shields. Excited cheers rose as two knights, one clad in deep purple, the other in bright yellow, emerged astride their mounts onto the jousting field. They stopped at opposite ends of the field and faced each other, waiting.

Trumpets blasted as Nicholas rose. Cheers from the crowd crested for another two minutes before they finally died. Silence vibrated around them. Excited tension hung thick in the air, as if the entire crowd held their breaths. 'Let the games begin!'

Lauren started to laugh at Nicholas's cliché, but a startled gasp tore from her throat when the knights charged one another. Before she could draw a breath to scream, the yellow knight's lance struck the purple man in the shoulder, knocking him from his mount. He landed on his back with a harsh thud and the rattle

317

of armor. The crowd went wild. The soldier didn't move.

Unable to take her eyes off the man, Lauren grabbed Nicholas's arm and asked in a hoarse whisper, 'Is he dead?'

Her husband chuckled and patted her hand. 'Nay, love. Unconscious, most likely.'

Four squires ran out and struggled to lift the knight and lay him on top of his shield. Amid grunts and reddened faces, the four boys lifted him and carried him off to the side. The yellow knight returned to his starting place and another knight, this one wearing green and gold, took the opposite end.

Lauren pressed her hand to her throat, felt the wild beat of her pulse, the gleam of sweat on her skin. 'How long does this go on?'

'Until there is a winner.'

'How many men are competing?' she asked.

'Twenty.'

'Oh, jeez.' She took a deep breath and looked away as the two horses set off toward each other. She squeezed her eyes shut and flinched when she heard the thud of crashing lances. When there wasn't a cheer, she dared a peek. Neither knight had fallen, but both had broken their wooden poles. Retrieving new ones, they turned and charged again.

This time she couldn't look away as they raced past each other, their lances splintering as they caught each other's shields. 'They're crazy.'

Nicholas looked at her, his eyes lit with amusement. 'This is a test of skills.'

'They could be hurt or killed.'

'Their weapons are blunt. Serious injuries are a rare event, and usually only happen when someone is careless. This is a contest of endurance as well as ability in striking a well-placed blow while avoiding one.'

Lauren realized that in a time of constant unrest what these men learned on the jousting field might save their lives in a real battle.

'Do you ever do this?' she asked her husband, feeling a wave of nausea roll over her. She breathed in a lung full of dust from the field, the scent of horse and sweat.

'Aye.'

She took his hand. 'But you're not today?'

'I did not wish to distress you.'

Lauren grunted and pressed her other hand to her stomach. 'Distress? I'd probably faint if I saw you out there.'

Looking incensed, he leaned toward her. 'Have you so little faith in your husband?'

She kissed the firm line of his mouth and squeezed his hand. 'I have all the faith in the world in you. I just don't think I could watch you fight.'

Two hours passed before a champion was announced – the yellow knight who had started the games, a man named Sir Redmond. The satisfied crowd headed toward the inner bailey where a feast would be held in Sir Redmond's honor.

Lauren leaned against her husband as he slid an arm around her back. She closed her eyes, absorbed the sound of laughing children as a group of them dashed past, followed by a pack of excited dogs. The scent of cooked meat and rich spices floated on the cool breeze. She opened her eyes and sighed.

Dusk crept closer, turning the sky soft blue, tinged with pink. She paused, trying to commit every detail to memory. Not so much what she saw, but what she felt. The sense of belonging, the happy laughter of children, the good-natured scolding of mothers. Through it all she sensed everyone clinging to the moment, as if the entire village knew each day together was precious, a gift of time so easily snatched away.

'Lauren? Where have you gone?'

She looked at her husband's questioning gaze and smiled. 'I was thinking about how happy I am here.'

He kissed her brow and led her through the dozens of tables that filled the inner bailey. Torches had been lit in preparation for the encroaching darkness. Women hurried about, carrying trenchers filled with fresh vegetables, bread and meat. Others carried pitchers of ale.

Making her way to the raised dais, Lauren stopped when she came face to face with Lady Kenward. She hadn't seen Nicholas's mother all day. A familiar tension gathered inside her, chasing away the serenity she'd felt. Damn! For once she wished they could have a simple meal without walking on eggshells. Especially tonight, with everyone in such good spirits. She took a steadying breath to prepare herself, determined to make tonight different.

'Good evening, Lady Kenward. It's good to see you out.'

The older woman stared at her, her wrinkled jaw flexed as if she clenched her teeth to keep from speaking.

'We missed you at the jousting field.' Lauren's voice faded, as did her effort to make peace with the woman. How could there possibly be a truce when Lady Kenward refused to acknowledge her? Like a reassuring touch, she felt Nicholas's presence behind her.

'Mother,' Nicholas said with quiet patience.

Lady Kenward tilted her chin in acknowledgment. 'My son, the festivities are going well. Elise has done a superb job seeing that all was made ready. A duty your *wife* should have seen to.'

'I did not wish the burden to be placed on my wife in her condition,' Nicholas said in response.

Lady Kenward's hard gaze sliced to Lauren's rounded stomach. In an unconscious move, Lauren raised her hands to cover her unborn child.

At that moment, Elise hurried forward. 'We must take our seats. Please,' she said, her voice stressed, 'everyone is watching.'

Lauren took her place while Nicholas raised his tankard and made a toast to his people. She didn't follow what he said. Her mind lingered over finding a solution to ease Lady Kenward's hostility. But the festive cheers rose, breaking through Lauren's futile thoughts. Mentally shaking herself, she lifted her cup, took a small sip of her cool, thick milk and joined the revelry.

The pleasant buzz of chattering people filled the air as people loaded plates with an overwhelming array of food. Lauren passed on the roasted peacock, its bronzy-green and blue feathers splayed in a beautiful arch, and settled for a lean cut of beef.

Once finished with her dinner, she pushed the plate away and sat back to watch and enjoy the people around her. To her right Elise took occasional bites of food as she spoke with Sir Redmond, a handsome man in a rough, stoic way. Lauren half hoped Elise was working past her feelings for Ronan Armstrong.

Though Nicholas was in deep conversation with a neighboring lord, he constantly touched her. His hand covered the side of her stomach, as if waiting for a kick. When the baby moved, Lauren saw a slight smile lift her husband's mouth. Then his hand lowered to her thigh, where he gave her an affectionate squeeze.

The blast of a trumpet rent the air. People were startled, and a hush fell over the grounds. All eyes turned to the curtain wall of the lower bailey where the trumpeter was stationed.

Nicholas rose to his feet.

The horn blasted again. With torches lighting his path, a guard ran toward them. Lauren's heart thudded against her chest as she rose and gripped her husband's arm.

A deep rumble joined the alarm, then a loud, clattering sound. 'What is that noise?' Lauren asked, though in her heart she knew the answer.

'The alarm to lower the portcullis.'

'Oh, God, no,' Lauren whispered.

The guard stopped before the dais. It was Thomas. The young archer still wore Lauren's felt riding hat, dented and filthy as it was. His brown eyes widened with anxiety, or perhaps it was fear. His chest heaved as he fought for breath. 'My lord, an army approaches!'

'Do you know who it is?'

'No, my lord, they crept near the castle after night fell.'

'God's death! Jacobson, Kenric!'

Lauren tried to draw a breath, tried to speak, but her chest clenched with suffocating force. The two soldiers leapt to Nicholas's unfinished command. Then, all at once, people rose from their seats and ran. Crying women clutched their children and dodged the men, who shouted orders for armor and weapons to be prepared. Others moved the tables to clear the area.

Nicholas grasped her arms and turned her to face him. 'Go inside the castle with Elise and remain in our bedchamber!'

'No!' Lauren cried. 'Nicholas, tell me it's not Armstrong! Tell me!' Tears fell, clogging her throat, choking her.

He drew her against him. 'Please, love,' he whispered against her hair. 'Go inside. I must see to my men.'

Lauren pushed against his chest, breaking free. 'You can't!' Her voice broke as she neared hysterics. 'You promised you wouldn't fight.'

Nicholas raised his hand toward her, but she slapped it away. His eyes narrowed. 'I never promised I wouldn't fight, Lauren.'

'Yes, you did.'

'I promised to do whatever I could to keep from being harmed. I shall keep my word, but I cannot let my men fight without me.'

'But . . .'

Elise put her arm around Lauren's shoulder. 'He must go, Lauren, or we will all suffer. 'Tis his duty.'

Shivering with helpless fear, Lauren took a step back and looked at her husband. In the flickering torchlight, his raven hair was a shade darker than his eyes. His squared jaw was set, and a wild pulse beat at the base of his throat. He was everything she loved: strength, passion, and scars. He was slipping through her fingers. And there was nothing she could do about it.

'It's happening, Nicholas. Don't you see?' She looked around the bailey, feeling strangely detached, yet horribly connected, as armed men hurried up the stairs to the parapet. 'The legend is coming full circle tonight.'

'No, Lauren!' He shook her by the shoulders. 'There is no legend. All will be well. Just do as I say and go inside.' He pressed a hurried kiss to her mouth, then turned to leave. 'Thomas, stay with my wife and make sure she does not leave her bed-chamber.'

Lauren watched her husband run through a throng of panicked villagers, then head for the stairs leading to the curtain wall. She shivered and gulped air into her lungs, terrified she might faint, praying she would. Accusations bombarded her mind. Silent screams raged inside her.

She'd risked everything by loving Nicholas, sure she could save him. But she hadn't done enough. *Not enough!*

Now it was too late.

CHAPTER 20

Lauren sat in the corner of the window seat with her back rigid and her hands clasped in her lap. She refused to lie down, as Elise suggested, or drink the spiced wine to calm her nerves. Hours had passed since Thomas had escorted her to her bedchamber. Unbearable hours of sitting and waiting for news, for something to happen.

She pressed her hand to the cold pane and searched the dark bailey below her. Each time she saw a man dash across the grounds her heart stopped, her hope soared, thinking it might be Nicholas. Each time she realized it wasn't her husband returning to the castle fear pressed harder against her. It breathed down her neck like a dangerous beast.

'Thomas,' Lauren said, her voice sounding distant to her own ears, 'I want you to find Nicholas and learn what's happening.'

'Nay, my lady,' the boy answered from his stool by the fire. 'My lord would have me head if I leave ye here alone.'

The helplessness, the dread, the defeat she battled

pushed itself to the surface. Rounding on the boy, her fists clenched at her sides, she ordered, 'You think I won't do the same if you don't listen to me? Go! I have to know who has come to attack us.'

Thomas looked from her to Elise. The younger woman nodded her agreement. As Thomas rushed from the room, Elise took Lauren by the shoulders and led her to the bed. 'You must lie down, Lauren. Nothing will happen tonight.'

Lauren followed only because she was too exhausted to argue. Sitting on Nicholas's side of the bed, she picked up his pillow and wrapped her arms around it. She buried her face into its softness, breathed in her husband's spicy scent. 'How do you know?'

'It is difficult to fight in the dark. Nicholas will prepare his men tonight. At dawn, the fighting will begin, unless Nicholas can come to terms with the other lord.'

'Oh, God,' Lauren cried softly. She rubbed a hand over her brow and tried to think. How could she prevent the battle? What could she do to make a difference? Go outside the wall to speak with Armstrong? As if she could manage to escape the castle grounds! There was the opening the soldier had forced her down, but she couldn't risk climbing a rope ladder in her condition. Besides, she didn't believe the Laird would listen to her. Ronan, perhaps . . .

'You must rest. Think of the baby and Nicholas. You do not wish to worry him, do you?'

No! Yes! Oh, heaven help her, she wanted him here, safe with her. She wanted to touch his face, feel his

327

arms around her. A jolt of reality struck her, and she sucked in a panicked breath. She might never be able to do those things again. Their child might never know its father.

Lauren squeezed her eyes closed. She couldn't think that way. Nicholas wouldn't be harmed. He would come back to her. He would. He wouldn't leave her. Not when they'd finally found each other. Not when they had a child on the way.

'Lauren?' Elise touched her shoulder. 'What did you mean about the legend coming full circle tonight?'

Lauren massaged her stomach for reassurance. 'If it's Armstrong out there, then this is the end of everything.'

The sound of running footsteps interrupted Elise's next question. Thomas hurried into the room and stopped beside them. He bent over, panting, and rested his hands on his knees. Between gulps of air, he said, 'I could not find my lord. But I did find Jacobson.'

'And? What did he say?' Lauren asked, fear rising up her throat.

''Tis Laird Armstrong. The old man shouted that he's come to finish the Kenward line at last.'

'Thomas!' Elise scolded.

Lauren couldn't hear if Elise said anything else. Her mind had already shut down, denying Thomas's words. She felt herself slide into darkness, felt hands grab at her arms and body. Then she felt nothing at all.

★ ★ ★

Lauren awoke to the muted sound of shouting. Her eyes flew open. Sunlight washed across her bed. The bright glare reached the cold fireplace, the two heavy chairs placed before it and the oversized tub that sat in the corner.

The shrill cries came again. Lauren rolled onto her side and pushed herself to her feet as fast as her swollen body would allow. She swayed as her mind spun with the quick action. The instant it passed, she made her way to Elise, who stood at the window with her arms wrapped around her waist.

'Elise, what is it? What's happened?' Lauren demanded.

The younger woman turned and tried to stop her. 'No! You must . . .'

'Oh, my God!' Lauren pressed her hands against the window pane. She moved her palms over the glass, hoping to wipe away the scene outside.

Nicholas's men filled the parapet. They took turns at the crenels, stepping forward to release their arrows on the encroaching army, then retreating to prepare another shot. Armstrong's men sent arrows over the curtain wall, close to her soldiers' heads. Some landed without harm in the lower bailey. One man was struck in the shoulder, his cry filtering into the safety of her room.

'I've got to go to him!' Lauren turned toward the door, but Elise and Thomas caught her arms. 'Let me go! I have to help.'

'There's naught ye can do, my lady,' Thomas said with quiet emphasis.

Lauren stilled. She could hardly breathe for the

pounding of her heart against her chest. Pulling free, she returned to the window and sank onto the padded bench. Flames leapt from the thatched roof of the mason's lodge. Boys too young to fight, along with men too old, hauled pails of water to extinguish the blaze. She watched in disbelief as a ball of fire sailed over the wall and landed in a pile of hay.

'My lady,' Thomas said from behind her. 'I must go 'elp them.'

'Of course.' Grabbing his hand, she pulled him toward the door. 'We'll all go.'

'No, my lady,' Thomas argued.

'It is too dangerous,' Elise said in unison with him.

'If I can't stop the battle then I can at least help keep our home from burning down!'

Her wardens only stared at her, their expressions unrelenting. Another cry of pain reached her room and made her insides go cold. 'All right. I won't go into the bailey.'

Thomas and Elise sighed in relief.

'I'll turn the hall into a hospital.' Lauren retrieved her basket of herbs from a nearby table. 'Thomas, tell everyone the injured men are to be brought here.'

'But . . .' Elise said.

Lauren laid her hand on Elise's shoulder. 'No buts. This is the only way I can help Nicholas. There are men . . .' She tried to say 'dying' but she couldn't force the word past her throat.

Elise started to argue once more, but Lauren stopped her.

'I have to do this.'

* * *

Time passed in a haze of blood and cries for help. Lauren automatically moved from one man to another, cleaning and wrapping their wounds, then moving on. Blood stained her hands and her green silk gown, but she refused to think about whose it might be. When she found a soldier beyond her help, she fought the endless sting of tears as she made him comfortable while he slowly bled to death.

Each time another injured man was carried through the door she paused to see who he was, her body tensing as she searched the man's face. Only when she was certain it wasn't Nicholas did she breathe a shameful sigh of relief.

'Come, you must rest.'

Lauren looked into Elise's tired blue eyes. The young woman had worked hard all day, following Lauren's instructions, never complaining or shrinking from the acrid smell of blood and gruesome body wounds.

Lauren looked around the crowded hall. 'There are men who still need to be treated.'

'The worst have been tended to. Please, Lauren, return to your bedchamber and lie down.'

With a trembling hand, Lauren pushed a strand of hair out of her eyes. She realized she was beyond exhaustion. She couldn't remember the last time she had eaten – not that she could stomach the thought of food right now. But she had to think of the baby. She couldn't be ill when Nicholas returned. He would need her.

'I have to go upstairs anyway. I'm out of yarrow to

stanch their wounds.' Lauren gathered her empty basket and headed upstairs.

She spotted Lady Kenward near the front door. The old woman twisted a strand of rosary beads in her bony hands. Throughout the grueling day, Nicholas's mother had not spared a glance or shown any concern for the wounded or slain brought inside. She'd paced the foyer and watched the battle progress.

Lauren knew Lady Kenward had eyes for only her son. In a way, Lauren was comforted by her mother-in-law's vigil, because she couldn't possibly have stood by and watched while Nicholas risked his life in the madness outside.

Entering her bedchamber, she felt the quiet, familiar surroundings envelop her like a welcoming hug. It was the one place she felt Nicholas's presence. In this room they had lain in bed and planned their future. She held onto those plans now. She wouldn't give up. She believed in her husband, not in a four-hundred-year-old legend that had to be more myth than fact.

It had to be.

She filled her basket with a batch of freshly clipped yarrow leaves, then paused by the window. The sun had started its descent behind the castle. In the dimming light, shadows crept across the bailey floor, reaching toward the curtain wall. Most of the soldiers were descending the steps. She saw Nicholas give another command, then follow the other men down. She stifled a cry with her hand. The fighting had stopped! Maybe it was over. Maybe . . .

Nicholas crossed the bailey, his strides long and

even. A laugh broke from her chest, but quickly turned into a sob. She clasped her hands over her mouth and drank in the sight of him.

Dark stains splattered his armor. *Blood.* So much blood. Somehow she knew it wasn't his. He was whole, and healthy, and alive! As he reached the inner bailey, he paused and lifted his head, his loose hair clinging to his sweaty face. As if sensing her presence, he immediately spotted her standing at the window. His eyes lit up. He gave her a devastating smile and raised his arm to wave.

Then she saw it. Time slowed as she drew a breath to scream. '*Nicholas!*' She dropped her basket and hit the window with her fists.

His smile vanished, and he turned. The single arrow struck his side, knocking him off his feet. He hit the ground with a thud of metal and flesh she could hear in her room.

'*No!*' Lauren's legs gave out from under her. Her knees hit the wooden floor. Shards of pain shot up her thighs. She couldn't draw a breath, couldn't release the screams inside her head.

Clutching the window seal with one hand and her stomach with the other, she pulled herself up. Her breath became wrenching sobs. 'Nicholas, no, oh, God, please, no.'

A dozen people were at his side in an instant. Lady Kenward fell to the ground and collapsed across her son's chest. Her frail body shook, and the wrenching sound of her wails carried through the castle walls.

Lauren's mind snapped into action. She grabbed

her basket of herbs. She had to get to Nicholas. She could save him. She knew about healing and repairing wounds. She had to reach him. *She had to!*

Sweat coated her skin. The acrid stench of fear clung to her as she raced through the long corridors. Rounding a corner, she felt a hot flash of pain pierce her stomach. She stumbled and caught the wall before she fell. Her breath turned harsh and she bit back the need to cry out.

She heard shouts and running feet in the hall. She couldn't stop now, not when Nicholas's life depended on her. Clenching her side, she limped to the stairs and made her way down. She skirted injured men lying on the stone floor and hurried to the courtyard. She stopped on the landing and stared in confusion.

Nicholas was gone!

She staggered a few steps, then turned around. Her mind swam with dizziness and her vision darkened at the edges. She gulped air.

'Where? Where is he?' she pleaded to no one. Then she spotted Thomas slumped on the ground near the smoldering remains of a wagon. His head was bent and his narrow shoulders shook.

Running, she dropped to her knees in front of him. She gripped his arms and jerked him upright. Tears streaked his soot-covered cheeks. His eyes were red and swollen and filled with agony.

'Where is he, Thomas?' Lauren asked, tears blinding her own eyes and choking her voice.

'He's . . . he's gone, my lady.'

Panic pressed against all sides of Lauren's mind.

She shook his shoulders. 'He was just here! Where did they take him?'

Thomas drew a shuddering breath. 'Lady Kenward took him.'

Lauren moved to leave, but Thomas clasped her wrist, sobbing. 'There's naught ye can do for 'im, my lady. He's dead.'

'No.' She shook her head. 'No, he's not dead. I can save him. I know I can.'

'They took 'im to the chapel.'

Lauren raced across the bailey. Tears streamed down her face – as much from the fear of losing Nicholas as from the pain knifing through her stomach, cutting off her breath. *Oh, God, not the baby.*

When the chapel came into view, her steps faltered. Villagers and soldiers had amassed around the old stone structure. The women wept into their skirts. The soldiers who'd served at Nicholas's side throughout the day seemed to fight against doing the same. Gradually they all turned to her, quietly staring at her with sorrowful eyes.

Suffocating pressure squeezed Lauren's chest. She pressed a hand to her mouth, smothering her cry.

Jacobson came forward, his rugged features haggard and drawn. He clasped her free hand. 'I'm sorry, my lady.'

She jerked free. 'I have to see him. Where is he?'

The old soldier nodded toward the chapel. 'Inside, but Lady Kenward refuses to allow anyone to enter.'

'We'll see about that.' Lauren climbed the chapel

steps, but two guards blocked the door. 'Move out of my way!'

'Nay, my lady, we 'ave orders not to permit anyone to pass.'

She stared at them in disbelief, then pushed one guard with all her strength. Two more men in uniform appeared and gripped her arms, pulling her back. 'He's my husband, damn you! I can save him if you let me through.'

The men exchanged distressed glances. ''Tis too late, my lady,' the one she'd hit said.

'He's my husband. I have a right to be with him.'

'We must take our orders from Lady Kenward.'

'*I'm* Lady Kenward!' She turned to Jacobson and Kenric. 'Why are they doing this? Why won't they let me see him!' She grabbed a handful of yarrow from her basket and shook it in the air. Her voice shrieked with helpless hysteria. 'I can save him!'

The heavy oak door opened and Elise slipped between the guards. She pulled Lauren against her, but she pushed free. She didn't need comfort. Nicholas wasn't dead. *He wasn't!* She would know it, feel it in her soul.

'Lauren, you cannot help him now,' Elise whispered through her tears.

'He's not dead.' Lauren clung to each word. She had to believe.

'Lauren . . .'

'He's not!'

'He is . . .' The truth haunted Elise's eyes.

'But I could have helped him.' Lauren held up the

336

crushed green herbs in her hand. Her arm shook violently. The sharp pounding of her heart struck her chest like a knife, striking her over and over again. 'He promised. He promised to stay out of the way!'

Her voice broke into a helpless sob as her mind replayed the last time she'd seen him. He'd spotted her at the window and had paused to wave. Had he kept walking, the arrow would have missed him. 'Oh, God, it's my fault! He's dead because of me.'

'No, Lauren.' Elise gripped her shoulders and gave her a firm shake. 'You are not to blame.'

Panic and guilt closed over her like a iron fist. 'Yes, I am! I knew this would happen. I've always known.' She struggled to breathe. 'It . . . it was in the legend, and I didn't do enough to stop it!'

'I knew you would be the death of my son.' The cold voice came from behind Lauren.

She caught her breath and turned to face Lady Kenward. The older woman stood at the top of the chapel steps. As if to protect her, two guards were positioned close beside her.

'Why are you keeping me from him?' Lauren demanded.

'You no longer have a place here,' Lady Kenward answered, her tone deadly calm.

'As his wife, I have every right.' Anger joined the fear trembling inside her limbs. The pain in her stomach burned hotter, spreading like streaks of fire, but she couldn't give in to it. If she left now, she might never see Nicholas again.

'My son's murderer has no rights in this household.'

'No.' Lauren shook her head. 'He's not dead. I won't believe you until I see him.' Then she whispered, 'I have to see him, please.'

'Lauren,' Elise urged, 'let me take you to your room.'

Lauren felt the last of her strength crumble beneath the weight of her living nightmare. Numb, she let Elise pull her away from the chapel. She hadn't given up. She would come back to see her husband. She had to. But with guards posted at the door and Lady Kenward standing vigilant, they'd make sure she couldn't get inside now.

As she neared the edge of the crowd, her mind kept repeating, *This isn't real. This isn't real.* But everyone around her openly wept with grief. A woman reached out and touched her sleeve and whispered a prayer for Nicholas's soul.

Lauren clenched her hands to her stomach. She didn't want to believe this was happening, but how could she not? Everyone was suffering. They'd lost as much as she. Life without Nicholas? Her mind began to shut down.

'I'll tell ye, with Lord Kenward dead, we'll have to surrender to Armstrong.'

Lauren halted her steps and looked at the soldier who had spoken to another man. Both men were streaked with dirt. One soldier had a bloody bandage wrapped around his forearm. Their eyes were red-rimmed, their faces drawn and hollowed with the look of defeat.

338

She stared at the pair in horror. 'You can't quit.'

'Beg pardon, my lady, but we 'ave no lord to lead us.'

A vicious tremor struck her body. She drew a quivering breath. 'Nicholas would want you to continue the fight without him.' Raising her voice, she said, 'This is your home. You can't give up.'

Lady Kenward descended one step and pointed a finger at her. 'I order you to leave here at once. Now, or the guards will forcefully remove you!'

Finding Jacobson, Lauren clasped his hand. She moved on an impulse she couldn't understand, an emotion buried deep inside her. 'I need Nicholas's sword. Please get it for me.'

Jacobson's gaze shifted from Lauren to Lady Kenward. He clenched his jaw and his ruddy complexion deepened. His eyes blazed. 'Aye, my lady. Wait here.'

When Lady Kenward refused to allow Jacobson to pass, Lauren said, 'I will not leave without his sword.'

Shooting Lauren an angry glare, Lady Kenward turned and entered the chapel. She reappeared a moment later with the broad, gleaming sword in hand. It was too heavy for her, and the old woman dragged it across the stone steps. The eerie screech sliced the air like a death wail.

Jacobson took it and brought it to Lauren.

She closed her fingers around the hilt. The finely tooled metal was smooth and cold against her skin. With both hands, she raised the sword above her, and felt the symbolic move rip the last of her heart from her body.

Lauren staggered beneath its weight. 'Listen to me!'

Silence fell over the bailey. She felt the eyes of every man, woman and child on her. She felt their despair, the fear that rose above them. She wouldn't let it end this way. She'd lost everything, but she would give them hope and the future they deserved. It was what Nicholas would want for them.

'This isn't over,' she cried, her voice breaking. Tears burned hot behind her eyes. 'We have to stand and fight. Now! We'll make Armstrong regret the day he stepped foot on Kenward land.'

No one spoke. Silence linked with doubt pulsed around her. Lauren held the sword, her raised arms growing numb. The heavy blade swayed above her. She willed herself not to drop it. Then Jacobson laid his hand over hers, lending her his strength. Kenric joined them and clasped his over Jacobson's.

Tears rolled from her eyes. 'Do we fight? Or do we allow Nicholas's death to stand for nothing?'

The battle cry she had waited for came in a deafening roar. Men waved their fists and weapons in the air. Women hugged and cried on each other's shoulders. Lauren released her grip on the sword, allowing Jacobson and Kenric to take the weight.

Tension filled the air as the two soldiers issued orders for the attack. She watched, not feeling, not thinking, forcing her own loss into a shadowed corner of her mind. She'd done everything she could. The rest was up to Nicholas's men. They would defeat Armstrong's army. Of that she had no doubt.

340

It was in the legend, and every part of it had come true.

She'd lost Nicholas despite all her warnings, all her fears. Waves of despair rose inside her. She pushed away from the crowd and headed for the castle in a numbed daze. Once in her bedroom, she slammed the door shut, feeling empty, feeling as though she'd left a part of herself in the chapel, lying alone in a cold, vacant room. She clenched her fists. She couldn't do this! She couldn't let go of the pain, give it space in her heart. The hurt was too big, too powerful. It would kill her.

She paced the room, frantic, unsure of what to do and too terrified to sit still and do nothing. The anguish she fought to keep at bay would overwhelm her. Destroy her.

The legend.

Lauren sat on a chair beside the cold hearth. Nicholas had died and now his men were rallying to defeat Armstrong. The next part of the legend came to her like a solid blow to her chest. She was supposed to leave! But this was her home, the place she'd been the happiest. *But only because of Nicholas.* Could she stay without him? Could she sleep in their bed, knowing he would never be there to make her laugh, hold her or make love to her?

Stifling a sob with her hand, she rose and crossed the room to her dressing table. Lifting the enameled jewelry box Nicholas had given her as a wedding gift, she ran her fingers over the painted depiction of the woman and child. She pressed its cool surface to her face, wanting to remember the love in his eyes when he had given it to her.

She couldn't leave. This was the only place she felt close to her husband. Her home. And there was their child, Aurora, to consider. She wanted her daughter to know her father's world. She would stay, wanted to stay. She hadn't lost everything. She still had Nicholas's child.

'You have destroyed everything.'

Lauren gasped and turned toward the door. Lady Kenward stood inside the threshold, her thin body rigid, her eyes burning with a hatred so deep Lauren trembled with fear.

Clutching the jewelry case to her chest, Lauren said, 'I've lost as much as you. I loved Nicholas with all my heart.'

'You have no heart, witch! And I give you fair warning, you have no home. You will be gone before sunrise.'

Lauren straightened her shoulders at the threat. 'As Nicholas's wife, I have every right to remain here.'

'Aye, you can stay, but who's to say how long you will live if you do?' Lady Kenward's lips twisted into an evil grin and her gaze flickered to Lauren's stomach.

A new kind of fear chilled Lauren's soul. 'You wouldn't hurt the baby?'

'Being the witch ye are, ye foretold that it would be a girl-child.'

Lauren swallowed the bile rising in her throat.

'Another one the likes of you! I'll not have it. You

can leave safely before dawn, or stay. And reap your due. The choice is yours.'

Lady Kenward turned and left the room. Icy sweat prickled Lauren's skin. Her nerves felt frayed and raw. She couldn't breathe, could hardly stand. Sinking onto a stool, her mind spun with her mother-in-law's threat.

Lauren ran a trembling hand over her stomach. She couldn't let anything happen to the baby. Nicholas's child. To her horror, she didn't doubt Lady Kenward would try to kill them both.

A wave of nausea roiled through Lauren as she realized what she had to do. She had no choice. The last part of the legend had to be fulfilled. She finally understood the events behind the legend, and she felt as if she'd been set up by some great, sadistic power, helpless to change it.

A wrenching sob caught in her throat as she clutched the jewelry case to her. She rose, her legs trembling, and left the room. Using the wall for support, she went to Nicholas's solar. Cloaked in darkness, she found a candle, lit it. On the oak table behind his desk sat a leather-bound chest. The same one her grandmother had found in the dungeon. Opening it, Lauren removed the papers and placed the jewelry box inside.

With the chest in one hand and the candle in the other, she left the solar and wound her way through the empty halls. Battle sounds found their way into the dark corridor. She heard the endless clang of metal against metal, the cries of men, some triumphant, others not. She said a prayer for Nicholas's soldiers, then hurried down a spiral staircase.

After descending two levels, she navigated a narrow passageway. Candlelight reflected off stone walls, damp and slick with mildew. The tight space closed around her, starving her of air. Lauren forced herself to go on. She had nothing to be afraid of in the dungeons. Nothing more could hurt her now.

She pushed open the heavy oak door. A black cavern waited across the threshold. She hadn't returned to the dungeon since Nicholas had released her from the oubliette all those months ago. She didn't want to be here now, but she had to go inside. She stepped onto the landing, lit a candle supported by a wall bracket. Descending the worn steps, she lit more candles, gradually pushing back the clinging shadows.

Reaching the bottom, she surveyed the dark, hollow room. She could imagine whispering voices echoing off the stone. A chill of foreboding tightened her spine. She'd always hated this part of the castle. Now she knew why. Forcing herself not to turn and run, she set the chest down and felt along the base of the walls. She grimaced as her hands slid over cold, wet stones. She searched most of the room, growing more desperate with each moment she stayed there alone.

At the far corner, mortar came loose in her hands. Her soft cry echoed in the quiet room. Using her nails, she pried a square stone free. Pushing the block aside, she held the candle in front of the hole and saw the space was large enough for the chest to fit inside.

Tears streamed from her eyes as she lifted the

chest's lid and removed the enameled box. She slid her wedding ring from her finger and felt as if her heart had been wrenched from her chest. Polishing the gold band with the hem of her skirt, she held it to the flickering light. The lion rampant stood brave and tall. Like her husband once had. Though she knew it by heart, she read the inscription. '*My love, my life I give you. N.*'

'Oh, Nicholas,' Lauren whispered, and kissed the ring. Her heart pounded against her breast as she placed the ring inside the case and closed the lid. She sealed the box in the leather chest then put the chest in the space behind the wall. Returning the stone to its proper place, Lauren leaned back and stared at it. A welcome numbness slipped over her mind, blocking the endless grief waiting to tear apart her heart.

'There's only one thing left for me to do,' she said, her voice a quiver in the empty room.

God help her, she didn't know if she could do it.

CHAPTER 21

Lauren tightened the girth of her side-saddle, then led Jessy to a mounting block. After struggling into the saddle, she glanced around the empty stable. Empty except for Hades, who watched her from his stall. He nickered softly, as if sensing she was leaving and not coming back.

She had to look away. She couldn't bear to see the black stallion without Nicholas by his side. It only added to the devastation of leaving her home without seeing her husband one last time. But Lady Kenward's guards had refused to let her inside the chapel. She'd walked away without seeing Nicholas's rugged face, feeling the silk strands of his dark hair. She hadn't been able to tell him goodbye, tell him she loved him. Or give him one final kiss.

Nudging the mare, she entered the bailey and headed for the gate. Frantic activity bustled around her, but no one took notice of her or called out for her to stop. It was nearing dawn, and Jacobson had returned with his soldiers half an hour ago, having driven Laird Armstrong back across Hadrian's Wall.

But their triumphant cries had sounded hollow, carrying the underlying price this battle had cost them.

At the curtain wall, Lauren paused in the shadows, drew her cloak tighter around her, and looked at the bailey one last time. Torches lit the relieved faces of women, who hugged their returning husbands. Children raised their arms and cried for their fathers to hold them. Horses were led away. Weapons were gathered. Squires helped soldiers remove their burdensome armor.

An emptiness gathered so deep and tight inside her heart she didn't think her body could withstand it. These people's lives would return to normal. They wouldn't have Nicholas to lead them, but they had Elise. She was strong, and more than capable. As much as she wanted to, she couldn't help these people with their precious struggle to survive. Lady Kenward had seen to that.

Lauren imagined her life spinning out of control, as if she were caught in a raging storm that scattered her dreams to the wind, leaving her battered and helpless to stop it. Bending her head, she turned her back on the life she loved and headed into darkness.

Her heart pounding against her chest, Lauren stared at the cave's entrance, afraid to move or breathe. She didn't know for sure if the Gaelic words had sent her here. She'd only guessed. Maybe it had been the sudden storm. What if she couldn't leave? What would she do then? She couldn't return to Westbourne Castle. She had no doubts that Lady Kenward would carry out her threat.

But what if saying the words didn't send her to the future, but to another time? Sweat gathered on her brow and her nerves tightened along her body. The baby kicked in response. Lauren rubbed her swollen stomach and drew a deep breath. She couldn't think any more. She knew what she had to do.

Leading Jessy inside the cave, she stopped at the back wall and knelt on the ground. As she'd done months before, she touched the snake-head staffs that formed an X, then the six-spoked wheel, and finally the silhouette of a woman with red hair.

'Are you Arianrhod?' she asked, half expecting the walls to answer her.

At the ensuing silence, she drew a deep breath and ran her fingers over the carved words, reading them aloud as she went. "'*Co Sam-bith beir Arianrhod uachta gearr a bolg de uair scoilt curfola steach an de.*'"

Nothing happened. Lauren held her breath and waited, afraid it wouldn't work . . . terrified it would.

She looked at the mare, who watched her with wide eyes. Still nothing happened. Frantic, Lauren touched the words again. Perhaps she had to read them a second time. She started to repeat the verse, but Jessy's whinny stopped her.

Then she felt it, a tingling over her skin, grazing her like a cold breath. It was happening, like before. She sat on the ground and leaned against the wall. This time she wouldn't fight it. She took deep breaths and tried not to think about the life she was leaving behind. She forced her mind to become blank, but images crept into the darkness: Nicholas's smile, the sound of his laughter. The flavor of his lips against hers.

Her love for him pressed against her chest, turning painful, unbearable. Like the devastating loss of her parents, but so much more. This pain ran deeper, linking with the root of her soul.

Her heartbeat changed, matching the rhythm of the low-pitched hum. The sound grew, like a wave rushing to shore. Reaching higher, gaining in strength. It pulsed against her skin, her mind. Her body grew heavy, almost smothering. Her lungs were tight and empty, yet she couldn't move to breathe.

She heard a loud crash. Thunder, perhaps. She couldn't open her eyes. Too heavy. The howl of wind filled the small cave. It echoed off the walls. The pulsing noise quickened its beat. It filled her body, making her numb. She welcomed it. She wanted to sink away, disappear where feelings couldn't follow.

She saw the blackness behind her closed eyes and reached for it.

CHAPTER 22

Standing in the foyer of the Great Hall, Lauren felt out of place, disconnected. As if looking through another person's eyes, she studied the flags of noble families hanging from the ceiling. Furniture from Henry VIII to the Victorian time filled the room. Polished swords, battle axes and bows and arrows, either hung along the walls or were displayed in polished glass cases.

Lightbulbs glowed from a chandelier above her. Lamps and indirect lighting filled every nook and cranny, giving the massive room a lived-in look, though she knew that was far from true.

This Westbourne Castle didn't house families and their children. Herds of livestock weren't grazing outside the curtain wall. There were no vendors haggling over their wares or teenage boys practising with swords. Only memories filled this place. That, and an old couple who had spent their life preserving each one of them.

Lauren stepped further into the hall, the rustle of her skirts invading the austere silence. She paused, looked down at herself and gasped. She couldn't let her grandparents see her this way. Dried blood and dirt covered her hands, caked her nails. Red hair fell over her shoulders in tangles. She still wore the tattered green silk gown from the day before. She hadn't thought to change. Hadn't been able to think that far ahead.

Hot, white pain sliced through her stomach, sudden and sharp. Crying out, she gripped her waist and fell to her knees. Above the sound of her gasps she heard running feet, then loud voices. *Please don't let it be Grandpa and Grandma. Please don't let them see me like this.*

'What on earth?' It was her grandfather's voice.

Hands were on her shoulders, her face. Lauren looked up into her grandmother's worried green eyes. They widened and filled with tears as recognition took hold.

'Lauren? Is it you, child? Oh, my heavens – what – how?' Her grandmother caught Lauren in a tight hug, pressed her cheek to hers and cried. Lauren held the frail woman against her, needing the safety of her grandparents' love more than ever.

'Come, Morna,' her grandfather coaxed. 'Let's get the lass to her room. Can you walk?'

Lauren nodded as the pain ebbed. She pushed to her feet and let her grandparents lead her to the wing designated as the living quarters for the staff. Her room contained a white wrought-iron bed with a colorful quilt Morna had made for her years before. The walls were papered in a small yellow and green flowered print. Pictures and relics from her child-hood all sat in their usual places, as if waiting for her to visit.

Her grandfather turned to leave. 'I'll go call a doctor.'

Lauren sat on the bed. 'There's no need, Grandpa. I'll be fine. I just need to . . . to . . .' The events of the past twenty-four hours crushed against her until she didn't know what she needed or what more she could stand. Her shoulders began to shake as tears gathered and fell. Tears she thought she had cried when she'd made the trip to the cave.

'Oh, my dear. Here now, I don't know what has happened to you,' Morna cooed in a quivering voice, 'but you're back now. Everything will be fine.' Her grandmother's tear-filled gaze dropped to Lauren's swollen stomach.

'I have a lot to tell you.'

'Aye, lass,' Morna said, 'that you do. But after you rest.'

'I'd like to bathe first.'

'Of course. Here, let me help you off with your dress.'

Touching the once-elegant gown, Morna said, 'My mind is bursting with questions, but they'll wait. What matters is that you're here and safe. We've been out of our minds with worry.'

Guilt buckled inside Lauren, adding more pressure to her chest. 'I'm sorry, Grandma. There wasn't a way for me to send you word that I was all right. I didn't even know if I could return or not.'

'What nonsense! Of course you can return here. This is your home, the place where you belong.'

Lauren held still while Morna unfastened her gown, thinking this was the place she belonged – just not the time.

Her grandparents entered the room as Dr Reynolds snapped his black medical bag shut. When Lauren had awoken this morning, Morna had insisted she see the doctor. Out of her concern for the baby, Lauren had agreed. Only now that the examination was complete, terror added to her despair.

'Her blood pressure is much too high,' Dr Reynolds told her grandparents in a scolding tone, his bushy gray mustache twitching as he spoke. 'Besides exhaustion, she has already dilated two centimeters and she has at least another six weeks to go.'

'Will she be all right, Dr Reynolds?' Morna asked as her hand gripped the silver cross hanging from her neck.

'Yes.' The doctor nodded. 'With complete bed-rest and no emotional stress. Do you hear, Lauren? The most taxing thing I want you to do is take an afternoon nap.'

'Complete bed-rest, Doctor? Can't I at least . . .?'

'Do you want the baby to come now?' he interrupted.

'No,' she whispered. God, no! She couldn't lose Nicholas's baby. It was all she had.

'Then be a good girl and do what I say.' Finished, he nodded to her grandparents and left the room, closing the door behind him.

'Well, then,' Morna said with forced cheerfulness. 'It's settled. With plenty of rest, you and the baby will be fine.'

Lauren ran her hands over her stomach, tried to think about the baby, its health, the joy it would bring her. Except she could only think of Nicholas and everything she'd lost.

'Grandma, I don't think I can spend six weeks alone with my thoughts. I can't bear it,' Lauren said as a stray tear slipped from her eyes.

'There now, what can I do to help?' Morna asked as she sat on the bed and covered Lauren's hands with her thin, papery ones.

'I have to tell you what happened.'

'No, dear,' Grandpa Angus said. 'Dr Reynolds said you were not to get upset.'

'I have to,' Lauren cried and bit down on her lip. 'It's all inside me, hurting. I have to let it out to know it's real. That I've lost him.'

'Who?' Morna asked. 'Who have you lost?'

'Nicholas.' Lauren could barely say his name.

'Nicholas who?' Angus asked.

'Nicholas Kenward.' Lauren held her breath as her grandparents exchanged doubtful looks.

'Oh, dear,' Morna whispered. 'The same name as our own lord.'

Lauren shook her head. 'Not just the same name, but the same man.'

'Oh, dear,' Morna muttered again. Rising from the bed, she straightened her black cotton skirt. 'I think I'll make us some tea.'

As her grandmother hurried from the room, Grandpa Angus watched Lauren with assessing eyes.

'I'm not making this up, and I'm not crazy.'

He patted her hand. 'Whatever happened to you, lass, we'll always be here for you.'

Was he patronizing her? Or did he think she had already lost her mind and didn't want her screaming through the halls and frightening the tourists? She laid her head against the bed-rails. 'I don't blame you for not believing me. Nicholas never believed me either. And I wouldn't have believed it if I hadn't lived through it.'

They passed the minutes in silence, waiting for Morna's return. She finally bustled in, carrying a tray with cups, saucers, the teapot and accompaniments. Once she'd served everyone, Morna sat in a chair beside the bed as if they were going to have a nice afternoon chat.

Lauren took a sip of her tea as she searched for a starting place. The hot liquid slid down her throat and helped soothe her raw nerves. Beginning with the cave, she explained the ancient words and their power, warning her grandparents not to reveal the secret to anyone, or even to go near the cave. They listened, spellbound, and nodded for her to continue.

She described the way Nicholas had captured her. His mistaking her for Armstrong's daughter, the destruction of Gowan Castle, and her return to Westbourne as his captive. She left out her stay in the oubliette, wishing to banish that event forever from her mind.

355

She told them about the people she'd met. The community that had shared the suffering as well as the joy. Then she told them about Nicholas: the hard man she'd first met, then the one who had slowly emerged from a shield of hate. She described him in detail, the rides they'd taken, the conversations they'd had.

When she reached the part about her trying to escape and being injured with an arrow, Morna's cup clattered against her saucer.

Lauren reached for Morna's hand. 'It was only in the shoulder.'

'You were trying to come back to us?' she asked, then shook her head as if she didn't quite believe she had asked the question.

'At first, yes.' Lauren looked at both her grandparents. It hadn't been an easy decision to make then, and explaining it so they would understand now was no easier. 'Nicholas's mother hated me because she thought I was Armstrong's daughter. She arranged for me to escape, but she also sent men after me to kill me.'

Morna gasped.

'I was on Jessy. They couldn't catch me.' When Morna seemed to accept that answer, Lauren continued. 'When I reached the grove of trees hiding the cave, I realized I couldn't leave. I was in love with Nicholas. I couldn't leave him.'

'You're in love with a man from the sixteenth century?' Her grandmother's brow dipped in a disbelieving frown.

'Yes, and I'm married to him, and this is his child.'

356

The antique teacup and saucer crashed to the floor. 'Oh, heavens. Angus?' Morna said, her voice wavering. 'Do you hear this? What shall we do?'

'We're gonna hear the rest of her story, Morna.' Her grandfather filled his own cup with more tea and handed it to his wife. Picking the shattered porcelain up off the floor, he said, 'Go on, Lauren, tell us the rest.'

'I was happy,' she said simply. 'Happier than I've ever been in my life. Except for one thing.' She set her cup aside and slipped out from the covers. Despite her grandparents' disapproval, she stood by the window and looked across the bailey, which wasn't a bailey any longer, but sparse green grass to one side and a parking lot to the other.

'I knew about the legend. I knew Armstrong was going to attack and that Nicholas . . . that Nic – ' Her voice broke and her tears returned. 'I tried to stop it. I told Nicholas what would happen, but he didn't believe me. I kept hoping maybe, just maybe . . .'

She stared out the window and imagined the last instant she had seen her husband alive. Smiling, his eyes shining his love for her. Her breath shuddered out of her. She couldn't put the rest into words.

She felt her grandfather's hands on her shoulders. She turned and buried her face against his chest, his comforting hold closing around her.

'There now, lass. Cry for your Nicholas. Cry the hurt away.'

'I know you d-don't b-believe me,' she sobbed.

'Nicholas didn't, but he married me anyway. He never said he loved me either, but I know he did. I know he did.' The eruption of tears slowed and she drew a full breath. He had loved her.

She pulled away and blinked her eyes dry. She placed her hands over her heart. She could still feel it. Nicholas's love was still a part of her, warm and nurturing.

'Come, darling, please lie down. Dr Reynolds can be a bear if you don't follow his instructions.'

Lauren saw the doubt tugging at her grandmother's pale green eyes. Lauren managed a smile to ease the worry she'd caused the older woman. 'Thank you for listening.'

Climbing back into bed, she let Morna fuss over her for a few minutes. They hadn't believed her, but for some reason it didn't surprise or upset her. The story was beyond belief. Still . . .

'Is there anything I can get you, dear?' Morna asked.

'Yes,' she said, feeling stronger now that she knew what she wanted to do. 'I need some paper and a pen. There should be some in the desk in the corner.'

After retrieving a writing tablet and pen, Morna left Lauren alone with her thoughts. Only this time she welcomed them. Having told most of her story had helped ease the pain bottled inside her. But she needed something more.

Putting pen to paper, she wrote: *My name is Lauren Ferguson Kenward. I was born in England in the year 1973. This is my story . . .*

She didn't know what she would do with it when she'd finished, but perhaps some day someone would read it . . . and believe.

CHAPTER 23

Lauren pressed her ear against the door and held her breath. She detected no sound from the hall beyond. No footsteps or voices. Her heart thudded against her ribs as she turned the knob and stepped into the hall. She knew she shouldn't leave her room this morning. Her grandparents would scold, lecture and shake their fingers at her if they ever learned of it. But she couldn't stand it anymore.

She'd lain in bed for the past three weeks, thinking, writing and crying. The horror of losing Nicholas hadn't lessened, it had become unbearable. She had to see him, look into his eyes, and remember.

Wearing a smock dress of dark blue cotton that stretched tight around her stomach, she tiptoed down the corridor. After spending months donning heavy gowns, chemises and wool stockings, she felt strangely underdressed. Keeping to the shadows, she passed the cavernous Great Hall without being seen, and hurried down the east wing.

The instant she saw Nicholas's portrait tears sprang to her eyes. Her sigh ended with a weak sob. She reached out and touched the heavy gilt frame. Her trembling hand hesitated over the hard lines of his face. His eyes were so blue, so intense, she could believe they were real.

'Oh, Nicholas,' she whispered. 'I miss you so much.'

'Everyone come close now. I'll be tellin' you a sad tale about our most famous knight.'

Lauren turned away from the approaching crowd and wiped the tears from her eyes. Moving to the opposite wall, she leaned against the cold stone. She knew it would be torture to listen to Edith's enthusiastic speech, but she couldn't stop herself.

'Now, this is none other than Lord Nicholas Kenward,' Edith beamed with pride. 'He ruled these lands from the tender age of twelve, when his father and brother were ambushed by a Scotsman named Laird Armstrong. Vowing revenge against the Scotsman, Lord Kenward grew into a hard man and always wore black to symbolize his hatred.'

Edith tucked a piece of fraying gray hair back into her bun. 'The villagers loved Lord Kenward, but were wary when he took an outlander as his wife. It is said she had a strange way about her. Not only was she Scots, which was bad enough back then, but it was rumored she had the power of sight.'

'What was the woman's name?' a man near the front asked.

Her name was Lauren! Lauren wanted to scream. She pressed her hand to her mouth and tried to slow her heartbeat. She shouldn't listen to this. It would make things worse.

'Regrettably, we don't know her name or where she came from.' Edith turned to the portrait and her hand fluttered to her chest. 'In 1530 the vile Laird Armstrong laid siege against Westbourne Castle. Lord Kenward was struck down by an arrow. It was Lady Kenward who, heavy with their first child, raised her husband's sword and rallied his men. After a long, wearying battle, they forced the Scotsmen back across the border.'

Lauren closed her eyes and steeled herself as Edith finished the tale of Nicholas's death.

'But that is not the end of the story. Once the wounded had been cared for, it was discovered Lady Kenward had disappeared. No one can truly say what happened next, but there is a myth. It's said Lady Kenward's tears woke the mystical Light Elves from their eternal slumber. Upon seeing the mistress's fiery red hair, they knew she was a *dergflaith*, a woman chosen by the Celtic Goddess, Arianrhod, to possess the power of sight.'

Arianrhod. The power of sight. Lauren wanted to scream at the mystical goddess. She had possessed all the knowledge needed to save Nicholas's life, and still she had failed.

'But the most tragic part of this tale,' Edith said in a sorrowful tone, 'is what happened to Lord Kenward afterward.'

Startled, Lauren pushed away from the wall. This wasn't part of her normal speech.

362

'When Lord Kenward recovered from his wound, he would not accept that his wife had left him.'

'What?' Lauren choked, stepping forward.

Edith's gaze swerved to her. The old woman's thin mouth pulled into a frown as she continued. 'It is said Lady Kenward predicted the battle and made her husband promise to protect himself. He had worn chain mail beneath his armor.'

Lauren pressed her hands over her mouth to stifle her cry. She couldn't breathe as an icy chill swept over her skin. 'Oh, God.'

'He scoured the countryside for her, and sent a messenger to Laird Armstrong's hold to see if the Scotsman had somehow captured his wife and unborn child. No trace of her was ever found. Some say Lord Kenward went insane with grief. He would leave the castle and go to a forest west of here, where he would wait for days on end. Waiting as if he expected his wife to appear. He never remarried. Instead he grieved for the wife he loved and the child he never knew. His family line ended with his death many years later.'

'He's alive?' Lauren's desperate plea drew the crowd's attention. Heat rushed up her body, dimming her vision. A loud buzzing filled her mind.

'Child, what are you doing here?' Edith scolded as she rushed to Lauren's side. 'You're as pale as death. If your grandmother sees you, you'll give her heart palpitations.'

Lauren clasped the older woman's arms. 'Edith, did you say Nicholas survived the siege?'

'Well, of course he did. You know that as well as I do. Heavens, what's wrong with you?'

'Lady Kenward lied!' She sucked in much needed air, afraid she might faint. 'He wasn't dead. I . . . I left him!'

'Who, dear?' Edith asked as she pressed a palm to Lauren's brow.

She pulled away, tears streaming down her face. Her mind fought to grasp what was real and what wasn't. 'I have to go back . . . now . . . I have to leave.'

Searing pain ripped through her stomach. A scream tore from Lauren's throat. She doubled over, dropped to her knees. Living fire spread beneath her skin. Drawing in one breath, then another, she struggled against the blackness creeping in.

'Lauren!' Edith cried. 'What is it? What's wrong?'

'The baby . . .' was all she could manage.

The pain took over. She squeezed her eyes closed and fought to breathe, fought the burning tearing her apart. A warm gush flowed down her legs. 'Edith, oh, my God. My water broke.'

She was barely aware of the two male tourists who lifted her and carried her to her room. She heard people talking, the rush of running feet. Her head dropped back. She saw bright light streaming through the windows, heard her own breath rasp in her ears. Streaks of pain spread down on her stomach, but she smiled and a sobbing laugh caught in her throat. *Nicholas is alive.*

Her grandmother appeared at her side. 'Dr Reynolds will not be pleased when he hears you were out of bed.'

364

'Aye, that he won't,' Edith concurred.

Lying on top of the quilt, Lauren clutched her stomach and gritted her teeth. 'I don't care what *pleases* Dr Reynolds right now. This baby is coming.'

'Yes, I know.' Her grandmother stroked Lauren's brow. 'We'll be fine until the doctor arrives. You just lie back and try to relax. Try that breathing thing everyone does these days.'

A sob clenched Lauren's throat. She tried to hold Nicholas's face in her mind, but it blurred in a sea of fire. 'The pain, Grandma, it's not stopping.' Fingers of agony wrapped around her body like a tight, relentless fist. Sweat glazed her skin and streamed down her face, mixing with her tears. 'I'm afraid for the baby,' she cried. 'Something's wrong.'

'Lauren, you've got to relax,' her grandmother coaxed gently, and patted her hand. 'Take deep breaths, focus on something happy.'

'Nicholas,' Lauren moaned. 'All this time . . .' A fierce white blaze seared her body. She tensed and gripped the wrought-iron headboard, screaming her husband's name. 'It's coming, Grandma,' she cried, terrified for the baby, for herself. 'The baby is coming.'

Panting, she tried to gain control of the agony, but the endless pressure shattered her thinking. Pain, there was so much pain. Her body was being pulled apart from the inside out. How could the baby survive this? How could she?

A heavy weight pressed against her stomach, spreading downward, harder, tighter. 'I have to push.'

Her grandmother looked to Edith, then shook her head. 'You can't. The doctor isn't here yet.'

'I don't care,' Lauren grunted, and gripped the headboard harder. 'I have to.'

'Could you not try and wait?'

Another contraction began. Moaning, Lauren bore down, willing the baby out of her body.

Situated at the foot of the bed, her grandmother gasped, 'I can see the baby's head! Oh, my, he has black hair.'

Lauren panted and laid back. 'He's a she.' Groaning, she gripped her knees and pushed again.

'The baby's head is out. Oh, Lauren, it's almost over.'

'Try to work a shoulder free,' Edith urged.

'Oh, dear, oh, dear, the baby's so small.'

Lauren shuddered as she resisted the urge to push. A cry rose from deep within her chest. Unable to wait any longer, she bore down and felt the baby slide free in a gush of warmth.

Collapsing against the bed, Lauren listened to her grandmother and Edith cry and fuss over the baby. Then came the beautiful wail of her newborn daughter.

'Just a moment, dear,' her grandmother cooed. 'As soon as we tie off the cord you can see this beautiful little one.'

Lauren closed her eyes and smiled. The baby was fine. They'd both survived. And Nicholas was alive. Alive! She put her hands to her face and sobbed tears of exhaustion and relief.

Minutes later, Morna moved to the bed with the baby wrapped in a white towel. 'Would you like to hold him now?'

'It's a girl, Grandma,' Lauren said, her voice thick with pride.

An indulgent grin spread across the older woman's wrinkled face. 'No, darling, it's a boy.'

Lauren's mouth dropped open. Her breath hung on a gasp as her grandmother laid the baby in her arms. Because of the legend, she'd been sure the baby would be a girl; she hadn't considered the possibility of having a boy.

In awe, Lauren stroked her fingers over the patch of black hair on his head, still damp from his quick bath. He opened his mouth and wailed, the cries healthy and strong. Then he looked at her with eyes so blue, so intense, she couldn't help but see a part of Nicholas in them.

The legend had changed . . . *again*. She couldn't have been happier.

Lauren stared at the empty page in front of her. She picked up her pen, unsure how to finish her journal. The blank piece of paper was so much like her future . . . and Nicholas's. It hadn't been written yet.

Should my story ever be read, and the cave be found, I caution the reader about doing what I have done: changing history. Though I would save Nicholas's life again, I would only do so because I believe history will be altered for the best.

Nicholas and I will be together, as we should be. His family line will not end prematurely; the healthy son I gave birth to a week ago assures me of that. God willing, we will have more.

His people, and this castle, will undoubtedly benefit from all that has happened.

In closing, I assure you everything you have read is the truth.

Today is the day I will return to my husband.

My name is Lauren Ferguson Kenward and I was born in 1973. I pray my death comes very late in the sixteenth century.

Descending the worn dungeon steps, Lauren clutched a metal box in her arms. Her heart hammered from excitement instead of fear. The last time she had entered the dark, decaying room it had been to leave her wedding ring behind.

This time she was leaving a legacy.

Safely sealed inside the container was her hand-written journal.

A naked lightbulb cast gray light over the damp, empty room. She crossed the packed dirt floor and knelt on the ground. Finding the right stone, she worked it loose and pulled it from its resting place. Her own private time capsule.

She placed the metal box inside the dark hole and stared at it for a moment. Everything she'd been through was locked inside. Every fear, every joy, every dream. It had taken over four hundred years for the chest with her ring to be discovered. How long would it be before someone found this one? Would it ever be found?

Lauren pushed the stone back into place. It didn't matter what happened in the future. She only cared about the past.

CHAPTER 24

The baby cried, a tired, mewling sound that told Lauren he was fighting sleep. She secured the make-shift sling that held him against her chest and hummed a lullaby. He soon gave up his struggle, closed his eyes and grew still.

She watched the small rise and fall of her son's chest, then grazed her finger over his soft cheek. She hadn't named him yet, wanting to wait until she was with Nicholas.

Her son. She touched his smooth brow. It amazed her how something so small, so innocent could bring so much love. Already she couldn't imagine her life without him. The thought sent a chill over her skin and pulled her gaze from her sleeping son to the ancient words written on the cave wall.

Wearing her cleaned and mended gown, with her cape draped over her shoulders, she sat on the dirt floor. She ran her fingers over the carvings and worried how the trip back through time would affect the baby. She assured herself she and Jessy had gone through twice with no lingering side-effects. Her son should be fine. But still . . .

Lauren shook away her doubts. There was only one choice to make, and she'd already made it. 'All right, Arianrhod, this is the last time for me. I won't be coming back.'

She'd said her goodbyes to her grandparents. At first they'd insisted she give up her fantasy, but as she'd packed a few items for the baby they'd realized she would leave them. Hurt and confused, they'd struggled to believe her. As much as she would miss them, she couldn't stay. Her life wasn't in this time.

Bringing her mind back to the moment, she drew a deep breath. She imagined the tension in the cave had shifted, intensified. Her son frowned in his sleep and squirmed in her arms. Sweat broke out over Lauren's brow and ran in rivulets down her sides and between her breasts. Jessy whinnied from behind her. Lauren glanced around, suddenly uneasy. Something was different. Maybe it wouldn't happen again. Perhaps there was a limit as to how often a person could go through time. Or maybe her own fear was causing the change.

Squeezing her eyes closed, Lauren willed herself to calm down. Her pulse gradually slowed. She envisioned Nicholas's face, the moment she would see him again. Smiling, she opened her eyes, and read '"Co Sam-bith beir Arianrhod uachta gearr a bolg de uair scoilt curfola steach an de."'

* * *

371

Lauren woke to darkness, feeling drugged and weighted down, as if the air had compacted and pressed against her. She drew in a cold breath that smothered instead of relieved her. She breathed in a deeper gulp, trying to pull herself fully awake.

She blinked her eyes open to a deep void with texture and depth. She tightened her hands around the bundle secured against her chest and felt the baby move. She sighed in relief. He hadn't been harmed.

Gathering her cloak around her, she used the wall to pull herself up. She held the baby with one arm, and reached out in front of her with the other, searching blindly for Jessy. Finding the mare, she gathered the reins and went to the mouth of the cave.

Black shadows in eerie shapes and deceiving valleys surrounded her. A wary prickle slipped down her spine. She hesitated, afraid to move forward and even more frightened to stay.

Who knew what lived in these woods? There might be a pack of wolves nearby or even an outlaw. Lauren shivered. She hadn't considered arriving here at night. How long had she slept? It had been a little past noon in her time when she'd whispered the Celtic words.

The forest lay quiet. No wind stirred the trees. No crickets sang. No night owls called out. There were no sounds at all. Nothing! As if nothing else existed in the world. Only her, the baby and darkness.

She tightened her hold on the reins and licked her dry lips. God! Where was she? *When* was she?

Cold sweat bathed her body. Fear rose like a scream inside her mind, but she fought it back. Draping the reins over Jessy's neck, Lauren tried to mount the mare. She clutched the baby to her and struggled to keep her skirt out of the way. On the third attempt she gained the saddle, not caring that her gown was twisted around her legs.

Bending over Jessy's neck, she shielded the baby from sharp limbs that struck out of the dark, and urged the mare east. Time crawled past, with every rustle, every snap of a branch making her heart race faster and her imagination run wilder.

Finally they reached the open field. A cold, biting wind whipped around her. Smoke-black clouds rolled across the sky, blocking the moon and stars. Lauren pulled her cape tighter over her and the baby.

She bit down on her bottom lip and searched for a landmark indicating which way to the castle. Fleeting moonlight revealed deeper shadows. The forest behind her seemed more like a tomb, dark and quiet. But at least in the woods they would be out of the wind. Deciding to wait until daylight to go to the castle, Lauren reined the mare around.

She heard a snap, then a whisper. Halting Jessy, Lauren tensed and listened. Was someone here with her? Or was it an animal? She drew a deep breath that trembled in her chest. It had to be the wind. Or perhaps it was Nicholas. Edith had said he'd come here for days at a time, as if he were waiting for something. For her? Had he been waiting for her to come back?

'Nicholas?' Lauren called above the wind. 'Nicholas, are you here?'

A vise gripped Lauren's arm and jerked her from the side-saddle. Her feet hit the ground and her shoulder slammed into a hard chest. She sucked in a breath and tightened her hold on the baby. 'Nicholas?'

Her son wailed – a loud, angry sound.

'Nay, lass, I'm no' Nicholas. And hush that bairn or I will.'

'Armstrong!' Lauren choked. Even in the dark she recognized his harsh voice. She stared at the silhouette beside her. Tall and fiendish, like a ghost from hell.

'Aye, in the flesh.' He chuckled low. 'I canna believe me own luck. Here I am searching for the Lord of Westbourne Castle and I find his lady instead.' He pulled her cloak aside. 'And Kenward's get as well. I'd say luck is shining down on me.'

'What do you want?' Of all people to find her, why did it have to be him?

'Lady Kenward, I believe that should be obvious. I want your husband dead.'

She pulled against his hold on her arm, but he jerked her against him.

'Do not try tae escape. You're mine now.'

Panic rose inside her. He was right. She couldn't escape. Even if she could mount Jessy and get away, she couldn't race across the moors on a night as pitch-black as this. She'd end up killing herself and the baby.

Another man stepped up behind her and lifted her back into the saddle. She clasped his arm. 'Please, let me go. Nicholas doesn't want to fight with you.' Sensing the man's hesitation, she went with her instinct. 'Ronan?'

He didn't respond. He took her reins and led her to a group of men waiting a few yards away in the open, where the icy gusts buffeted them. As smoky clouds filtered past, she made out four shadows in the darkness.

The baby squirmed, then released a high-pitched cry.

'Quiet,' Armstrong growled.

'He's hungry.'

'Then give 'im a tit and shut him up!'

Lauren trembled with fury as she secured the cloak around her and unlaced her gown. She swore if Nicholas didn't kill Armstrong, she'd gladly do it.

As they headed north, the laird rode up beside her. 'Where 'ave ye been for the past month?'

Lauren turned her head away, ignoring him, refusing to let on how terrified she was. Armstrong had murdered Nicholas's family in cold blood. What would he do with her?

'Your husband sent a messenger demanding tae know if I had captured ye. Imagine my disappointment when I had to answer nay.'

She thinned her lips to keep from saying something that would only enrage him.

'They say he's insane, ye ken. Staying near the forest day and night, waitin' for something.'

'That's why you're here?' she blurted. Guilt assailed her from all sides. Once again she'd put Nicholas's life in danger. 'You thought you could capture him? Shame on you, Armstrong,' she jeered. 'He's ten times the man you are.'

'We'll see what kind of man he is when he learns I have his wife.'

Lauren glared at him and cursed the fact that he couldn't see her disdain. She had to escape. She couldn't allow Nicholas to be led into a trap. She had to make a run for it. It was dangerous, but she had to try – as soon as an opportunity presented itself. Shifting the baby to her other breast, she heard a thump. She turned and saw shadows against shadows. An eerie quiet seemed to breathe in the dark, alive, watching them.

The Laird turned his mount. 'Keane? Thady?'

Another thud, and then the sound of prancing hooves stirred the night. A shiver of anticipation curved over her spine. Was it a wild animal? Thieves? Oh, God! Were she and the baby next?

Armstrong's horse reared. 'Ronan!'

'Aye.' The young Scotsman leading Jessy turned both horses about so Lauren was sandwiched between the two men. Her eyes wide in the darkness, she tried to see what was happening.

'I believe you have something that belongs to me,' a deep, vibrant voice said from somewhere in front of them

'Nicholas!' Lauren cried, and pressed a hand to her mouth.

Ronan and Armstrong drew their swords, the screech of metal slicing the air. 'That I do, Kenward,' the Laird said. 'And ye'll not be gettin' the woman or the babe alive if ye move any closer.'

'Touch my wife, Armstrong, and you will be the one to die.'

'Brave words, Englishman. But I am the one who'll be victorious this time.'

Lauren gasped when the flat of Armstrong's sword pressed against her throat. Cold steel bit into her skin. Oh, please, no. She couldn't allow them to use her to trap Nicholas. 'Ronan, don't let him do this.'

'Shut up,' the Laird ordered.

'You're not like your father.'

'Lauren, don't,' Nicholas said, sounding closer than before.

'I said, quiet, woman!' the Laird bellowed.

The blade dug deeper into her flesh. She felt a warm trickle of blood run down her neck. 'Oh, God.'

'That's right, lady,' Armstrong sneered. 'Start praying tae your maker. You're likely tae meet 'im soon.'

Lauren tried not to swallow, afraid the sword would cut her deeper. She gripped Jessy's mane and urged the mare back. Tilting her head, she noticed the black sky was now tinged with purple. Dark shadows became trees and bushes. The silhouette before her became her husband, mounted on Hades.

If she hadn't been in love with him, the sight of him would have terrified her. The Black Knight. Harsh angles defined his face. Twin pools of black replaced his eyes. With his sword drawn, he urged his raven mount forward.

'Another step and she dies, Kenward,' Armstrong warned.

In a move so fast she barely followed it, Nicholas raised his arm and released a dagger. Laird Armstrong cried out. The sword against her neck dropped to the ground. Gasping, she glanced to the side and saw the jeweled hilt of a dagger protruding from the Laird's arm.

Nicholas pointed his sword at Ronan.

The younger man resheathed his weapon. 'I will no' fight you, Kenward.'

'Ronan! Are ye coward, or no'?' the Laird bellowed. 'If there be an ounce of Armstrong blood in ye, kill the woman.'

Ronan ignored his father and said to Nicholas, 'I have no wish for the war between us to continue.'

'Then why are you here? And why do you have my wife?' Nicholas bit out.

In the growing light, Lauren saw Ronan's jaw clench. 'I owe my father loyalty, though I don't always believe as he does.'

'Yet ye betray me?' his father raged as he grasped his bleeding arm.

Still looking at Nicholas, Ronan said, 'Let this be an end to the feud between us, Kenward.' He handed Lauren the reins.

She kicked Jessy's sides and moved next to Nicholas. The mare whinnied and rubbed Hades's neck.

Safely beside her husband, she faced the two Scotsmen and was struck by the differences between them. While one lived with hate, the other struggled to survive in spite of it. Not so different from Nicholas and his mother, she realized.

Regardless of what had just happened, Lauren felt a tug of empathy for Ronan. 'What about Elise?'

The question startled all three men into looking at her. A rueful smile broke over the young Scot's face. 'Tell her she has nothing tae fear from the Armstrongs ever again.'

'Is that all?' Lauren asked.

'My lady, that is all there ever can be.' With a nod, Ronan spurred his mount and led his cursing father away.

As the hoofbeats faded, Lauren met Nicholas's gaze. The unreachable coldness of his eyes tore her heart. She'd done this to him, brought back the invincible knight. She tried to smile, but couldn't quite manage it. Did he no longer trust her? Did he hate her for leaving him? She swallowed the knot stuck in her throat. 'Well, this isn't how I had planned our reunion.'

Nicholas touched the wound at her neck. The bleeding had stopped and she hardly felt the sting. He leaned close and cupped her face between his hands, his thumbs stroking the curve of her cheeks.

Without warning, his mouth bore down on hers, hard and devouring. An anguished sound rose from his chest, conveying the depth of his feelings. An agony she shared. The feel of him, his scent, his taste, filled her mouth, shocking her mind. It wasn't that she had forgotten him. This was like waking up and finding her dream was real.

She secured her hold on the baby as he gripped her waist and lifted her to sit before him.

With her fingers, she traced the line of his jaw, the crease at the corner of his eyes, his brow. She rubbed her palm over the rough stubble on his cheek. A face she knew so well, loved so much.

Laughing softly through her tears, she said, 'I thought I'd lost you forever.' The tears came harder. She shook her head, then hugged him to her. 'I'm sorry, Nicholas. I never would have left if I'd known you were alive.'

He stroked her hair, the side of her face. Kissed her tears. 'Why *did* you leave?' The question sounded ripped from his heart.

She gripped him tighter, afraid to let him go. 'Your mother said you were dead. She wouldn't let me see you.' Her breath shuddered as she added, 'She threatened to kill me and the baby if I stayed. I had to leave.'

'My mother kept you from me?' He sucked in a breath and looked toward the sunrise. Rage darkened his eyes to a dangerous black.

Lauren could only nod.

'I promise you, love . . .' he pressed his lips to her brow '. . . she'll never come between us again.'

'What will you do?'

'Send her to live with her brother.'

'I'm so sorry, Nicholas. I know how much this hurts you.'

He kissed her temple, and whispered, 'I am the one who is sorry. The past weeks without you have been the hardest of my life.'

She rubbed her forehead against his jaw. From the corner of her eye, she caught a glimpse of Armstrong's retreating back in the morning light. 'I'm surprised you let him go. After hating him all these years, you had the perfect opportunity to kill him.'

Nicholas followed her gaze. 'I'm probably a fool, but I believe young Ronan. He shall rule in his father's place soon enough. I'd much rather have one good ally in Scotland as another enemy.' He caught her hand and touched it to his lips. 'When you left, where did you go?'

'To my home in the future.'

'Through the cave?'

'Yes.'

Nicholas nodded his acceptance. 'But you came back.'

'I'd been in my own time for three weeks before I could work up the courage to see your portrait. I listened to the tour guide tell your story. When she reached the part that said you spent the rest of your life mourning my disappearance, I was so shocked I went into labor. You were alive.' Her voice hitched. 'All that time . . .'

He moved her cape aside. Pale sunlight touched the infant's face. Dark curls escaped the edge of the white

381

cotton blanket. Small hands were clasped together beside rosy cheeks.

'I thought she would look like you,' he said.

'She's a he.'

Nicholas's head jerked up, his eyes wide with surprise. 'You said it would be a daughter.'

'Well, the legend was wrong – again.'

'Again?'

'The legend said you died. You didn't. If I hadn't believed it so much, things might have been different. It wouldn't have been so easy to convince me you had been killed.' She touched the scar on his face. 'We wouldn't have been separated.'

Nicholas shook his head. 'No, love. The legend was true – or at least I believe it was at one time.'

She frowned. 'What are you saying?'

'Because of you, I wore more armor. If I had not, I would have died during the siege.'

'Oh.' She swallowed. 'Your injury, was it bad . . .? I mean . . .'

'It is healing now that you're here.' Nicholas stroked the baby's plump cheek. 'Was it difficult?'

She watched the lines around her husband's eyes soften. A smile touched the corners of his mouth. 'The delivery?'

'I was concerned.'

'It wasn't fun, but we both did fine.'

Some of the tension eased from his shoulders. He kissed her temple. 'So you can have another child?'

'Nicholas, please, this one is only a week old.'

His gaze met hers. 'I would like a daughter. One with your hair and eyes. But only if you believe it safe.'

'I think I can manage one more child, eventually.'

'I would not risk losing you again, Lauren.' He kissed her, his hands framing her face. 'I love you.'

She placed her hand over his. 'Do you know how many times I've wanted to hear you say that?'

'As many times as I've wanted to say it to you.'

Laughing, she kissed him. 'I love you. With all my heart.'

He pulled her back against him and spurred Hades into a walk. Looking over her shoulder at the sleeping baby, he asked, 'What have you named my son?'

'I haven't. I waited so we could do it together. But I do have a suggestion.'

Nicholas nudged the baby's hand until his small fingers wrapped part-way around his father's larger one. 'And what is that?'

'James David.'

Nicholas stilled and looked at her.

'After your brother and my father,' she explained.

Nicholas's eyes crinkled with tenderness as he studied his son. 'James David Kenward. It suits him.'

With her husband's arms wrapped around her, she relaxed against his strong chest. The rising sun pushed away the lingering shadows. A pale blue sky, dotted with orange-tinted clouds, appeared above them. Lauren closed her eyes and tried to hold onto the moment. The safety, the love, the feeling that she was finally where she belonged. And all because of a goddess named Arianrhod. Smiling, she whispered, 'Thank you.'

She tilted her head to see Nicholas's face. 'What about Jessy? We're leaving her behind.'

'Don't worry,' he said, and kissed her brow. 'She knows where her home is.'

Wanting a better kiss, she reached up and said, 'So do I.'

EPILOGUE

'Here, now, everyone gather round,' Edith beamed. She waved her hands, gathering the tourists like a sheepdog herding its flock. 'I'll now tell you about our most famous knight, Lord Nicholas Kenward.

'He ruled these lands from the age of twelve, after his father and brother were murdered by Laird Armstrong. Driven to claim vengeance against the Scotsman, Lord Kenward grew into a hard man, but one the people of Westbourne Castle loved. That is until he married an outlander. Not only was she a Scot, which was bad enough in those days, but she had a strange way about her. 'Tis said she had the power of second sight.

'Well . . .' Edith sighed and looked at the portrait. 'Nicholas loved his wife so much, the people eventually lost their fear of her. But their happiness was not meant to last. Tragedy struck. Laird Armstrong laid siege against Westbourne Castle. After grueling hours of battle, a lone arrow struck Lord Kenward down.

'Lady Kenward, heavy with their first child, raised

her husband's sword and rallied his men to continue the fight. They forced the Scots back across Hadrian's Wall and managed to save the castle.

'But what happened next is what tears my heart,' Edith added dramatically, pleased to have captured everyone's attention. 'After the wounded were finally cared for, it was discovered Lady Kenward, who had believed her husband had been killed, had disappeared. Once Nicholas recovered from his injury, he searched the countryside for her. Never to find her. Some say he went insane with grief. He spent days on end at a forest not far from here, waiting. He refused to eat, to sleep. He stayed there as if he expected a miracle to occur.

'Then, after his wife had been missing for a month, she mysteriously returned. She stepped out from the forest as if she knew he would be there waiting for her. And what did she have with her, but Lord Kenward's newborn son?'

'Where had she been?' an old man asked as he swiped at the mop of gray hair hanging in his eyes.

'No one knows for sure,' Edith explained. 'But there is a legend. It's said Lady Kenward's tears woke the mystical Light Elves from their eternal slumber. Seeing her fiery red hair, they knew she was a *dergflaith*, a woman chosen by the Celtic Goddess, Arianrhod, to possess the power of sight.

'Well,' Edith went on, 'feeling pity for the lady, the elves pleaded with Thorr to ease her pain. Thorr swept her way to the celestial palace, and there Lady Kenward bore her child.'

Smiles broke out on the tourists' faces. A young woman raised her hand and asked, 'What was the woman's name?'

Edith's grin came slow and easy. She turned to a man who stood in shadows along the far wall. She sighed and stepped back as he moved closer to the group.

Sunlight caught the blue highlights in his black hair. His eyes, a deep, startling blue, were focused on the portrait.

'This is Lord Richard Kenward,' Edith explained, and pressed a hand to her heart. 'He is a direct descendant of Lord and Lady Kenward. He can answer your questions about the lady.'

The man, whose angled features were so like those in the painting, smiled and said in a deep, steady voice, 'Her name was Lauren.'

**THE EXCITING NEW NAME
IN WOMEN'S FICTION!**

PLEASE HELP ME TO HELP YOU!

Dear *Scarlet* Reader,

Don't forget we are now holding another super Prize Draw, which means that **you could win 6 months' worth of free *Scarlets*!** Just return your completed questionnaire to us **before 31 January 1998** and you will automatically be entered in the draw that takes place on that day. If you are lucky enough to be one of the first two names out of the hat we will send you four new *Scarlet* romances, every month for six months.

So don't delay – return your form straight away!*

Looking forward to hearing from you,

Sally Cooper

Editor-in-Chief, *Scarlet*

QUESTIONNAIRE

Please tick the appropriate boxes to indicate your answers

1 Where did you get this Scarlet title?
Bought in supermarket ☐
Bought at my local bookstore ☐ Bought at chain bookstore ☐
Bought at book exchange or used bookstore ☐
Borrowed from a friend ☐
Other (please indicate) _____

2 Did you enjoy reading it?
A lot ☐   A little ☐   Not at all ☐

3 What did you particularly like about this book?
Believable characters ☐   Easy to read ☐
Good value for money ☐   Enjoyable locations ☐
Interesting story ☐   Modern setting ☐
Other _____

4 What did you particularly dislike about this book?
_____

5 Would you buy another Scarlet book?
Yes ☐   No ☐

6 What other kinds of book do you enjoy reading?
Horror ☐   Puzzle books ☐   Historical fiction ☐
General fiction ☐   Crime/Detective ☐   Cookery ☐
Other (please indicate) _____

7 Which magazines do you enjoy reading?
1. _____
2. _____
3. _____

And now a little about you –
8 How old are you?
Under 25 ☐   25–34 ☐   35–44 ☐
45–54 ☐   55–64 ☐   over 65 ☐

cont.

9 What is your marital status?
   Single ☐   Married/living with partner ☐
   Widowed ☐   Separated/divorced ☐

10 What is your current occupation?
   Employed full-time ☐   Employed part-time ☐
   Student ☐   Housewife full-time ☐
   Unemployed ☐   Retired ☐

11 Do you have children? If so, how many and how old are they?
   _____
   _____

12 What is your annual household income?
   under $15,000   ☐   or   £10,000   ☐
   $15–25,000   ☐   or   £10–20,000   ☐
   $25–35,000   ☐   or   £20–30,000   ☐
   $35–50,000   ☐   or   £30–40,000   ☐
   over $50,000   ☐   or   £40,000   ☐

Miss/Mrs/Ms _____
Address _____
_____
_____

Thank you for completing this questionnaire. Now tear it out – put
it in an envelope and send it, before 31 January 1998, to:

Sally Cooper, Editor-in-Chief

USA/Can. address	*UK address/No stamp required*
SCARLET c/o London Bridge	SCARLET
85 River Rock Drive	FREEPOST LON 3335
Suite 202	LONDON W8 4BR
Buffalo	*Please use block capitals for*
NY 14207	*address*
USA	

DADRE/11//97

***Scarlet* titles coming next month:**

HARTE'S GOLD   Jane Toombs
No-nonsense rancher Carole Harte can't believe that she, of all people, would fall for a film star. But that's exactly what she's done! Trouble is, she's never heard of 'the star', Jerrold Telford, and fears he's out to con her grandmother!

THE SECOND WIFE   Angela Arney
When Felicity decides to marry Tony she thinks the decision is theirs alone, and that love will conquer all. What she's forgotten is that other people have a stake in their future too, and then Felicity realizes just how difficult it is to be *the second wife* . . .

WILDE AFFAIR   Margaret Callaghan
Rich, powerful, ruthless – the Jared Wildes of this world don't make commitments. Oh yes, Stevie has come across men like Jared before. Her daughter Rosa's father for one!

A BITTER INHERITANCE   Clare Benedict
'A scheming little gold digger. Her husband not cold in his grave and she's involved with another man!' That's how Sam Redmond thinks of Gina. How can she change his mind, when he clearly can't forget or forgive how badly she treated *him* in the past?